Rosalind's eyes had adjusted to the dark, allowing her to see farther into the ballroom. There, almost hidden by the deeper shadow under the musicians' gallery, lay an odd black bundle. It might have been a rolled-up rug, except it was too uneven, and it gleamed, in patches, as if the torchlight from outside were catching on glass or metal. She thought it might be a pile of burlap sacks, perhaps delivered by the workmen downstairs. But such things wouldn't have been so inelegantly dumped in the Almack's ballroom, no matter the time of day.

And if it were a pile of sacks, what was the pool of thicker darkness that spread out around it? That wasn't a shadow. It was the wrong shape.

"Is there something the matter, miss . . ." Rosalind felt Mr. Whelks move to look over her head. "Great God!"

Propriety forgotten, Mr. Whelks shoved past her. The boards echoed under his shoes as he bolted across the ballroom.

Rosalind grabbed up her hems and ran after him as quickly as skirts and coat allowed. Even so, Mr. Whelks had dropped to his knees beneath the gallery by the ⟨…⟩ reached his side.

It was not a rug ⟨…⟩ not have long white hands, or ⟨…⟩ shadow he knelt in, but thick ⟨…⟩ whose still, startled eyes stared ⟨…⟩

"Who i⟨…⟩ now . . ."

"Dear L⟨…⟩ Rosalind. "It's Jasper Aimesworth!"

A
Useful
WOMAN

A ROSALIND THORNE MYSTERY

DARCIE WILDE

BERKLEY PRIME CRIME, NEW YORK

Published by the Berkley Publishing Group
An imprint of Penguin Random House
375 Hudson Street, New York, New York 10014

This book is an original publication of the Berkley Publishing Group.

Library of Congress Cataloging-in-Publication Data

Names: Wilde, Darcie.
Title: A useful woman / Darcie Wilde.
Description: Berkley Prime Crime trade paperback edition. | New York :
Berkley Prime Crime, 2016. | Series: A Rosalind Thorne mystery ; 1
Identifiers: LCCN 2015035789 | ISBN 9780425282373 (softcover)
Subjects: LCSH: Women detectives—England—Fiction. | Private
investigators—England—Fiction. | Murder—Investigation—Fiction. |
London (England)—Social life and customs—19th century—Fiction. | BISAC:
FICTION / Mystery & Detective / Women Sleuths. | GSAFD: Mystery fiction. |
Historical fiction.
Classification: LCC PS3623.I5353 U84 2016 | DDC 813/.6—dc23
LC record available at http://lccn.loc.gov/2015035789

PUBLISHING HISTORY
Berkley Prime Crime trade paperback edition / May 2016

PRINTED IN THE UNITED STATES OF AMERICA

10   9   8   7   6   5   4   3   2

Cover art by Matthieu Forichon.
Cover design by Lesley Worrell.
Interior text design by Laura K. Corless.

Penguin
Random
House

To Tim and Alex,
the light and the mystery of my life.

PROLOGUE

When the Dance Finishes Early

When she told the story afterward, Rosalind would say the noise woke her. The truth was, however, she had never actually been asleep.

She'd come home unusually early from the Wednesday ball at Almack's. She'd been tempted to stay, but if she did, she knew she'd have blurted out her secret. As it was, she feared she'd given herself away.

No. That is not possible. No one noticed anything. They would have spoken out.

Her acquaintances among the assembly would just assume her high color and her breathlessness came from the dancing. Who wouldn't be excited? It was every well-bred girl's dream to be allowed to waltz in Almack's famous rooms.

Perhaps I should have stayed. Rosalind tiptoed into her own, far more modest chamber. Annie, the upstairs maid, trailed behind with the lamp, yawning and blinking. No. Leaving looked odd, but staying would have been far worse. Rosalind wasn't sure whether she should laugh or cry at her own lack of discretion and discipline. She'd been unable to keep her eyes from Devon. She smiled and blushed every time he glanced toward her, and that was a countless number of times. Worse, she was tripping over everybody else's feet because she kept looking for him in the crowd instead of paying attention to her partner. She'd needed to have a headache and leave before someone said something out of turn to Mother. She'd write to Devon later, probably through his cousin Louisa, and explain the reason for her sudden departure. He would understand.

Mother had been put out, of course. Mother never left any party early if she could help it. She did, however, agree that Rosalind could take the carriage and her maid, as long as she sent both straight back as soon as she got home.

Rosalind peered into the boudoir she shared with her older sister, Charlotte. Charlotte had stayed home with her own headache, which might or might not have been real. Rosalind was inclined, this once, to believe that it was. Despite the fact it was barely midnight, Charlotte looked to be asleep in bed, wrapped up tightly in her covers.

It's just as well. Rosalind closed the door so as not to disturb Charlotte while Annie, fumbling, and still yawning, got her ready for bed. *I have to think. I have to plan.*

Because tonight Devon Winterbourne had made his intentions perfectly clear. He hadn't gone so far as to actually propose, of course, but he nearly had. Rosalind felt her blush rising again, and was glad the room was dim enough that the maid couldn't see her color.

I must calm down.

She also must decide exactly how to tell Charlotte about Devon. She couldn't be giggling and girlish when they spoke. Depending on her mood, Charlotte was as likely to laugh in her face as she was to help, and Rosalind was going to need help. Neither Mother nor Father was going to look favorably on an alliance with Devon Winterbourne, certainly not at first.

Mother had ambitions for Rosalind as well as for Charlotte, and Father was determined the girls should marry into fortunes, not just titles.

"My bright stars are not to be hidden out on fusty old estates!" Father cried. "They are meant to shine in the heights of heaven!"

Father was fond of making speeches like that. But he truly meant this one, and therein lay the problem. Devon was the son of a duke, but he was a *scorpion*, a second son, with limited prospects of his own. By prospects, of course, everyone meant money. His brother, Hugh, was young and strong, if profligate. Hugh Winterbourne also had women trailing after him in long strings, any of which he might marry at any moment. So there was next to no chance of Devon ever inheriting the title. Worse, Devon had a reputation of being under the thumb of his devout, reclusive mother. This wasn't true, of course, but it was the gossip.

But if Rosalind could get Charlotte on her side, she'd stand a much better chance with both parents. Charlotte had Father's ear, and she always knew best how to manage Mother.

Rosalind climbed into her bed and let down the curtains, but she lay awake with her blood fizzing in her veins and her mind tumbling over every detail of the moment: Devon's hesitation, the way his hand felt in hers, how they'd danced and they'd laughed and stepped on each other's feet. Neither one of them could waltz worth a ha'penny, and they whispered in merry agreement that this surely meant they'd get on famously all their lives.

Lady Blanchard had taken note. She was another problem and she'd have to be talked 'round quickly. Maybe even before Charlotte. Thankfully, Lady Blanchard wouldn't go to Mother, at least not yet. She had warned Rosalind, though.

Be careful, my dear. Do not fix your heart on someone who can do so little when your family needs so much.

It's my marriage, not theirs! Rosalind squeezed her eyes shut. She'd have to apologize for that, and quickly. Lady Blanchard's title and standing, not to mention her longtime attachment to Mother, would be a marvelous help if Rosalind was to navigate the tricky shoals of parental approval.

But one way or another she would do so, because Devon waited on the far shore.

That was when Rosalind heard curtains rustle, followed by the stealthy slide of fabrics. She turned over and tried to ignore it. Probably Charlotte just needed to make use of the chamber pot. But that particular noise did not occur. Instead, there was more furtive rustling, and the grating noise of something heavy dragging across the floorboards. Curiosity got the better of her. Rosalind hooked one finger around the velvet bed curtains and eased them back to peek.

A single candle flickered on the bedside table. Rosalind had to blink before she could correctly make out what she was seeing. There was Charlotte, fully dressed and kneeling down by her bed, pulling out a bandbox from underneath. Another, larger box sat beside her.

Rosalind flung the curtains back and scrambled out of her bed. Charlotte whirled, clutching her coat to her chest.

"Rosalind!" Charlotte hissed. "What are you doing? Go back to bed, you little idiot!"

Rosalind ignored this. "What's happening? Are you *eloping?*"

Charlotte hesitated for a single heartbeat and then began pulling her coat on. "Yes," she answered acidly. "How very clever of you. I'm eloping. He's waiting downstairs now."

"You can't! Mother will have a fit! And Father . . ." *If you elope now, they'll never consent to Devon! They'll lock me in the attic!*

But Charlotte wasn't listening. "I'll write, I promise." She grabbed up her boxes, pushed past Rosalind, and shouldered her way out the boudoir door. Rosalind ran out into the corridor in time to see Charlotte struggling to get herself and her luggage down the back stairs. Charlotte was not naturally stealthy or subtle, especially when encumbered, and she banged and clattered down the stairs.

If the servants aren't all awake now, they will be soon.

"Who is he?" Rosalind demanded as she thudded down the stairs behind Charlotte. "At least tell me that!"

Charlotte didn't so much as pause. They reached the kitchen and she marched to the garden door. "Go back to bed, Rosalind! You'll ruin everything!"

"I won't!" Rosalind grabbed her sister's wrist. "Not until you tell me. You don't understand, Charlotte." She added more softly. "Something's happened to me as well."

"Something's always happening to you. Now get off!"

Charlotte yanked her wrist from Rosalind's startled grip and shoved through the door to the back garden. Rosalind stared, but only for a moment. Then, her determination hardened and she ran out behind her sister. The cold of the flagstones bit into the soles of Rosalind's toes despite her woolen stockings. Beyond the garden wall, the watchman shouted, "Five of the clock and all's well!"

No it's not!

Even running gingerly on her toes, Rosalind still managed to catch up with Charlotte, who was wrestling with boxes and hems. This time when she grabbed Charlotte's arm, Rosalind hung on tight. "Tell me who it is, or I'll wake the house!" She wanted to believe she was thinking of her sister and her good. She wanted to help, to do the right thing. An elopement would be a scandal. Mother and Father would be beside themselves and they'd never listen to her or hear reason about Devon. Ever.

Charlotte brought her booted foot down hard on Rosalind's toes. Rosalind squeaked in pain, and surprise, and let go. Charlotte ran, or at least trotted, for the gate.

What doesn't she want me to see? thought Rosalind as she staggered behind. *I must know the man.*

Rosalind reached the gate. A hired coach and four waited in the muddy lane outside. The coach door was open and Charlotte was climbing in. Rosalind hesitated, straining for a glimpse of the man, afraid she'd made the wrong decision, that she should have run back at once, screaming to wake their parents as well as the servants . . .

Her father leaned out of the carriage to pull in the step and shut the door.

The world froze. At least, Rosalind froze. In front of her eyes, the hired driver touched up the sturdy horses so that the coach rattled and creaked into motion. The curtains in the coach's back window were down. They did not lift to afford her any last parting glimpse of the occupants, and yet she knew she had not been mistaken. She knew Father's profile—his hooked nose and his strong brow—in any light.

Rosalind's thoughts leapt from a standstill to a full gallop. She turned on her sore and frigid feet and dashed back into the house. She ran through the dining room to Father's book room.

The door stood open. The smell of burning paper hung in the air, and the last embers of various ledgers and papers smoldered on the hearth. The imported Italian desk was completely clear for the first time in Rosalind's memory, except for the one letter left lying squarely in the center of the blotter.

It was addressed to her mother. Rosalind barely attended to that. She just broke the seal and read:

Althea, My Dearest Wife:

How difficult it is to write these words! How many tears roll down my cheeks to stain this page as I think of you even now sleeping so soundly in your bed, blissfully unaware as to what this cruel, cold morning holds in store for you.

I have always worked diligently at business in order to provide the living that you and our lovely daughters deserve. Alas, several recent speculations have not turned out as well as I had hoped. This failure has weighed heavily on my mind for some time, but I have labored unceasingly to free myself of the obligations and restore our fortunes. Of course, I could not tell you, for I had no wish to risk any perturbation in that domestic harmony which I know means the world to you, as it does to me.

But now—oh, the pain of having to write this!—certain men who swore me friendship and assistance have treacherously gone back on their word. And worse—far worse!—they have spread infamous lies about my character and conduct, such that I now am hounded without stint by moneylenders and false friends seeking restitution for debts I never contracted and do not legally owe.

Because of the calumnies spread by these smiling fiends who once shook my hand and behaved to all appearances in the manner of gentlemen, I am left with no choice. I must run! I must fly! I am to become a fugitive in my own country lest I be taken up for these false debts.

Now, you must be strong, my darling! You must remember when these men come to you that they are liars and infamous customers. You must hold your loving heart firm against the falsehoods they will seek to pour into your ears. I know your courage. You will never lose faith in your dearest Reginald. You know in the depths of your soul that I will return to restore our family's reputation and fortune, as soon as I am able.

To help you in this time of greatest trial, I leave you our daughter Rosalind. Her steady good sense will surely serve to keep and comfort you until I am able to return and clear my good name of these libelous charges and unjust debts. Our loyal and thrice-darling daughter Charlotte has bravely consented to be my companion and helpmeet in the toils of my exile.

Adieu, my dearest! Have courage! Know that my heart is breaking as I write. Think of your darling Reginald alone in the cold world without one friend to succor him. His only thought is of the day he will be able to reunite all our family and restore tranquility to our home.

May God bless and keep you both!

Your eternally loving husband,
R.T.

It was Mrs. Kendricks, the housekeeper, who found Rosalind an hour later, still sitting in the book room, breathing in the scent of burning papers, and holding her father's parting letter in her numbed fingers.

CHAPTER 1

The Little Scandals of the Little Season

The lady patronesses of Almack's . . . carried matters—to say with a high hand seems almost inadequate—shall I write, with a clenched fist?

—E. Beresford Chancellor, *The Annals of Almack's*

LONDON, FEBRUARY 15, 1817

"Are you sure we may expect callers this early?" asked Mrs. Kendricks.

Rosalind Thorne smiled up at her housekeeper. She was breakfasting in her parlor with the small table drawn up close to the coal fire. In addition to providing extra warmth, this arrangement allowed her to surreptitiously toast bits of muffin on her fork. Rosalind made sure she'd eaten the evidence of this unladylike occupation before ringing the bell.

"They will be here," she told Mrs. Kendricks firmly. "I expect we'll be seeing Miss Littlefield first, followed by Mr. Faulks. I have laid the most tempting bait possible in front of them. Power is about to change hands. The world will not wait for polite visiting hours to discover the details." Courtesy dictated that morning visitors did not present themselves before eleven o'clock, but the church bells, which tolled solemnly outside the frosted windows, declared it had just gone on nine.

"Well, that should make for a busy season after all."

"Indeed it will, Mrs. Kendricks, if we're lucky. I trust we are ready to receive?"

"Of course, miss." Mrs. Kendricks was a thin, dark woman with severe eyes and narrow, calloused hands. Her long years in service had erased the element of surprise from her being, and taken a goodly portion of her ability to smile with it. "The coffee is ready, and I've baked some of my ginger biscuits as well."

Rosalind had no time for further remarks, for at that moment the doorbell jangled, not once, but four times. She and Mrs. Kendricks exchanged a knowing glance before the housekeeper departed to open the door for the insistent visitor.

Or visitors. It was possible that Alice Littlefield had met Sanderson Faulks on the way to Little Russell Street. Gentleman that he was, Mr. Faulks would surely offer Alice a ride in his well-sprung and—more importantly—warm carriage. Winter had clamped down hard this year, and London's streets were ankle deep in snow and frozen mud.

Rosalind folded her newspaper beside the large stack of her correspondence and stood to receive her early callers.

Upon first impression, Rosalind Thorne was often considered either striking or imperious. Unusually tall, she possessed the figure and bearing of a grand dame from a previous era—statuesque, confident, and thoroughly poised, despite the modesty of both her surroundings and her made-over blue dress with its sparse lace trim. Although her rich golden hair had been called her finest asset, she habitually wore it in a severe knot at the nape of her neck. Her wide-set blue eyes, on the other hand, were considered generally unremarkable, except for the unsettlingly direct way they had of looking at a person, any person, of any rank.

"Cold" was another word frequently applied to Rosalind Thorne.

As such, she was as much of a contrast to the persons who entered her diminutive parlor as they were to each other. Pretty, brisk, tiny, and dark, Alice Littlefield breezed into the room, and straight up to Rosalind.

"I am not speaking to you!" Alice announced. "You've been keeping secrets and I'm quite put out!" Despite this declaration, she kissed Rosalind soundly on the cheek.

"May I also bid you good morning, Miss Thorne?" drawled Sanderson Faulks as he bowed over her hand with the weary politeness that was the hallmark of the dandy set. Mr. Faulks was tall, lean, and pale, and if he had ever moved briskly, Rosalind expected it was because either his life or his fortune was in imminent danger. "If you had not already discerned it from Miss Littlefield's eloquent exclamation, you see here two wretched pilgrims come to present their humble petitions at the shrine of truth and knowledge."

"Fiddlesticks, Mr. Faulks," announced Alice. "Lovely, of course, but fiddlesticks still. Is there coffee?"

"Mrs. Kendricks is bringing it now. Good morning, Mr. Faulks. Good morning, Alice. Do sit down. I am so sorry my note forced you both out so early."

"Really, Miss Thorne!" Mr. Faulks's long, mobile face became the very picture of woe as he drew out a chair for Alice. "I strongly suspect you are now the one talking, as Miss Littlefield so quaintly puts it, fiddlesticks." Dandy though he might be, Mr. Faulks betrayed no hint of discomfort or fastidiousness as he took his own place on Rosalind's worn velvet sofa.

"Of course it's fiddlesticks." Alice plumped herself down in the cane-bottomed chair, flipped open her notebook, and took up her pencil. Alice had been trained in deportment by the same masters who had drilled Rosalind in the rigors of their art. Unlike Rosalind, however, Alice had cast off this early instruction almost as soon as she had ceased to be a minor heiress and begun supporting herself by writing for the newspapers and magazines. "Rosalind's been up for at least two hours waiting for us. One can tell by the breakfast table, and the morning papers, already half read."

"All right, you've caught me out." Rosalind moved her letters and papers to one side so Mrs. Kendricks could set down the coffee tray. Very little of the ancestral plate had passed unscathed through the abrupt transitions in the Thorne family fortunes, but the silver coffee set had been kept intact. Rosalind at once set about the business of pouring out and fixing the first cup with two sugar lumps and a delicate dollop of milk. "But surely we should wait until you've had your coffee before we discuss business?"

"Mr. Faulks, I may be about to commit murder." Alice turned a cold shoulder toward her hostess, but not before she took her coffee.

"Heaven forbid, Miss Littlefield. I've not had my morning cup yet, and Miss Thorne knows my taste to perfection." Faulks accepted the second coffee, took a long sip, and sighed like a man who has experienced true greatness. "Ah! Now. Miss Thorne, I beg you to spare your life and my susceptible nerves and tell us quickly. Is it true? Is one of the mighty Lady Patronesses from Almack's Assembly Rooms about to retire her post?"

It was tempting to tease her friends a moment longer, but Rosalind decided against it. She needed their goodwill for several important matters yet today. "Yes, it is true," she said. "I've received confirmation from a highly reliable source. One of the ladies is to step down, and there will be a new patroness at Almack's."

"I knew it!" cried Alice. "Oh, George will be furious that I got to you before he could!"

A stranger to London and its gilded social season might have been startled to hear such breathless suspense raised over the question of a single woman on the governing committee of a single suite of assembly rooms; especially when the popular press regularly mocked Almack's as a dull place that foolishly clung to tyrannical rules regarding dress and manners, not to mention its meager bread-and-butter refreshments.

Despite this, however, Almack's remained far more than a set of assembly rooms where dances and dinners might be held. It was nothing less than the gateway to the uppermost strata of London society. To be admitted to one of Almack's weekly subscription balls was to be given the chance to shine before the women who controlled social life across the length and breadth of the United Kingdoms. To be turned away, on the other hand, marked one indelibly as second rate.

Only a member of the Almack's board—a lady patroness— could decide who would be admitted to the assemblies. Without their approval, it did not matter what a person's rank or fortune might be. That person would be left to languish in the cold.

"Now quickly, Rosalind, which lady is leaving?" Alice Littlefield's eyes shone with childlike enthusiasm—or perhaps it was simple greed. The lady patronesses were petted, courted, feted, and discussed throughout the fashionable world, and the newspapers observed their movements as closely as if they were royalty. "It can't be Lady Jersey. She'll die in harness. The Princess Esterhazy? Or is it Lady Blanchard? There've been whispers that Lord Blanchard is in line for a post abroad."

Rosalind raised her coffee cup. A small smile played about her mouth as she took a swallow.

"I'll tell you, but I'll need something in return. From each of you."

"Mr. Faulks . . ." Alice gripped her pencil as if she meant to squeeze blood or gold from it.

"Now, now, Miss Littlefield. Might I advise you to consider the look of delight on your editor's face when you deliver this news, piping hot for his delectation? Not to mention the jealousy of your dear brother, George?"

"All right, all right," muttered Alice. "You win, Rosalind. What is it you want?"

"A friend of mine, Mrs. Nottingham, is giving a party at her London house to help brighten the little season." The "little season" was the name given to the time between Parliament's opening and Easter Week. Usually it lasted most of February and on into March. During this time, fashionable society made its way back to London from the country and set about preparing for the gaudy pageant that was the social season.

"I spy Miss Thorne's meaning." Mr. Faulks gave Alice a significant nod. "Mr. Nottingham, MP, has something up his sleeve for the coming session of Parliament and Mrs. N. wishes to rally support in the drawing rooms."

Alice rolled her eyes. "Thank you, Mr. Faulks, I do read the papers as well as write for them."

"It will be an elegant and exclusive event," Rosalind went on, unperturbed by Mr. Faulks's aside. "Here is the guest list." She lifted a sheet of paper from her correspondence and handed it to Alice. "I hope you'll find a few lines in your column to mention it will be a magnificent affair; a sign of a delightful season to come for one of our most sparkling and sagacious political hostesses."

Alice made a small, strangled noise. At the same time, her

pencil flew across the page, setting down Rosalind's words in practiced shorthand. "Any further dictation?"

"Not at this time, but I will let you know if anything else occurs."

"You always do."

"And what is the ransom I am to pay for this information which you guard so jealously?" inquired Mr. Faulks.

"You're to attend the party."

"In fact, your name's already on the guest list." Alice squinted at the page Rosalind had given her. "Sanderson Faulks, noted collector and art critic. You forgot pride of the dandy set, Rosalind. I'll make sure it's added."

"Oh, no." The blood drained from Faulks's cheek. "Not a political party. You may speak as much flummery as you please about Mrs. Nottingham being sparkling, but she's a fusty old cat and we all know it. I will not open my season in an overfilled drawing room being bored to tears about reform bills."

"Mrs. Nottingham's son is an artist," Rosalind told him. "He's back from the Continent. They've some of his work in their gallery. If you like what you see there, you'll have a new find to grace your season."

"I said *no*. Not even should you refuse to name the retiring patroness."

"Mr. Faulks," said Alice darkly. "Rosalind is not the only one risking her life at this moment."

"A political party given by a *parvenue* mama from a pocket borough whose son has artistic pretensions? You won't have to kill me, Miss Littlefield. Miss Thorne has done the deed."

"I have seen young Nottingham's work." Rosalind leveled her direct gaze at the collector. "He is worth a few hours at the start of your season, or any other time."

Faulks held his silence under Rosalind's full attention for

almost ten seconds, which was more than many men could manage. At last, he sighed. "Only for you, Miss Thorne. Now, out with it." He rapped his knuckles smartly against the sofa's arm. "Which of the lady patronesses will retire this season?"

"Alice guessed it," replied Rosalind. "Lord Blanchard has received a diplomatic posting to Konigsberg. At the first ball of the season, Lady Blanchard will announce she is withdrawing from the Almack's board so she can accompany her husband abroad."

Both visitors expelled the breaths they had been holding.

"Who is to be her replacement?" Alice turned a fresh page in her notebook.

Rosalind shook her head. "That I cannot yet tell you."

"And won't be able to for some months," said Mr. Faulks shrewdly. "If I know Lady Jersey and her cronies, they'll spend the entire season vetting the candidates, and incidentally setting the cream of ambitious *haut ton* matronry at each other's throats."

"There'll be blood in the ballrooms." Alice tapped her chin with her pencil. "Unfortunately, I don't think my editor will care for that turn of phrase."

"An affable affray to light afire betting books in White's and Brook's," said Faulks. "And you may not quote me on that, Miss Littlefield." He reached out and closed Alice's notebook firmly. "That is a bon mot of my own composing and I don't care to hear myself repeated all over the gossip sheets."

"Besides," said Alice, "you'll need it for your own use when you've a wider audience than a couple of spinsters."

Faulks laid one manicured hand over his breast. "I would never use such a vulgar epithet when describing two such excellent ladies. But otherwise, you are correct."

"Excuse me, miss." Mrs. Kendricks entered, carrying a silver tray with a single letter in its center. "This just came, by hand. The boy said he was to wait for a reply."

"Thank you, Mrs. Kendricks." Rosalind picked up the letter and looked at the direction. "You can stop craning your neck, Alice. I recognize the hand. It's from Tamwell House."

"Is it?" Alice opened her book and began writing again. "That means Honoria Aimesworth and her mother are finally back from Switzerland? They left so very suddenly last year . . ."

"Alice," said Rosalind sternly. "Leave this one alone. You know very well that the Aimesworths have been back for months, and spent a quiet Christmas at their country house."

"I do know it," said Alice. "I was just wondering if you did."

"Of course I did. Why wouldn't I?"

Alice bit the end of her pencil and made no answer. Rosalind frowned.

"How stimulating it is to see a professional engaged in the delicate cut and thrust of social intercourse." Mr. Faulks rose to his feet. "I could watch all day. Alas, however, I have business of my own and must bid you ladies adieu. Miss Littlefield, is there anywhere I may drop you?"

Alice hesitated, apparently debating whether Rosalind might be convinced to yield more information. This time, however, discretion proved the better part, and Alice also rose.

"Thank you, Mr. Faulks. It seems I also have work to do and should go at once to my paper's offices."

"My carriage and my person are entirely at your service, Miss Littlefield. If I may?" He rang the bell for Mrs. Kendricks and requested his hat and cape as well as Alice's wrap. "Adieu, Miss Thorne." He bowed to Rosalind.

But although Mr. Faulks turned to go, Alice didn't move.

"I'll be there in a moment. I've dropped my pencil." Alice

said this directly to Rosalind and so missed the significant way in which Mr. Faulks glanced from her to their hostess before he retreated into Rosalind's small foyer.

"Rosalind," Alice said as soon as the parlor door shut, "if you are going to be spending any time with the Aimesworths this season, you should know you will probably be seeing a great deal of Devon Winterbourne. Only, he's Lord Casselmain now."

Rosalind did not blanch. She had too many years of practice at self-control for any such display.

"I knew, of course, his brother had died," she said softly. "But why should he be connected to the Aimesworths?"

"There are rumors in the air beyond the ones regarding Almack's, and they're linking Lord Casselmain with Honoria Aimesworth."

Rosalind lowered herself gracefully into her chair. She was certain Alice noted how she kept her hand pressed flat against the table to prevent it from trembling.

"It, of course, can mean nothing to you personally," Alice prompted her. "But it is always good to be informed."

"Yes, that's it exactly. You needn't be concerned about me."

"Only I had thought you once cherished a certain preference for Lord Casselmain."

The smile that turned up the corners of Rosalind's mouth was entirely artificial. She was sure Alice saw that, too. "Once. For about an hour, I think, when we were both younger and my social standing was rather different."

"I don't suppose you'll consider staying away from Tamwell House?" Alice asked.

"I might, but as things are . . . Lady Aimesworth has been generous in displaying her gratitude for my assistance in the past."

"You mean with helping smooth things over when Honoria got jilted by Phineas Worth."

Rosalind didn't bother to answer that. "If she invites me for even part of the season, I may not be able to turn her down."

"I do understand." Alice pressed Rosalind's hand once. "Good luck. Be sure to call on me if you need anything."

"I will, dear Alice. Thank you."

They made their farewells and Alice took herself off after Mr. Faulks. Rosalind Thorne stayed as she was for a very long time. It was only when she was certain her hands had stopped shaking that she picked up the new letter and broke its seal.

CHAPTER 2

The Bosom of the Family Home

Everyone knows in England, ton *governs everything.*
—Marianne Spencer Stanhope Hudson, *Almack's*

"Mother! You've invited that Thorne creature here! What are you trying to do to me?"

Lady Edmund Aimesworth, *née* Sophia Inneswell, did not so much as lift her eyes from her visiting book. "Honoria," she said as she finished crossing the last *T* in her latest entry, "you will compose yourself and you will not speak again until you have." She moved Mrs. Chadwell's visiting card from one stack to another.

"I beg your pardon, Mother." Acid leeched all trace of sincerity from Honoria's words, but at least she achieved something approaching an even tone. "But you did invite Rosalind Thorne to spend the season with us, did you not?"

"I have not yet, but I will." Lady Edmund wondered which servant let slip this information to Honoria. The person would have to be dismissed. This would naturally lead to all the trouble and aggravation of finding a replacement, but that could not be helped. "Miss Thorne is a most useful woman. If we are to continue our recovery from last year's unfortunate occurrences, we need to manage your season most carefully."

"She is . . ." Honoria began, but Lady Edmund turned, and let the girl see her expression. Calm was always the right answer to a tirade: calm, and a cool, patient regard. A display of temper only made one look ridiculous.

"I do not want her in the house at this time, Mother."

The soft scratching at the door indicated the arrival of the maid. For a heartbeat, Lady Edmund considered sending Honoria away. Contrary to what they might think, she did not underestimate the intelligence or determination of either of her children. She'd had a year to repent ever having done so.

The door opened and the white-haired parlor maid stepped in, carrying a neatly folded letter in both hands.

"Is that Miss Thorne's reply, Gillingham?" Lady Edmund did not shift her gaze from Honoria's as she held out her hand for the letter. "There's nothing further. You may go."

As soon as the door closed, Lady Edmund broke the plain seal and opened the letter. "It would appear you are somewhat tardy with your request, Honoria. Miss Thorne writes she will call here this afternoon. Was there anything else you wanted?"

Honoria clamped her teeth tightly together. She wanted to storm. She wanted to rage. Lady Edmund could read it in the bright, brown eyes the girl had not yet learned how to mask. But Honoria straightened herself up, and—thank heavens!—drew back her out-thrust chin. It was all done too obviously, but it was good to see her make some effort at self-control. Perhaps there was still hope.

"No. There was nothing else, Mother. Thank you."

Lady Edmund gave her daughter a small nod, and let her

withdraw. Then she smoothed her own countenance and turned back to her desk. It was going to be a busy day.

Honoria slipped through the door into the conservatory and locked it behind her. Damp heat surrounded her, instantly dragging down the curls her maid had worked so diligently to set that morning.

The conservatory of Tamwell House was Lord Edward's particular pride. Not that Honoria's father had any genuine interest in exotic plants. His lordship employed a botanist to tend the palms and orchids. It was building that was Lord Edmund's passion. He'd designed the glass walls and central dome with their intricate hexagonal panes and laid out the system of pipes that delivered both heat and water and, incidentally, clanked and hissed so constantly that one could barely hear the central fountain's soothing trickle.

It was that noise that Honoria sought to cover her own. She backed away from the door, balled up her fists and shouted, "This is not happening! I will *not* permit it! We don't need Rosalind Thorne!"

"Why, what's all this? Poor little puss!" called a voice from the next room. "Someone put vinegar in your milk, poor puss?"

Honoria whirled around. Behind her waited the curving chamber that was labeled CARD ROOM on Father's cherished blueprints. Not that anyone actually played cards there. The conservatory's damp heat wilted any pasteboards within minutes, no matter how tightly one closed the French doors.

"Jasper!" Honoria cried. "What are you doing in here?"

The question was reflexive. Honoria could see for herself that her brother sat by the hearth with his feet on the fender, a poker in one hand and a glass in the other. The noise from the pipes had disguised the crackle of the cheery little fire kindled in the grate.

"Poor, poor puss." Jasper waved the tip of his ashy poker in time with his words. "Poor puss."

Although two years younger than Honoria, Jasper was the taller of them by a good six inches. Despite this, there was no mistaking the connection between the Aimesworth children. They shared the family's chestnut hair, egg-shaped face, and deep-set, dark eyes. They also both possessed a talent for turning those eyes either sultry or intimidating, as the situation required.

"Are you drunk?" Honoria demanded as she strode into the card room. There was a sharp, familiar smell in the air under all the odors of damp greenery. She'd place it in a minute. She grabbed the tumbler out of Jasper's hand and sniffed. *That* was definitely whiskey.

"Probably." Jasper grabbed the glass back and hugged it to his breast. "I take it Mother intends for the Thorne woman to stay after all. How very humiliating for you."

"If that's the sort of thing you've got to say, you may clear off."

"I was here first, sister dear. You may clear off." Jasper jabbed the poker vaguely toward the door. "I still have some drinking to do."

The unsteadiness of her brother's hand, and the slur in his voice, made Honoria look at him more closely. Jasper's normally saturnine face was flushed and swollen from far more than the room's artificially tropical atmosphere. Concern flickered through her. "What's the matter with you?"

"None of your business, Honoria." Jasper dug the poker tip deep into the fire. "None. Of your. *Damn*. Business."

"If you're drunk before noon, it is very much my business." Honoria yanked the glass from his hand again. This time, she set it on the mantelpiece, well out of reach. "What's happened?"

"Nothing. Nothing new at any road. The world's just a revolting mess, and I can't seem to make it any better." Jasper tossed the poker down so it made a hideous clanging and scattered ash across Father's beloved gold and blue Roman tiles. "I try, Honoria, 'pon my soul, I do. But I just . . . *can't*."

"Well, that makes two of us, doesn't it?" Honoria dropped into the opposite chair. Mother would be appalled to see how she fell backward, and threw out both arms. Had it not been for her corset, she would have positively slumped.

"Poor puss," Jasper said again, but this time there was genuine affection in it. "Is the Thorne creature really the problem?"

"Of course! Her entire family is a disgrace. By rights everybody should have dropped her years ago, but no! Phineas jilts me, and I can't show my face in town for a year. But *her* . . . She's everywhere one looks, prying and poking and managing everybody's business and all of *them* going on and on about how well she's carried on in the face of her troubles and how wonderfully useful she is! It makes me sick."

"Not to mention the fact that she was once all but engaged to the man you are currently all but engaged to."

Honoria made no answer. She just stared at Jasper's little fire. It was sinking quickly, like her spirits.

"I know I made a mistake," she said to the fire, and her brother. "I've admitted it. I've apologized for it, and heaven knows I've paid for it. I mean, wasn't that the point of that dreary trip to Switzerland?"

"Oh, come now, it can't really have been that bad."

"Oh, no. I only endured endless rounds of dinners and so-called parties in cramped little houses with the same tiny crowd of English expatriates. Then there was the dragging one-self up mountains and down vales on mule back, and squinting at buildings and paintings one had no interest in at all. But what would you know about it? You got to stay in London."

"So I did," murmured Jasper. "For my sins, I did indeed."

"Jasper, for heaven's sake, what is the matter? Please tell me."

"I won't. But." Jasper leaned forward, his voice and manner both steadier than they had been a moment before. "I will say this. If you want to drop the Casselmain engagement, I'll back you with the paternals. It was a bad idea from the first."

"It's not a bad idea," Honoria said. "It's the best idea. That's the real problem." It was also the quickest way out from under her mother's authority, because Lord Casselmain was a man of sufficient rank and wealth that even Mother couldn't muster any objection to the social position he'd bring the family.

Jasper stuck the poker back into the fire and stirred the ashes thoughtfully. "If it helps, I don't think Mother is bringing Miss Thorne here to shepherd you to the altar."

"What else could it be?"

"I suspect that our beloved mother is set on gaining revenge for all the snubbery she suffered after that business with Phineas."

"Snubbery? Now I know you're foxed. If I rang for coffee, would you drink it?"

"I might. For novelty's sake." Jasper heaved himself to his feet, caught up the whiskey glass from the mantle, and downed the remaining spirit. "There!" He slammed the glass back down. "Bring on your black brew, Medea, and do murder to the morose spirits of my soul!"

Honoria rolled her eyes, but she also rang the bell and ordered the footman to bring coffee at once.

"Speaking of novelty, I've had an idea." Jasper leaned back

against the hearth and looked down his long Aimesworth nose at her. "It goes against the tide of all civilized opinion and feeling. It is, in fact, positively radical in nature . . ."

"Stop it, Jasper. If you've got something useful to say, say it."

"I'm drunk, remember? A man gets to ramble when he's drunk." He flashed at her that particular smile which had enabled him to cut a wide swath among London's more susceptible women.

Honoria huffed out a sigh and folded her arms. "Well, get on with it, or I shall hold your nose and pour coffee down your throat until you can speak to the point."

"You could try talking with her."

"Mother won't listen! I've just left her room. She's set on this. She—"

"Not Mother, you goose." Jasper tweaked her ear and Honoria slapped his hand impatiently. "The Thorne creature."

Her brother's words so stunned Honoria, she had to repeat them to herself several times before she was sure she understood correctly. "What could Rosalind Thorne and I possibly have to say to each other?"

"She's useful, isn't she? That's the whole point of her. She offers to help everywhere she goes. Ask her to help you."

"I don't want her help! I don't want her anywhere near me!"

"But you've got her, haven't you? If you can't get rid of her, you might as well get her on your side."

Silence fell between them, broken by the crackle of the fire, and the rattle of Father's steam pipes.

"It won't work," Honoria said finally. "Rosalind Thorne hates me. She's never forgiven me for putting her in her place when we were girls. Which she deserved, by the way."

"Tish-tosh, pish-posh. Water under the bridge."

"She's sure to be jealous as well. She made herself positively ridiculous over Devon for a whole season. We all saw it. She's as likely to try to sabotage things as she is to help them along."

"Ah, but my sister dear, you have what the Thorne creature desperately needs, and I do not mean a titled husband."

"You mean money?"

Jasper nodded, slowly and significantly. "I mean money. A little bird told me that since she left the protection of Lord and Lady Blanchard's house to set up her own establishment, several of our finest London hostesses are rather less comfortable with their martyred Miss Thorne. Living on her own shows a shocking independence at odds with the gentility that our *grande dames* expect from their charity children. As a result, Miss Thorne may find this season a lean one, and she won't be as fussy about where her assistance comes from." He paused and groped across the mantle. His hand found the whiskey glass and he looked into the bottom, seemingly in disbelief that it was empty. "Sticky, greasy stuff, money," he muttered. "Oozes into all sorts of corners like you wouldn't believe, and drives out all thought of everything else." He started for the table and the decanter, but Honoria grabbed it first.

"Is that why you're drunk? Over money?"

"Among other things. Don't worry, though, the money's not mine. As to the rest . . ." He touched the side of his nose. "Now, here's my coffee. Do you mean to stay and watch me drink it all up like a good boy?"

"No, I trust you." Honoria stood, but she made no other move to leave. "Do you really think Mother's up to something?"

"Oh, I'm sure of it." Jasper poured coffee from the silver pot into the Sevres china cup, and added an appalling amount of sugar.

"Very well. I will talk to Miss Thorne. I will bribe her, if necessary." Honoria glowered at the doors as if she expected them to open at any moment and reveal Rosalind in all her shabby triumph. "I will *not* let anyone make a fresh ruin of my life, and that includes our mother. I'll ruin her first."

"I wish you all the luck in the world with that, sister dear." Jasper raised his coffee cup. "Do let me know if you need my help."

CHAPTER 3

Invitations and Insinuations

*To be introduced to that magic circle was considered at one
time as great a distinction as to be presented at Court, and
was often far more difficult of attainment.*

—E. Beresford Chancellor, *The Annals of Almack's*

"Miss Thorne, how good of you to come."

Watching Lady Edmund cross a room was very much like watching a prima donna take the stage. Every movement was perfectly smooth, but in no way relaxed. Lady Edmund was always on the alert, and she controlled not only her person, but the space around her.

Controls it, thought Rosalind. *But does not inhabit it.*

"Thank you for inviting me, Lady Edmund." Rosalind made her curtsy and took her seat on the round-backed tapestry chair her hostess indicated.

"Will you have a cup of tea?" Lady Edmund was already pouring out as she spoke. "And do try a slice of this apple tart. We've a new cook, you know, and I shall be most interested in your opinion."

Rosalind slid etiquette and expectation firmly across her impatience. She drank the tea and inquired as to its provenance.

She ate the tart and pronounced it excellent. The nutmeg was a perfect touch, much to be preferred over cinnamon as an accompaniment for apples, especially if one was also enjoying a good cheddar cheese with them. The roads were, of course, bad, the weather was worse, and all families of their mutual acquaintance were last heard to be in excellent health.

As the polite and practiced chatter flowed, Rosalind cast any number of surreptitious glances about her. Lady Edmund had clearly taken advantage of her time away to institute sweeping changes to her household decor. The frescoes, tapestries, and gilding Rosalind remembered had been replaced by plain paint: dusky red for the upper walls, pure white for the panels, trim, and ceiling. Only a few plaster rosettes and garlands were suffered to remain. These were relieved at reasonable intervals by tasteful oil paintings, mostly copies of great masters, with one or two family portraits between them.

Lady Edmund had also changed. Not in her *toilette*; that remained perfect. Her sage green morning dress was exactly what the moment called for, being elegant and expensive without overt ostentation. Her dark hair was swept back and pinned beneath a cap that was little more than a scrap of tissue. Nonetheless, Rosalind detected fresh lines around Lady Edmund's wide mouth, and a furrow between her ruthlessly plucked brows. These small signs showed Rosalind that Lady Edmund had hardened herself. As with the rest of the room, everything that was not of immediate use to the leading lady had been put away.

"Now, Miss Thorne." Lady Edmund set her empty cup and its saucer down on the new teakwood table. "I fear I must beg your pardon. The truth of the matter is, I have invited you here to ask a favor."

"There is no pardon necessary, Lady Edmund. How can I be

of assistance?" Rosalind put her plate aside with a small twinge of regret. The tart really was excellent, and there was still a bit left. But it would not have been polite to keep eating now that the business portion of this conversation had commenced.

"I was wondering if I might persuade you to come stay with us for the month? As you know, Honoria and I are only just returned from the country, and before that our tour abroad. Everything is at sixes and sevens. We stand in sore need of your calming influence as we prepare for the new season."

And that, Rosalind mused, was as close as Lady Edmund would come to mentioning the fact that Honoria had been jilted in favor of Emma Ibbotson-Davies and her bewitching ways, not to mention her fifty thousand pounds.

"Lady Edmund, I thank you for your kind invitation," said Rosalind, "but I'm afraid I must decline."

Another woman would have huffed, or even cried out in surprise. But in twenty-five years of close and glittering confine- ment in London society, Lady Edmund Aimesworth had never been required to so much as raise her voice.

She said, "I trust, Miss Thorne, that I may be frank without giving offense?"

"I much prefer plain speaking, Lady Edmund."

"A quality of yours I particularly admire. Now, while your skills and connections would prove invaluable to helping make up the ground my daughter lost last year, it is not Honoria's situation that persuaded me to invite you. At least, not entirely."

This took Rosalind aback and, unfortunately, piqued her curiosity. A hint of a smile flashed behind Lady Edmund's eyes. "Since Lady Blanchard is your godmother, she has no doubt told you that she and her husband will shortly be leaving London for a diplomatic posting."

"I have heard something of it," agreed Rosalind.

"I want the position she's deserting. I want to be named a lady patroness of Almack's."

It was as if Lady Edmund had announced she wanted to be married to King George. In point of fact, arranging that match might have been easier. Mad as the king was, he might be persuaded to at least like her.

Rosalind did not say that. She said, "A great number of ladies will wish to be named to the Almack's board. Many of them will be close friends of the current patronesses."

"But will any of them guarantee your future if they get it?"

The cold sensation of having been cornered crept across Rosalind. "I beg your pardon?"

Lady Edmund fixed her gaze entirely upon Rosalind's, and when she spoke, it was in the same ringing tones a barrister might use upon summing up his case. "I understand that since last season, you have set up your own establishment. I suppose that's in preparation for your godmother's departure?" She paused, but Rosalind did not answer. "It is also, of course, an expensive undertaking. If you assist me in becoming a lady patroness of Almack's, I will sign over to you a house my family owns in Westminster for use during your lifetime. With it will come an annuity of seventy-five pounds per year. It is not a great deal, but it will enable you to live quietly, comfortably, and without reference to anyone else."

A house? It took every ounce of Rosalind's pride and self-control not to stare at Lady Edmund. This cold, practiced woman was offering her a house? It was unheard of. It was ridiculous.

It was a bribe of the very first water.

What was it for? Yes, Almack's lady patronesses had prestige and power, but so did Lady Edmund. Her daughter had been jilted, but a good marriage would erase all memory of that unpleasantness. As the mother of the Duchess of Casselmain, Lady Edmund would have access to the very heights of London society. She did not need the patroness post. Certainly she did not need it enough to offer Rosalind a house and a pension.

"That's very generous of you, Lady Edmund, but—"

She got no further. "Miss Thorne, there is no reason at all we should not work together on this. It's not as if you retain any friendly feeling for the lady patronesses and their smug little assembly."

"If I may, Lady Edmund, that is hardly the point. There is very little chance that I could even begin to help with what you're asking. Lady Jersey is notoriously high in the instep. If someone's name so much as sounds disagreeable to her, she will blackball them from the assemblies. If a girl is not pretty enough, or her mama comes from trade, she will keep them out of Almack's forever. Any person she allows onto the board will be someone she is certain is loyal to her first and to Almack's second."

"Then we will have to remain alert for opportunities to demonstrate that loyalty. Perhaps you could consult Lady Blanchard herself?"

"I do not believe Lady Blanchard will be receptive to inquiries on the subject."

"Should that prove true, I'm sure you will be able to think of something else. You have always demonstrated such impressive invention. In the meantime, we will make sure that the world understands you are here to assist with arrangements for my daughter's season, which, I should tell you, will likely culminate in a ball celebrating her engagement to Lord Casselmain."

Rosalind had been ready for this. She'd been ready since Alice broke the news this morning. She should have been ready since she heard of the previous Lord Casselmain's death. Her readiness didn't matter, though. The words still hit her dead center.

"I tell you this in strictest confidence, of course," Lady Edmund went on.

"Of course." *For heaven's sake, don't let her see how she's upset you.* "I regret to say that I must still refuse." Rosalind stood. "I am sorry I could not be of more help."

Lady Edmund did not move. "It's clear you need a little time to think. I am certain that once you've considered all aspects of the situation, you will find yourself able to accept my offer."

There was a scratching at the door and a footman in the dark Aimesworth livery entered. He carried a silver salver with a single card on it. Lady Edmund read the card and nodded. Rosalind looked away and suppressed her sigh of relief. The etiquette of paying calls dictated that if another visitor arrived, the first was required to make a quick, polite exit.

Her relief, though, lasted only until the footman admitted the visitor: an elegant, broad-shouldered man with waving black hair.

Devon. This was Rosalind's first thought as Devon Winterbourne, Lord Casselmain, entered Lady Edmund's salon. Her second was, *You've changed.*

His shoulders were broader and his bearing more decided than she recalled. His eyes had changed as well. Not the color. They were still that remarkable steel gray, made all the brighter by the contrast to his black hair and dark brows. But the man behind those eyes had darkened. Was he tarnished or closed off? It was impossible to tell from so brief a glance.

Rosalind had prayed this first meeting would occur someplace that offered easy escape—some concert or rout, where there was a balcony, or a retiring room to which she could retreat.

"Lord Casselmain." Lady Edmund executed a perfect, polite curtsy. "How charming. We did not expect you today."

Devon's—Lord Casselmain's—answering bow was as smooth and as polite. "Lady Edmund. How do you do? I was coming to see Jasper, but **wished to** stop a moment to pay my respects."

"You are always welcome here, sir. And I believe you know Miss Thorne?"

Devon turned. Their eyes met for a single instant. "Of course," he said. "But it has been a very long time since I've had the pleasure." Then, he was bowing once again and she was curtsying because that was what the moment called for, and they must all conform to etiquette's expectations. "How do you do, Miss Thorne?"

"Very well, Lord Casselmain, thank you. I trust I find you well?"

"Perfectly, thank you."

He certainly looked well. His clothing—a blue coat, tan waistcoat, and buff breeches—was sparingly elegant. His white cravat had been tied in crisp folds, but without any trace of the dandy's fussiness. He had foresworn the stiff, black Hessians so many gentlemen considered indispensible. Instead, he wore a pair of plain top boots, scuffed from long usage and clearly soft as kid gloves. Devon Winterbourne had become a practical man, and one who followed inclination rather than fashion.

Why on earth is he agreeing to marry Honoria Aimesworth? The question was shamefully petty, but Rosalind could not clear it from her thoughts.

"Won't you sit down, Lord Casselmain?" Lady Edmund resumed her own place. "I'm afraid my son is not at home. He left us before luncheon and has not yet returned."

Lord Casselmain sat. He also looked quite perplexed.

"Did you have an appointment?" Lady Edmund inquired.

"It's of no matter. I'm sure to run into him at White's later."

"Well, I know Honoria will be delighted to see you." Lady Edmund reached for the bell to summon the parlor maid. "Please tell Miss Aimesworth that Lord Casselmain is here."

Lord Casselmain turned toward Rosalind. Naturally. It was the time to make polite conversation. "Have you plans for the season, Miss Thorne?"

"They are not yet fixed." Rosalind kept her gaze on the tea table. If she looked up, she might yet see pity in Devon's eyes.

"I have been attempting to persuade Miss Thorne that she should come stay with us for a short time, Lord Casselmain," Lady Edmund said as she passed him a cup of tea. "As you two are old acquaintances, perhaps you could help me."

The words jolted Rosalind's gaze away from the safe contemplation of the china. That was no accident. Lady Edmund must have heard whispers of their old attachment. Now she was testing them.

If Devon realized as much, he didn't even blink. "Lady Edmund, I have never observed that you require any assistance to achieve your ends. I am quite sure Miss Thorne will be brought 'round to your way of thinking without my intervention."

"You make me sound like a managing woman."

"Then I must apologize, for that was not my intention. I only meant that you are sensible, resolute, and determined."

Rosalind felt a twinge inside her. This polite banter was exactly right for the moment, but it was entirely wrong for Devon. Devon was always a little awkward and searching for his balance. Devon was sincere, and he was kind. He wasn't polished. He wasn't graceful in company. He laughed. He teased. He returned small, lost things to their proper owners.

Only this wasn't Devon in front of her, of course. This was Lord Casselmain.

Lady Edmund laughed. "As flattery, sir, that has the virtue of being original. What is your opinion, Miss Thorne? Shall I accept his apology?"

"As it is sincerely offered, Lady Edmund, I think you should."

As Rosalind spoke, the doors opened to show Honoria Aimesworth poised on the threshold.

"Oh, Lord Casselmain is never less than sincere," Honoria declared. "It is one of his great virtues."

Honoria entered the room with a stride closer to a soldier's march than a lady's delicate glide. Rosalind glanced at Lady Edmund in time to see how quickly she smoothed out her frown of disapproval. As for Devon, he watched the approach of the girl he was supposed to marry with indifference, and perhaps a little amusement. Not that Honoria's face exactly lit up with joy at the sight of her future bridegroom. Perhaps it might have, if she had not been so busy scowling at Rosalind.

"Lord Casselmain was calling on Jasper," said Lady Edmund. "Do you know where he's gone, Honoria?"

The question turned Honoria's attention back to her mother.

"I didn't know he had. He said nothing at breakfast about going anywhere."

"Well, you and I must entertain his lordship until your brother returns."

As a hint, it was hardly subtle, and Rosalind at once got to her feet. "I'm afraid I must be on my way. Thank you for the tea, Lady Edmund."

Devon—Lord Casselmain—rose as well.

"Oh, must you go, Rosalind?" said Honoria brightly. "I was so hoping we might have a chance to chat."

The small, false politeness of social conversation had never been Honoria's forte. If the truth were to be known, it was something Rosalind actually liked about her. Honoria might be sharp as a knife, but she was also entirely straightforward.

Lady Edmund wasn't frowning, but maintaining her placid demeanor was obviously costing her. Rosalind felt curiosity prick. Honoria was giving her an acceptable excuse to stay, but that would mean angering Lady Edmund. She might not have any intention of accepting her outrageous proposal, but Lady Edmund was a prominent figure in society, and Rosalind could not risk falling into her bad books.

"Thank you, Honoria, but I'm afraid I've several calls to make. Perhaps another time?" Rosalind found her polite smile and bestowed it evenly on the little assembly. "Thank you so much for your invitation, Lady Edmund. I will have an answer for you regarding the other matter shortly."

"I look forward to hearing from you, Miss Thorne."

Then, because it was expected and therefore required, she turned to face Lord Casselmain and receive his polite bow. Rosalind bobbed her curtsy. But her eyes raised themselves a heartbeat too soon and caught his.

Memory wrapped her in summer darkness, and Devon's gentle eyes were filled with moonlight and kindness and something else she did not yet have the courage to put a name to. His hand caught hers, and she felt how he shook. She remembered thinking how this was only fair. She was shaking, too.

Six hours later, Rosalind was chasing her sister Charlotte down the servants' stairs, out to the coach and four their father had hired to make his escape.

Rosalind forced herself back to the present, where Lord Casselmain stood a polite distance away and touched her only with his light, gray gaze.

"Oh, I nearly forgot," he said. "But I believe you know my cousin Louisa, Miss Thorne?"

"Yes, indeed. How is she?"

"Very well, thank you. She and my aunt are staying with me for the season. She mentioned she hoped to meet you while you are in town. May I tell her you will call?"

Rosalind did not for a moment believe this invitation actually came from Louisa. Lord Casselmain was contriving to bring them together again, right in front of the girl who was supposed to be his fiancée.

Unfortunately, because of the way Lord Casselmain phrased the request, and because they were in company, Rosalind could not refuse without appearing ill-mannered. "Certainly you may, Lord Casselmain. I'll be delighted to see Louisa. Now, you must excuse me."

Annoyance at having been so neatly cornered gave her the strength to turn smoothly away.

Outside, January's cold wrapped around Rosalind, digging under her collar and into her finger ends. There was a livery stable nearby where she might be able to hire a hackney carriage, but as she mentally counted the meager number of coins in her reticule, Rosalind sighed, and started walking in the direction of Blanchard House.

Why? she thought again. *Why are you doing this, Devon?*

But still there was no answer.

CHAPTER 4

The Secrets of a Diplomatic House

*"How will this look in Almack's" was as insistent a question
as "How will this look in the universe?"*

—Thomas Carlyle

Blanchard House had been built on a grand scale. Unlike Lady
Edmund, however, Lady Blanchard had attempted to find some
harmony between her home's past and its present. The lower
rooms maintained much of their old grandeur, with their fres-
coed ceilings and gilded trim. Since it was not easy to make such
vast painted and paneled chambers comfortable, Lady Blanchard
did her receiving in the private rooms above the first floor.

Because Rosalind was expected, the stout footman took her
up the sweeping central stair without any of the formal delay of
sending up a card or inquiring whether the mistress of the house
was at home. As a further mark of distinction, she was led to
the private parlor off Lady Blanchard's boudoir.

"Rosalind!" Lady Blanchard held out her hands in welcome.
"At last! Sit down, my dear, and tell me of your success."

"It was not at all difficult, you know." Rosalind took her
godmother's hands and pressed them warmly. Her encounter
with Lord Casselmain had left her more troubled than she
would care to admit, and being able to throw herself into Lady

Blanchard's business was a welcome distraction. "The news that you are leaving your post as lady patroness of Almack's should appear in A. E. Littlefield's 'Society Notes' this Sunday."

"Excellent." A determined satisfaction that Rosalind had not seen for a very long time lit Lady Blanchard's green eyes. "I know tea and sandwiches are poor payment for a successful effort, but you shall have them all the same."

When Rosalind had first come to London in preparation for her debut, Lady Blanchard was a society hostess at the height of her powers. To say that the intervening years had not been kind to her was to do a grave injustice to the pitched battle each had waged against the other. Lady Blanchard still charmed, but like her beauty, that charm had dimmed. She propped up her diminished personal luster with the perfection of her houses and entertainments, much in the way the faded gold of her hair had been reinforced by a special recipe known only to her lady's maid. She applied the art of conversation and of arranging a guest list as carefully as she did her rouge and powder. Nothing, however, could conceal the fact that her pallor was no longer fashionable, or that years of holding back any unseemly show of feeling had sharpened the once gentle lines of her face.

The business of pouring out tea and selecting sandwiches of delicate farm cheese, or thinly sliced ham, or spicy preserved meats occupied the following several minutes, and gave Rosalind time to consider her next words.

"You understand, of course, your fellow patronesses will not be best pleased by our actions." Rosalind settled onto the sofa with her plate of sandwiches and biscuits. "I expect Lady Jersey at least would prefer some say in the form and timing of the announcement."

"Which is why I'm making sure the word is put about now." Lady Blanchard sipped her own tea, but left the food untouched.

"I never should have gotten involved with Almack's. It has been a disaster from beginning to end, but I thought it would help my husband. He was so pleased when I was tapped for the post."

"And now you're both going away."

"Yes, we are, and it's high time." As she spoke, Lady Blanchard smiled, a soft, distant, contented expression.

"It's good to see you happy," Rosalind said warmly. "I will say, though, that when I'm offering my assistance to a friend, I'm generally told what it is they are after."

Lady Blanchard colored at this, but only a little. "I know it. But you know that in society two people can keep a secret only when one of them is dead, even if one of those persons is you, Rosalind."

"I think I should be insulted."

"Probably you should. I'm using you rather shamelessly, and what makes it worse is that you are the one person I will truly miss after I am gone."

Rosalind waited, and she hoped, but Lady Blanchard was too practiced a political hostess to allow one moment of intimacy to loosen her tongue. "Enough of my dreary business. Tell me how you are doing."

Had Rosalind been speaking to Alice Littlefield, she might have ignored the attempt to change the subject. Her difference in age and station to Lady Blanchard, however, made that impossible, not to mention severely impolite.

"To speak the truth, Lady Blanchard, I find myself in a quandary. I've just come from Tamwell House. Lady Edmund Aimesworth wants me to stay with her for the little season."

The pause between Lady Blanchard's taking hold of her cup and her lifting it from its china saucer was small, but it was there. "I'm sure she wants you to help manage her daughter's return to polite society, just as you helped with her exit."

"That's what I thought at first, but Lady Edmund wanted to discuss a different matter. She'd heard about your leaving London, and the Almack's board, before I got there."

"Oh, well." Lady Blanchard attempted a careless attitude. "We knew it could not be kept quiet for long. Men talk as well as women, and all of Blanchard's ministry friends knew about the posting days ago."

Rosalind fixed her attention on her hostess. She did not dare blink lest she miss some subtle point of her friend's reaction to what she said next. "Lady Edmund wants to become a patroness."

Lady Blanchard froze, a heartbeat of absolute stillness. "She *what?*"

"She asked me to use my influence with you to smooth her way."

Lady Blanchard set her cup down. She rose then, and walked to the window. Rosalind watched with a growing sense of alarm. For Lady Blanchard, such a gesture was as forceful as another woman's shout.

"Tell me what she said," ordered Lady Blanchard without turning around. "And what she did. Tell me exactly."

Rosalind did, describing as best she could the scene and the conversation she had endured. She even told Lady Blanchard about the offer of a house and an annuity.

"Who was there when she did this?"

The question took Rosalind aback. How could that matter? *No*, she stopped herself. Of course it mattered. Who heard a thing was at least as important as who said it. "No one at that time. We were alone until Lord Casselmain arrived."

"Ah. Yes. He'd be there to visit Honoria. I've heard the rumors coming from that quarter, and I'm sorry."

"There is no need," murmured Rosalind, trusting the distance between them to mask any telltale note of falsehood. Lady

Blanchard had, after all, been the first to warn her that setting her heart on Devon was a mistake.

Lady Blanchard maintained her post by the arched window, staring out at her walled garden and the cobblestone street beyond. Rosalind felt something very close to panic bubbling up in her. It was ridiculous, and she knew it. She was behaving as if her friend were threatening harm or dissolving into hysterics. But that was how she felt. For all the time she had known Lady Blanchard, she had never seen her betray such indecision that she could not even look at the person to whom she spoke.

Then, just as Rosalind was certain she could endure no more, Lady Blanchard turned, and it was not indecision Rosalind saw shining in her expression. It was triumph, cold and absolute.

"This is an excellent turn of events," Lady Blanchard said. "Lady Edmund should not only seek the post of patroness, she should have it. It's perfect."

"Lady Blanchard . . ."

"No, no, you must trust me, Rosalind." She returned to her seat and took both of Rosalind's hands. "It is positively providential. Lady Jersey will not approve of her at first, but we can change her mind. I'll enlist the Countess Lieven to help. She can persuade Mrs. Drummond-Burrell and Lady Sefton. Then we'll all work together on Sarah . . . yes." Lady Blanchard's eyes darted back and forth, following the thoughts that flickered through her mind. "You'll have your work cut out for you as well. We must build up Lady Edmund's social presence, and show off her hostessing skills. That will be your work. She must hold a series of routs and supper parties, and they must be exquisite. You will send me the guest lists and I will make sure the required persons, in fact, attend. Getting Lady Edmund out into the most useful settings without tipping our hand might be a little more difficult. I can arrange only so many invitations . . ."

"Stop, please, Lady Blanchard." Rosalind withdrew her hands so she could smooth her brow. "Just a moment so I can catch my breath! I am ready to stand by you, and do whatever you need and whatever you ask. But please, can't you take me into your confidence? How can I truly help if I don't know what it is you hope to accomplish?"

If Lady Blanchard had any intention of answering, it was cut short by the knock at the door.

"You'll excuse me, I hope, ladies," said Lord Blanchard as he entered.

Morgan Newcombe, Viscount Blanchard and Third Under-Secretary for Foreign Affairs, was a broad man who exuded an air of physical strength in spite of his advancing years. Although his clothing was both conservative and immaculate, his gray hair was perpetually shaggy, as were his eyebrows. Taken together with his small, hooded eyes, strongly arched nose, and prominent chin, he had the look of a highly annoyed hawk.

"Oh, I hadn't realized you'd arrived yet, Miss Thorne." His lordship nodded distantly to her. "All is well, I trust?"

"Very well, thank you, Lord Blanchard." Rosalind made both her curtsy and reply as if she and Lady Blanchard had been discussing nothing more serious than the latest Drury Lane comedy. "May I congratulate you on your new appointment?"

"Yes, yes. Lovely place, Konigsberg, and there's a good deal of work to be done now that we've finally gotten rid of that damned upstart, Napoleon. No one wants the Prussians getting ideas about taking too much of their own back from France." He smiled thinly. "Has Jane secured your agreement to her plans?"

Lady Blanchard colored. "Morgan," she murmured.

"We had not yet talked about it, sir." Rosalind put a great amount of effort into keeping the statement casual and her countenance cheerful, but Lord Blanchard's attention remained entirely on his wife.

"That's me putting my foot in it, I suppose." He laid his hand on Lady Blanchard's shoulder. "Still, no harm. We were hoping you might come stay for the season, and perhaps even through the summer." His words were meant for Rosalind, but he spoke them directly to his wife. "There are a thousand details to be seen to before we leave. Jane was saying how glad she'd be of the help, and I must concur."

Throughout this speech, Lady Blanchard sat with her husband's hand on her shoulder, stiff as a wax doll, her smile fixed in place. It was as well he could not see her expression from this angle, because he would surely be at least as shocked as Rosalind. She could not believe Lord Blanchard really wanted her to stay. He had put up with her for his wife's sake, and as long as she did not presume too much on her status as his goddaughter. Her father's dramatic, though blessedly brief, reappearance last season had eroded even that tolerance.

"I was just telling Lady Blanchard how I'm glad to be of whatever help I can."

"Excellent." Lord Blanchard squeezed his wife's shoulder. "Jane was certain we could count on you. Now, I'm sure you have a thousand things to talk about. My dear, I have to go and see Hildebrand, but I should be back in time for dinner." He kissed Lady Blanchard's hand, nodded to Rosalind, and took his leave.

Rosalind waited until the door closed again, and until her friend's attention had returned to her.

"I suppose I should thank you for your kind offer," she said. "I see you've been preparing Lord Blanchard for my presence this season." *You've been lying to your husband so that you'd have an excuse for bringing me back into the house. Why? And why on earth has he decided to agree?*

"You mean to remonstrate with me, and I'm sure I've earned it," Lady Blanchard said. "I trust to our years of friendship to make you understand I would not be doing all this were it not completely necessary."

"Which means something is wrong." Several very unpleasant possibilities rose up in Rosalind's mind.

Lady Blanchard did not answer at once. Rosalind bit her tongue. She must let Lady Blanchard find her own words.

"The truth is, Rosalind," said her godmother softly, "I need the world distracted while I, that is we, make our departure."

"That's why you're playing this game with the patronesses. This is the distraction."

Lady Blanchard nodded. "Society and the newspapers will speculate madly about who will take my place, and the sooner that begins the better. Lady Jersey and the others will do everything possible to use the publicity to their individual advantage. In the face of all that commotion, the fact of our leaving will fade into insignificance."

You don't want anyone asking questions; not the papers, or the Lady Patronesses, or me. And you've found the only possible way to guarantee that silence. But why all this trouble? What's happened?

Now it was Rosalind's turn to look away. Outside, snow had begun to fall on the Blanchard gardens. Rosalind watched it while she struggled to gather nerve and composure.

This woman stood by me when the rest of the world would have tossed me and Mother onto the ash heap, Rosalind reminded herself. *She showed me how to live, and keep at least a teaspoon's worth of my gentility and pride.*

Because of this, instead of asking the obvious and obviously unwelcome question, Rosalind only spoke the obvious warning. "If Lady Jersey realizes you're using her and the board for your own purposes, she will ruin you."

Lady Blanchard only smiled. "Soon, I will be beyond the reach of Lady Jersey or any of the rest of them. Then, they may whistle for their vengeance. I will not hear." She spoke this softly, almost as if she did not wish to hear herself. "And now, what will you do, Rosalind? Will you stay and help me, or will you leave? You should know that either way, I remain your friend."

Rosalind suppressed her disappointment and her confusion. They would not serve. She had to think clearly, and see the future as well as the past.

"I will stay," she said. "You may be assured of my best assistance." *And may heaven help me*, thought Rosalind as the words of the promise echoed in her heart. *But at least if I've erred in this decision, it's out of friendship, not cowardice.*

Even as she thought this, she exchanged smiles with Lady Blanchard, as if some tender secret had been shared.

"Well." Lady Blanchard's manner turned brisk. "I fear that the day is getting on without us. The patronesses are meeting to approve each other's voucher lists for Almack's first month of assemblies." The Almack's balls were subscription affairs. Upon being deemed acceptable by the board, each subscriber paid a fee of ten guineas. In return, they were granted a voucher guaranteeing them a set number of tickets to a set number of dances. "It will all take hours, even if Lady Jersey is in one of her more charitable moods. I dare not be tardy, especially now that we have such plans. How did you come?"

Rosalind put down her cup and stood, because that was what one did when one had been dismissed, whether one wanted to or not. "I came on foot."

"Well, you will ride out with me, and Preston will drop you at home."

"Thank you, Lady Blanchard, but I've several errands yet to attend to." This was not strictly true, but she wanted the time to think about all that she had seen and done on this long, strained day.

"How would this be? You ride out with me, and once I'm safe at Almack's, I'll give Preston instructions to take you wherever you wish. You may return for me at half five. That should give us both time enough to take care of our business. Perhaps you would care to dine with us afterward? It will be entirely informal, no need to make any fuss." Meaning there was no need for Rosalind to change her dress.

"Thank you, Lady Blanchard. That is most kind. I'd be happy to accept." *And perhaps I can get a few more answers from you.* Because Rosalind was certain of one thing. It was there in every word her friend spoke, and in the way her new plans shone so brightly in her tired eyes.

Lady Blanchard was leaving London, and she did not intend to return.

CHAPTER 5

At the Gates

Kings Street, St. James, is, as all the world knows, the link between London's most fashionable street and its most aristocratic square; it is within calling distance of Pall Mall, which had then a royal palace on each hand, and in the very center of club-land.

—E. Beresford Chancellor, *The Annals of Almack's*

It could not be described as a madhouse. A madhouse had keepers, rules, doctors, and other such attendants to calm and confine the inmates. Kings Street on a Monday evening had no such civilizing influences. It was every man, woman, and horse for themselves.

Carriages jammed the cobbles and were forced up onto the walks in front of the plain building described as "the seventh heaven of the fashionable world." Those pedestrians unfortunate enough to be caught in the crush squeezed themselves through narrow windows of space afforded by such breakwaters as thresholds and lampposts.

"Confounded nuisance!" exclaimed one portly gentleman to his companion as they attempted to force themselves past Rosalind's borrowed carriage. "What's it all for?"

This was an excellent question. Rosalind smiled to herself.

She suspected a number of the people crammed into the street were asking themselves the same thing. At the same time, it seemed no one quite knew how to stop.

It was Monday. The lady patronesses were meeting to decide who would be allowed to the first of the Almack's assemblies. Considering that hopes and dreams, not to mention marriages and fortunes, could hang on their decisions, it was not perhaps surprising that the world treated this meeting as a moment of vital importance. Therefore, everyone in the general vicinity had to linger to witness the emergence of the grand imperial ladies of the board, whether they wanted to or not.

Not that Rosalind could claim to be entirely immune to Almack's allure. When she'd first been allowed up to London as a girl, she'd spent the better part of three solid weeks pacing the drawing room while waiting to hear how Mother's application for an Almack's voucher would be answered. Every waking moment was spent contemplating the sublime possibility that she might not just attend the exclusive assemblies, but make her debut there. If only she could have this one night, she prayed over and over, she'd never ask for anything else. She'd never need anything else. It wouldn't matter how Honoria and the others treated her. Even Charlotte's spite wouldn't matter anymore. One night at Almack's, and the whole world would open wide for her.

And for a little while, it had.

Rosalind shook her head. She never knew whether she should be angry at her world for turning out to be so small, or at her own naiveté for believing one night of dancing could force that small world to deliver up its keys.

And yet, look at me, still standing at the crossroads of that world and hoping to find some way home.

"Hello again, Miss Thorne."

Rosalind was so deep in her own past that it took her a moment to realize the voice was not just another memory. Devon Winterbourne, real and present, spoke to her from the cold, crowded street. She could not possibly mistake the tone and timber of his voice for another, even through the closed windows of her borrowed carriage.

Rosalind thought, a little frantically, about not turning her head. She thought about drawing the curtains and sitting alone in the chilly dark until he went away. But it took a great deal of hardened nerve to behave like a coward, and Rosalind found she did not have so much in her.

Therefore, Rosalind did turn her head, and she did look, politely, of course, at the dark man in the black coat trimmed in beaver fur, who had stopped beside her carriage.

When she saw Devon in Lady Edmund's sitting room, she'd noted how he'd changed. Now that she was separated from him by nothing more than the thickness of a carriage door, Rosalind noted how he'd stayed the same. His full mouth had kept that slight curl about the edges, as if he wanted to smile, but was uncertain if this was the right moment. The cold still brought a pleasing color to his ruddy cheeks. His breath steamed in the deepening twilight, and the light from the lanterns and flambeaux caught in his gray eyes, which had always been a little too wide and too bright to belong on a man's face.

She must stop noticing things about Devon's person, just as she must quash the rising curiosity about what brought him to this street at this moment. She must also stop thinking of him as Devon. His father and infamous older brother were both dead. This man was the Duke of Casselmain.

But since she had looked at him, she could not fail to speak without giving him the cut direct, which, considering the difference in their stations, was a ridiculous idea. Reluctantly,

Rosalind unhooked the window glass and let it slip down. The winter cold flooded the carriage and she shivered.

"Good evening, Lord Casselmain," she said.

He touched his fashionably curled hat brim. "Good evening, Miss Thorne. How are you?"

Rosalind found she had no interest in answering that question. "How is it you happen to be here?"

"I stopped by Blanchard House earlier, and saw you leaving in Lady Blanchard's carriage." He waved his stick vaguely up the street. "It was not much of a guess that you might be here about this time."

"You had business with the Blanchards?"

"A friend asked me to deliver a message to Lord Blanchard," he answered placidly. He might even have been telling the truth.

"You also had an appointment with Jasper Aimesworth this same day."

The corner of Lord Casselmain's mouth twitched. Twice. *Stop noticing.* "Do you suspect me of following you, Miss Thorne?"

"Should I?"

"Yes."

His blunt, graceless answer gave Rosalind an excuse to feign anger, which was better than giving in to any of her other churning emotions. "That, sir, is unworthy of you."

"Yes, I suppose it is. I'm sorry." The soft apology sounded so much like the Devon she remembered that Rosalind felt something twist inside her. He was still there, underneath the shell of Lord Casselmain—her Devon, who was both too direct and too kind for the rest of the fashionables. Rosalind closed her eyes and wished she hadn't noticed that as well.

When she was able to open her eyes again, Casselmain was no longer looking at her, which was a relief. Instead, he stared over the hats of the crowd, toward the wide stone steps leading up to Almack's closed doors. "Are you going to ask me about it?"

"About what, sir?"

"My soon-to-be-announced engagement to Honoria Aimesworth."

Rosalind found she wanted nothing more than to climb out of the opposite side of the carriage and disappear into the London streets. Had there been any chance she could even get the door open, she might have done it.

"I have no right to inquire about your personal business," she reminded him, and herself.

"Not even though we are such old friends?"

"Not even then. Propriety forbids."

"Propriety. Ah, yes. Where would any of us be without it?" A sneer slipped underneath those words. Rosalind found she had no answer to it. That anger had also always been part of her Devon. Like her, he'd learned to suppress it, because it was of absolutely no use.

There was something else she needed to say. Propriety demanded it, but so did common feeling.

"I got your letter when Mother died. It was kind. Thank you."

Lord Casselmain, still struggling with his own bitterness, only shook his head. "I should have come myself."

"No, you shouldn't have. What you did was enough."

"Since you say it is so, I must accept that."

For a brief moment, Rosalind considered adding something along the lines of, "I hope we are still friends." She dismissed this. To begin with, it was untrue. Whatever she might want of Devon Winterbourne, such a polite and noble sentiment as friendship was not on the list. He rested his hand on the window's edge. He was so close. If she lifted her own hand, she could touch him. As easily as that. She could feel his warmth again, know the shape of his strong hand, even if it would be through the double thickness of their winter gloves. No one was paying them any attention. No one would ever have to know. Except her. Except him.

"You're truly not going to ask why I'm marrying a girl I'll never love?"

The smile that formed on Rosalind's lips was a small, bitter thing. "If you want me to know, you can tell me. Here we both are, alone and unobserved."

Devon paused again. He had become a careful man, one who didn't like to say a thing he might regret. But she could tell he did want her to know his reasons. Slow, heavy understanding tumbled over Rosalind. He wanted her to know, but more than that, he wanted her to ask. He wanted her to be the one who broke confidence and propriety.

He wanted to see she was humbled, and brokenhearted. He hoped that she was pining for him and the life he could have given her if only he had not stayed away after Father fled.

Anger surged through Rosalind, raising a flush to her cheeks despite all the bitter cold. "It is better if you say nothing, sir. After all, we don't know each other that well, do we?" She did not look at him. She must not look. She must remember the whole, dreadful arc of her life. She must remember the ongoing whispers, and the constant little reminders of exactly who she had become.

Because Devon was now the one required to uphold the position and fortune of his great and ancient family, much to that family's relief, Rosalind was sure. Devon's older brother, Hugh Winterbourne, had been a careless, coarse, intemperate man and no one was at all surprised when he died by falling drunk from his horse and breaking his neck.

No one knew better than Rosalind the heartbreak that would follow if Devon failed in his duty. He needed a wife who could manage the vast household, and provide heirs and income to bolster the bloodline. Honoria Aimesworth could bring him those things. Any other reasons Lord Casselmain might have for choosing this particular bride meant nothing at all to the obscure Miss Rosalind Thorne.

Since she couldn't look at him, Rosalind knew Devon was leaving only because his wavering shadow slipped off her lap. She sat alone in the cold, the noise, and the flickering lights of torches and tapers as the coachmen moved about lighting the carriage lanterns.

"Good-bye, Devon," Rosalind murmured, but only after she felt sure he couldn't possibly hear her.

CHAPTER 6

The Empty Ballroom

Many Diplomatic arts, much finesse, and a host of intrigues
were set in motion to get an invitation to Almack's.
— E. Beresford Chancellor, *The Annals of Almack's*

Fortunately, Rosalind was not left with much time to sit and brood upon the cruelties of fate, much less her many deficiencies of resolve and good judgment. Around her, the crowd was shifting, its assorted conversations and curses overwhelmed by that low, murmuring gasp which indicates a mob has spied something of interest. Rosalind's gaze lifted itself reflexively to Almack's, and its low doors.

Just as she did, those doors opened. A small flock of servants in assorted liveries hurried out. The crowd's massed murmuring turned awed, and excited. People crammed, craned, and crowded—or at least they attempted to crowd. The footmen, prepared with staves and very firm manners, descended the steps to keep the way open for the lady patronesses.

First to emerge was Sarah Villiers, Lady Jersey. Swaddled in burgundy velvet, with white plumes nodding above her ruffled bonnet, Lady Jersey was the acknowledged queen of the patronesses. They might all have some say in what happened in

Almack's, but Lady Jersey's word reigned over the rest, and she made sure the whole world knew it.

Mrs. Drummond-Burrell, garbed in forest green and a positive acre of fur, came up beside her. Delicate, pale, and younger by far than most of the rest of the patronesses, Mrs. Drummond-Burrell was reckoned to have her position because Lady Jersey knew she could always count on her vote and agreement, no matter what the question. But Rosalind saw something in the keen way the young woman turned her face toward the crowd, and wondered.

The Princess Esterhazy glided forth from the doorway. Lady Sefton bustled. The Countess Lieven rolled her dark, imperious eyes in an attitude of exaggerated suffering. She also picked up her hems with ostentatious fastidiousness before descending the stairs.

Rosalind unlatched the carriage door and waited.

Lady Blanchard did not appear. The footmen closed the doors. Rosalind frowned, but composed herself to patience. She also remembered to raise the window glass again.

Around the carriage, the crowd began to crack apart. The bystanders on the walks drained away first, presumably prodded by the cold and encroaching dark, as well as the looming necessity of dressing for dinner and the evening's entertainments. The scrum of carriages loosened much more slowly, urged on by the shouts of drivers and postilions.

But Almack's doors remained closed.

All around, church bells began their ponderous tolling of the hour. Rosalind shifted on her seat. What could possibly be keeping Lady Blanchard so far behind the others? The memory of their conversation that afternoon filled her. How could it not? Especially after Lady Blanchard had made it so clear she meant to use her position at Almack's for her own purposes. Rosalind remained certain those purposes included leaving London behind for good and all, but what else did they include?

As Rosalind contemplated this unpleasant question, the driver, Preston, called down from his box. "Shall I go speak to the porter, miss? Perhaps he can find out what's keeping her ladyship?"

Rosalind shook herself. This idle speculation served no purpose. "Thank you, Preston, but I'll go."

"Yes, miss." Preston climbed off his perch and opened the door to help her out.

"She's probably just been detained on some matter of committee business," Rosalind ventured. Never mind that all the rest of the committee had already gone.

Preston touched his hat. "That's sure to be it, miss. These meetings do take up a mountain of Lady Blanchard's time."

Rosalind picked her way across the cobbles and around the frozen puddles. As she did, she performed several small adjustments to her attitude. By the time she reached the doors, she had assumed an air that managed to be brisk, unassuming, and completely at home all at once. Almack's might fill others with terror, but not Miss Rosalind Thorne. She did still belong here. Although it was not quite on the same terms as in earlier days, she knew everyone. Oh, not the patronesses, but all the others—the ones who kept the door, who staffed the rooms and made sure the patronesses' plans were fulfilled, down to the last detail. These were the persons who constituted Rosalind's Almack's now.

"Good evening, Molloy," Rosalind said to the porter at the door. "Is Mr. Whelks still inside?"

"I believe that he is, Miss Thorne." Molloy bowed and held open the door so Rosalind could step through.

Almack's entrance hall was spacious. The lusters overhead were quite dark, but several candles shone in the brass wall sconces. Their yellow light reflected on velvet drapes and gleaming floorboards. Mr. Whelks was indeed within, at the foot of the grand staircase. He was also engaged in what could be described as an animated consultation with several stout gentlemen wearing dingy shirts and stained leather aprons.

"It is simply insupportable!" roared Mr. Whelks. "We must have the new chairs for the card room *before* next week, you b—"

Rosalind cleared her throat. Mr. Whelks clapped his mouth shut and turned toward her.

Thorvald Whelks was Lady Jersey's personal secretary and the tallest, thinnest man Rosalind had ever met. Rumor was Lady Jersey had chosen him as her assistant because he could be easily seen in any room, no matter how crowded. He was also reputed to be a harpsichordist of unusual talent, but as Rosalind had never heard him play, she could not judge.

What was no way in doubt was that when Lady Jersey wasn't in the building, Mr. Whelks was the voice of the Almack's patronesses. Mr. Willis might occupy the building's offices, reviewing the books and counting the receipts, but Mr. Whelks was the only person trusted to handle the sacred voucher lists once they were completed by the board. Rosalind had never seen him wearing anything other than a black coat, no matter the time of day or night. The only reason he changed his black trousers for white breeches when evening came was that if he did not, he would not have been admitted into the ballroom, no matter how pressing his business. The rules for gentleman's attire in Almack's admitted no exceptions.

"Miss Thorne!" Mr. Whelks greeted her with a long, deep bow, this being the only sort his elongated frame was capable of. "Good evening!"

"Good evening, Mr. Whelks. I'm here with Lady Blanchard's carriage. Is she still upstairs?"

"I confess, I don't know, Miss Thorne. Shall I enquire?"

"If you please."

Mr. Whelks glanced at the aproned tradesmen and coughed. A lady, he was clearly thinking, could not be left alone with such rude mechanicals as these. "Perhaps you'd care to step upstairs? As it's you, I'm sure no one will mind."

"Thank you, Mr. Whelks."

The secretary ordered the tradesmen to wait and took up a candle from the nearest table. Rosalind followed.

The great marble stair curved grandly upward to the right. The light from Mr. Whelks's candle flickered across its polished banisters and was reflected warmly in the painted glass of the arched windows. The air smelled of cold and wax, faded smoke, and old perfume. It had been a long time since Rosalind had been this far into the sanctum sanctorum, but she still remembered it perfectly. The stair ended at the broad open gallery, which furnished a fine view of the entrance hall below. To the left waited the grand ballroom and, beyond that, the famously modest tea room. To the right was the card room. Rumor whispered that Lady Jersey had fought bitterly against the introduction of cards at Almack's, as it would take the gentlemen away from the dancing. It was one of the few battles she'd ever lost.

The committee rooms and business offices waited one more floor up, but Mr. Whelks hesitated—delicately, of course.

"If you'll just wait here, Miss Thorne? I think I see a light on in the committee room. I'll go and knock for you."

"Thank you." Rosalind nodded her understanding. While Rosalind might be welcome here and even accorded a certain amount of latitude, no outsider could be allowed into the patronesses' office—not even the Prince Regent or the Lord Admiral.

Mr. Whelks bowed with perfect aplomb and started up the last flight of stairs. Rosalind strolled across the gallery to keep the cold from settling more firmly into her bones. As she turned, she could not help noticing that the ballroom doors were less than two yards from her left shoulder. Somewhat to her surprise, they were slightly ajar.

I will not look.

This resolution lasted even less time than her initial resolve not to look at Devon Winterbourne. The ballroom, at least, could not look back.

Rosalind glanced up the stairs but saw no hint of motion. Slowly, she let herself drift toward the ballroom doors. When neither Lady Blanchard nor Mr. Whelks appeared, she gently nudged the right-hand door open a little farther. The hinges were, of course, perfectly oiled and made no noise.

Inside the ballroom, the draperies were closed, turning the evening's twilight to a deeper gloom. Pale gold light seeped under the velvet from a few remaining torches and lanterns in the street outside. It made a pretty sheen on the floorboards, but did little to alleviate the darkness. She could only just make out the shape of the musicians' gallery at the farthest end.

She'd seen this room when the curtains were fully open and light from great lusters and chandeliers sparkled on gilded pillars and framed mirrors. She'd felt like the queen of the world when she walked into the ballroom on Father's arm. She remembered the weight of the pearls around her neck—a gift from her then-fond father—and the pink roses in her hair. By contrast, her white dress had seemed light as air. The music had swelled, as if that particular passage had been chosen specifically for her entrance. Every head turned. The ladies whispered and nodded. The gentlemen looked her up and down again. She'd blushed. She'd adored it.

She'd curtsied to Lady Jersey and heard herself praised.

So slender, so modest, such a pretty girl, Althea. And, ah! Here is my particular friend Mr. Hammond. He will make you an excellent partner for the first waltz, Miss Thorne, should you agree to accept him.

Of course she'd agreed. She would have agreed to the Man in the Moon. She'd just been given permission to waltz at Almack's, and at last, life would begin.

She trembled a little at this memory, and felt an unfamiliar trace of shame. *It's all right*, she told herself. *It's your life, after all. Why shouldn't you remember being happy?*

But it wasn't memory that made her ill at ease, at least not entirely. Rosalind frowned at the empty ballroom. There was something odd about the dark, still, soaring space in front of her, but she couldn't quite make out what it might be.

It was then she heard Mr. Whelks's measured tread descending the stairs.

"I'm sorry, Miss Thorne, but Lady Blanchard isn't in the committee room. You must have missed her in the street."

"Yes, I'm sure that's it," Rosalind replied, but didn't turn to look at him. Her eyes had adjusted to the dark, allowing her to see farther into the ballroom. There, almost hidden by the deeper shadow under the musicians' gallery, lay an odd black bundle. It might have been a rolled-up rug, except it was too uneven, and it gleamed, in patches, as if the torchlight from outside were catching on glass or metal. She thought it might be a pile of burlap sacks, perhaps delivered by the workmen downstairs. But such things wouldn't have been so inelegantly dumped in the Almack's ballroom, no matter the time of day.

And if it were a pile of sacks, what was the pool of thicker darkness that spread out around it? That wasn't a shadow. It was the wrong shape.

"Is there something the matter, miss . . ." Rosalind felt Mr. Whelks move to look over her head. "Great God!"

Propriety forgotten, Mr. Whelks shoved past her. The boards echoed under his shoes as he bolted across the ballroom.

Rosalind grabbed up her hems and ran after him as quickly as skirts and coat allowed. Even so, Mr. Whelks had dropped to his knees beneath the gallery by the time she reached his side.

It was not a rug he turned over. Rugs did not have long white hands, or dress in buff and blue. It was not shadow he knelt in, but thick blood—the blood of the young man whose still, startled eyes stared up at them both.

"Who is this?" cried Mr. Whelks. "How . . ."

"Dear Lord," whispered Rosalind. "It's Jasper Aimesworth!"

CHAPTER 7

Persons in Inappropriate Places

What is so dreadful, what is so dismal and revolting as the murder of a human creature?

—Thomas De Quincey, *On Murder Considered as One of the Fine Arts*

Rosalind stumbled backward. An odd choking noise teased at the edge of her awareness, but all she could truly understand was that Jasper Aimesworth lay stretched out at her feet with his eyes wide open— perplexed, sad, and quite certainly dead.

Arms, warm and solid, wrapped around her and turned her away. Soft fur and woolen cloth pressed against her cheek and she caught the scents of leather and sharp soap.

Devon.

Rosalind jerked away sharply and would have stumbled again, but Devon did not let her go.

"Gently, gently, Rosalind," he murmured. "It's all right. You're safe."

"Don't talk nonsense!" Of course she wasn't safe. She was being held by Devon Winterbourne with Jasper Aimesworth lying dead just a few feet away. "What are you doing here!"

"Never mind that," Devon said. "You must come away now,

Rosalind. Whelks, is Willis still about? Get him down here at once!"

"Yes, your lordship."

Whelks was past them in an instant, stretching his long legs to their utmost. Rosalind attempted to push Devon away from her, but he had turned himself and her so that somehow he was beside her, holding her under both elbows in a way that pinned her arms to her sides. Rosalind seethed, but she did not struggle. It would have made her look ridiculous. But she also did not let herself feel grateful for his support, or acknowledge how badly her knees were shaking.

"We're getting you out of here," he said firmly.

Which may have been an excellent plan, but their retreat was blocked by Lady Blanchard, who hurried toward them across the broad expanse of the floor.

"Rosalind!" she cried. "Lord Casselmain! What on earth . . ."

"Oh, no!" Rosalind tried to pull away from Devon to intercept her godmother, but she was too late. Lady Blanchard had already come up level with them, and seen past them.

The blood drained from her face, and slowly, as if her strings were being cut one at a time, Lady Blanchard sank to her knees.

"This can't be," she breathed. "How can it be?"

Dignity forgotten, Rosalind yanked herself away from Lord Casselmain's importunate grip. She knelt beside her godmother and grasped her shoulders. Lady Blanchard looked up at Rosalind, and her green eyes were almost as still and staring as Jasper's.

"I was waiting. I had to wait." She wasn't even looking at Rosalind. She was looking past her, toward the doors.

"Now, now, Lady Blanchard." Devon crouched down beside her. "There's no need to be talking so. Miss Thorne, will you help her ladyship away?"

Rosalind nodded and took Lady Blanchard's ice-cold hands. "Hush, Lady Blanchard. Lord Casselmain is right. You need to get out of here."

But Lady Blanchard didn't move. Her hands did not even clench around Rosalind's. Light flickered overhead and more footsteps sounded. The thick-set Mr. Willis, who managed the building, was racing across the ballroom, a globe lantern held high. Mr. Whelks towered over him, carrying a branch of candles.

"He wasn't supposed to be here!" cried Lady Blanchard. "It's not what we *agreed* . . ."

Willis came to a halt beside their chilling tableau. He slapped a beefy palm over his mouth as he took them all in. Mr. Whelks looked down on Lady Blanchard, his face flushed and as close to angry as Rosalind had ever seen him.

"Damme," Willis muttered. "Damme! Who is this young idiot? And what in God's Holy Name . . ."

"Mr. Willis," Devon said, "we have to get the ladies out of here, then we can deal with the rest." He glanced at Rosalind. Another time she might have bristled at his high-handedness, but Lady Blanchard still wasn't moving and that demanded all her attention.

"Mr. Whelks," Rosalind said. "Run down and alert Lady Blanchard's coachman. He must be ready to leave immediately."

Whelks glanced at Willis, clearly uncertain about whose orders were to take precedence in this ghastly moment.

"Go, go," snapped Willis. "Damme! A complete disaster. Would you, Your Grace, help the ladies out of here?"

Rosalind tried to raise her friend, but Lady Blanchard didn't budge. "Lord Casselmain, I'm afraid I will need your assistance." Devon, murmuring quiet nonsense, moved around Lady Blanchard until he could get his hands under her elbows. Between the two of them, he and Rosalind lifted the trembling woman to her feet. She lurched heavily to the right and Rosalind caught her.

"Don't look." Rosalind turned Lady Blanchard's head so she would not see the corpse, or the great splotch of blood that stained her skirts. "Close your eyes. Lean against me. I will take you out of here."

Thankfully, Lady Blanchard obeyed and pressed her face against Rosalind's shoulder. Rosalind glanced over her head at Devon, who simply nodded. Together, they half supported, half dragged Lady Blanchard across the great expanse of ballroom and down the long, curving stairway.

They emerged onto Kings Street and were plunged instantly into the damp and the cold of the February night. Rosalind drew as deep a breath as she could manage. She must clear her head. The bells were tolling seven. Barely an hour had passed since she had walked through Almack's door and into, as Mr. Willis so succinctly described it, a complete disaster.

Lady Blanchard had begun to shake. She had no wrap and was as cold as death. Devon slipped off his own top coat and wrapped it around Lady Blanchard's shoulders as Preston threw open the carriage door and put down the step.

"Here we are, my lady," Preston said. "We must get you inside, and wrap you up warm." Rosalind scrambled inside first, ready to receive her godmother as the driver handed her through.

"Why?" Lady Blanchard whispered. "He wasn't supposed to be here. I told him. I told him! Everything was already arranged!"

"Hush now." The carriage was well stocked with rugs, and Rosalind piled them all over Lady Blanchard. "You must not agitate yourself."

Devon closed the door, and stared in through the window. "Will you be all right?"

"I'll get the ladies safe home, Your Grace, you may depend on it," said Preston stoutly, and a trifle defensively.

"Good man," said Devon, but he was still looking at Rosalind. "See she stays wrapped up, and you as well. Neither one of you can get chilled."

The knowledge that she had a task to perform rallied Rosalind's strength and spirits more thoroughly than anything else could have. "I'll take care of her."

Something else scrabbled at the back of her crowded thoughts, something vitally important. But with her attention divided between Lady Blanchard's state of nervous collapse and Devon's solicitous presence, Rosalind couldn't think clearly.

Preston hoisted himself up onto the box and the boys clambered up behind, all jostling the carriage. Lady Blanchard moaned.

And still Rosalind did not give the order for them to move. She looked into Devon's face. The play of shadow and flickering lamplight made his familiar features dramatic and mysterious.

"Devon?" she said, as if it were perfectly natural to use his Christian name.

"Yes?" he answered just as reflexively.

"Why were you in the ballroom?"

His gray eyes had gone confused, and unkind. He was helping her, looking after her, but was irritated with her. "I followed you in. I didn't like to leave you as I did. I bungled things. Then I heard you scream . . ."

"I didn't scream."

"I'm afraid you did. At length."

She wanted to deny it again, but did not seem able to muster the strength. Besides, she was becoming uncomfortably aware of a raw burning sensation in her throat.

"What . . . what will happen to . . ."

Devon glanced over his shoulder. "Willis means to send for his physician. They'll get poor Aimesworth back to his people."

"Someone must go tell them. Prepare them." But how on earth did you prepare parents for the death of their son? Not even Lady Edmund deserved such horrible news.

"I'll do it," said Devon. "Don't worry."

A small, utterly inappropriate laugh escaped her. "A man is dead. It seems worth a bit of worry."

"Let Willis worry about it. They're his rooms. You worry about yourself and Lady Blanchard."

"Yes, yes, of course." She should not keep them sitting here. Except there was something important she still needed to ask, but she couldn't remember what it was. Devon stepped back from the carriage. "Drive on!" he ordered Preston. Preston touched up the horses, and Rosalind uneasily turned her attention to comforting Lady Blanchard.

It felt like a year before the carriage finally reached Blanchard House. The whole way, Lady Blanchard lay still and silent in her swoon. Rosalind held her friend close, trying desperately to impart some kind of warmth, but she had none of her own to spare.

Preston had barely brought the horses to a halt before he tossed the reins to the groom and leapt down. He barked an order to the footman, who had come out onto the steps with a lamp. The footman ducked into the house, presumably to summon help, while Preston threw open the carriage door and put the step down.

Good man, thought Rosalind dazedly. She gathered her godmother into her arms, trying to sit her up a bit straighter. "Come now, Lady Blanchard. You are home. Can you climb out, do you think?"

In answer, Lady Blanchard clutched Rosalind's wrists. "His eyes," she murmured. "I will never escape his eyes."

There was no answer to that.

The entrance hall of Blanchard House was lit only by a single branch of candles. They had meant to dine informally at home this evening, Rosalind remembered. As Rosalind supported Lady Blanchard inside, a house maid, followed by a woman in black whom Rosalind recognized as Lady Blanchard's maid, came running down the stairs, with Lord Blanchard at their heels.

"Jane!" Lord Blanchard cried. "What *happened?*"

As soon as the maids reached Lady Blanchard, they pulled her away. Rosalind's arms flopped to her side.

"Well?" Lord Blanchard roared at her. "Speak up, girl!"

"I saw . . . that is to say . . ." Rosalind swayed on her feet. Now that her godmother was home and safe, her strength fled. She couldn't even feel her hands anymore. "Jasper Aimesworth is dead. In the ballroom at Almack's."

Lady Blanchard slumped forward, making the maids who held her stagger. Lord Blanchard stared.

"You can't tell me *Jane* found him!"

"She saw him. I . . . happened on him first."

"Damme!" Lord Blanchard shouted. "But how? What did you see? Tell me exactly what you saw."

"His eyes," whispered Lady Blanchard. "I saw his eyes."

Lord Blanchard whirled around. He muttered another oath, but this time he also moved to his wife's side. "Jane, Jane, you must bear up. Lacey, get her upstairs into bed. She'll need hot water bottles and plenty of quilts."

"Yes, m'lord."

Lord Blanchard glanced at Rosalind in apology, and she waved him away. He needed to be with his wife.

Master and servants left in a crowd around their fainting mistress. Rosalind found herself alone in the echoing front hall. She began to shiver, then to shudder. The painted salon was to her right. She managed to reach the hearthside chair just as her knees collapsed, dropping her into the round-backed chair beside the hearth and its bright fire.

Rosalind rubbed her arms hard and tried to force some order upon her thoughts, but there were too many of them and they would not quiet. She remembered Jasper from when they were both younger. She saw him astride his chestnut hunter in the cool morning, raising his hat to the girls gathered to see him off. She remembered the breezy and utterly disinterested way he led her through country dances at the parties and the balls where they were urged together. She remembered him standing in a corner with Honoria, attempting to make her at least smile at what she saw around her.

She thought about Honoria. She thought about Lady Edmund, and Lord Edmund, who spent his days hidden away with his books on classical architecture and his blueprints. Had Devon reached them yet?

What was Jasper even doing *there?*

I was waiting. I had to wait. He wasn't supposed to be here! It's not what we agreed . . .

The papers were going to feast on this. Alice and George Littlefield would be describing every detail for the rest of the season, perhaps even the rest of the year. They'd be mad to interview everyone involved.

Like her.

It is the least of your worries, Rosalind told herself. *You must think clearly.*

Because she was missing something. Some important idea was trying to run away from her.

Before she could grasp it, though, light flickered in the front hall, and a maid entered the salon carrying a freshly lit lamp.

"Excuse me, miss. Lord Blanchard sends his apologies, but says you are to stay here for the night. I'm to take you up to the Summer Room, and Bertram has been sent to your house for your servant. I'm to help you until she arrives."

"Of course. Please convey my thanks to Lord Blanchard." Her gratitude was genuine. The thought of another frigid, jolting carriage ride across London was too much to endure.

The Summer Room got its name from its bright yellow walls and dusky gold draperies. Maids bustled to and fro, unfolding the bedding and stuffing pillows and bolsters into fresh slips.

"You must forgive us, Miss Thorne," said Mrs. Pauling, the Blanchards' housekeeper. "The house is just opened, and the rooms are not all yet in order. You sit yourself down. Cook will be sending up a hot meal directly, and you can eat and rest. Forgive my saying, but you must be exhausted! Such a thing . . ."

Rosalind did sit. She let Mrs. Pauling's exclamations and orders to the staff roll over her like a warming breeze. As promised, a hot meal was brought in and placed on a table. The rich smells of beef broth, veal in white sauce, and cheese tart were all enticing, but Rosalind found herself only able to pick at the food. Her mind could not settle and she could not understand why. This was, after all, the accepted prescription for shock and tragedy. While the men decided what to do, the women were to retreat until any possibility of making a public scene had passed. She must eat and drink what was given, take her *sal volitale* as she required. Probably she should lie down.

Rosalind pushed her tray away. "Where is Lady Blanchard?" she asked the nearest maid.

"Her ladyship is in her rooms, but . . ."

Whatever it was she had to say after that could be safely

ignored. Rosalind got to her feet and started down the dim corridor.

Rosalind had lived in Blanchard House for quite some time after her father deserted them. She therefore had no difficulty finding her way to Lady Blanchard's rooms. She knocked on the door. When no answer came, she took a deep breath, prepared to instantly apologize, and slipped into Lady Blanchard's private sitting room.

The room was lit by several lamps and a good fire. Lady Blanchard's personal maid, Lacey, was just closing the door to the boudoir.

"Oh, Miss Thorne." Disapproval dripped from the maid's words. "I did not realize that was you."

"I came to inquire as to how Lady Blanchard is," Rosalind said. "May I see her?"

"I'm afraid not, miss," answered Lacey, who, despite her name, was one of the straightest, plainest women Rosalind had ever laid eyes on. "My lady needs rest after her ordeal."

But I need to know what she meant! I need to know what had been arranged, and with whom! Was it Jasper Aimesworth? Mr. Whelks? Lord Casselmain? Someone else entirely?

But Lacey simply stood in front of the closed door, with her chin raised. She might be only a lady's maid, but in this, her authority was inviolate. She and she alone looked after Lady Blanchard, and she was not to be gainsaid.

Pressed hard by the twin weights of exhaustion and convention, Rosalind's resolution collapsed. "Please tell her ladyship I was asking for her," she murmured.

"I will deliver the message, miss," said Lacey, although, of course, she did not say when.

Rosalind returned to her room. There was nothing she could

do at the present. She could hardly go looking for Lord Blanchard. He might not even be in the house anymore. She sat in her comfortable chair and stared at her comfortable fire.

He wasn't supposed to be here, it's not what we agreed . . .

What agreement is this? Which he *are you talking about?* The questions ran back and forth through Rosalind's mind, chasing out all other thought, but bringing her no answers. Something about Jasper Aimesworth's death had left Lady Blanchard shaken to her core. Was it the location? The suddenness of it? But people died suddenly every day from accidents or illnesses of all sorts. Lady Blanchard had endured the deaths of all three of her children. Why would the loss of this one young man leave her so devastated?

Unless, somehow, the relationship between the two of them was much closer than she knew. This, however, was not a possibility Rosalind cared to examine closely. No good at all could come of it.

Eventually, a nightdress, cap, and wool stockings were brought in, doubtlessly from Lady Blanchard's own store. Rosalind let herself be undressed and re-dressed, brushed, braided, and eventually laid down in the bed and covered over with a thick layer of quilts. The soles of her stockinged feet touched hot bricks wrapped in flannel. The heat was a blessing and she savored it as the servants snuffed the candles and closed the door behind them.

Rosalind burrowed into her covers and waited for sleep. But a moment later, her eyes flew open, and she stared into the darkness. In all her confusion, she had grasped only half of the problem.

Lord Casselmain had been first to the ballroom after Rosalind and Mr. Whelks found Jasper. He shouldn't have been there at all. That was obvious. That was understood. But all that time, while the uninvited and the inappropriate had clambered freely through Almack's, where was the one person who should have been there?

Where was Lady Blanchard?

CHAPTER 8

Things Seen in the Correct Light

Lady Jersey's bearing, on the contrary, was that of the theatrical tragedy queen.

—Captain Rees Howell Gronow, *Recollections and Anecdotes of the Camp, the Court, and the Clubs*

When Rosalind awoke the next morning, she found herself lying in a comfortable bed in a sunny room that she didn't recognize. She shoved herself upright and stared about, unable to account for her surroundings, or her sudden fear. Slowly, memory filled itself in: of Almack's, of Devon, and of Jasper Aimesworth.

"It's all right." Rosalind gulped air and groped for the bell rope. "You're in Blanchard House and you're perfectly safe."

The maid who answered the bell was a dark slip of a girl carrying a breakfast tray. Immediately behind her came a well-known and entirely welcome figure in a severe black dress.

"Mrs. Kendricks!" Rosalind struggled to find a way out from under the mountain of covers.

"None of that, miss." Mrs. Kendricks took the breakfast tray from the maid and deposited it across Rosalind's lap. "Thank you, Melon. I'll look after Miss Thorne now." As soon as the girl curtsied and departed, Mrs. Kendricks bolted the door and came at once to grasp both of Rosalind's hands.

"My poor miss! Are you all right? Were you hurt? I wanted to stay in the room with you, but they said I might disturb—"

"I'm all right, truly." Rosalind squeezed her hands back, hoping a show of strength would convince Mrs. Kendricks that she spoke the truth. "I was not hurt at all. Only badly shocked."

"I should think! They said it was young Mr. Aimesworth that died."

"It was." Rosalind leaned back against the bolsters. "I don't understand it, Mrs. Kendricks. It seems so impossible."

Mrs. Kendricks just shook her head. "Some things are not for us to understand."

"But—"

"No more talking now, if you please, miss." Mrs. Kendricks lifted away the cover on the breakfast dish to reveal a generous helping of kedgeree. There was toast and marmalade on the tray as well, alongside the universal restorative: a pot of tea. "You need to eat to get your strength back."

This second statement was something Rosalind could readily agree with. She was famished, and parched. "Is Lady Blanchard awake?" she asked as she poured herself some tea. "If she is, I should—"

"I am under strict instructions from her ladyship that you are not to come down until you have eaten."

This may or may not have been the truth, but Rosalind was not inclined to argue. Instead, she tucked into the kedgeree, rich with golden rice, raisins, and hard-cooked egg.

This evidence of a healthy appetite clearly relieved Mrs. Kendricks's mind. She bustled around the room, opening the bronze-colored curtains and bringing out a tapestry bag from the wardrobe to extract a clean chemise and stockings, as well as Rosalind's violet sprigged morning dress.

"I'll go see this is ironed, miss. You are not to stir until I get back."

It was easier than it should have been to follow Mrs. Kendricks's instructions. Rosalind allowed herself to believe that if she was issuing orders, Lady Blanchard must be recovered from her collapse. Thus comforted, she cleaned her plate and drained the teapot. When she'd finished, she leaned back against the bolsters. The warmth and stillness of the room wrapped around her, as thick and comfortable as the quilts. She wanted never to move again. Especially since moving would inevitably drag her back into the current of yesterday's dreadful events.

"It was an accident," Rosalind said to the canopy above her. "That's all. Some sad and terrible accident."

Too soon, Mrs. Kendricks returned with Rosalind's freshly ironed dress. "I've told her ladyship that you are awake, miss. Lady Blanchard hopes you'll be so good as to join her and Lord Blanchard in the morning room, but only if you're feeling quite well."

"Of course I am well, Mrs. Kendricks." To prove her point, Rosalind threw back the covers. Much to her own relief, she found she was perfectly able to stand, and stand steadily.

Mrs. Kendricks helped Rosalind into her clothes, and combed and dressed her hair. Feeling much refreshed and ready to meet the questions that were sure to follow, Rosalind made her way to Lady Blanchard's formal morning room.

Although the door was open when Rosalind reached it, neither of that room's occupants noted her arrival. Lady Blanchard sat straight as a ramrod on the Louis XIV sofa by the fire, with both her hands wrapped around a teacup. Lord Blanchard leaned over her. One hand gripped the sofa back, the other clutched her shoulder. He was saying something soft and harsh, and the effort of it twisted his lined face.

"Of course," murmured his wife in answer. "Of course."

Rosalind swallowed. She also quickly knocked against the open door. Lord Blanchard sprang back from his wife. His face flushed red as he glared at the source of the interruption.

Lady Blanchard merely turned her head. "There you are, Rosalind!" she cried as brightly as if Rosalind had been strolling about the gardens. "I trust you are quite recovered?"

"Perfectly, thank you, Lady Blanchard." Rosalind sank to the sofa beside her. Lady Blanchard was made of stern stuff, tempered by long years in society and politics. Even so, the complete and utter calm of her demeanor this morning was a marvel. The disloyal thought passed through Rosalind's mind that Lady Blanchard's earlier show of shock and extreme grief might have been just that—a show. She dismissed this almost at once. A woman of Lady Blanchard's breeding would pretend to feel less than she did, rather than more, even in the midst of an unfolding disaster. "I must thank you both for allowing me to trespass—"

"Nonsense! What else should we have done?" boomed Lord Blanchard. "Do you feel up to talking, Miss Thorne?"

"Of course, sir," said Rosalind. This was true, although she very much doubted that Lord Blanchard wanted to discuss the same subjects she did.

Lord Blanchard planted himself directly in front of the sofa and clutched the lapel of his coat with one hand, his gaze and stance as severe as if he were facing down an opposing member in the House of Lords. The last time she had seen him like this, he had been explaining to her why she had to leave his house.

Rosalind concentrated on keeping her shoulders straight and her face placid.

"Now, Miss Thorne," said Lord Blanchard. "Just where did you find Aimesworth?"

"He was under the musicians' gallery." With an apologetic

glance toward Lady Blanchard, Rosalind told his lordship what she had seen, as simply and quickly as she could. Lady Blanchard sipped her tea and listened quietly.

Lord Blanchard's gray brows knitted. "How was it you who found him, Miss Thorne? You can't really have been there alone?"

"Mr. Whelks had gone up to the offices." *To look for Lady Blanchard.* "I saw the ballroom door was open, so I looked inside. Mr. Whelks came then and noticed something was wrong in the room. We went together to investigate the matter. Then . . . I'm afraid I screamed."

"Quite natural." Lord Blanchard nodded as if granting her a favor by allowing this evidence of feminine weakness.

"Shortly afterwards, Lord Casselmain arrived . . ."

"Casselmain?" Blanchard snapped. "What the devil would Casselmain have to do there?"

"Morgan," murmured his wife. He waved his hand, annoyed.

"I could not say," Rosalind told them. She was certainly not about to disclose that Devon might have been there because of her.

"Had he . . . that is to say, Mr. Aimesworth . . . was it a fit, possibly?" murmured Lady Blanchard. She had lowered her gaze to contemplate her teacup. "A stroke? He hadn't . . . had he been ill?"

A stroke would not have produced so much blood. But this was another thought Rosalind kept to herself.

Lord Blanchard, however, spared Rosalind the necessity of making any answer. "I know exactly what it was. Stupid not to have thought of it before. Young Aimesworth was a member of White's, wasn't he?"

"I'm sure I don't know," said Rosalind. White's was one of the most exclusive gentlemen's clubs in London. It numbered the Prince of Wales and several of the royal dukes among its membership.

"Well, I do, and he was. Probably, the young idiot was up in the gallery as part of some fool bet." White's was as famous for its members' outrageous gambling as Watier's was for its chef and its wine cellar. "Grab a tassel off the curtains, write your initials on the wall of Almack's, bet you five pounds you can't, that sort of nuisancy thing. He got up there, overbalanced on the rail, or a ladder, or some such. Then he fell and broke his fool neck."

"I don't think Mr. Aimesworth was the sort—" began Lady Blanchard, but Lord Blanchard was already shaking his head.

"Depend on it, Jane, that is what happened. Young idiot," he repeated. "Sorry for his parents. Only son, wasn't he? Shouldn't have been playing with his life like that."

It was a simple explanation, and perfectly plausible. Lady Blanchard should have seized on it, but Rosalind saw the doubt shining in her friend's eyes.

A scratch at the door signaled the arrival of the footman. "Lady Jersey and Mrs. Drummond-Burrell for Lady Blanchard," he told them all. "They beg my lady's pardon but say the matter is very urgent."

"It has to be gotten over with, Jane," said Lord Blanchard quietly. Rosalind bit her tongue to keep from blurting out her own impatience. She couldn't possibly ask Lady Blanchard her own questions while the lady patronesses were calling.

"Simmons, you may show the ladies in." Lady Blanchard rose to her feet. "Then send Mrs. Pauling with more tea. No, coffee. Lady Jersey prefers coffee at this hour."

Simmons bowed and left to carry out these instructions. Lord Blanchard closed his hand briefly on his wife's shoulder, just exactly on the curve where shoulder joined neck. A bare heartbeat later, Lady Jersey strode in.

Society's daughters were routinely drilled in the art of elegant deportment. Lady Jersey, however, seemed to have neglected these lessons, or skipped them altogether. All of her movements were brash, abrupt, and expansive. The moment she entered any room, she became the focus of attention, much the way a charging horse might.

Mrs. Drummond-Burrell, on the other hand, spent all her energies in an attempt to be unassuming. She shadowed Lady Jersey closely, like a Spanish duenna. Her dark eyes met Rosalind's, and narrowed. Young, she might be, but that sharp look told Rosalind she understood the endless internal calculations and compromises that made up a moment in society, and that she was good at them. Neither she nor Rosalind spoke. It was for Lady Blanchard as hostess to perform the introductions, and until then, they had to remain silent.

"My dear, dear Jane!" Lady Jersey sailed up to Lady Blanchard, shawl and hems billowing. "I knew we would find you home. Lord Blanchard, you will excuse the intrusion at such an hour, but we are in the midst of a crisis!" She favored him with a glance that mingled annoyance with tepid apology.

Lord Blanchard bowed. "Not at all, not at all. In fact, let me take myself out of here so you ladies can tend to your business. You will excuse me, Jane? Lady Jersey? Mrs. Drummond-Burrell?"

All necessary courtesies were exchanged, and as soon as the door closed, Lady Jersey dropped into the chair directly in front of Lady Blanchard. "I have sent messages to all the other patronesses. We must convene an emergency meeting at once, but I wanted to come to you personally!"

Lady Blanchard remained standing. When she spoke, her voice was perfectly even and disinterested. "Lady Jersey, Mrs. Drummond-Burrell, I believe you know Miss Rosalind Thorne?"

Lady Jersey turned in her seat, frowning. By the rules of strict propriety, she should have stood, but then, by the rules of strict propriety, she should not have sat down until introductions were completed. As if she were a servant, Rosalind dipped a curtsy to the seated lady, but she was not going to be seen as anything less than polite. If she was, it would reflect badly on her hostess.

In return, Lady Jersey lifted the quizzing glass that hung on the chain from around her neck, and looked Rosalind up and down. Rosalind knew this sort of look. Lady Jersey wasn't taking note of her face. The lady patroness examined Rosalind's plain, cheap dress, her hair, which was entirely devoid of fashionable ringlets, and the simple gold necklace at her throat. By these signs, Lady Jersey added up Rosalind's taste and level of *ton* and rendered her judgment accordingly.

"Miss Thorne," Lady Jersey drawled. "Sir Reginald Thorne's daughter, I believe? I have perhaps heard Mrs. Holywell speak of you? A friend of her daughter's or something? And of course, you were . . . *there* yesterday?"

"I am Sir Reginald's daughter, Lady Jersey, and yes, I was there yesterday." Doubtlessly, Mr. Whelks had informed her of this, and all the other details. "As to what you have heard from Mrs. Holywell, I could not say."

"Well. Well. This is very good." With a great rustling of brocade, Lady Jersey turned to their hostess again. "How clever of you, Lady Blanchard, to bring the young woman here so quickly. It is vital, *vital* that we suppress any word, any possible hint, of this terrible accident. Think of the papers! Almack's will be under siege! There will be writers and gawkers and all sorts of vulgar persons clamoring to get inside . . . It will be impossible! So, you first, Miss Thorne." Lady Jersey gestured impatiently for Rosalind to come stand before her, like a headmistress to a schoolgirl.

Fortunately, at that moment, the housekeeper entered with

the coffee tray, and Lady Blanchard was able to interrupt the scene. "Ah, thank you, Mrs. Pauling. Will you please pour for us, Rosalind? You take sugar, do you not, Lady Jersey?"

Checked, Lady Jersey waved her quizzing glass negligently. Rosalind concentrated on fixing and passing cups of coffee, and on keeping pique out of her expression.

Lady Jersey gulped her coffee. "As I was saying, Miss Thorne. I've made inquiries, you should know that. Mr. Whelks says you're a sensible and useful sort, and Lord Casselmain speaks for you."

Rosalind felt a fresh heat rising in her cheeks that had nothing to do with modesty. "I will have to remember to thank him."

"You should, and of course, your association with our own Lady Blanchard speaks volumes. Despite your excellent connections, however, I'm sure you recognize that your being in the ballroom at all was a serious breach of conduct. If you were to find yourself censured by the board of patronesses, the consequences to a young person such as yourself could be most severe."

Merciful heavens. She's threatening me. And there beside her was Mrs. Drummond-Burrell, nodding with such vigor Rosalind was surprised her head didn't drop off and land in her coffee cup.

Lady Blanchard took a small sip of coffee and set her cup down. "Sarah, I can entirely vouch for Miss Thorne's discretion. She has been my dear friend for many years, and ably assisted me in many delicate matters."

"I'm sure that's so, Jane, since you say it is. But you understand our situation, do you not? There cannot be one breath, one hint of this matter abroad. It is only by perfect and complete secrecy that we will be able to keep the institution of Almack's free of vulgar scandal or speculation. We must have your solemn promise, Miss Thorne, that you will say nothing to anyone!"

The women's attention all fixed on Rosalind.

Had it not been for Lady Blanchard, Rosalind felt sure she would have told the lady patronesses to all go hang. When her father and Charlotte ran off, Almack's slammed its doors in Mother's face, and in hers. She also knew perfectly well that if she brought up this fact now, Lady Jersey would look surprised. In fact, she would not understand why Rosalind might even think to protest the matter. One did not allow an abandoned, degraded, or divorced woman into Almack's.

Rosalind lifted her chin.

"I promise you, Lady Jersey," she said. "That you are already far, far too late."

CHAPTER 9

In the Lion's Den

I think her a fearful kind of person, she dares do or say anything to anybody.

—Marianne Spencer Stanhope Hudson, *Almack's*

Silence fell, thick, heavy, and disapproving. Lady Jersey lifted her quizzing glass to once more scrutinize Rosalind's figure and bearing. That glass was an odd affectation for a woman who was still in her prime. Rosalind found herself wondering if Lady Jersey might be shortsighted in more ways than one.

"I hope, Miss Thorne," said Lady Jersey sternly. "That you are not accusing Mr. Whelks or Lord Casselmain of improper talking."

"No, m'lady," answered Rosalind promptly. "But there were servants and tradesmen in the rooms, not to mention bystanders outside. Also, by now, all the servants in all your houses know what happened." She paused and let each of the women see the seriousness of her expression. "Your own movements, Lady Jersey, are closely watched by members of the press and public. Those who make it their business to know such things are already aware something of import has occurred, and depend on it, they will be avidly seeking details."

Mrs. Drummond-Burrell cleared her throat hesitantly. "There might be something in what she says, Sarah." This statement evidently cost her no little effort, because she pulled a kerchief from her sleeve and blotted her upper lip. Lady Jersey, however, was already drawing in an enormous breath, preparing to launch her own speech.

"There is also the fact that Mr. Aimesworth's death will not remain a secret for much longer," Rosalind went on. "The pieces will be put together, no matter what the patronesses do, no matter what power or discretion they exercise. It will be published abroad, and probably sooner rather than later."

Lady Jersey's chin quivered. Rosalind knew the grand dame of Almack's was frightened by what she'd heard. Unfortunately, Lady Jersey was the sort who reacted to things that frightened her by dismissing them.

"Such indiscretions as you allude to, *Miss* Thorne, might be a danger among low, chattering sorts, but I may assure you that in the very best society—"

"Almack's will die a death by parlor gossip," said Rosalind evenly. "London's matrons will panic. They will rescind their subscriptions and refuse to let their daughters cross the threshold lest they be murdered in the retiring room."

"Murder!" cried Mrs. Drummond-Burrell, the drama of her exclamation somewhat muffled by her lace kerchief. "How horrible! You cannot be serious, Miss Thorne!"

"It does not matter whether I am or not," replied Rosalind. "The papers will use the word, you may depend upon it." *Oh, Alice, you're going to get to use your "blood in the ballroom" bon mot after all!* She had to look away lest she accidentally smile at the thought.

"What are we to do!" exclaimed Mrs. Drummond-Burrell to Lady Jersey. This time she remembered to lower her kerchief. It occurred to Rosalind that Mrs. Drummond-Burrell could hardly be more than one and twenty. She might be a veteran of tiny ballroom skirmishes, but this moment was entirely outside her experience.

"Clementina, you will collect yourself!" Lady Jersey thundered. "We cannot allow ourselves to be terrified, or compromised, by an unlucky accident."

Lady Blanchard leaned forward. "Lady Jersey, if I may suggest you listen to Miss Thorne. She has assisted many of our finest ladies through murkier waters than these. I will be quite relying on her in the coming days." She paused as if she'd just hit on some beneficial notion. "Perhaps Rosalind could speak with some people she knows. She has, in the past, been able to make sure that the newspapers put things in the *correct* light."

"Has she?" Lady Jersey sniffed. "I, of course, have no experience with newspapermen myself. Tawdry gossip merchants, and the women! Ten times as bad. All of them spreading rumors for the lowest sort of person to dine upon. I would be the last to praise anything that detestable little Corsican did in France, but his control of the popular press seems an entirely sensible measure. I do hope it's a question you might persuade Lord Blanchard to put forward in the coming session," she added to Lady Blanchard. "Still, if your Miss Thorne has some experience in these matters, with your imprimatur, Lady Blanchard, I think we may consider any suggestion she might have."

The ladies all turned to her expectantly. Rosalind folded her hands, in case there was any possibility they might start trembling, or curl into fists. "My suggestion, Lady Jersey, would be to make no attempt at secrecy. Any denial about what happened will increase the amount of attention paid to the matter."

"As Shakespeare tells us, 'The lady doth prostest too much, methinks,'" murmured Lady Blanchard.

"Just so," Rosalind agreed. "At the same time, if anyone inquires as to the details of the incident, it is only necessary to speak with sympathy of the family and their loss." *Incident.* Even as she spoke, Rosalind felt uneasy. *I am reducing the loss of a man's life to an incident.*

Lady Jersey tapped her quizzing glass thoughtfully against her palm. "What you are saying is that the matter is like that of a girl refusing a troublesome suitor. The more she demurs, the more that suitor will be certain there's something worth having. Yes. There is some sense in that. And being sure to place the emphasis on the Aimesworths is also an excellent scheme. It was after all the young man's own fault. He was in a place he had absolutely no business being. The family must bear the burden of what he has done, not us."

Yes, because what could a family's grief matter when compared to the reputation of your little club?

Rosalind's teeth came together with a sharp click, grinding down on words and anger before either had a chance to escape.

But Lady Blanchard heard, and she saw the flash in Rosalind's eyes. "Rosalind, my dear, I feel a draft. Could I trouble you to go fetch my new cashmere shawl? You know the one I mean."

It was, of course, a discreet invitation to withdraw before she said something they would both regret.

"Of course." Rosalind rose to her feet. "If you will excuse me, Lady Jersey? Mrs. Drummond-Burrell?"

She received the polite nods of permission and took herself out of the room as quickly as she decently could. Out in the hall, she stopped and pressed her hand against her stomach, trying to get her breathing under control for a moment. But she could not be caught standing here. She started down the corridor toward the family rooms. Lacey would probably be in Lady Blanchard's room. She would know which shawl was meant.

"Miss Thorne. May I have a word?"

Rosalind was so intent on recovering her composure that Lord Blanchard's voice seemed to come out of nowhere. Rosalind stared about herself in momentary confusion before she realized she stood beside the open door of a small library. It was a chilly room, as it contained no fireplace, but the curtains were thrown open to make the most of the winter sun. Map cases as well as bookcases lined the walls. Sturdy, practical tables took up most of the remaining space, waiting for the occupant to spread out papers and plans so they could be examined in detail. Lord Blanchard was in the act of rolling up one such set of plans as she entered.

Rosalind was struck afresh by how tall Lord Blanchard was. His shaggy gray hair gave him an eccentric, almost absent-minded appearance, but one glance at his sharp eyes put any such idea to rest. This was a man who might be distant, but he would never be absent.

"This is a sad, hard business, Miss Thorne," he said, deftly knotting the black ribbons around his roll of papers. "I'm sorry you were drawn into it."

"Thank you, Lord Blanchard. But you needn't worry for me." She paused, and then decided to dare a remark. "I'm only sorry Jasper would have to meet with such a strange accident. His family will be devastated."

"Yes, yes. Aimesworth is many things, but he's never been the strongest of men. And Lady Edmund . . . well." Lord Blanchard pulled a ring of keys from his waistcoat pocket, unlocked one of the cabinets, and laid the roll of papers inside. He then settled into the wingback chair beside the room's small writing table and gestured for her to take one of the stools beside the table.

"I trust . . ." He stopped. "No. Let me begin again. I very much hope, Miss Thorne, you will be here to help Jane through this. She needs a friend by her, I think even more than she realizes. I would hate to find that you could not because some hard feeling exists between us."

Rosalind kept her gaze level and her face calm. Despite her close connection with his wife, she and Lord Blanchard had never been friends. She'd often wondered if the viscount ever had financial dealings with her father, and if he'd lost money, but she was never able to find out for certain.

"Lord Blanchard, all that happened between us was perfectly comprehensible. My father broke into your house in a drunken state. He demanded money of you and created an unforgivable scene." *Among other things.*

Rosalind could still see Father clearly, lurching forward across the front hall, stinking of gin, rumpled and unshaven and leering.

I know what you're doing, keeping my girl in your house, you old satyr, he'd growled to Lord Blanchard. *Well, b'ghad, if you're going to have her, you're going to pay the one that owns her!*

"You were perfectly right to request that I leave," she continued. "I would have done so in any case. If there are any apologies to be made, I am the one who should make them."

They'd never told Lady Blanchard about their last conversation, either of them. She would have refused to let Rosalind go if she'd known Lord Blanchard had ordered her goddaughter out, even with such causes as he had. Rosalind did not like secrets, but she also could not stay with her godparents when Father might return at any moment. Better she should face that possibility in an obscure house in an obscure street than somewhere the world might find out, and tear the last of her reputation to shreds.

Lord Blanchard waved her words away. A thought occurred

to Rosalind then. "Lord Blanchard, may I ask a question? White's Club keeps a betting book, I believe?"

"Famous for it." Among the rules of society's sporting men, a bet not only had to be made, but had to be witnessed. There should also be an opportunity for friends to make their own side wagers on the outcome of whatever question was to be settled. Thus the excitement, and chance for gain, was spread as widely as possible. To this end, many clubs kept a ledger of bets entered into between the members.

"If, as you suggested, Mr. Aimesworth was at Almack's because of some wager—"

"He may have entered it into the book!" cried Lord Blanchard. "Of course. I should have thought of that myself. I'll go have a look at once." He pulled on the bell to summon the footman. "Thank you, Miss Thorne. I knew you would not let Jane down." He shook his shaggy head. "The truth is Almack's has been more of a burden than a help, to us both. I admit, I badgered her into it. That was a mistake. Jane's an admirable woman. The consummate hostess. Man couldn't ask for better. But she's not really ambitious, do you see? At least, not in that way. I sometimes think she'd be just as content in a Shropshire cottage having the vicar and his wife to supper on Wednesdays, as long as she could pull it off neatly."

"I think you may be right, sir."

"What she can't bear is shabbiness. Can't stand to sink below standard, and thinks nothing at all of those who do. And, by Harry, she's always managed it, come stormwrack or strife. She keeps her head and her house all above water. But this . . . this may finally be too much. Still, it's important for her, and for us as a family, that her exit be well managed. Have to leave all in good order for our return. We need the world to be looking forward to it, you understand?"

A slow chill spread over Rosalind as Lord Blanchard spoke his carefully chosen words. She did understand, although she also desperately wished she didn't. There was only one reason Lord Blanchard would talk to her about managing both his retreat and his return. He was not being given this new posting because of his personal merits or because he'd requested the transfer.

Lord Blanchard was being gotten out of town.

CHAPTER 10

Willis's Rooms

Almack's advertised that it was built with hot bricks and boiling water: Think what a rage there must be for public places if this notice, instead of terrifying, could draw anybody thither.

—E. Beresford Chancellor, *The Annals of Almack's*

For such a famous building, Almack's Assembly Rooms was in truth a graceless, squared-off edifice. There was no gate or garden to soften the facade, just an iron area railing and a porter in a plain greatcoat to guard the unprepossessing doors. Only the arched windows of its first floor lent it any sort of distinction.

Thankfully, as this was neither a Wednesday nor a Monday, Kings Street was relatively clear of traffic and Rosalind was able to make her way up the walk without hazarding her limbs or her hems.

After her unsettling conversation with Lord Blanchard, Rosalind had returned to the patronesses with Lady Blanchard's shawl and the news that Lord Blanchard was going to investigate the betting book at White's.

"Excellent man!" cried Lady Jersey. She had taken a seat at Lady Blanchard's writing desk and was scribbling away furiously even as she spoke. "It would certainly be most considerate of Mr. Aimesworth to have left proof of his folly in writing, but what a waste and bother! I shall speak with my husband imme-diately about putting an end to the practice of that book in the club. Should any child of mine display so little taste and discre-tion . . ."

"Young men must be allowed their follies, Sarah," said Lady Blanchard softly.

"But not a complete disregard for taste and *ton*. It is up to us to demonstrate the benefits and advantages of living according to the best of both. What are we for otherwise?" Lady Jersey jabbed her quill onto her page. "Miss Thorne, we have been considering your recommendations and have agreed. I hope we may prevail upon you to carry a note to Mr. Willis at Almack's asking him to come to us this afternoon? We will not be meet-ing in the offices after all, but rather at the Countess Lieven's during the confidential hour."

Of course, Rosalind had agreed, and was duly dispatched in Lady Blanchard's carriage with the letter, and a hundred other instructions, most of which she fully intended to ignore.

The porter was not happy to let her in, but as she invoked the lady patronesses' names, backed by the letter she carried, he even-tually relented and conducted Rosalind up to the second floor. If her hand trembled against the banister as they climbed the curving stair, she was determined not to let it trouble her, or slow her step.

For the second time in as many days, Rosalind walked into Almack's great ballroom. This time, however, it was a bright and busy hive of activity. The double doors were wide open and all the draperies had been tied back to allow in as much light as possible. Three women wielding stiff brushes knelt under the musicians' gallery and scrubbed at the floorboards. The sloshing, swishing noise of their labor carried through the room along with the acrid fumes of lye soap.

"Gently, lads, gently!" Mr. Willis's gruff voice rang out overhead. "Tear those and it'll be coming out of your hide, and your pay!"

Mr. Willis stood in the musicians' gallery, calling his directions to a pair of men in aprons and shirtsleeves. One held a folding ladder so that two others could climb up and unhook the red velvet curtains that framed the gallery. From this vantage point, Mr. Willis soon saw Rosalind crossing the room. He gestured to the workmen and a moment later she heard him thumping down the hidden stairs.

"Look sharp now, my girls," he said as he passed the scrubwomen. "Be sure to get it all. Can't have the ladies worrying about their lace and hems, now can we?"

"No, sir," they answered in a ragged chorus. Mr. Willis did not stop to acknowledge this, but faced Rosalind and tucked two thick fingers into his waistcoat pocket.

"Miss Thorne, isn't it? William Willis, at your service." Mr. Willis gave a perfunctory bow, which Rosalind answered with a polite nod.

Mr. Willis was several inches shorter than Rosalind. His crooked nose sloped sharply forward, and his shining brow sloped sharply back. Although he had not yet reached his middle years, his dark hair was beating a hasty retreat across his mottled scalp. His reputation, Rosalind knew, was that of a clever man of business. Certainly, his round face was both intelligent and lively, even though he must have had even less sleep the night before than she did.

"You'll forgive a man if that service is a little distracted today." Willis shook his head up at the workmen in the gallery, carefully gathering up the costly, and heavy, draperies. "Dreadful business. Got to get it all cleaned at once, you see, otherwise we'll be replacing the lot on account of the stains."

"Of course, Mr. Willis," replied Rosalind. "And I'm sorry to be interrupting your work, but I have a letter to you from Lady Jersey."

"Well, we was expecting more of that, wasn't we?" said Mr. Willis placidly. "Would you care to step up to the office? I'm sure her ladyship wants an answer as soon as may be."

Rosalind assented and followed Mr. Willis to the upper floor and through the first door on the right-hand side of the corridor. Her gaze did stray down the hall, wondering which of the closed doors that lined the hall led to the patronesses' sacred and secret meeting space.

Willis's office was an airy and well-appointed room. A good blaze burned in the hearth, and the draperies were pulled back from the tall windows. Shelves were filled with carefully labeled ledgers, account books lined the walls. The center of the chamber was taken up by the biggest desk Rosalind had ever seen. It was a "partner's desk," built for not one occupant, but two, and it was currently being used by a plump woman with a serious face.

"Mrs. Willis!" boomed Mr. Willis. "This is Miss Thorne, with a letter for us from Lady Jersey."

Mrs. Willis looked up at Rosalind, removed her spectacles, and looked again. It was only after this second inspection that she heaved herself to her feet to make her courtesies.

Like her husband, Mrs. Willis was sturdily built. Her dress was dark green woolen stuff, and while her white cuffs might be rumpled, they were edged with lace, as was her stiff collar and ruffled cap. A great ring of keys hung at her waist, and a gold locket hung about her neck along with the chain for her pince-nez. A small notebook and pencil dangled from yet a third chain. The whole of her appearance proclaimed the Willises' middle class prosperity as firmly as Mr. Willis's white stockings and the silver watch chain stretched across his peacock waistcoat.

"I do apologize for disturbing you, Mrs. Willis," said Rosalind. "I understand you are extremely busy."

"All in a horrid muddle is what we are," Mrs. Willis snorted as she resumed her seat and set her spectacles back on her button nose. "Had to take on extra help to get the cleaning done. The men understand they're to take up the gallery carpet as well, Mr. Willis?"

"I made that quite clear, Mrs. Willis." Her husband drew his chair up to the other half of the desk and broke the seal on Lady Jersey's letter. "I will say, Miss Thorne, I'm a bit surprised that Thorvald Whelks didn't bring this."

So was Rosalind. Normally, Mr. Whelks followed Lady Jersey like an extremely elongated shadow. Cartoonists and satirists were constantly amusing themselves with the image. "I'm sure Mr. Whelks is occupied with other commissions."

"To be sure, to be sure. Our Lady Jersey is doubtlessly busy as a whole hive of bees today."

"And probably enjoying herself to the full," muttered his wife.

"Now, Mrs. Willis." Mr. Willis tipped the edge of the letter down to better regard Mrs. Willis. "That's a bit harsh, I do think."

"But it is true, Mr. Willis, and as none of our grandees is here to listen, I will speak as I please."

Mr. Willis gave Miss Thorne a glance of apology.

"As it happens, I don't think Lady Jersey is enjoying this morning very much," said Rosalind. "She does like a spectacle, but not an unpleasant one. It is in bad taste."

"Ha!" laughed Mrs. Willis. "You've put your finger on something there, Miss Thorne, I will say. Well, Mr. Willis? What are her ladyship's instructions?"

"Says we won't have to worry about having the fire lit in the

office after all, Mrs. Willis," he answered. "And you can tell
Molloy he needn't send over to the Gray Goose for luncheon.
The ladies will be meeting elsewhere this afternoon."

"Thank heaven for small mercies." Mrs. Willis took up the
memorandum book and made a note with the tiny pencil that
hung beside it. "Harding has had to chase off a couple of newspapermen this morning. If all the ladies showed up off their
usual time, we'd never be rid of the nuisances."

"Those nuisances help shape the reputation of these rooms,
Mrs. Willis," answered Mr. Willis placidly.

"No doubt, Mr. Willis, like flies help shape the reputation of
a jam pot."

Willis chuckled. "I'll just pen a reply for you, Miss Thorne."
He pulled out a fresh quill and a knife to trim it. "Although I
expect her ladyship will not be best pleased with what I have
to say."

Mrs. Willis eyed her husband over the rims of her spectacles.
"I hope you're not going to change your mind."

"Have no fear, Mrs. Willis," he replied as he put quill to paper.
"It's already in hand. I had a reply to my application less than an
hour ago, and I expect the man himself shortly."

"I don't mean to appear inquisitive, but may I know what's
the matter?" asked Rosalind. "If there's the possibility of an
objection, I might be able to help smooth things over with the
patronesses."

Mrs. Willis looked skeptical, but in the end she shrugged.
"Willis is hiring a runner from Bow Street to find out if anybody helped Mr. Aimesworth on his way."

Surprise robbed Rosalind of her voice for a moment. "But it
was an accident!"

Mr. and Mrs. Willis shared a significant look. "Of course,

the patronesses regard our rooms as their property, but they're not, are they?" Mrs. Willis sniffed. "They belong to Mrs. Pitcairn, and she's trusted their management to Willis and me. We're the ones who must oversee the staff and servants and all the rest. We're the ones who must make sure there's money enough to pay the mortgages and the taxes *and* show a profit besides. We need to be sure of our people, don't we? There's a deal of wickedness in the world," she added piously. "It's for the likes of me and Willis to make certain the grand ladies remain untroubled by it, isn't it?"

Or those grand ladies might just choose to move their exclusive gatherings to other quarters. Rosalind nodded her understanding. It was not only the lady patronesses who stood to lose by a scandal at Almack's. Even stone walls had to worry about their reputations. "Do you have reason to suspect Mr. Aimesworth might have died because of a robbery?"

Willis frowned as he blotted his letter. "We've no reason but to suspect it. Young toff—I beg your pardon—gentleman, being where he's got no business being, loaded down with seals and chains and a note case and I don't know what all, probably all ready for a night at his club. We've men in and out of here all day when we're getting ready for the season. Furniture, carpets, painters, plasterers, all's got to be repaired and made ready, hasn't it? Might be there's somebody's brother or cousin brought in to do a bit of fetching and carrying in return for a day's wages decided to relieve Mr. Aimesworth of his burdens."

He wasn't supposed to be here. I told him. I told him. Everything was already arranged! Lady Blanchard's words came back to Rosalind.

"Ah, I see I've shocked you, Miss Thorne," said Willis. "I'm sorry about that."

"No, no, Mr. Willis. It was . . . a passing thought. That's all." She considered mentioning the wager that Lord Blanchard theorized about, but quickly decided against it. "A runner seems to me an entirely prudent measure. I'm sure the patronesses will agree, but if you think it will help, I'll be sure to emphasize the point."

"Thank you, Miss Thorne," said Willis as he handed over his sealed letter. "That would be most welcome."

Rosalind slid the letter into her reticule. "I will not take up any more of your time, Mr. Willis, Mrs. Willis. I expect, however, we will be seeing more of each other. I'm sure the ladies will also find a great deal of extra work needs to be done in the coming weeks."

"There's no doubt about that." Mrs. Willis flipped her account book open again. "Oh, Mr. Willis, you'd best give over . . ." She pointed toward his half of the desk.

"Ah, yes. Thank you, Mrs. Willis. Miss Thorne, I don't want to presume, but I've some articles here . . ." Mr. Willis unlocked his desk drawer and took out a ring of keys and several coins. The key ring had a pitted and spotted brass fob in the shape of an elaborate scrollwork *A*. "They were found this morning in the gallery. Those keys, I expect they belong to Mr. Aimesworth, and probably should be returned to his people."

"I'll see that they are, Mr. Willis," murmured Rosalind. She tried to tell herself they were only objects, and of no particular meaning or import, but she shivered as she took them to add to her reticule.

"I'll show you out, Miss Thorne." Mrs. Willis pushed her chair back from the desk.

"Please don't trouble yourself, Mrs. Willis. I know my way. Thank you again. I'll make sure the keys reach the Aimesworths."

With this, Rosalind took her leave. The meeting had gone very well. In any social endeavor, the goodwill of a house's master was pleasant and useful, but the goodwill of those who ran that home was essential. Whatever might be coming next, she needed to cultivate the Willises' good opinion.

But why should anything else be happening? she asked herself as she tied her bonnet ribbon. *Surely, Lord Blanchard will be able to show Jasper's death was an accident, and all will be laid to rest.*

But even while she occupied herself with this firm and sensible thought, a door down the hallway opened, and Mr. Whelks stepped out. Very carefully, he locked the door behind him and tucked the key into his waistcoat pocket. He turned and saw her, and was visibly startled.

"Miss Thorne! I did not expect to see you here so soon. I thought after yesterday . . . yes, well. Perhaps it is better not to speak of it."

Rosalind smiled. "You may be sure, Mr. Whelks, I would not be here had Lady Jersey not sent me with a note for Mr. Willis."

"Her ladyship sent you?" Although he spoke softly, Rosalind did not miss the note of jealousy underneath the words.

"Only because you were engaged," she said quickly. "And you know I am anxious to do anything I can to assist Lady Blanchard, and Lady Jersey, of course. I could hardly refuse a trifling errand." Which might have been laying it on a bit thick, but Mr. Whelks did not seem to notice. "Lady Jersey was kind enough to tell me you spoke on my behalf, Mr. Whelks. Thank you very much for that." If it was important to be in Mr. and Mrs. Willis's good books, it was utterly vital that she have Mr. Whelks's trust. If he took against her, Lady Jersey would as well.

Mr. Whelks bowed. "You are most welcome, Miss Thorne. You have always been, may I observe, a young lady of superior

understanding and sensitivity. Of course, all of us who have the
honor of the lady patronesses' confidence must feel very keenly
the importance of these next days. How we conduct ourselves is
bound to reflect on Almack's and the patronesses more than
ever." Rosalind nodded in solemn acknowledgment of this. "If
you require any assistance, Miss Thorne, you have only to ask."

"Thank you, Mr. Whelks. I will remember that."

Rosalind descended the curving stair in a state of abstraction.
Something was out of place, but she could not lay her finger on
what it was. Certainly it was nothing about the Willises. They
had been properly taken up with wiping away any physical trace
of unpleasantness that might disturb their guests and patronesses. Neither was it anything to do with Mr. Whelks. It was the
most natural thing that he be in the ladies' private office, taking
care of whatever business the lady patronesses, and specifically
Lady Jersey, might have. On the other hand, he might simply
have been making sure that nothing had been disturbed.

Has anything been disturbed? Rosalind wondered. Then she
wondered how she might find out.

The sound of quick footsteps jolted Rosalind out of her con-
templations. A man was climbing the stairs in front of her. He
dodged neatly sideways so she would not have to disturb her
own path down to the ground floor.

Rosalind could not afterward say what made her turn. Perhaps it was the way he trotted so easily up that long, steep stair.
Perhaps it was the light glinting in his golden hair, or the sight
of a plain coat and dark trousers in a place where she expected
magnificence. Then, too, there was the startling combination of
his scarlet waistcoat and black cravat.

Whatever the reason, Rosalind did pause, and when she did
turn, it was to see him looking back down at her.

He had a weathered face, but a strong one. There was a stillness about him and a sense of patience and attention. Here was a man prepared to wait for a year and a day to get what he wanted.

The man bowed pleasantly, but with a small smile Rosalind did not know how to interpret. She turned and started down the stairs again slowly. Suddenly, Rosalind felt deeply determined that whoever this man was, he should not see her hurry away from him.

CHAPTER 11

A Fresh Summons

If once to Almack's you belong, like monarchs, you can do no wrong; But banished thence on Wednesday night, By Jove, you can do nothing right.

—Henry Luttrell

When Preston brought the carriage up in front of the Jerseys' great house, Rosalind gave him Willis's letter with instructions to hand it directly to Lady Jersey. Lady Jersey would naturally expect Rosalind to deliver Mr. Willis's letter personally, and Rosalind considered it. She very much wanted to hear what was happening in the patroness's meeting, but she must hope that Lady Blanchard would give her a full account later. She had other business to attend to.

Preston, fortunately, did not consider it his place to ask her any questions. He simply did as she asked and then drove the carriage to Little Russell Street, where Mrs. Kendricks met Rosalind in the foyer.

"How are you, miss?" she asked as she helped Rosalind off with her coat and bonnet.

"I'll do. Eventually anyway," Rosalind answered. "Lady Blanchard's carriage is outside. You might take them a drink and tell Preston I won't be needing them for at least another hour."

"Very good, miss, but I need to warn you . . ."

Before Mrs. Kendricks could finish, the parlor door opened to reveal Alice Littlefield, and her older brother, George.

"It is not Mrs. Kendricks's fault," announced Alice.

"She tried to deny us the premises," said George.

"She was quite firm about it," added Alice.

George nodded. "But we were rudely adamant and insisted on waiting for you."

Rosalind looked to Mrs. Kendricks.

"It is all perfectly true, miss," she replied staunchly.

"I'm sure it is, and I in no way blame you. In fact, I was expecting them both. Shall we go into the parlor?" Rosalind added to her guests.

The Littlefield siblings agreed at once. George even held the door.

George's close kinship to Alice was easy to see. Like Alice, he was dark and fine-boned and possessed a pair of cheerful black eyes. Also like Alice, George Littlefield seemed to have fallen down into working life without a single regret or backward glance, although Rosalind knew how carefully the pair of them husbanded their housekeeping money during those long months when the season was over and fashionable London was closed up tight.

Even with the tension of the Littlefields waiting on pins and needles to talk, Rosalind's tiny parlor enfolded her with a homey embrace. There were letters on the table and a fire in the grate, and her worn but comfortable armchair in its accustomed place.

"All right." She picked up the great pile of letters to glance through them. "Why don't you tell me . . ."

Words written in a firm, masculine hand caught her eye and Rosalind stopped. *Devon?*

"What's the matter, Rosalind?" asked Alice.

Rosalind set the letters down at once and turned away. "Nothing. A bill." She smoothed her skirts and her expression as she sat. "I was going to say perhaps we should start with you telling me what you already know?"

"I don't believe you," said Alice. "About the letter, that is, but I will let that pass because we haven't the time. Where have you been, Rosalind? Were you with Lady Blanchard? Is it true? Was Jasper Aimesworth found dead in the lady patroness's office at Almack's?"

"It's said he had a petition for a voucher clutched in his fist," added George.

"And was stabbed in the back with thirty pens like Caesar?" cried Rosalind. "Dear heavens, surely you don't believe such nonsense!"

"Should we?" Alice shot back.

"No," answered Rosalind firmly. "But it is true, Jasper Aimesworth is dead."

"Poor fellow," murmured George. "Not someone I liked, but no one deserves to shuffle off that young. And the rest?"

Rosalind's eyes wanted to stray toward her letters. She kept them fixed on her friends, and she made a decision. *This is to protect Lady Blanchard*, she said silently. *I'm so sorry, Alice, George. I hope you will understand. But there are places I cannot go, nor can I lead you there.*

"He was not found dead in the lady patroness's office. It was near the back door."

Alice's eyebrows shot up. "What was he even doing in the building?"

"At the moment, it seems most likely he had made a bet with

someone about being able to get into the rooms without a ticket, perhaps to steal a memento. He fell, and hit his head. It was a terrible accident."

George let out a long sigh. "Well. Won't Major Alway be disappointed." "Major" Algernon Alway was the publisher and editor-in-chief at the *London Chronicle*, for which both George and Alice wrote.

Alice had not stopped looking at Rosalind. "How do you know all this, Rose?"

Rosalind didn't blink. "I found him."

"What?"

"Lady Blanchard had invited me to dine. I was at Almack's to collect her after the patronesses' meeting. She was late, and I went around the back to avoid the crowds." She paused. "I found him there."

"Oh, Rosalind!" Alice dropped her pencil and ran at once to wrap her arms about her friend. "How awful! I'm so sorry!"

"It was an ugly shock," Rosalind said as soon as she could extricate herself from Alice's abrupt embrace. After being surrounded by an atmosphere of careful restraint all morning, this flood of emotion was a little overwhelming. "It's also why Lady Blanchard insisted I stay with her last night."

"Quite right, too." George pulled out his notebook and scribbled down a few lines. "So, you went to Lady Blanchard's right from Almack's? I imagine you didn't want to go home alone."

There was something in the way he asked the question that set Rosalind on the alert. "I couldn't go home. I had to see Lady Blanchard to her house. She was still at Almack's when Jasper was discovered." She paused. "As I told you."

George made no answer. It was Alice who asked the next question. "Was anyone else there? We can still get several stories out of this, you know, if we can talk to other witnesses."

"Mr. and Mrs. Willis were there, of course. I do not think they'll be all that eager to talk with you. Mr. Willis has, however, hired a runner from Bow Street to interview the staff and make other inquiries, so the public can be assured that everything at Almack's is exactly as it should be."

"You'll be taking on my job next." Alice peered at her shorthand, crossed out one notation, and added another. "It does mean that someone is not entirely certain it was an accident." She glanced up at Rosalind. "What do you think, Rose?"

"I think . . ." Rosalind stopped. "I think that Jasper was doing something foolish, and he paid too heavily for it. I think there will be some trifling wager found in White's book with his name on it and that will close the matter." *Whether it should or not.* Rosalind kept her face still and her gaze steady as she spoke.

George heaved a great sigh and tucked his notebook away in his coat pocket. "Well, sis, I warned you it would turn out to be a very little thing after all. Another case of mischief gone tragically wrong among the idle young men of the aristocracy. Or something of the kind."

"Yes," said Alice reluctantly. "You did. *C'est le vie, n'est-ce pas?*" But she was looking at Rosalind again. "Perhaps we can work up a few fulminations on the scourge of gambling and the ruin it is wrecking upon our finest young men?"

"That always goes over," agreed George. "And I'm sure we can add in a little something about having spoken to someone entirely informed on the subject, all right, Rosalind?"

"If you leave out my name, certainly."

"Well, come on then, Alice." George got to his feet and slipped his book into his pocket. "We can still get this in the early edition, but we'll have to hop it."

"Yes. Of course." But Alice didn't move. "Just one thing,

Rosalind. Did you decide whether you were going to go to the Aimesworths' this season?"

"As a matter of fact, I'm going to be staying with Lady Blanchard until she and Lord Blanchard leave for Konigsberg."

"I see," said Alice, and Rosalind had the uncomfortable idea her friend might see more than she wished. She nodded once, and turned away. Rosalind suddenly wanted to cross the room, to lay her hand on Alice's arm and say, "I've told you everything I can."

But she stayed where she was and watched her friends leave. She could not escape the feeling she had gotten off rather easily. Should she have told them about Devon also being a witness when the body was found? Or Mr. Whelks? They might still find it out. She bit her lip and chided herself for her indecisiveness.

When she heard the outer door close behind her friends, Rosalind turned back to her letters. There were indeed several bills—from the grocer, from her seamstress, and from the collier. None of these was enough to make her hesitate, but that letter addressed in a man's bold script was. There was also one note that had come by hand with just her name scrawled across the front. She decided to open this one first. She would face the other in a moment.

Rosalind broke the black seal and unfolded the letter.

If you are not nursing too many old grudges, come see me as soon as you get this.

Honoria A.

Rosalind pinched the bridge of her nose. A headache was beginning. Honoria Aimesworth had never been one to waste charm, or overmuch courtesy. It was something her mother, Lady Edmund, had never been able to correct or comprehend. Of course, Lady Edmund could never understand how much of Honoria's permanent disdain for the fashionable world came from her mother's endless insistence on perfection within it. In that at least, Honoria and Rosalind had a great deal in common. The difference came in how they'd dealt with that insistence.

A memory of a country house party flashed through her, though it was impossible to recollect whose. But it was before her debut; that much she did recall. She also remembered Honoria's scornful voice ringing out over the lawn.

"Oh, yes, do go and consult Miss Thorne about the dress! If anyone was born to be the world's lady's maid, it's her!"

Rosalind laid Honoria's note down and picked up the other. It was from Devon. She was sure of it. At least, she was sure until her reluctant fingers turned it over and she saw the red wax seal impressed by a signet ring—it featured a linnet perched on a stone with its beak open, presumably to sing.

Rosalind frowned. That was not the Casselmain crest. In fact, she didn't recognize it at all. She looked at the direction again. She'd been mistaken. That wasn't Devon's writing. Frowning, she broke the seal, unfolded the letter, and read.

Dear Miss Thorne:

You'll excuse the impropriety, I'm sure, but since I am not able to see you face to face, I was left with no choice. My being seen calling at Little Russell Street wouldn't be good for either of us, a fact I know you'd be the first to point out.

I'll skip the usuals. I'm sure you're in excellent health and you may assume the same for us. I'm writing about my sister, and my mother. Miss Thorne, I don't know whether you're actually considering Mother's suggestion that you come to stay and do whatever-it-may-be you do so well to get her enthroned on the board at those ridiculous assembly rooms, but if you are, I beg you pay attention to what I have to say. It would be infinitely better for all concerned—and this includes your very good and respectable self—to steer clear of us, and them.

There, now I've been as mysterious as a Gothic hero and rude in the bargain, but I can't help either. Miss Thorne, I know you've every reason to wish us, and Honoria in particular, to the devil. But if ever I've been capable of sincerity, I am sincere now. Do not get yourself involved with us this season.

Your humble and honest, if not terribly faithful, servant,
Jasper Aimesworth

CHAPTER 12

The Arrival of the Robin Redbreast

At the top of Wellington Street, and close to the more crowded portion of the busy Strand . . . has always been the center of criminal as well as of theatrical life.
—Percy Hetherington Fitzgerald, *Chronicles of the Bow Street Police Office*

When Principal Officer Adam Harkness returned to the ward room at the policing station, a most unusual chorus of greetings rose around him.

"Oooo, my stars! If it ain't the Earl of Bow Street 'imself! They do say 'e dances so trippingly!"

"Give us a turn, then, your lordship, show us how it's done!"

"My word! So 'andsome! Iffen 'e don't favor me with a waltz directly, I shall surely perish!"

"And who'd let you waltz in them boots, Dickinson?" Harkness pulled off his tricorn hat and took a swipe at the constable who made the jibe. "You'd stomp a hole right through the floor, and God help the lady whose foot got in the way!"

The room dissolved into general laughter with Harkness joining in as he hung coat and hat on their pegs.

There was little fancy or comfortable about the Bow Street Police Office. Its ward room was a plain, whitewashed space fur-

nished with benches and scarred tables where the patrol constables and captains could gather to rest or receive their assignments.
Even when it was empty, the place smelled of beer, tobacco, cold
mutton, and damp wool. Maps of the various city neighborhoods
had been pasted to the walls, along with printed notices of crimes
and criminals from around London and the provinces.

It was unusually crowded just now, as it was late afternoon
and the men of the night patrol were gathering to hear their
orders and assignments. They were a rough lot, and sported
every shade of skin from Michael Dougherty's pale Irish white
to Sampson Goutier's midnight black. Drawn largely from the
laboring classes, the fellows had signed on mostly in hope of
steadier work than doing the city's digging and hauling.

"Speakin' serious now, Mr. Harkness." Dickinson took his
outsized boots off the table where he'd been resting his feet and
planted them on the floor. "Did you see the ballroom? My
sister'll strike me dead if one of our own was inside Almack's
an' I can't tell her what it was like."

Harkness surveyed the round of hopeful faces and sympa-
thized. He was sure his own sisters, not to mention his mother,
would be pressing him for details when he got home tonight.

"Well, lads, I'll tell you." He leaned toward them, and to a
man, they leaned toward him.

"It was very, very big," he said. "And very, very empty."

With that, Harkness walked out of the room and let the
curses of disappointment swirl against his back.

The patrol room, which waited on the far side of the ward room,
was somewhat smaller and scarcely more luxurious. In truth, it
resembled a cross between a bank office and the reading room of
a circulating library. In the ward room, the cabinets and shelves

held lanterns, pistols, and alarm bells. In the patrol room, they held bound volumes of newspapers and clippings. More recent papers from across the length and breadth of England hung on racks or were stacked on the tables. Among them were issues of Bow Street's own publication, *Hue & Cry*. Circulated among the policing offices of London and its outskirts, its pages were given over to descriptions of crimes and descriptions of stolen property that was either still missing or had been discovered in pawn shops or other inappropriate places.

The world in general might call each and every man who worked out of the Bow Street station a "runner," but the men themselves did not use the term. Those who walked the streets or rode the highways were patrolmen, and each patrol was headed by a captain. Principal officers, like Harkness, were separate from the patrols, although they did sometimes assist them in the same way they assisted the river police or the watch. Principal officers had no fixed rounds to keep—rather, they went where the magistrates sent them. Generally what occurred was that a gentleman or other worthy citizen, such as Mr. William Willis, would write the magistrates to complain of some loss or injury, or to warn that they expected trouble. The magistrate reviewed the details, and assigned a patrol captain or a principal officer, as he felt the case merited. The worthy who contacted the office was afterward required to pay the fees of the men they hired.

At the moment, only one other man was at his desk in the patrol room. Samuel Tauton looked up from the paper he was perusing to give Harkness a friendly wave.

"Hello, Harkness."

"Tauton!" Harkness grasped the other man's hand. "I hadn't heard you were back. How was Bath?"

Tauton smiled and folded his hands across his paunch. Samuel Hercules Tauton was older than Harkness by at least ten years. He was also as crafty as they came and had a memory for faces that was second to none. He could spot a thief years after the crime had been laid away as unsolvable, and unlike some thief takers who'd just go after whoever was handy, Tauton's man—or woman—would generally be found out to be the right one.

"Bath gave me and my fellows some rare good fishing, I can tell you," said Tauton cheerfully. "Thinned the schools of the London dips for you lot."

The Prince of Wales had been in Bath the week before, which meant a host of swells, fashionables, and nabobs had followed him, along with a herd of pickpockets and other ne'er-do-wells. The city officials had written at once to the magistrates, begging to be supplied with some Bow Street men to help clear out the traveling predators.

"I hear you've climbed the mountain of the fashionable world, Harkness." Tauton folded his paper. "A dead man in Almack's, is it? I'm surprised Townsend didn't take this on himself."

Harkness allowed himself a brief, bitter smile. "It might take him away from the Prince of Wales's side, and then who would hold His Royal Highness's watch while he's gaming?" John Townsend was the principal officer best known to the public. Very few weeks went by without Townsend's name being mentioned in the papers. As far as Harkness could tell, the man was useful in that he kept the aristocracy, which controlled the purse strings, well disposed toward the idea of Bow Street and stations like it, but that was the beginning and the end of it.

Tauton grimaced. "Still, I expect it's nothing," he went on breezily. But when Harkness remained silent, Tauton's face grew solemn. "It is nothing, isn't it?"

"Everyone wants it to be."

"What did you see?"

"Not a thing, Tauton." Harkness perched himself on a stool at one of the writing desks. "It wasn't as if they were going to leave the corpse, or anything else, lying about all night until I could get a look at it."

"What did you find, then?"

Harkness rubbed his jaw. "I found Mr. Willis being harassed by his wife to make sure no rogue had accidentally slipped inside the rooms. I found doors with surprisingly stout locks thrown wide open for men and women to come and go. I found charwomen and porters, all more than ready to talk and asking for details about the corpse. I found a great, mostly empty, set of public rooms that could have hidden a small army. I found a very strange story," he added, "of a lady patroness, the young Duke of Casselmain, a private secretary, and a rather undefined gentlewoman with the dramatic name of Rosalind Thorne who in some order all found the body." He paused again. "It's a damned odd crowd to be hanging about a corpse."

"You suspect something?" Tauton asked him.

Harkness shook his head. "I suspect that young gentlemen are fools, young ladies are pretty, old ladies are nosy, and confidential secretaries are shocked and horrified."

"And you're going to talk to them all anyway?"

"All the ones who will talk to me. Probably come to nothing, but I'll have a good report for Townsend and the magistrates, and it will read well in the papers."

"Bit of a step down for the hero of the highways, ain't it?"

"You did warn me it was dull work when I accepted the promotion," answered Harkness. "Still, there's fewer chances I'll get my throat cut asking questions at Almack's."

Tauton chuckled. "My boy, that all depends on who you dance with."

Harkness spent the rest of the afternoon writing up what he'd learned from Willis and from the magistrate. No one was sure yet if an actual crime had been committed. Nothing appeared to have been stolen, but the Willises were still completing their inventory. Mr. Willis did state confidently that the young man's note case and gold snuff box had been found near him, and returned to the family. Despite this, it was good to start a full description of the crime—if a crime it proved to be—circulating generally among the other policing offices. One never knew where a useful tidbit of information might turn up, or when.

Once Harkness gave his report to the clerk to copy out, he wrote up a pair of letters in his best fist—one to Sarah Villiers, Lady Jersey, and one to Devon Winterbourne, Duke of Casselmain. Both requested the favor of an interview regarding the recent unfortunate occurrence. He'd have liked to send off a third letter to Miss Rosalind Thorne, but while it was public knowledge which houses the nobility resided in, he had no direction for Miss Thorne. Maybe Mr. Willis could supply one. He'd been fairly cooperative today. Of course, that might change if he thought Harkness was about to start bothering his patrons and their friends.

Once the letters were put in the mail bag, Harkness turned his attention to the files, and the *Hue & Cry*. Finding a description of a similar crime was only a faint hope. If he'd read about any other dead gentlemen who were not obviously killed in a duel, he would have remembered. Still, Harkness liked to be thorough and he knew the value of patience.

By the time Harkness straightened up and knuckled his eyes, daylight had faded to twilight. The boy came in to light the lamps. Out in the ward room, he heard the sounds of the patrol captains calling out names and assignments to the men, accompanied by the usual complaints and taunts, and the tramp of boots as the patrols took to the streets to do what they could for another night.

Tauton looked up from his own report. "Have you found anything?"

"Not a bean." Harkness returned the last pages to their file, and the file to its cabinet drawer. "Wasn't really expecting it, but . . ." He shrugged. "I've gone over the ground now. If I find something tomorrow, I might just know what I'm looking at."

Tauton eyed him. "You really do think this is more than just some tomfoolery gone wrong?"

Harkness pushed the drawer shut. "I can't get it out of my mind that there was a damned odd crowd hanging about for it to be only tomfoolery."

"I wouldn't get too bothered about them. Your man, if there was one, was out the door and down the street as soon as Aimesworth's head hit the boards. Even one of the gentry'd know better than to hang about with the man they'd just killed."

"If they could get out fast enough," said Harkness. "It's a big place, and not as empty as it might have been. Maybe they got spotted before they could get to the door and had to play at being as surprised as everybody else."

"Now there is a thought," said Tauton slowly. "Well, well. You'll let me know if you need any help?"

"I will that."

The men said good night. Back in the ward room, Harkness claimed his great coat and tricorn hat and wound his muffler tight around his neck. A glance out the narrow windows showed that the snow had started up again, and it was getting worse. A good night for one of his mother's hot dinners at home, and the cheerful riot in the parlor afterward. Harkness had six brothers and sisters, most of them still at home, or near enough. There was seldom any peace about the place, and very little quiet.

Harkness's musings on home and hearth, though, were interrupted by the sight of the man waiting at the bottom of the station's stairs, hands shoved deep into his pockets and a look of determined hope on his sharp-boned face.

"Well now, George Littlefield," Harkness hailed the newspaperman. "What brings you to Bow Street today?"

"Well now, Mr. Harkness," the other man answered amiably, "I expect you already know."

"I expect I do." The news of Aimesworth's death might not be in the papers yet, but that didn't mean that their hounds weren't already on the scent. "I'm a little surprised that you worked out so quick it'd be me on the case."

Littlefield shrugged. Probably his work had consisted of laying a shilling across the clerk's palm. "Care to get a pint and talk the matter through?" He jerked his chin toward the Staff and Bell public house across the busy street.

Harkness shook his head slowly. "I've got nothing to say to the *Chronicle*, Littlefield. Not for beer, love, or money." And nothing to say to George Littlefield that was worth keeping his dinner waiting.

"Not for love or money maybe." George smiled. "But how about for information?"

CHAPTER 13

A Comfortable Pint

> *. . . the dramatic element always was supplied by the "Bow Street Runner," popularly supposed to be a miracle of detective skill.*
>
> —Percy Hetherington Fitzgerald, *Chronicles of the Bow Street Police Office*

The Staff and Bell public house was full to overflowing with noisy, convivial men pushing up to the bar and coming away with tankards of beer. The landlady and her daughters shouldered their way between the tables and benches, bestowing trays of cheese and bread and bowls of mutton stew on the waiting customers. Not a few of the men raised a pint in salute to Harkness as he and Littlefield doffed their hats and shook the snow off their shoulders. One or two, however, pulled their own hat brims down low and hustled out the door.

Harkness claimed a spot on the bench by the fire, and waited while Littlefield acquired two pints of the Bell's dark, rich beer from the innkeeper. They toasted each other's health and drank.

"Thanks, Littlefield." Harkness wiped the foam from his mouth. "Now, what have you got for me?"

George contemplated the depths of his beer, as if he had a

choice to make. "By now you'll have heard the name 'Rosalind Thorne.'"

"I have," Harkness acknowledged. "Do you know Miss Thorne?"

"She's a friend of my sister's. She's also a source for the gossip pages, and usually a good one. But today . . . well, she tried handing me and Alice some false coin about this business of Jasper Aimesworth."

"Any idea why?" A reliable friend deciding to lie, that was interesting. Even more interesting than a gentlewoman who also had dealings with a newspaperman such as Littlefield.

"Two possibilities." George took another swallow of beer. "I think she's protecting someone. Alice, though, thinks she really wants to get us looking toward the possibility of some nefarious deed regarding Jasper Aimesworth, but can't tell us so directly."

Harkness felt himself go still, a reflex he'd acquired while hunting highwaymen with the horse patrol.

"What sort of nefarious deed would that be?" he asked.

"No idea," said George. "But Rosalind knows everybody, and everything, about society. She just might know more about this business than she can say out loud."

Harkness rubbed his chin. "You said she might be protecting someone. Who might that be?"

"Well, herself, for starters, as well as Lady Blanchard. Lady B is Miss Thorne's godmother, and a fair way of being all the family she has. Lady Edmund Aimesworth's another. She might also be protecting Almack's itself, although Alice says not and Alice usually knows best."

"What about the duke who was there?"

Littlefield lowered his tankard. "A duke?" he said. "Not the Duke of Casselmain, by any chance?"

"The same."

The newsman pulled a face as if his beer had turned to water on him. Then he whistled. "Well, well. All my pretty chicks and their dam, and she said not a word . . ."

"Then, I take it Miss Thorne does know the duke as well?"

"Oh, yes." Littlefield drained his pint. "They were secretly engaged once."

"Says Alice?"

George nodded. "Less secretly, Alice says that Lord Casselmain's about to become engaged to Honoria Aimesworth, sister of the dead man."

"Then I may take it Miss Thorne knew Aimesworth as well?"

"As it happens. They weren't friends, but she's on visiting terms with the family."

Harkness took another swallow of beer. Miss Thorne was changing in his estimation from an undefined gentlewoman to a remarkably prominent figure in this strange and gaudy incident. Not only did she seem to know every member of the crowd around the dead man, but she was setting her friends out to run her errands, and failing to mention the presence of the prominent man for whom she once cherished a regard.

"Tell me about Miss Thorne. How is it she knows so much?"

George considered his empty tankard. Then, he considered Harkness. "Back in the old days, our parents sent Alice to school to gain the usual set of ladies' accomplishments. Once she got there, she met the Thorne sisters."

"Sisters?"

"Rosalind, and her older sister, Charlotte. They became good friends—or at least Alice and Rosalind did. Alice was at her coming out at Almack's and all."

Harkness frowned. "So Miss Thorne's another one out of the first circles?"

"Oh, she isn't now. But she was. Her father is Sir Reginald Thorne and the family was once welcome in all the best houses. Then—" George snapped his fingers. "There's a crash in the markets, and we all fall down. It turns out Sir Reginald had been living beyond his means for a good long while. He scarpered, and took Charlotte with him. Rosalind stayed with her mother to face the music."

"Why did she stay? Why not leave with her father?"

George shook his head. "Not even Alice knows that much. She says that Rosalind never got on with her mother, but it's possible she stayed out of simple decency when Sir Reginald scarpered."

Harkness very carefully kept the doubt out of his face. "So, her father's vanished, and she's not married. Her mother?"

"Dead."

"How does she manage?"

"Carefully. When you fall, everything depends on who's there to help you land. With me, it was some school chums who remembered I won a few prizes for essays and were able to put me in the way of some newspaper work. With Rosalind, it was Lady Blanchard. Lady Blanchard helped set her up as a sort of private secretary to society ladies. She helps out with their guest lists and parties and that sort of thing, and they invite her to dinner and to stay and give her little presents, and so on."

"Why doesn't she marry?"

"No money and no title," said George. "None of the tonnish mamas will let her near their fair-haired boys."

"And yet you think enough of her to be running errands for her," said Harkness.

Littlefield set the tankard on the floor beside the bench. "Miss Thorne's a good sort, but she's in a tough spot, being a

woman alone trying to keep up with all the demands of gentility. When her father and sister left, it hurt her, and that's made
her very loyal to the people who stayed by her side. So loyal, in
fact, she sometimes gets caught up in trying to protect the
wrong people." A muscle in his cheek twitched. "We're not just
after the story on this one, you see?"

Harkness did see. George and Alice Littlefield wanted him
to find out the truth so they could pull their friend out before
she sank under the weight of trying to protect some criminal
who had the good fortune to be well born. That also was very,
very interesting.

"I'll need an address for Miss Thorne, if you please."

Littlefield gave him the number of a house in Little Russell
Street. "All right then, Harkness. I've shown you mine. What
about yours?"

Harkness considered the man beside him. George Littlefield
was honest, by the standards of his profession. He wanted his
story, and he wasn't above embellishing the facts to add color to
the page, but unlike some others Harkness dealt with, he never
outright invented his news. He'd also as much as said he was
willing to help on this Almack's matter, provided it would also
help this Miss Thorne.

"Littlefield, you can tell your readers that the principal officer
of Bow Street has thoroughly and exhaustively questioned all
the staff of Almack's Assembly Rooms who were on hand at the
time of this dreadful incident. He is pleased to report they all
are honest and hardworking and answered his questions in a
forthright manner." Which included a lot of slurs about what a
Tartar old Mrs. Willis was, how miserable it was to try to get
blood out of the boards, complaints about the cousins of the
Irish carters brought in to help with the new chairs, not to men-

tion some asides about the famous Lady Jersey and her constant schemes for improvements, which generally meant more work for persons other than herself.

"How very reassuring," said Littlefield blandly. "My editor will be delighted."

Harkness nodded as if he'd been thanked, and took a last swallow of beer. "Call around Bow Street in the next couple of days. I'll know more than I do now."

"Come on, Harkness. That's less use to me than reassurances about the honesty of the working classes."

"Tell your readers Watchdog Harkness is on the scent, and closing in on the true facts of this dreadful and mysterious case."

Harkness met Littlefield's gaze and held it. Littlefield whistled low.

"You think it was murder."

Harkness made no answer. Littlefield leaned closer. "You do! Why? What's tipped you?"

"Call 'round in a couple days," Harkness repeated, firmly and finally.

Littlefield raised both hands in surrender. "All right, Harkness, you win. You've got your two days, and then . . ." He leveled his ink-stained finger at Harkness's chest. "I'm coming for you."

"Fair enough," Harkness agreed. "Oh, and don't tell your Miss Thorne you talked to me, all right?"

"Why?"

"Because I want to talk to her myself, but after I've talked to the Aimesworth household. You tip her the wink, and you'll get nothing from me for the rest of this case. Understand?"

Littlefield's mouth twitched as a bitter battle between conscience and profession churned inside him. Harkness found himself wondering if Littlefield cherished a soft spot for Miss Thorne.

He was certainly right about falls. But it wasn't just about who was there to help you up, was it? It was also all about who'd been there to help put you down.

CHAPTER 14

The Uneasiness of
a House in Mourning

*Gentlemen, I'll tell you the plain truth. Every day of the
year we take up a paper; we read the opening of a murder.*
—Thomas De Quincey, *On Murder Considered as
One of the Fine Arts*

**BLOOD IN THE BALLROOM!
EXCLUSIVE DETAILS!**

The drear calm of February was suddenly and brutally
shattered last Monday by the discovery of a death in
that haven of exclusivity and gentility—the Almack's
ballroom. While the lady patronesses pored over their
lists of candidates, determining which new young
misses and first circle families would this month
be favored with a coveted Almack's voucher, the terrible and the inexplicable were occurring beneath their
delicate slippers, in the very heart of the *sanctum sanctorum.*

Mr. Jasper Aimesworth, only son of Lord Edmund
Aimesworth, was found dead in the hallowed hall of

the *haut ton*, apparently having fallen from the musicians' gallery. The mysterious circumstances of this accident, if an accident it should prove to be, have not yet been revealed.

The most worthy Mr. William Willis, manager of Almack's Assembly Rooms, did not let a moment lapse before displaying prompt and sound judgment. As soon as the tragedy was discovered, Mr. Willis sent to the Bow Street Magistrate's Court to procure the services of Principal Officer Adam Harkness, known to his colleagues as "the Watchdog." Faithful Readers of the *Chronicle* will be familiar with that name from several years ago when we reported how the same Mr. Harkness, then a member of Bow Street's horse patrol, proved instrumental in tracking down the vicious highwayman Peter "The Red Hand" Lowell . . .

"And that's done," Rosalind murmured as she read over George and Alice's hurried, and sensational, work spread across the front page of the *London Chronicle*'s special edition. At least if any of the lady patronesses asked, she could honestly say she'd tried to tell all and sundry that there was nothing to find out. She had failed, and she would apologize. Initially, it would cost her in terms of their goodwill and trust. She would have difficulty regaining that lost ground, but she would think of something. In the meantime, she had calls to pay, and she knew she must start by answering this extraordinary summons from Honoria Aimesworth.

It had been some time since Rosalind had been in a house of mourning. Not that the Aimesworth house was quite there yet. Like any public occasion, mourning required a great deal of preparation. Rosalind's hired hack drew up behind the funeral furnishers' black carriage. A dark-skinned groom dressed in a long black coat and white wig watched solemnly as Rosalind stepped down. The footman who opened the door wore a black band on his arm, black stockings on his legs, and black ribbon on his powdered wig.

"I'm sorry, Miss Thorne," he said. "Lady Edmund is not at home to anyone."

Rosalind showed the man Honoria's note. He hesitated, but then bowed her inside. While the downstairs maid helped her off with her coat and bonnet, Rosalind had a fine view of the activity in the front parlor. Inside, more men in black coats and trousers hung lengths of black cloth around the walls. A maid carried a mirror out.

That would be where Jasper would be laid in his coffin. The undertaker would be upstairs even now, taking Jasper's measure with his rod and quietly discussing the appropriate woods, finishes, and linings for his coffin with Lady Aimesworth. He would lie in the box in the parlor for two or three days, with candles burning continuously at his head and feet. If the family did not care to hold vigil themselves, the funeral man would supply professional mourners to take on the chore. That way, not only would Jasper be properly mourned, but the family could also be confident that their son truly was dead, not just sleeping.

Rosalind did not think there was much possibility of Jasper waking from the sleep he had been sent to.

When Rosalind entered Honoria's apartment, she found her sitting at her dressing table and staring into the mirror. She didn't turn, but the reflection showed Rosalind how pinched and pale her face had become. The circles under her eyes might have been drawn with kohl. Her black crepe dress was of an older cut that strained across her bosom and shoulders.

She tried to remember the last time she'd spoken directly with Honoria. Surely it was during her second season. Yes, at Beryl Wentworth's wedding breakfast. Charlotte had been a bridesmaid. Everyone had been talking about how the lovely older Thorne girl was sure to be betrothed before the year was out.

Which only went to show how little anyone knew about the future.

"Hello, Honoria," Rosalind said.

Honoria didn't answer. Rosalind looked at her pale reflection and saw the way her hand rested beside her brush and comb, as if she'd forgotten what to do with such objects.

"They won't let me see him," Honoria snapped. "They want the mortuary men to be finished with him first."

"I'm sorry," said Rosalind, both because it was true and because she had no idea what other answer she could make.

"Lord Casselmain says you found him."

"I did, yes."

"Did he . . . did he look like he suffered?"

Rosalind found her throat had gone dry. She had been prepared for many different possibilities, but Honoria Aimesworth's genuine distress was not one of them. The Honoria she knew was quick with a barb and didn't just profess disdain for the fashionable world, she genuinely meant it. Rosalind felt a bit ashamed.

"No, I don't think he suffered. I think it was very quick."

"Jasper was a coward," Honoria told her. "He wouldn't have managed it well if it had hurt."

Rosalind made no answer. Honoria was watching her in the mirror. They made a strange pair in this luxurious and tasteful boudoir—Rosalind in her plain dark blue dress, and Honoria in outmoded, ill-fitting black, both of them wan and hesitant. Well, perhaps not both hesitant. Honoria seldom hesitated.

"I imagine you're wondering what I want with you." Honoria

finally turned around. As she looked up, Rosalind watched her
face struggle. Pride, confusion, and anger all warred for their
place. Her dark eyes blazed with fury and with tears, but her
voice was as steady and cold as stone.

"I want you to find out who killed my brother."

The words were shocking and the request outrageous, even
ludicrous. It was a long moment before Rosalind could even
begin to formulate a response. "No one killed your brother,
Honoria. It was an accident."

"Don't be stupid," Honoria snapped. "He was killed. I know
he was."

"How do you know?"

"Because he was hiding something from me. He never hid
anything from me. But when I saw him yesterday . . . he was
burning papers in the hearth."

"Papers?" A blunt and brutal memory assaulted Rosalind—
the smell of burning paper, the ashen remains of ledgers and
letters, a single note on an empty desk . . .

Stop it, Rosalind Thorne. Concentrate!

Honoria frowned at Rosalind's evident inattention. "He was
in the card room off the conservatory. When I found him, he
was sitting there half-drunk although it wasn't yet noon." She
paused. "Before you say it, no, that was not normal for him.
Anyway, there was a smell. It took me a while to recognize it,
but it was burning paper. I'm certain of it." She took a deep,
steadying breath. "He was troubled and burning papers in the
morning, missing at lunchtime, and dead before nightfall. Do
you still expect me to believe it was an accident?"

Again, Rosalind found she had no answer. "May I sit down?"
she asked instead.

Honoria waved her to the overstuffed white satin chair by
the fireplace. Rosalind sat carefully and smoothed her skirts.

"Honoria, why would you ask this of me? If there is anything to be discovered, surely your parents will hire a man . . ."

Honoria barked out a laugh. "My parents! My father is drunk. He will be for the next three days. After that, it's likely he'll forget he ever had a son. My mother . . . my mother wants Jasper buried as quietly as possible so she can get on with her return to society."

"Then why—" Rosalind cut the sentence off.

"Why do I care?" The question fairly dripped with scorn.

"I was not going to say that." But she was going to say something close to it, and the embarrassment reddened Rosalind's cheeks.

"I care because Jasper cared," said Honoria. "The rest of the family sees me as a pawn or a distraction, depending on the day of the week and whether we are in season or out of it. Jasper was an idiot and a romantic and a drunk. He was bored and he was dissolute, but he actually gave a damn about *me*, his sister—the real girl, not the Aimesworth daughter. I want whoever did this found!" The fury in Honoria's words pulled her to her feet.

"I understand, Honoria," Rosalind said, but the way Honoria's face twisted said the other woman very much doubted that. "And it is possible that Jasper surprised a burglar."

"Nonsense. Who is going to burgle Almack's, and for what? There's no silver plate or money in the place. Did they mean to steal the new chairs out of the card room?"

"I don't know," Rosalind admitted. "The one is as likely as the other. A burglar might just be acting in hopes of luck and on the reputation of the rooms."

"One would think if a man was risking the gallows, he'd know what he was after."

That Honoria would have such an elevated opinion of London's criminal classes was yet another surprise, but Rosalind also kept this to herself.

"Mr. Willis has hired a Bow Street runner to look into—"

"Oh, yes, I've read all about the runner!" sneered Honoria. "With a dramatic pet name and I know not what else. How grand! Just how far do you think such a man will get? No lady of quality will talk to someone from Bow Street, and you know it. They'll see him as a sordid thief taker and shut up like oysters. The *gentlemen* will do their best to protect their houses and their names, and they'll be utterly insulted if the fellow presumes to look anywhere above the servants' quarters for his answers!"

It finally sank in to Rosalind what Honoria was truly suggesting. Her first reaction was dismay at having taken so long to understand. Her second was surprise.

"You think Jasper was killed by . . ."

"By someone he knew. One of us. The *haut ton. Society.*"

Rosalind would have sworn she harbored no illusion that any sort of inherent moral superiority clung to the members of the "first circle." She knew the sorts of things they did, and the sort they paid to do. Young men destined to lead the kingdom regularly paid to enjoy their vices, or made a blood sport of each other over the turn of a card or the fall of a pair of dice. Ladies turned, laughing, from their marriage vows almost as soon as they'd made them, or at least as soon as they'd made a legitimate heir and a spare. But this . . . every fiber of her being screamed out that this was different.

And yet Jasper had known something was wrong. And Mr. Whelks, who never left Lady Jersey's side, had been absent on this all-important morning. And Lord Blanchard was being forced out of London, and Lady Blanchard, at least, did not intend ever to come back.

And Devon was in the ballroom.

"It does not have to have been a friend," Rosalind offered. "Perhaps Jasper met with a gambler or a money lender, someone of that stripe."

"Why would he meet such a person in Almack's? They'd meet in a tavern, a club, a gambling hall. Do you even *hear* yourself?"

Rosalind swallowed. "I do, Honoria, and I hear you. There's something else." She reached into her reticule. "I hear Jasper." She laid the letter onto the tea table.

Honoria all but dove for the paper. Rosalind would not have thought it possible for the other woman to turn any whiter, but as she scanned the words her brother had left behind, the last drop of blood drained from her hollow cheeks.

"You cannot ignore this," she whispered. "You have to help me."

"I don't want to ignore it, but neither do I know how to proceed. Honoria . . ." She hesitated. "Honoria, I organize guest lists. I decorate ballrooms and leave visiting cards at houses for women who want to be seen as doing the right thing, but who can't be bothered to go themselves. I find tickets and talk to newspaper writers. That's all." Her cheeks were burning. Why should this make her blush? There was nothing wrong in it. It enabled her to keep her place in the only world she knew. "Discovering a criminal act, a murderer, is something else entirely."

"You could do it if you tried."

"Why would you think so?" *You, who never believed one good thing about me. Who saw before anyone else I was born to be nothing but another's servant.*

"Because people talk to you. Because you're one of us." Rosalind tilted her chin up and Honoria had the decency to pause at least a little. "You've done such a careful job of guarding your gentility. People talk about 'poor Rosalind,' but they still see you as somebody who's got to be sheltered by the bosom of the ton."

"How very kind of them," Rosalind murmured.

"You are in and out of everybody's house. You talk to everyone about everything they can't be bothered with. There must be some sign, some reason why Jasper was in Almack's in the first place."

And why Devon was there to help find his corpse. Do you even know Devon was there? Did he tell you? This, too, suddenly seemed a very important question.

"I should think any sign would be here." Rosalind gestured toward the house. "Have you looked in his papers? His appointment books? Talked to his friends?"

"Oh, yes. All those single gentlemen. I, the unmarried girl, just called on them at their rooms and asked indelicate questions about my brother."

"But that's what you're asking me to do."

"I'm asking you to exercise those vaunted talents of organization and finesse for something beyond a ball or a triumphant season! Whatever you think of me, Rosalind Thorne, leaving Jasper to the grave is cruel and it is unjust!" She paused and added. "I'll pay you, if that's what you want. I have quite a bit of my own money."

Rosalind's first instinct was to fling the offer back in Honoria's face. But she bit back her retort. Honoria was asking for help, in the extremes of her grief. But what she was asking, and what she was offering . . . there was no rule, no social guide to follow for how to accept, or even demur. Yes, Rosalind had meant to find out what had happened to help Lady Blanchard through her troubles, but what Honoria was asking was fundamentally different. She was asking for the means to start a public prosecution. For that, there was no correct answer except to refuse and to pretend this conversation had never happened. Or rather, that would have been the correct answer except for one small detail: Honoria was right. On some fundamental level, it was unacceptable to leave the question of Jasper's death unanswered.

"I'll do what I can, making no promise beyond that," said

Rosalind slowly. And then, because it was Honoria she spoke to, she added, "If I fail, which I almost certainly will, you must swear to believe that I have done my utmost."

Honoria nodded once. "Very well. How will you begin?"

Rosalind swallowed. She felt the enormity of the situation looming over her but forced herself to set that aside. It was a task. A complex task, to be sure, but all that meant was that she must take each piece in its turn.

Fortunately, the first piece was already at hand. "Mr. Willis found a ring of keys dropped in the musicians' gallery." She pulled them out of her bag. "Are these Jasper's?"

Honoria took the ring and peered closely at it. "Yes," she said. "I recognize the fob and the seal."

"What are they for?"

Rosalind seldom thought of Honoria as careful, but she was being careful now. She turned the keys over one at a time, examining each closely. "This is the front door of the house." She touched one. "One of the others might be to his rooms. He has—had—bachelor rooms." Most young gentlemen did, even those who still officially lived with their parents.

"Where are his rooms?"

Honoria shook her head. "I don't know. He moved while we were out of the country, and I hadn't had any reason to ask for the new address. Ridiculous, isn't it? Not to know where my brother's living?"

Or for him to have avoided telling you. The thought startled Rosalind, but it could not be dismissed.

She touched the smaller key where it lay on Honoria's palm. "Is there a strong box or anything of the kind in his room here?"

Honoria shook her head. "I've had no chance to look. They've been busy in there with . . . with his body. I could look once he's moved to the parlor."

"I think you should." That would account for three of the keys, but there was a fourth, and it also looked to be for a door. Rosalind touched it. "What of this one?"

Honoria shook her head. "I don't know it."

"May I keep these?"

"If you think it will help."

"I don't know, but perhaps." Rosalind returned them to her bag. "If there was a matter of honor or business behind this, there might be papers or letters left behind."

"Jasper was burning papers," Honoria reminded her.

"Perhaps he missed some." Rosalind paused, staring at nothing, just watching her own thoughts as they turned back to the smoldering ashes that had been left behind when Father fled. "Has that grate been swept yet?"

Honoria sat up straighter. "I don't know. The house has been in such an uproar, it might have been missed. We should check."

Both women rose to their feet and hurried out into the corridor.

"Honoria! What are you doing?" Both young women winced and turned.

Of course it was Lady Edmund, directly behind them.

CHAPTER 15

The Understanding Between Them

As it is impossible to hammer any thing out of it for moral purposes, let us treat it aesthetically, and see if it will turn to account that way. Such is the logic of a sensible man, and what follows?

—Thomas De Quincy, *On Murder Considered as One of the Fine Arts*

Of course Mother chose now to make her appearance. Honoria swallowed the scream that threatened to burst out of her. It was, after all, exactly the wrong moment.

"I didn't realize you were here, Miss Thorne." Mother's gaze darted back and forth between her and Rosalind, searching for reasons and faults.

Honoria watched Rosalind draw herself up and a dreadful moment of doubt shivered through her. If she'd made a mistake in judging the fallen Miss Thorne's essential character, she'd pay the price for months, possibly years.

But thankfully, Rosalind seemed willing to make do with those comfortable and appropriate platitudes she was so expert at. "I came to offer my condolences, Lady Edmund," she said. "I did not like to disturb you, as you were much engaged."

"That was most kind. Thank you." Not that there was any

feeling in Mother's reply. She wasn't even looking at Rosalind. She was watching Honoria. "I've just been told that Lord Casselmain has arrived, Honoria. Perhaps you could go down to him while I have a word with Miss Thorne?"

"Oh, very well." Honoria didn't take any leave of Rosalind. It might have looked odd to show extra consideration, especially taking into account her previously stated opinions of the other girl. Mother had already scented that something was wrong. If she got her teeth into the matter, it was all over.

Honoria swept down the corridor. A glance behind assured her that Mother and Rosalind were already out of sight. She ducked into the green sitting room and rang the bell.

"Tell Lord Casselmain he's to meet me in the conservatory card room," she directed the girl who answered. Then she hurried out again, down the east stairs and into the conservatory.

Honoria slammed the door's bolt home, startling little Mr. Shelly at his potting bench. "Oh, Miss Aimesworth, I wasn't expecting anyone . . ."

"I'm sure." She darted past him to the card room.

"May I say how very sorry . . ." he called to her back.

"You may, but I haven't time to listen." Honoria closed the French doors and drew their curtain.

For once, luck seemed to be with her. A pile of black ash lay heaped beneath the grate. Whoever left this should thank their stars she'd found it before Mother did. Honoria grabbed the brush and shovel from the fire irons and knelt on the hearth. For her own part, she had to thank her stars for black skirts. There would be no obvious smears of grime for Mother to notice. Honoria brushed the ashes forward and spread them out on the hearthstones, raising the acrid scent of old smoke.

There. A tiny scrap of paper lay among the ash. Honoria plucked it out and squinted at it. With the door shut, the light in here was abysmal, and she could make out next to nothing about it.

Someone knocked. Honoria groaned. She also jumped to her feet and dropped the scrap into the plain vase on the mantel that held the spills used to light the lamps and candles.

"Come in," she called, folding her dirty hands quickly behind her back.

The door opened, and Casselmain, looking unusually hesitant, stepped inside.

"Hello, Honoria."

"Hello," she answered. "Close the door, won't you? There's no need to have Father's orchid farmer listening in."

Casselmain did as she said. "How is your father?"

"How am I to know? I haven't seen him since . . . since you came to tell us Jasper died."

Sorrow's black wave threatened again. That night had been inconceivable. First had come the great banging at the door. Honoria remembered waking up, befuddled, and ringing for her maid to find out what was the matter. The stupid girl came back already in tears and choking out nonsense about Jasper.

Honoria remembered brushing past her, not even stopping to pull on a wrap or slippers. The gallery had been abysmally cold, but she'd rushed to the top of the stairs anyway. There was Casselmain down below in the entrance hall. There were Father and Mother standing with him. She couldn't hear what they were saying. Thoroughly irritated, she'd started running downstairs, the marble steps cold and slick as ice beneath her stockinged feet.

Before she reached the bottom, Father fainted. Not Mother, of course. It was not the done thing. But Father crumbled as if his bones had all suddenly dissolved. It took the butler, the valet, and two footmen to carry him away.

Honoria stood on the bottom stair, facing Mother. Her breath was gone, stolen from her by a host of imagined disasters: They were ruined. There'd been a fire at the warehouse, a ship had been lost, the funds had crashed, the money was gone.

Where's Jasper? she had thought. *If the world's ending, where's Jasper?*

"Your brother is dead," Mother said.

Just like that. No warning, no attempt to shield her or soften the blow. Just the blunt statement of facts. *Your brother is dead.*

Honoria closed her eyes before her tears could begin again. *I have to get out of this house.*

"Should I go?" Casselmain asked from behind her.

By rights, he should. They weren't even officially engaged, after all. They should not be alone behind closed doors. And heaven knew she was in no mood to make conversation.

"No, you'd better stay, for a little while anyway. It's what Mother wants. If we're being left alone together, more people will think the engagement's a done thing." Weariness overcame her and Honoria collapsed into the chair. Jasper's chair. "You can sit if you like."

"Thank you." Casselmain sat down in the other wing-backed chair and rested his hands on his knees.

Honoria looked at the man she meant to marry. He had a decent figure, thank goodness, and dressed simply and with reasonable taste. Unlike his late brother, Hugh, Devon Winterbourne had a reputation for being sober. A bit too sober, some said, but if that was a fault, it was one Honoria could live with. And Jasper had trusted the man.

Jasper.

His death was a great formless mass that filled all the spaces, inside and out. It left no room to think about what she ought to be doing.

"I'm sorry, Honoria," said Casselmain. "He was a good man."

Honoria shrugged and turned her face away. Probably Jasper was a good man. He was certainly better at being a man than she was at being a girl. He could drink and gamble and dress and live as he was expected to do.

I try, 'pon my soul I do. She closed her eyes. She was going to start crying again. She was sick to death of crying.

"Is there anything I can do?" Casselmain asked.

"There's nothing anyone can do."

Silence. Casselmain moved one hand from his knee to the table beside him. The room's damp was wilting his shirt points and cravat. He was trying to be kind. She should try to accept that kindness. Unfortunately, that wasn't something she was any good at.

"Your maid told me Lady Edmund was with Miss Thorne," Casselmain said. "Honoria, did you . . . ask Rosalind here?"

Of course. Honoria felt her jaw tighten. "Why should you care about that?"

"I was just curious."

"About Miss Thorne. Yes. She's a great object of curiosity with you yet, isn't she?"

"We are all friends, Honoria, and she . . ." He stopped. In the walls, the steam pipes hissed and pinged sharply.

Honoria rolled her eyes. "She found Jasper. You can say it. It will take much more than words to break me down. You should remember that."

He didn't rise to the bait. He had plenty of practice at keeping his temper, and his own counsel. That was something she'd need to remember. It would take time to learn how to handle this man. Weariness washed over her again.

"Honoria, I don't want to quarrel with you."

"Then what do you want?" she snapped.

"I want to tell Rosalind about why we decided to get married."

Honoria straightened up in her chair. He couldn't mean it, except from the frank and direct way he looked at her, he evidently did.

"Well, I do not want to tell her."

"We can trust her."

"You can."

"What has Rosalind done to you?" asked Casselmain. His tone turned waspish. She had insulted his lady love. Good. She had more practice at dealing with anger than with kindness.

"She's done nothing yet, that I know of, but she wants too much to be trustworthy."

"I don't understand you."

This was not the safest ground, and prudence dictated she should tread lightly, but Honoria discarded that. Casselmain should understand her opinion of Rosalind Thorne at once, and she must wrangle his as far out into the open as it would come. No one was going to keep secrets from her in her own house. On that point, she was determined.

"Rosalind Thorne wants to get back into society," Honoria told him. "She's been hanging about like a cat at the back door for years. She picks up everybody's scraps and makes herself as lovable a stray as she can. But for all that, she hasn't found a home yet. She had to leave the only one she did find, and no one seems to know why. Now, she's getting a second chance, and she's going to grab hold of it and not let go."

Casselmain's jaw hardened, but his voice when he spoke remained low and even. He wasn't a shouter, by any means. He probably knew full well what being overheard at the wrong moment could cost. "If you think Rosalind would let herself be ruled by that sort of base motive, you are very much mistaken in her character."

"I don't expect she'll want to be ruled by it, but it's there just the same. She's played the martyr for too long for there to be anything else. Oh, don't worry." Honoria waved her hand again. "I'm not going to forbid her the house or anything of the kind. In fact, I've my own plans for the ever-so-useful Miss Thorne." She paused for a long moment. She wanted him focused entirely on her, not lost in his own thoughts. "She's going to find out who killed Jasper."

It was a long time sinking in. Rosalind Thorne might be uppermost in Casselmain's thoughts, but this did not fit his rather limited view of her. In fact, the idea so distressed him, he had to get to his feet and cross the room to the mantle.

"No one killed Jasper, Honoria," he said when he at last found his voice. "It was an accident."

"That's a lie and you know it."

"How should I know it?"

"I'm not sure yet, but you may want to step a little carefully around Miss Thorne for a while."

"I have nothing to hide from Rosalind."

"Of course not. She loves you and you love her."

Did he realize she'd known all along? She wasn't sure. But by saying it aloud, she'd shocked him, as she knew she would.

"I'm sorry," he said.

"Don't be." The damp had plastered Honoria's ringlets against her forehead and she pushed impatiently at them. "One of the reasons I chose you for our bargain was that I knew your heart to be fully occupied."

He looked away. There. She'd made him feel sorry for her, and he was trying not to be angry anymore. That probably counted as some kind of victory. That flicker of doubt behind his gray eyes was another. Dear Lord, what a thing to adore someone. It made one risk so much and play so many games when no good could come from them.

Maybe she should change her mind and become an old maid. An old maid with money was not such an object. Mother would hate it and nag at her endlessly, but Mother at least was the devil she knew.

I'll back you with the paternals, Jasper had promised. *It was a bad idea from the beginning*, he said.

No, she didn't have the patience for any more waiting. She knew Devon as well. They'd grown up together as neighbors, and he had the advantage of not being much of a devil at all. The sooner she married him and escaped to that great empty house in the country, the better. Honoria imagined what it would be like having whole long days where no one would be watching her and constantly correcting her. There would be no expectations beyond keeping peace between the servants and handing out prizes at the occasional garden fete. She could be alone. Finally and truly, she could be alone, and that would be freedom.

But she would not go until she was certain Jasper's murderer had been punished. If she had to cut his throat herself, or poison his soup or any other thing, she did not doubt her own ability. She must, however, be sure of her target.

Until then, however, there was Casselmain, who was kind, and horribly, mistakenly in love, and whom she needed rather more than he needed her.

"Please do not tell Miss Thorne about us yet," she said. "Wait a little so we can see what she'll do about Jasper. There will be time afterwards to tell her whatever you like."

"Very well." She wondered if he realized that his relief showed in his face. She had removed the decision from him. "But you're misjudging her."

"Probably. I misjudge a lot of people. It's my own bad character, I suppose."

"You don't have bad character."

She shrugged one shoulder. "I act badly, and that's all the world cares about."

Casselmain wanted to argue the point. She could see it in his hesitation. He wanted to remind her that she could change her actions at any moment. She turned fully toward him, showing him plainly what she thought of such platitudes.

As a result, Casselmain said nothing. He just stood and bowed. Another point in his favor. He had always been fairly quick on the uptake.

"I should go condole with your father."

"Yes, probably." Honoria also stood, so he'd leave that much sooner. She was unbearably tired and there was the paper from the fireplace. She only hoped Rosalind was giving some good news to Mother; otherwise there would be no peace for anyone this whole horrid day.

"I do mean to be a decent husband while we're together," Casselmain said. "It's little enough, I know, but I promise it all the same."

"I know," she told him, grateful he was willing to be so honest. "And I promise I will keep up your name and appearances. People think I don't care for them, or that I don't understand them, but I do know what must be done."

"I never thought that you didn't care, Honoria," he said quietly. "I'll leave you now."

"Thank you."

Casselmain bowed once more and she curtsied. He remembered to close the door behind himself.

As soon as the sounds of his footsteps vanished beneath the eternal clank and hiss of the conservatory's steam pipes, Honoria turned to the mantle again and fished the scrap of paper out from the vase. More ash smeared her fingertips as she carefully turned it over. She squinted at it. The thing was barely the size of her thumb, so there wasn't not much to see—just a carefully written .0 in red ink, and beneath it, another. But that and the faint grid of lines told her enough.

Jasper had been burning a ledger.

CHAPTER 16

A Mother's Heart

She consents to become a victim of ambition and the slave to the world of fashion.
—Marianne Spencer Stanhope Hudson, *Almack's*

Rosalind followed Lady Edmund, her sense of misgiving sinking deeper with each step. Despite this, she did not permit herself to hesitate. She did, however, glance over her shoulder in time to see Honoria rush from her room and down the hallway. Probably on her way to the conservatory's card room. What would she find there?

And what will you talk with Devon about?

Rosalind forced her thoughts away from this question. If Honoria's conversation with Lord Casselmain touched on anything to do with Jasper's death, Honoria would surely tell her. She could count on that, given the task she'd been set, that she'd agreed to.

What have I gotten myself into?

First, she had agreed to help Lady Blanchard, then the lady patronesses. These two promises at least were linked. Lady Blanchard was in distress and had been even before Jasper Aimesworth died. But had Rosalind now actually promised

Honoria she would look into the circumstances surrounding his death? What kind of a fool was she becoming?

Lady Edmund led Rosalind into her private sitting room. Through the threshold to the boudoir, where the lady's maid paused in the act of laying out several black dresses, doubtlessly looking them over to see which needed to be ironed or mended. She would probably be kept busy for the next several days re-dying some dresses and ordering others. A black bonnet waited on the dressing table, beside a neat row of black kerchiefs.

"You can go, Hiller."

Her maid left without comment, closing the door behind herself. Lady Edmund gestured Rosalind to the tapestry chair beside the fireplace. No fire had been lit yet today, but despite that, the room felt stuffy, as if it had not been properly aired in some time.

"Now, Miss Thorne." Lady Edmund settled herself gracefully onto the tapestry sofa. The death of her son had done nothing to alter the woman's bearing. She held herself as straight, proud, and determined as when Rosalind had last entered her house. "May I inquire what it was Honoria wanted to speak with you about?"

"It was said in confidence, Lady Edmund."

This was very clearly not what the other woman wanted to hear. "Miss Thorne, Honoria is deeply distressed over her brother's death. When Honoria is distressed, she forgets herself. It is my duty as her mother to protect her from public comment during this difficult time."

"I understand perfectly, Lady Edmund, but I still cannot answer you."

Lady Edmund glared daggers at her. Rosalind brushed that off, and fairly easily. She had been glared at by experts. "Will you assure me that Honoria does intend to carry forward with her planned engagement to Lord Casselmain?"

Here, at least, Rosalind could tell the truth. "I believe that she does. She has not said otherwise."

"Good. That will help restrain her actions until the worst of this is over." Lady Edmund glanced toward her boudoir and the black dresses lying on the bed. "You must think me quite unfeeling, Miss Thorne."

Again, this was something she could answer truthfully. "No, Lady Edmund. That is not at all what I think."

"I would not blame you if you did. But I have lived a long time in the world, and I know the world does not reward sentiment. It will expect a proper funeral show, and appropriate mourning decorously stepped down at regular intervals. Nothing else will be tolerated, at least not for long, so that is what I must provide. Honoria will not, and my husband cannot."

Rosalind looked at Lady Edmund, with her proud demeanor and her blunt declaration of social responsibility. In that moment, she felt suddenly and strongly sorry for the woman. Lady Edmund was right that her daughter would be no help with any expected arrangements. Honoria was too far gone in her own grief and anger. As for Lord Edmund . . . he might very well be drunk as Honoria suggested. That left Lady Edmund entirely alone. Probably she had felt herself to be alone for many years now.

"I cannot spare you much time," Lady Edmund went on. "But I wished to speak with you regarding the matter of my previous invitation for you to stay with us. I wanted to be sure you know that it is still on offer."

Which meant she was still holding out her bribe of the house and pension in return for being named Lady Blanchard's successor to Almack's board of patronesses. Rosalind looked at her hands, folded neat and still in her lap. The gesture was so reflexive, she hadn't even been conscious of arranging them that way.

"I do thank you, Lady Edmund. And I . . . it seems wrong to speak of this now."

"You may speak to me with perfect freedom, Miss Thorne. Unlike my daughter, my feelings are well regulated."

"Honoria's regard for her brother does her great credit."

"Yes." The single word made for a frigidly polite acknowledgment. "But that is neither here nor there. This matter will cause talk and attract vulgar curiosity. We must put an end to that as soon as possible. I'm certain I am not alone in this opinion?" It was a question.

"Far from it, ma'am," murmured Rosalind. "I am given to understand that many others on whom this tragedy touches hold that view."

"And may I take it you've spoken with those others about this?"

"I have," Rosalind acknowledged. "And I can tell you that I did have the opportunity to speak with Lady Blanchard regarding your interest in being named to the position of lady patroness."

For just a moment, Lady Edmund's calm mask slipped. A light came into her eyes, along with the coldest, hardest hope Rosalind had ever seen. The back of her neck prickled.

"Lady Blanchard seemed to feel that it was a distinct possibility," Rosalind told her. "She, in fact, spoke with great approval of your candidacy and its chances."

Even as she spoke, Rosalind was aware of a fresh shiver crawling up her spine. This was wrong, all of it. That Lady Edmund should aim for such a position, and that Lady Blanchard would be willing to help her to it. The women knew each other, but did not like each other. The games of social success and triumph that Lady Edmund played were the very sort Lady Blanchard avoided whenever she could. Why was this thing happening? And why was it happening now?

Lady Edmund pulled a black kerchief from her sleeve. She pressed it against her mouth and against her temple. "I had not believed . . ." Lady Edmund began, but she stopped herself. "I had expected her to demur for rather longer. But of course, of course, now things have changed."

"Yes," agreed Rosalind. "However, while you are in mourning, it will be more difficult for you to present yourself in any public fashion."

Lady Edmund busied herself with folding her handkerchief into a tidy square. Her mouth was moving silently, and her brow furrowed. But Rosalind's years in noisy, crowded rooms had developed in her the skill of guessing what was said by watching a lady's mouth move.

. . . ruined it all, Lady Edmund said silently. *Cannot have ruined it . . .*

"Fortunately we have barely begun the little season," Lady Edmund reminded her aloud. "And it is my son who is dead, not my husband. There is time to indulge in a respectable period of mourning, and yet still join in with the proper season once it begins. Especially as this was an accident." She paused. "I imagine Lady Blanchard was greatly shocked. Lord Casselmain said she found Jasper's corpse."

"Yes. She did, and she was. Terribly shocked." Rosalind found she could not meet the other woman's eyes.

"Did she . . . no. We will not speak of it further." Lady Edmund stood. "I must bid you good morning, Miss Thorne. There is a great deal to be done here, and I am sure to have other callers."

Thus dismissed, Rosalind rose to her feet. "I will speak with Lady Blanchard further on the subject, and let you know what she has to say as soon as I can."

Because I have to maintain my entrée into this house. Because I promised your daughter that I would help her.

Lady Edmund pulled on the bell rope. "But you have not yet said whether you will be staying with us. It is a little irregular, but I'm sure . . ."

"I thank you for your offer of hospitality, Lady Edmund. However, I have already accepted an invitation from Lady Blanchard."

"I see. Well. Perhaps that is for the best."

Rosalind meant to turn to go, but memory of the letter from Jasper she carried in her bag made her hesitate. "Lady Edmund, may I ask you a question?" When the lady nodded her assent, Rosalind went on. "Did you tell Jasper you intended to seek the patroness's position?"

Lady Edmund frowned. "No, I didn't mention it to either of the children. Why do you ask?"

"It is the details that will help us all through this affair," answered Rosalind easily. "Thank you for your time."

"Miss Thorne," said Lady Edmund, "I have said how very much I trust and value your judgment. I should be very disappointed to find out you might put past personal disappointments ahead of what is right, and what is to your future advantage."

What reply could she possibly make to this? The situation was beyond all those bounds that were understood and respected. While she might sigh over the limitations etiquette imposed, Rosalind also relied upon it. Without those boundaries to provide definition, she did not know who or where she was.

And isn't that the problem? murmured a soft and strangely shrewd voice in the back of her mind. *Hasn't that always been the problem?*

"I understand you, Lady Edmund," Rosalind said. "And I thank you for your candor."

She smiled politely and Lady Edmund smiled back with equal politeness before the footman opened the door to bow Rosalind out.

Rosalind let herself be shown down the stairs toward the front entrance hall. She passed the front parlor, where the servants still carried out their preparations under the funeral man's direction. She barely noticed them. All her thoughts were occupied with a new question.

If Lady Edmund had not told Jasper she sought the patroness's position, how had he discovered it? Could that be what took him to Almack's to meet his ultimate fate?

Suddenly, gaining access to Jasper's rooms seemed very, very important.

CHAPTER 17

All Necessary Preparations

It will soon be the hour when the committee are to meet ...
my dear, your fate will then be decided.
—Marianne Spencer Stanhope Hudson, *Almack's*

The bells were tolling seven and the February dark had settled in for its extended stay as Rosalind returned to Little Russell Street. Firelight and candlelight shimmered in the house windows, mingling with the steady glow of the streetlamps that had just recently been erected as part of a city plan for general improvements.

There was no question of Rosalind's decamping to Blanchard House that evening, or even the next. Since her visit was to be open-ended, she had to put matters at Little Russell Street in order before she left. Deliveries had to be canceled. Money must be put down on account with tradesmen and she had to leave a forwarding address. Otherwise, her assorted creditors might believe she had chosen to emulate her father and flee rather than meet her obligations. That required a thorough review of accounts and a careful rebalancing of income and outlay. A letter to her landlord informing him of her intentions was likewise advisable.

Mrs. Kendricks met Rosalind in the narrow foyer to take her outdoor things. She, of course, noticed Rosalind's distracted expression.

"Is everything all right, miss?"

"No, Mrs. Kendricks, I don't think it is." Everything that had occurred during her call on Honoria and her family had left Rosalind profoundly unsettled. She wanted a moment's peace to sort it all out, but at the same time, she wished for an excuse to call 'round at Blanchard House so she could find out what had happened at the lady patronesses' meeting. Had Lady Blanchard raised Lady Edmund's name to the others yet?

Mrs. Kendricks paused in the act of shaking out Rosalind's bonnet. "Is there any way I can be of help?"

"No," began Rosalind, but she stopped. "Yes . . . No."

Mrs. Kendricks waited. Rosalind hung her head in embarrassment. "Something is wrong," she said. "I knew that. I knew that Lady Blanchard needed help. But now . . ." She took a deep breath and told Mrs. Kendricks what had happened at Tamwell House.

Mrs. Kendricks stood silently for a long moment. "I think you'd best come in to dinner," she said at last, and Rosalind couldn't help smiling.

"I think that's an excellent idea."

The table in the little dining room was already laid and a modest fire burned in the hearth. Rosalind remembered how she'd gritted her teeth when the agent had first showed her through this house. She was used to the grand town residences that Father rented and the sprawling country homes of her friends from school. Here, she felt that if she stuck her elbows out too far, she'd knock holes in the walls. At the same time, her mind had run frantically back and forth over the tiny sums at her command, and she told herself she was deeply fortunate to be able to afford this much.

Tonight, she welcomed the small table, the stack of correspondence, and the warm little fire. While Mrs. Kendricks brought in Scotch broth, ham and gravy, and onion tart with steamed pudding to follow, Rosalind opened her letters with an enamel knife and, against all ladylike propriety, she read as she ate.

Isabella Yates was already back in town and inviting her to call as soon as she had time. Fredericka Tillman-Edwards was furious that her mother had decided to spend the little season at their country house. Fredericka was certain she was being sabotaged, since it was her fourth season and her chosen beau, Augustus Finley, still hadn't come up to scratch. Mrs. Tillman-Edwards didn't approve of Finley, and she might just be keeping Fredericka in her room until she was ready to admit she needed to set her sights elsewhere.

And the bill from the shoemaker for repairs.

And the bill from the grocer.

And the bill from the chandler.

Mrs. Hugo Beal, whom Rosalind had known when she was Aurora Hartwell, was in town and asking Rosalind to call. She had her younger sister's trousseau to arrange and wanted to get to the warehouses before all the best goods were snapped up for the season's new ball gowns and walking costumes.

And the bill for lamp oil.

And the bill from the milliner.

Elizabeth Oakfell would be here next week and would Rosalind remember to call? She had such news as could not be communicated in writing.

Rosalind laid down Elizabeth's letter and stared at the walls.

She listened to the wind in the eaves and the ticking of the clock. So many letters, so many lives. What would she write back to any of them? What could she tell them about her own life and what had been happening to her?

Nothing. Or at least, very little. But that didn't mean she couldn't write, and pay her calls. Her well-born friends and acquaintances would be as eager as the Littlefields to talk about Jasper and tell her what they knew of him and his dealings. One of them, or one of their brothers, or their husbands, ought to be able to supply additional details about his life of late, which might just lead in turn to his hidden enemy.

"Shall I take your plate, miss?"

"Yes, thank you, Mrs. Kendricks."

"If you're determined to go to Lady Blanchard, you'll be wanting to look over your dresses right away."

Mrs. Kendricks's phrasing, and her tone of resignation, brought Rosalind's attention fully back to the present day. "Yes, thank you. We'd best start on that first thing tomorrow. I'm afraid I'll be leaning on you rather heavily these next weeks, Mrs. Kendricks," she said. "And I will particularly require your assistance when we're in Blanchard House."

"Meaning I'll be keeping my ears open." Gossiping below stairs was, of course, frowned upon. It was understood that no good servant spoke of the master, or the master's business. It was, however, universally acknowledged that this understanding was breached far more often than it was upheld.

"Unless you've already heard something?" asked Rosalind.

Mrs. Kendricks didn't answer at first; she simply kept loading the dinner dishes onto her tray.

"I've heard nothing new yet." Mrs. Kendricks covered the dirty dishes with her towel. "But I worry. I have for a long time.

I've held my peace because we've always done so well by Lady Blanchard's friendship."

It was because Rosalind had been welcomed into Blanchard House that the other girls, the ones whose letters lay in a scented stack on the table, could continue to accept her into their homes and lives. If she lost Lady Blanchard, then the rest would fall away, no matter how useful she made herself. This last year was a testament to that fact.

That made it all the more imperative that she listen to Mrs. Kendricks's concerns. The woman had honed her instincts sharp. She could read the hidden currents lying under the still surface of a great house. Failing to pay attention to her was to risk falling into the depths.

"What is it that worries you?" asked Rosalind.

Mrs. Kendricks looked away, and Rosalind watched her calculate how much to say. "Lady Blanchard saved you. This is true and everybody knows it. But I have to ask myself, what did she save you for?"

Rosalind felt her brow furrow. "She saved me because she's my godmother, and she saw it as her duty."

"That's as may be," said Mrs. Kendricks, "but why's it you she calls on now? Especially when we've gone almost a year with barely a word from her."

Rosalind wanted to protest that the silence had been entirely necessary. First of all, Rosalind had left Blanchard House over Lady Blanchard's protests. Neither Rosalind nor Lord Blanchard had mentioned that it was Lord Blanchard who had asked her to go. After that, for their separate reasons, both she and Lady Blanchard had to wait until Lord Blanchard's temper had thoroughly cooled regarding Sir Reginald's outrageous behavior. Rosalind also waited for her own shame to dissipate, but in vain, it seemed.

It was really only the fact that the Blanchards were leaving London that made it possible for Rosalind to return to her former footing in the household.

Wasn't it? She remembered her own confusion about the sudden and entirely unexpected accord between the two ladies over the matter of the patroness position. What had happened between them during this past year that brought them together now? It was not new friendship. But what was it?

Rosalind lifted her letters up so Mrs. Kendricks could draw the cloth from the dining table to shake out and fold over her arm. "You will please listen carefully to any talk you hear when we go visiting Blanchard House, or anywhere else," said Rosalind.

"If I do, will you listen to what I find?"

"I promise."

"I will hold you to that, miss," her servant answered. "Now, the fire's going in the parlor."

It was. Rosalind tried not to think about the cost of the coal for the second blaze, not to mention the price of the oil in the lamp that was also lit. She settled herself at her desk to sort her letters—separating the bills from the social correspondence. Mrs. Kendricks arrived with a pot of tea and Rosalind's favorite cup. Rosalind brought the account books out of the drawers, arranged her work neatly in front of her, and then found she could not raise a hand to begin.

Something was nagging her, something she'd forgotten to say, or do, or ask. She shook her head. She must trust it would come back to her. In the meantime, there were, as always, letters to write.

Rosalind trimmed her quill, unstoppered her inkwell, and addressed herself to her social correspondence.

*Dear Isabella: I was so glad to get your letter, and I'll be glad to
call as soon as may be. I have barely caught my breath since
Jasper Aimesworth's tragic death . . .*

*Dear Fredericka: I am quite well, but you must imagine we are
still reeling here from the suddenness of Jasper Aimesworth's
death . . .*

*Dear Elizabeth: How wonderful to hear from you. Of course
I'll be glad to help with the trousseau. Have you heard about the
terrible accident at Almack's yet? Oh, it is beyond words . . .*

The letters were near copies of one another. Each contained
a sketchy (and only partly accurate) account of what had happened, laced with many exclamations of shock, and much speculation over Jasper's character and habits. Each, in the language
of society, was an invitation to an extended gossip on the subject
of Jasper and the Aimesworths.

Lady Jersey was going to be livid when she found out Rosalind had been talking freely about the tragedy. Lady Blanchard
would be shocked. But this was as necessary as talking with
George and Alice. These friends would have all the gossip about
Jasper. If there were debts, or bad company, or a woman in his
life who might have led him into danger, it should not take long
to discover. The gently bred ladies might not be meant to know
of such things, but their husbands, sons, and brothers all did,
and the ladies had sharp ears as well as busy tongues.

But there was also the question of where to tell her friends to
direct their replies. Rosalind paused in her work, and turned this
over in her mind. If she did return to Blanchard House, and if
Father reappeared as he did the last time she was living there, it

would be a complete disaster. There was no guarantee that he would again choose the evening of a quiet supper at home to make himself known. If he made his threats in front of company, she would not be able to keep the thing quiet a second time. Not only would she never find out what had happened to Jasper, but the precarious foundation she had built under her life would collapse. She would fall, and this time she would fall farther than ever.

Rosalind laid down her quill and unlocked the central drawer of her desk. Here was where she kept her purse, and her bank books. In the back, underneath all the other papers, waited one battered letter. Rosalind unfolded the plain paper, and read:

I'm sorry. It will not happen again.

C.

The letter had arrived the day after Father's scene. It was the first, last, and only communication Rosalind had had from her sister since Charlotte had left the house. There was no date or direction inside the letter, no hint of where it had come from. Only that brief apology and promise.

Rosalind had been angry and confused. She'd gotten Mrs. Kendricks to talk to the footman and the man at the post office, even while Rosalind herself prepared to leave Blanchard House. But those inquiries yielded nothing. She had told herself the letter made no difference. She still needed to leave, of course, because after her abandonment, and all the years of silence, there was no way to trust Charlotte to keep any sort of promise, and because of all the things Lord Blanchard said afterward.

But the fact remained that Father had not returned since

then. Was that luck? Or was it Charlotte's doing? She had no way to tell.

Rosalind folded the letter away and locked the drawer. She picked up her quill and dipped it in the ink. She addressed the unfinished letters in front of her, and in each one, she told her friends that they should direct their answers to Blanchard House.

And if I am wrong in this, then may Heaven help us all.

CHAPTER 18

The Bow Street Runner

In her own house, and especially in the winter, Rosalind cultivated the habit of rising early. Daylight was too precious to waste. This morning, she dressed in her oldest, plainest house dress and braided and pinned her hair tightly before she went down to a breakfast of Mrs. Kendrick's porridge, griddle cakes, and coffee. Once the meal was cleared away and the letters of the night before duly sealed and made ready to be posted, she and Mrs. Kendricks both donned their aprons and climbed to the attics. One by one, they hauled Rosalind's four great trunks down into the second bedroom, which had been converted to a workroom for Mrs. Kendricks.

These boxes held Rosalind's last legacy: her clothes.

This had become the most important ritual at the start of each season. Rosalind's small wardrobe of everyday wear was enough to allow her to look respectable on ordinary days. These were the visiting clothes, the costumes that belonged to the lady she was supposed to be.

Rosalind and Mrs. Kendricks folded back the layers of tissue and one by one brought out the gowns, the walking dresses, the morning dresses, the riding habit. Gloves. Stockings. Shoes. Each had to be shaken and brushed and minutely examined. This year's pattern cards and ladies magazines had to be consulted to see how trim might be altered, or augmented with Rosalind's handmade lace or careful embroidery to bring each closer to the look of current fashion. Did the sleeves need to be shortened or extended? Could the gloves be cleaned and mended, or would money have to be found for a new pair? What about this fan? These ribbons? This bonnet? Would the cashmere shawl, and the lace wrap with the fringe, do for another season? Nothing more could be done for this dress, but it could be pulled apart. Some components could be used to update other costumes, and the rest sold to a secondhand clothes dealer.

Usually, several days were dedicated just to the chore of inspection and at least two weeks to that of repair. But with Rosalind's planned departure to Blanchard House, all that work had to be compressed into a mere sennight. The careful inventories in Mrs. Kendrick's book and in Rosalind's were consulted and updated. The fine work was listed for Rosalind to attend to, while the mending, and the buying and selling, were given over to Mrs. Kendricks. Some light repair of embroidery or ribbons could be done after they were installed at the Blanchards, but there must be enough ready for Rosalind to be entirely presentable from the first. Especially since the lady patronesses would be watching.

Last of all came the ball gowns. There were three: the rich burgundy and antique lace that had once belonged to Mother,

Charlotte's prized sky blue silk brocade with its daring décolletage and silver netting, and Rosalind's own, splendid with white silk, pearlescent beading, gold net, and creamy velvet ribbons.

Rosalind ran her hands down the tucked and pleated skirt. "Perhaps it is time to retire this one," she murmured. "Surely I'm a little too long in the tooth for all this white."

She waited for Mrs. Kendricks's stout refusal. It came every year.

Instead, the doorbell sounded. With a huff, Mrs. Kendricks descended the stairs, leaving Rosalind to stare at her white debut gown. She tried to make herself see the thing dispassionately, to picture where the silk, the beads, and all that shimmering netting might be best put to use.

She had not made a great deal of progress by the time Mrs. Kendricks returned.

"There's a . . . person asking to see you, miss. I told him you were not at home and he should leave a message, but he insisted he would wait."

"What sort of person is he, Mrs. Kendricks?" Rosalind began frantically tallying her accounts. Was there one so delinquent that the creditor might be driven to demand immediate payment?

"It's a Mr. Harkness, miss. He says he's come from Bow Street."

Rosalind had never personally encountered a Bow Street "runner." They were creatures of the magazine serials and Sunday papers. In those breathless pages, "Robin Redbreasts" were depicted as either hard-eyed heroes of justice and public order, or corrupt thief takers, ready to do the bidding of whoever held up the ready money to pay for their services.

The man by her parlor fireplace did not much resemble either extreme. He didn't even wear the red waistcoat that was the runner's uniform. He was, however, a neat man, built spare and clean of limb and probably only a few years older than Rosalind herself. His bronzed face had pleasant and regular features, but deep lines marked the corners of his mouth and eyes. It was a good face, she decided, and graced by a pair of blue eyes that were both sharp and energetic. His fair, curling hair had been tousled by the winter wind and several locks slanted across his broad forehead as he bowed.

He was also the man she had passed on the stairs at Almack's, the one who made her stop and turn.

"Miss Thorne?" he said and Rosalind dipped her chin in acknowledgment. "I am Adam Harkness, Principal Officer of the Bow Street Police Office. I hope you'll forgive me for intruding on your morning."

From the way he spoke, it was plain that Mr. Harkness was a London man, and he'd had a decent education. His clothing was entirely that of a working man: dark trousers, dark coat and brown waistcoat with a single chain stretched across it, and a black cravat at his throat. His hands, though calloused, were well kept and his nails pared.

"You are not intruding, Mr. Harkness. Won't you please sit down?" Rosalind gestured toward the cane-bottomed chair and took her usual place beside the fire.

Mr. Harkness bowed again in thanks and took the seat she offered. "As I'm sure you'll have guessed, I'm here to speak with you about Mr. Jasper Aimesworth."

"Yes. Mr. Willis said he intended to hire a runner."

Mr. Harkness's smile tightened a bit at her use of the cant term. "You spoke with Mr. Willis about the matter?"

"I was delivering a letter to him and—"

"We passed on the stairs."

"Yes." She wondered if she should ring for Mrs. Kendricks to make coffee or tea, and then she scolded herself. She was only looking for distraction. "At that time, Mr. Willis mentioned he had contacted the Bow Street magistrates."

Mr. Harkness appeared to consider this. "Was there a reason Mr. Willis would tell you that?"

"He hoped I could convince the lady patronesses that it was a beneficial move. Some fear that inquiry into the circumstances behind poor Mr. Aimesworth's death might endanger Almack's reputation for gentility and exclusivity."

"What is your opinion?"

His question surprised her. "How could my opinion matter?"

"I believe you might have information I need. I'd like to know how you feel about providing it."

Now it was Rosalind's turn to pause and consider this person in front of her, with his habit of lapsing into stillness and his sharp eyes. He was, she decided, not an entirely safe man, but he was certainly not a stupid or a venal one—not unless he was hiding that tendency, and hiding it well.

"I believe it is better that the truth be known," she told him.

He nodded. "Very few ladies of your station would say as much."

"Have you spoken with many ladies of my station on the subject of secrets? Wait. I suppose that you have."

"An unfortunate necessity."

"But that's not true," Rosalind murmured.

Mr. Harkness drew back his chin. "I beg your pardon?"

She'd surprised him, and she was a little startled to find that she enjoyed doing so. Perhaps it was his casual reference to conversations with other ladies that did it. Rosalind found she did not care to be categorized with anyone he would so easily dismiss.

"Forgive me, Mr. Harkness. I did not mean to say that out loud."

"But you did say it, Miss Thorne, and now I require an explanation."

"Require?" She raised her eyebrows.

He smiled at her show of polite indignation. The expression lit his eyes, which were, Rosalind noted, a particularly stormy blue. "Request then."

"Very well. I do not think you find it unfortunate. I think you rather enjoy it."

Now a hint of mischief entered into that smile. "Talking with ladies?"

"Uncovering secrets."

"What makes you think that? We've not been acquainted . . ." Mr. Harkness glanced at her clock. "For even ten minutes."

Rosalind had had plenty of practice at providing meaningless answers for direct questions. It was, after all, one of the skills necessary to drawing room conversation. But she knew Harkness would recognize such diversion for what it was, and he would be disappointed.

"You carry an air about you, Mr. Harkness. Your manner is careful, but it is not that of a man who dislikes the position in which he finds himself." She paused. "And I will thank you to refrain from applying the words 'feminine intuition' to anything I have just said."

"I would not. For you've an air about you, too, Miss Thorne, and it tells me you are one of life's observers."

"Even though we've known each other for less than ten minutes?"

"Even though." He bowed his head in acknowledgment. "Which makes anything you have to tell me all the more valuable."

"I suspect I am being flattered."

"It is possible." Did he wink at her? Really, this was unacceptable. Mr. Harkness had a certain rough charm about him, and he clearly felt no hesitation about applying it. She, however, had no business taking notice of it, much less in permitting it to work upon her sensibilities. These were deeply serious matters. The course of lives, hers among them, would be affected by this conversation, and what followed.

But oh, what a relief it was to speak lightly after all the shocks and worries of these past days.

"What was it you were doing at Almack's on the unfortunate day?" he asked.

"I had arranged to collect my godmother, Lady Blanchard, after the patronesses' meeting, and she was late. I went inside to try to find her."

"And you thought she might be in the ballroom?"

He asked the question mildly, but there was nothing mild about the way he watched her. A more fastidious woman would have found his look insolent. Rosalind, though, just found the contradiction between his casual tone and his searching eyes unexpectedly disconcerting.

She took refuge in self-deprecation. "I confess, Mr. Harkness, I was indulging the sin of curiosity. The ballroom door was open. I had not been inside . . . well, in a long while. I wanted to take a look."

He smiled. It was a good smile, and it filled his lively eyes. "I'm sure I would have done the same, if I were there. That room is legendary. Did you see Mr. Aimesworth right away?"

She shook her head and described how she hadn't even rec-

ognized the object as the remains of a man and that it was
Mr. Whelks who had done so, and had run forward while she
followed.

"This next question is very important, Miss Thorne." Mr.
Harkness leaned forward and pressed his palms together, pointing
all his fingers directly at her to emphasize the point. "By the time
I was let into the rooms, Mr. Aimesworth had been taken home
to his family, and the place where he'd fallen had been thoroughly
cleaned. But you saw the blood clearly?"

"Yes. It was . . ." Memory rose up, still far too clear, and she
swallowed.

"You will not shock me, Miss Thorne."

"Perhaps I will shock myself, Mr. Harkness. I'm gently bred,
you know. It is hardly the expected thing for me to speak of . . .
physical matters."

"I understand," he answered solemnly. "Would you like to
take a moment and fetch some eau de cologne or smelling salts?
That way if anyone asks, you can say you fainted and so on."

Was he teasing her? She had not expected that at all. Despite
this new surprise, or perhaps because of it, the tightness underneath her ribs eased. "How considerate you are, Mr. Harkness,
but I believe we may carry on. Yes, I saw the blood clearly. It was
a large pool, surrounding his head."

"Nowhere else? Not on his face, or his chest, for example?"

"Not that I saw."

Mr. Harkness pulled a small memorandum book out of his
pocket and consulted something there. "Well. That is interesting."

"May I ask why?"

He glanced up from his book. "You're certain you don't want
those smelling salts?"

"I am quite able to hear whatever you have to say," she answered, and she endeavored to mean it.

"I'll take you at your word. We have two possibilities for how Mr. Aimesworth died. The first is that he was in the musicians' gallery for some reason, and that he overbalanced and fell. That makes his death an accident." He paused, judging her manner. Rosalind found herself unusually piqued.

"Yes? Go on. I assure you I am not in the least bit faint."

"No, I can see that." He also nodded his approval. The gesture irritated her. What business had this man approving or disapproving of her?

Stop that, Rosalind. You're turning missish!

"It is just barely conceivable that a fall from the relatively short height of that gallery would do for a man, if he was extraordinarily unlucky. It's a funny thing, though, but when it's a short, sharp fall that kills, it doesn't produce that much blood. No doubt one of our clever medical fellows could tell us why this is, but the fact remains. It would take a concentrated pounding, or some deep and penetrating wound to let out the amount of blood you saw. If I'd come across such a scene in the street rather than the ballroom, my first conclusion would be that an enemy had come at Mr. Aimesworth with a weapon in hand, and a determination to see him dead."

Rosalind was silent for a long moment. She was still forgetting something, something that had bothered her before. "Perhaps I was wrong. Perhaps there was not quite so much blood."

"I doubt that, Miss Thorne," replied Mr. Harkness. "You don't strike me as the sort who would exaggerate in that way." He ducked his head, trying to catch her eye. "You're trying to find a reason not to believe it. I understand that. It's an ugly thing."

But that wasn't it. She was trying to find that memory, that thing which did not fit. Then, she had it, and her hand flew to her mouth. "The draperies," she said. "Oh, heavens. The draperies *and* the carpet!"

Mr. Harkness waited. There it was, that stillness she had only glimpsed before. It was striking, because it was also an attitude of absolute concentration.

"When I arrived the other day, Mr. Willis was in the gallery directing some workmen to take down the draperies. He said . . . he said he needed to get them cleaned, or they would have to be replaced."

"I see," said Mr. Harkness slowly.

"I didn't." It was unreasonable for her to be annoyed, but she was all the same. "If . . . if Jasper died because he fell from the gallery, then the blood should all be on the floor. But if he were battered before he died . . ."

"There would be blood on the draperies and the carpet in the gallery, which would need to be cleaned up immediately before the stains set," Mr. Harkness finished.

"They also found Jasper's keys, dropped up there, and some coins." That significance had also escaped her. If he'd fallen, they should have been on the floor beside him, or in his pockets. The only reason things from Jasper's pockets would have fallen out in the gallery was if there'd been some sort of struggle there.

"How do you know the keys were Aimesworth's?" asked Mr. Harkness.

"I showed them to his sister, and she recognized the fob and seal."

"It would have been good to have those keys."

"But I do have them."

"You do?" Now she had shocked him, and she was rather strangely pleased about the fact. "The family left them with you?"

"The family did not. Mr. Aimesworth's sister, Honoria, did."

"Why would she do that?

"That is between myself and Miss Aimesworth." She paused. "And now I've disappointed you."

"It shows? Well, that's my own fault. I'd gotten my hopes up."

"I don't understand."

"You, Miss Thorne, are one of my very few potential windows into Mr. Aimesworth's life. Without your help, I'm afraid my inquiries can go no farther."

"And you do not collect your bounty," she murmured. She wasn't sure why.

He shrugged. "If I had my way, Miss Thorne, the city would pay a salary to trained and qualified men to do this work. The discovery and punishment of criminals should be treated as a public good, rather than a private affair."

"I take it you've read Sir Robert Peel's writing on policing?"

"I have, and I agree with his thinking. Violence and theft affect everyone, Miss Thorne. They cannot be banished by the hiring of yet more constables to clear those we are pleased to call riffraff from the streets. The proof is in front of us in the form of Mr. Aimesworth."

"Thus you bring me neatly back to the point."

"Conversation is an art, Miss Thorne, even for a man from Bow Street."

"I expect especially for a man from Bow Street." Rosalind fell silent, and Mr. Harkness let her. He'd gone still again, waiting and watching. It was not comfortable, especially not when she needed to think.

"Have you spoken with Mr. Whelks?" she asked. "He was there also."

"Yes, and he has imitated his namesake and clung stubbornly to his silence."

"You should have a word with Lady Jersey. Mr. Whelks is her secretary, and won't say anything until she gives permission."

"And so I would, if Lady Jersey would agree to speak with me," he replied blandly. "Her response to my note requesting an interview was to suggest, firmly, that I cease to bother persons of the highest rank and respectability and get about the business of apprehending those hooligans rendering the streets unsafe for respectable persons."

Which sounded very like Lady Jersey. There was, however, another response to ascertain, and she found herself extremely reluctant to ask about it. "Then I must assume you have also approached Lord Casselmain?"

"I have, but thus far, he has not condescended to answer."

"I see."

Mr. Harkness leaned forward again. Although there was still a good two feet between them, he felt unsettlingly close. Rosalind forced herself to keep her breath regular. There was neither room nor time for the unaccountable and ridiculous vagaries of attraction in this moment, especially with a man who was so clearly aware of his personal charm.

"I am going to suggest some facts to you, Miss Thorne," said Mr. Harkness quietly. "You found the body of a young man of your acquaintance, who was the victim of violence. You have already presented me with information that makes accident or chance robbery unlikely. Therefore, we must consider that this thing has been done by someone who knew Mr. Aimesworth."

Rosalind nodded in slow and thoroughly reluctant agreement. "Honoria—that is Mr. Aimesworth's sister—shares your opinion."

Rosalind rather wished Honoria were there to see the way Mr. Harkness straightened up, and how the look of surprise on his face swiftly melted into one of respect, and eagerness. "Has she said who?"

Rosalind shook her head. "She asked me to help her find out."

"That's why she left you the keys," he murmured. "You or she thought they'd come in handy." A muscle twitched high in Mr. Harkness's cheek.

"Is that a laugh you are suppressing, sir?" demanded Rosalind. His disappointment she could bear, just about, but not mockery.

"No. I promise it isn't. What I'm suppressing is the very strong hope that you told Miss Aimesworth that you would help."

"You're not going to tell me not to interfere or suggest that such inquiries are completely hopeless?"

"I've told you, Miss Thorne, 'society' has so far decided not to talk to me. If they will talk to you, it could be much to the benefit of my inquiries."

"But surely your warrant compels people to talk with you."

"No. My warrant allows me to ask questions and to make an arrest. It doesn't compel anyone to answer those questions so that I am able to make that arrest." He smiled grimly. "I'm afraid the popular press exaggerates our powers as much as it does our vices."

"You'd rely on an aging spinster? Surely I cannot be depended upon to divulge accurate information or make pertinent inquiry."

"And now, Miss Thorne, you are attempting to discover if I'm a fool." His tone was as close to anger as she'd heard it yet. "Well, I'm not and neither are you. With your help, I stand a chance of actually doing my job, not just what's wanted of me."

He was right, of course. Everyone—from Lady Jersey to Mrs. Willis herself—wanted Jasper's death tidied neatly and finally away, whatever the cost. She needed to make up her mind. Could she trust this man? Was she prepared to risk the consequences if she was caught assisting his official inquiries? If Jasper was killed by someone in society, and should that person's name be made known, there would be consequences. One of them might very well be that Rosalind herself, despite all her work and patient humility, might finally be fully ostracized. No one would tolerate her presence if they thought she would speak out of turn with someone beyond accepted circles.

But the alternative was to let the secret remain, and to live every day with the knowledge she had done so.

"Very well, Mr. Harkness. I am with you. How can I help?"

CHAPTER 19

Where the Evidence Might Lead

*In these murders . . . the hand which inflicts the fatal blow
is not more deeply imbued in blood than his who passively
looks on . . .*

—Thomas De Quincy, *On Murder Considered as
One of the Fine Arts*

Harkness held himself still and watched Rosalind Thorne make
up her mind. It was a sight worth paying attention to. But then,
there was a great deal about Miss Thorne to make a man wish
to pay very close attention indeed.

So far, their conversation had confirmed everything Littlefield
told him about this woman. That she had been gently bred was
obvious. It could be seen in each graceful, trained movement, and
heard in her polished accents. That she and her family had fallen
on hard times was equally obvious. What Littlefield had failed to
mention was Miss Thorne's lively intelligence, and an unexpected
amount of pure nerve. And when she turned to him, determination clear on her expressive features, he couldn't help thinking
that here was a sight he would have been sorry to miss.

Thank heavens old Townsend wasn't here to see the look that
was surely in his eye. He'd only chaff Harkness about his sus-
ceptibility to a pretty face. Again.

"Very well, Mr. Harkness," she said. "I am with you. How can I help?"

Triumph, unexpected and strong, roared through him, and it took every ounce of control Harkness possessed to keep his voice calm. "Thank you, Miss Thorne. What I need most is to know what your acquaintances, and Mr. Aimesworth's acquaintances, are saying about his death."

She paused. She'd say nothing in haste. She'd want what she told him to be correct, and scrupulously accurate. How could he be so sure so soon? Well, he was accustomed to observing hard cases with hidden lives. Who hid their lives so thoroughly as the women of the *haut ton*?

He realized he wanted to tell her this, and suspected she'd laugh at the comparison.

"Mr. Harkness, you know that Lady Blanchard, who is one of Almack's patronesses, was also there when Jasper's body was discovered."

"I do." Biddy Caulder, a charwoman brought in to clean the floors, had told him that tale, with gusto. She hadn't seen it herself, but she'd heard Mr. and Mrs. Willis exclaiming over the fact.

"Lord Blanchard believes that Jasper Aimesworth had made a wager with someone. He went to check the betting book at White's to see if anything had been recorded there."

"And what was the result?"

She shook her head regretfully. "I have not yet heard."

"That would certainly serve to explain Mr. Aimesworth's presence," said Mr. Harkness. "But it would do nothing at all to explain his death."

"It might point toward who was there with him."

"It might, or it might not." She frowned, but did not interrupt. She'd hear his reasons first. That was something else to like about Miss Thorne. "It all depends on whether that betting book could be opened and read by all members of the club, and also the staff," he said.

Rosalind was silent for a moment. "I think I see what you are saying. Anyone in White's perusing the book could have seen the record of the bet . . ."

"If there is one."

She accepted his correction with only a mild glint of annoyance in her eye. "If there is one. They could then use that to formulate the opportunity to commit the murder."

"That's it. Still, it would be a useful thing to know." Mr. Harkness pulled out a memorandum book of his own and made a note with the stub of a pencil he habitually carried. The mention of White's tickled something in him. Ah, yes. That was where "Tiny" Toby Fergus had fetched up, wasn't it?

"I can write to Lord Blanchard," said Miss Thorne. "Or if you can wait a day or two, I'll be able to ask him directly. I am going to stay with the Blanchards for a little."

"That would be very helpful, Miss Thorne. But I think I will still try to get a look at the book for myself."

"Why?"

"Men lie, Miss Thorne."

For a minute, Harkness thought she would protest Viscount Blanchard's innocence and honesty. In the end though, all she said was, "Yes, of course."

That was interesting, too, because she was thinking of something specific as she said it.

Not for the first time since he rang her bell did Harkness wonder exactly what Miss Thorne's relationship with Mr. Aimesworth had been. He'd had a chance to talk with the Aimesworths' coachman, and a couple of the grooms were more than willing to swap household gossip for a cup of hot punch on a cold night. Jasper Aimesworth wasn't often at the house these days, they said. Had his own rooms. Came around once a week to dine with his father and do the dutiful. But he had reason to keep to his own digs. Liked a nice bit of female companionship, did young Mr. Aimesworth, and he didn't have any trouble convincing them to like him neither.

Harkness didn't want to believe Miss Thorne would lose her heart, or her head, over a common womanizer, but then he'd known strong, sensible men, never mind women, to fall and fall hard without explanation.

Still, it didn't sit right. He told himself that it was his experienced judgment, and not his sentimentality, that made him think so.

"You won't be allowed in White's club room," Miss Thorne was saying. "There are a host of rules about it, and of course, none of the gentlemen will want to talk to a runner . . ."

He opened his mouth to tell her there were ways, but she'd already gotten up and moved to her writing desk. "I'm going to give you a letter for Mr. Sanderson Faulks in Bayswater Street. He's a member of White's, and he'll be willing to help you."

"Because you ask it?" What the devil made him say that out loud? It was outrageous. He steeled himself should she take offense, but she didn't even look up from her writing.

"Mr. Faulks delights in the unusual. He'll be able to tell the story of helping Bow Street at dinners every night for a month." That did make her pause. "Although you might not care to find you're the topic of dinner table conversation."

"Miss Thorne, if it helps me discover the truth in this matter, I am perfectly willing to become a nine days' wonder."

"Excellent." She blotted and sealed the letter. "I've written the direction." She handed it to him.

"Thank you, Miss Thorne. This will be most useful." *Although maybe not in the way you expect.* He tucked the letter into his coat. "You said you were allowed to keep Mr. Aimesworth's keys?"

"Yes." She unlocked the desk's central drawer and brought out a small reticule. She pulled a ring of keys from this and handed them across. "This one, Honoria said, was the key to Tamwell House. This she thought might be to Jasper's rooms. These two she didn't know."

Her fingers grazed his palm, ever so lightly, and Harkness much to his regret, had to draw his hand away.

"Where were his rooms?"

She shook her head. "Honoria didn't know. He'd moved recently, she thought."

Well, the grooms would know, or the footmen. Lady Aimesworth had a reputation for being a Tartar where talking was concerned, but Harkness had yet to find a house where that kind of threat shut people's mouths. It was only the ones who believed the master was loyal to them that actually kept quiet.

"I could find out, though," she went on. "I meant to inquire for myself."

She had changed. When she came into this room, she was entirely the society woman, aloof, careful in her motions and sparing with her words. Now that she had made up her mind to her course, she came fully alive. Miss Thorne was made for action, not passive acceptance.

"Miss Thorne, how did Miss Aimesworth decide you were the one to help her find out about her brother's death?"

Possible answers chased themselves behind her eyes. He found himself holding his breath, wondering if he'd pushed too quickly, and if she might lie. But she didn't. She said, "There's something I think you should see, Mr. Harkness."

Miss Thorne reached into her bag again, and brought out a

letter sealed in red wax. She unfolded it, and handed it to him. "This reached me shortly after Jasper died."

Harkness scanned the lines, noting how they'd been written in a hurry, and none too neatly. The correspondent, Jasper Aimesworth, had stopped and started several different times, and considering what it said, that was no surprise.

He read the dismissal of formalities, and he read the plea that Miss Thorne keep away from Almack's business, and from Lady Edmund, and from the Aimesworth family, for her own good.

It was a shocking letter, and it didn't answer any of the hundred questions filling Harkness's mind, not to mention his notebook. Except, perhaps, the one. If Aimesworth and Miss Thorne were on what polite society called "terms of intimacy," this note would have had a far different tone.

He lifted his eyes from the page and what he saw made his breath catch for a moment in his throat. Miss Thorne was staring at him. She'd been watching him as he read, absorbing the details of his face and now she was blushing furiously, aware she'd been caught out.

He turned away and scrubbed at his face so she wouldn't see how he smiled.

"This would make it seem Jasper Aimesworth knew something detrimental connected with the assembly rooms," he said.

"Yes. But if this whole matter sprang from a wager between gentlemen, why would he write me such a letter?"

"That is the exact question I am asking myself," Harkness told her. "Has his sister seen this?"

"She has, but she could offer no explanation."

"Do you think Miss Aimesworth would consent to grant me an interview?"

Miss Thorne smiled. "I am sure something can be arranged, although it may be on short notice."

Harkness brought his case out from his coat pocket and extracted a card. "A note sent to the magistrate's court will always find me."

"Very well. I will do what I can."

He should stand up now, and he should leave. He had all that he came for, and more. There was no reason for him to stay any longer, except there was. One more answer he wanted to hear, one more moment during which he wanted to watch and see what Miss Thorne might do.

"I have a last question, Miss Thorne, if I may."

"Please, Mr. Harkness." She gestured to indicate his perfect freedom.

"I'm afraid it's personal."

She considered this, but was not shocked or affronted. She was intrigued. "Very well. I am forewarned."

"How was it your parents decided on Rose Thorne as a name?"

She smiled and for once that smile was a little shy. "It's Rosalind," she corrected him.

He should stop. He should get out of here. He was entering into very, very dangerous territory with this lovely, lively Miss Thorne. "And no one calls you Rose? No one's made the connection?"

That was a mistake. Her eyes clouded over with some old hurt. "I'm sorry," he said swiftly. "I've overstepped." He had. She should dismiss him. He should take himself away.

But she didn't, and neither did he. "No, no. Of course I am Rose and Rosey and all such things. Especially when we were younger. But the name . . . well, therein hangs a very old tale, sir."

"I'd be delighted to hear it."

She looked at him for a moment, and evidently decided he meant what he said. "My mother's family name was Broadhurst," she said. "It's a very old and distinguished family, tracing its lineage back to the Domesday Book. However, there was a time when they were simple dairy farmers."

He nodded, encouraging.

"During the reign of Bloody Mary Tudor, the queen had her sister—then Princess Elizabeth—arrested and taken to the tower, supposedly for refusing to convert to Catholicism. According to the story, Elizabeth was taken away so early that the only persons awake were the dairy maids milking the cows. One little maid saw the princess with her escort of soldiers. She thought the princess looked very ill, and, not knowing what was afoot, ran to her with a cup of milk to help revive her. The soldiers were amused, and allowed the princess to drink the milk. Elizabeth inquired after the child's name. Later, when she ascended the throne, she sent the Broadhursts a purse of twenty pounds in gold, six cows, and the note of gratitude to Little Rosalind of the Dairies." She was still smiling and it looked well on her. Not that he had any business looking. "Since then, every generation of Broadhursts has named at least one girl Rosalind, for luck. Since my mother was the first of her family to have a daughter, she gave the name to me, despite the Thornes."

Harkness laughed and now he did stand. "Well, Miss Thorne, I will leave you with that. I deeply appreciate your help, and hope to hear from you again very soon."

"As soon as I have something to tell." She rose and rang for her housekeeper to show him to the door.

The housekeeper, when she arrived, was not at all smiling. In fact, her face was positively thunderous as she led Harkness to the narrow front hallway, and the door.

"Bad times," he remarked. "When something like this can disturb such a respectable house."

"Yes indeed," she said. "No scandal has ever been able to

attach itself to my mistress. It's a sin and a shame that the young gentleman's death should come so close."

Harkness nodded sympathetically, and accepted his hat and coat when she brought them. He made a few additional conversational sallies, but none of them elicited any answer. The housekeeper just opened the door and waited for him to go, and not very patiently either.

Which told Harkness this woman was loyal to her mistress, and had reason to believe her mistress was loyal to her. Considering her mistress's reduced circumstances, that was worth noting.

In truth, there was a great deal about Miss Thorne worth noting. Harkness glanced back over his shoulder as he descended the steps to the street. And much he wished he hadn't noted at all, because she was beautiful, and lonesome, and intelligent, and brave.

He could not, however, ignore the fact that Miss Thorne had spoken freely of Lady Blanchard, and Lord Blanchard, of her unusual promise to Honoria Aimesworth, of Almack's lady patronesses, and even Mr. Whelks. There was one person about whom she attempted to maintain a discreet silence: Devon Winterbourne, the Duke of Casselmain.

That, to Adam Harkness, could not help but be tremendously interesting.

CHAPTER 20

In All the Papers

Therefore, let us make the best of the bad matter ...
—Thomas De Quincy, *On Murder Considered as*
One of the Fine Arts

Rosalind stood by the front hall window and watched Adam Harkness turn the collar of his blue great coat up against the wind and begin walking down the street with an unhurried pace, despite the fresh flurry of snow.

Throughout their interview, he'd been waiting for her to say something in particular, but she could not tell if he'd heard it or not. This left behind a sensation of deep disquiet. Principal Officer Adam Harkness was the sort of man who kept looking until he found what he wanted, and he had so many directions to look in.

"Mrs. Kendricks?" Her housekeeper had come into the parlor behind her.

"Yes, miss?"

"I'm going to have to ask you to finish the inventory on your own. Make a list of what I'll need to do. I've some additional letters to write, and after that, I'll be going 'round to talk with Alice Littlefield. I think it's important I find out something more about this Mr. Harkness, and she and George may be able to help. After that . . . well, we shall have to see." She paused, and she shivered, as if caught in a sudden draft. "Am I being too sensitive? It seems like we're standing on very thin ice, and I can't tell which way the cracks are running."

Mrs. Kendricks did not answer at once. When she did, her tone was low and serious. "We have survived many disasters, Miss Thorne. It would be a wonder if you had not developed some sense of their approach."

"Wonderful. Some are blessed with a weather knee. I have a weather heart."

"There are worse things, miss."

"I'm sure you're right, Mrs. Kendricks. I just wish mine wasn't giving me so much to keep track of just now."

They shared a weary smile and Rosalind settled herself back at her writing desk. First, she penned a note to Lord Blanchard, asking what the betting book at White's had yielded. Then, with a wince at the hypocrisy of it, she wrote a note to Louisa Winterbourne, Devon's cousin, in which she informed the young lady she would be delighted to accept her invitation to take an outing to Taylor & Green's warehouse with her.

It was only when these had been laid on the tray with the rest of the post that Rosalind pulled on her coat, gloves, and warmest bonnet and left the house. She had to go quickly, before she changed her mind about the second letter.

Alice and George shared a flat in the neighborhood of Bloomsbury. Rosalind nodded to the charwoman she passed on the stairs and knocked at their unpainted door. She heard Alice's shout from the other side and let herself in.

"Good morning, Alice!" Rosalind called as she took off her coat and bonnet to hang on the pegs by the door. The flat was clean, but it was worn, and the Littlefield siblings for the most part did for themselves. Alice even confessed that George, if called upon, could boil a passable egg over the sitting room fire.

"Good morning, Rosalind!" Alice's greeting came from the sitting room. "Find yourself a seat, will you? I've got to get this translation for the Ladies Supplement finished, or we're going to have a dev—problem making the housekeeping next month."

Rosalind settled herself on the slightly lopsided sofa and took up an annual that had been tossed on the table. She perused this to the quiet rhythm of Alice's scratching quill, a sound that was punctuated by madly flapping pages as she consulted her French dictionary.

"There!" Alice stabbed her quill into the final full stop. "*A Concise History of the Dutch Masters and Their Works, Told in Plain Language*, accurately and clearly translated from the French to the English by A. E. Littlefield, to the tune of five whole lovely pounds. Thank you, Sanderson Faulks, for the good word to the editors, and to Madame DuFrense of blessed memory for beating all those conjugations into my head." Alice turned her eyes reverently toward heaven.

"Are you sure you're looking in the right direction?" asked Rosalind. "As I recall, she was quicker with a ruler than any other teacher at school."

"Well, today, because of the good she has done my household accounts, she shall be elevated. Now." Alice scooted her chair around. "What can I do for you, Rose?"

"Actually, it was George I needed to talk to. I was hoping we might walk 'round to the *Chronicle* together, if you're free."

"As it happens, I am, and I shall be glad of the exercise. But why are you honoring my dear brother with a morning call?"

"Will you allow me my secret, just until we see him, Alice? It may be nothing—"

Alice cut her off with a single sharp gesture that would have done Madame DuFrense proud. "Don't even bother finishing that. It's something, and it's to do with Jasper Aimesworth's death, isn't it?"

"Why would you think that? It could be to do with Mrs. Nottingham's political party."

"It could, but it isn't. Rose, darling, you can fool the rest of the world, but not your Alice. However, I shall allow you your moment of mystery. Let me get my hat and coat."

The *London Chronicle* was of a species of paper known as the "twice-weekly." Published on Sundays and Thursdays, it covered events from the trivial, such as speeches in Parliament (from a Whiggish perspective), to the momentous, such as which hostess's party was deemed a particular success.

The *Chronicle*'s home was a modest brick warehouse on the upper slope of Fleet Street. The noise of the place could be heard right out into the streets, with the constant squeal, creak, and thud of the great presses accompanied by the rhythm of mallets pounding rows of lead type into place in their wooden frames. Once through the barnlike doors, Alice and Rosalind dodged men pushing handcarts stacked with great piles of cut paper and other men in leather aprons carrying proof sheets while boys ran to and fro with trays of unset type. The tang of ink and hot metal filled Rosalind's nose and burned the back of her throat as she followed Alice up the stairs to the marginally quieter and cleaner floor that held the desks of the writers, not to mention the private offices of the editors and publishers.

"Good afternoon, Miss Littlefield!" cried out a host of voices as the women made their way through the maze of desks and stools.

"Make way for the Queen of the Sundays!" called someone else.

Alice smiled and nodded to all and sundry, making a great show of putting her best debut-day manners on. This earned her a number of smiles and laughs from the men, most of whom were in their shirtsleeves with leather cuffs on their arms to protect their sleeves from ink stains. There was also, Rosalind noted with wry amusement, a look of puppy love from a boy who was almost hidden by the great stack of manuscript pages he carried.

George had a desk near the windows that allowed him access to what passed for fresh air during the heat of the London summer, but in the winter his little corner was flooded with an icy draft that would have done credit to the Scottish Highlands. Indeed as they approached, it was to see George clutching a muffler around his throat with one hand as he scribbled madly at the page in front of him with the other.

"Good morning, brother dear!" cried Alice merrily. It took far more than a simple draft to chill her boundless spirits. "I've brought you a visitor."

"Miss Thorne!" George tossed his quill into the inkstand at the top of his slanting desk and stood to bow. "How very good to see you again." He grabbed two rush-bottomed chairs from the little line by the wall and set them in front of the desk. "Won't you sit down and tell me how may I be of service?"

Rosalind did sit, and she said, "I received a visit from a Bow Street runner, a man named Adam Harkness."

"I'd heard." George rubbed his hands together, whether in contemplation or from cold, it was difficult to say.

"Do you know him?" prompted Rosalind.

The Littlefields exchanged a look between them that was both long and significant. "Why, brother dear," said Alice. "I believe you and I may know something of interest to Miss Thorne."

"It appears so, sister dear." George nodded solemnly. "My. How shall we answer her?"

Alice tapped one gloved finger against her chin. "I would say it depends how contrite she is about that whopper she told us regarding where and how Jasper Aimesworth was discovered in Almack's."

"Ah," said Rosalind. "Yes. I should apologize for that."

The Littlefields nodded in perfect unison.

"I'm sorry. I was protecting . . ." Who? What? Rosalind found herself suddenly uncertain of how to finish her sentence.

"You have a great deal to protect," acknowledged George simply. "But you have to admit, it's pretty poor form to ask for our help but not be willing to give us any in return."

"Not to mention very unlike you," said Alice.

"I am sorry," said Rosalind, suddenly grateful for the covering sounds of boisterous men's conversation and constant industry. "Things have happened so fast, and gotten so complicated, I'm afraid I'm stumbling around in the dark. I hardly know what I am going to do next."

"Not a good position for anyone," said George. But Alice was looking at her in thoughtful silence, which also was not conducive to comfort.

"Well." George sighed. "What I know is that Adam Harkness is the youngest man ever promoted to principal officer. Old John Townsend thinks the world of him, or at least of how the papers are so taken with his exploits. He made quite the name for himself on the horse patrols. Had an uncanny knack for working out where the highwaymen would strike next." George paused, allowing himself to relish his next revelation. "So uncanny, in fact, there were some who said he was in cahoots with the gangs, or taking money from different bands to turn their rivals in."

This was concerning, especially when Rosalind remembered

how quickly she'd warmed to Mr. Harkness's banter and solemn teasing. "Is it true?" she asked. "Was he taking bribes?"

"I've never believed it," said George. "I've always found him honest, according to his type. He wants a man in the dock so he can collect the reward, but he also wants it to be the right man. I've known him to hand back his fee if he couldn't lay hands on the correct blaggard. There's others that'll just pick up some known housebreaker or dealer in stolen goods and swear it was them, on the grounds it's all one what a wrong 'un gets taken up for. They've surely done *something*."

"What is going to be said in tomorrow's paper about Almack's?"

Alice and her brother looked at each other.

"It's not going to wait until tomorrow, is it?" sighed Rosalind. "That's why it's such a madhouse downstairs. There's going to be a special edition tonight."

George sighed. "As it happens, yes. We've several people who say they saw shady figures hanging about in the alleys, possibly French. One of the men was at Waterloo, and so ought to know."

"That is patently ludicrous," said Rosalind.

"Have you got something better?" inquired Alice.

"Not yet," Rosalind admitted. "Soon, perhaps."

"Well then, mysterious lurking Frenchmen it will have to be," said George. "And I've got to get back to them."

"Good luck, brother dear." Alice gave him a kiss on his cheek. "I'll save some dinner for you."

Outside, the wind had driven off the clouds, and for a moment, at least, the sun shone down upon the cobbles. Arm in arm, Rosalind and Alice dodged puddles, traffic, barrow men, and secondhand clothes dealers, until the traffic and noise both thinned out and they could walk more easily.

"This," remarked Alice. "Was rather a long way to come for so little. You could have written a letter and gotten as much."

"Perhaps." Rosalind tucked her chin a little farther into her coat collar. The wind was still sharp and smelled of fresh snow, as well as stale London. "Alice, have you ever thought that of the two of us, you made the better choice?"

"Oh, yes," she answered loftily. "Because having to pinch every penny until it begs for mercy, not to mention pleading with the green grocer and the milliner for just another week to pay, is so much better than staying the winters and summers in the best houses and nights at the theater and the opera."

"Don't tell me you regret it."

"Regret? Not exactly." They turned a corner, only to find a crowd of men trying to free a cart that had become stuck in a mudhole. They backed up at once, and started down the other way.

"I do look around the ballrooms sometimes when I'm writing about the parties," said Alice. "I see all the wives and daughters, and I think how that could have been me. Then I read about the latest criminal conversation trial, or I write about somebody else's profligate brother gambling away house and land and dying in a duel and I think I'm well enough off as I am." She paused. "You could do it if you wanted to, Rosalind. I could put you in the way of some translation work. Your French is better than mine, and you have German as well. Or, oh! I know! You could write a novel."

"Don't be ridiculous."

"I'm not. I met a man at one of the publishers' evenings. His name is Harry Colburn. He says that people are clamoring for stories of the *haut ton*. He's had an enormous success with that thing, *Glenarvon*. You know it, the one that's supposed to be written by Caroline Lamb about her affair with Lord Byron? Mr. Colburn thinks more like it would sell outrageously well. He might even be willing to advance a sum to anyone who could promise him a manuscript. Describe a few dances, throw in a daring highwayman and a treacherous nun . . ."

"French or Italian?"

"Italian, I think. The highwayman can be French." They shared a smile, but it was brief. Alice stopped right in the middle of the walk. Ignoring the curses and growls that rose around them, she faced Rosalind directly. "Rose, will you tell me what you're doing? I swear I won't breathe, or write, a word of it until you give me permission. I'm worried about you."

"I . . . you really promise you will hold it in confidence?"

Alice held up her hand. "May Madame DuFrense's ruler strike me down if I don't."

Rosalind smiled. "All right. Honoria Aimesworth believes Jasper was murdered, and it's starting to look like she was right. She's asked me to find out who the killer is."

"*What?*" Alice exclaimed. "You loathe Honoria, and she returns the sentiment."

"Yes. And I'm not sure that's changed. But I have more freedom to ask questions than she does."

"With that mother of hers for a jailer, there's men in Newgate who have more freedom than she does." Then, Alice's hand flew to her mouth. "That's why you wanted to know if you could trust Adam Harkness! You're not just asking questions for Honoria! You're asking them for . . ." She dropped her voice. "Merciful heavens, Rosalind, you're working for Bow Street!"

Rosalind did not answer. She turned and began walking again, leaving Alice to trot to catch up.

"And you said you couldn't turn lady novelist!" Excitement raised Alice's voice to a squeak. "This is wonderful! Oh, you have to let me do a piece on it . . ." Rosalind frowned at her. "Once it's all over, of course, and the perpetrator is brought to justice. Have you any real clues?"

"That's the problem." She bit her lip. "Jasper was killed during the patronesses' Monday meeting, or right after it. Mr. Harkness thinks he might have been beaten to death."

"Rosalind." Alice reached out and gripped her wrist. "You are not seriously suggesting that one of the lady patronesses committed violent murder? I couldn't even sell that to the major!"

"I'm suggesting one of them might know who did commit the murder." *And heaven help me, it might be Lady Blanchard.*

They walked on in silence for a while, pressed close together by the passing crowds with their baskets and bundles. "Rose, according to what George and I . . . heard, there were other people in the building. Willis himself, for example."

She wasn't going to say it, so Rosalind did. "Devon Winterbourne was also there, and me, of course."

"Yes. I don't know if you've thought of this, but beating a man, it must make rather a lot of noise. Whoever was in the building when Jasper did die, they should have heard."

"Oh yes," Rosalind answered. "I have thought of that, Alice. Rather a lot."

CHAPTER 21

The Gossip in the Servants' Hall

*This will show you how reports spread in a moment,
and how little credit should be attached to the* on-dits *of
society.*

—Marianne Spencer Stanhope Hudson, *Almack's*

The clamor of the Tamwell House kitchen poured over Mrs.
Kendricks in a ragged wave of noise. "Mrs. Heath, is the pigeon
pie ready?"

"Just here. Alfred, you take care with that!"

"Mr. Barstow, they're about out of sherry upstairs."

"Take up the fresh glasses. I'll have more up from the cellar
directly. Martin, come with me!"

Not one person was sitting still. Everyone had a job to do,
from the sour-faced girl, Rebecca, who was mending linens so
extra rooms could be made up should any extra relations decide
at the last minute to stay, to Mrs. Kendricks herself, who was
helping arrange cakes and savories on the trays for the footmen
to take upstairs.

Although Mrs. Kendricks would have cut off her right hand
before she admitted it to Miss Thorne, she regretted having
left service in a large establishment. It was more than just the

company of her fellow servants she missed, it was the sense of moment and purpose that was brought to the job at hand, especially during an important party or event, even should that event happen to be a funeral.

A funeral was a terrible time for a family and a busy one for the house. Everything had to run as perfectly as for the finest dinner party. Any misstep would not only be noticed, but be profoundly embarrassing. All this left downstairs in a particular state of uproar, and when she'd offered to lend a hand, Mrs. Kendricks had been gratefully accepted.

Upstairs, the men were still off at the churchyard seeing young Mr. Aimesworth laid to rest. This initial reception was for the ladies, both relatives and visitors, whom tradition did not allow to attend the burial. For them, the refreshments had to be light and plentiful, and everything the finest the house had to offer. After the men returned, there would be a supper for the relations and choice friends. The table for that was already laid and the cold preparations waited in the larder, but there was still a great deal to be done.

"Hey now! You get off there!"

Even over the noise and bustle, Mariah Neill's exclamation made the whole room jump. A man's grinning face pressed up against the area railing outside the kitchen window. Alfred, the senior footman, said something he wouldn't have wanted his mother to hear and bolted out the kitchen door.

Mrs. Neill drew the curtains more firmly shut, but that did nothing to damp down the sound of Alfred shouting, "Clear off!" Probably there were a few swift kicks administered as well. News of the young man found dead at Almack's had spread and wide, and all manner of idlers lingered on the walkways outside and probably even around the church.

"For shame!" cried Mrs. Neill as she moved to hand a tray of dainties to one of the footmen. "Vultures."

Miss Thorne might not have friends in Tamwell House, but the head housekeeper, Mariah Neill, was Mrs. Kendricks's cousin by marriage, and they exchanged visits and news with each other on a regular basis, something Miss Thorne encouraged, even if Lady Edmund did not.

"An' it ain't gettin' any better," said Alfred as he came back in. "What's them constables doin' out there, I wonders?"

"No good," said Mrs. Neill. "Here, you get the decanters ready for Mr. Barstow when he comes up."

"Yes, ma'am." Alfred opened the glassware cupboard and began taking out the cut glass decanters.

"I thought Lady Edmund was going to go out there with a cutlass," muttered Rebecca as she bit through her thread. Mrs. Kendricks found herself eyeing the girl thoughtfully.

"You be quiet, Becky Lewis," snapped Mrs. Neill. "This is a house of mourning, and we don't need any talk like that."

"Mourning," snorted Becky.

"I heard that," the housekeeper warned her.

"It is a terrible thing, Mrs. Neill," said Mrs. Kendricks as she nudged the little cakes on the tray in front of her into tidier lines. "My mistress says Miss Honoria is ill with grief."

Becky snorted again.

"That's it!" Mrs. Neill snapped. "One more like that and I'll put you in the scullery with Sally until you can't remember what upstairs work looks like."

"Yes, Mrs. Neill." Becky bowed her head to hide her expression. "Sorry, Mrs. Neill."

"Honestly." Mrs. Neill shook her head as she held up another silver tray to inspect for smudges. "Girls these days. No respect."

"Not like when we were young, Mrs. Neill," murmured Mrs. Kendricks as she stood back to let Cook inspect her handiwork. The other woman nodded her approval and the filled tray was placed with the others waiting in readiness on the table.

"Nothing is, Mrs. Kendricks. Certainly not . . ." Mrs. Neill rolled her eyes toward the ceiling. "What's it all coming to, that's what I'd like to know."

"Do you think . . ." Mrs. Kendricks lowered her voice. "There's the possibility that he jumped?"

Mrs. Neill lowered the tray she was inspecting for tarnish. She also glanced over her shoulder toward Becky Lewis. Cook turned her attention to the sauces simmering on her stove and pretended not to listen. "Well, I don't know who told you that, but I would never believe it. At least, I wouldn't have."

Mrs. Kendricks waited for Mrs. Neill to enjoy her moment. She had a love of the dramatic, Mariah did. She leaned close. "Gambling, Mrs. Kendricks," she whispered.

Mrs. Kendricks let her brows shoot up. Mrs. Neill nodded solemnly. "He'd been worried about money. After his father about it. Now, what could that mean but a debt he had to pay, an' . . ."

Just then Mr. Barstow and the young footman, Martin, emerged from the cellar with a bottle of sherry in each hand. "Mrs. Neill," said the butler. "It occurs to me we should bring up some more of your dandelion and lemon cordials. The dowager ladies favor those over more spirituous drinks at such times."

"Oh!" Mrs. Neill slapped her palm against her forehead. "And I've had no time to bottle the new. I'll go to the still-room . . . oh . . ." She gestured at the cook and the trays.

"I can go, Mrs. Neill," said Mrs. Kendricks at once. "Then you can get on with the cakes and the service." She paused. "Becky can come help me, can't she?"

One look at Becky's screwed-up face told her all the girl thought of that task. Which, as far as Mrs. Neill was concerned, sealed her fate.

"Do as you are told," snapped the Aimesworth's housekeeper. "And remember, I've got my eye on you, my girl."

Becky put down her linens, stood, and curtsied. The whole time her face was about as cheerful as a wet January. Mrs. Kendricks nodded once. She'd made the right choice.

Most houses had a stillroom, but they were nothing like the ones Mrs. Kendricks remembered from her youth. Then, there'd been a separate maid to tend the fires, distill liquors and tinctures, and cook down the syrups both sweet and medicinal that the house might need. Nowadays, the stillroom was barely a closet off the kitchen where the cook made jellies or dried herbs on a small brick hearth. Occasionally, though, if a housekeeper had a special recipe, the copper-bottomed distillers might be brought out.

The tiled room smelled strongly of smoke and the savory herbs that hung in bundles overhead. It was warm and dry in there, and perspiration immediately prickled under Mrs. Kendricks's stiff collar.

"Now, just bring me two of the clean bottles, Becky, and a fine sieve," said Mrs. Kendricks as she reached up on the shelf for the crocks labeled in grease pencil. She found a pitcher as well and brought that down to the worktable.

"Oh, yes, Mrs. Kendricks," muttered Becky. "Right away, Mrs. Kendricks." She did, however, bring the bottles.

"You won't last long in this house with that kind of attitude, my girl." Mrs. Kendricks set the sieve over the top of the pitcher. "Even if you don't feel humble, you need to act as though you do. Her ladyship is not the forgiving sort."

"This house." Becky took hold of the sieve to keep it steady while Mrs. Kendricks poured the pale gold cordial from its crock into the pitcher. "Wouldn't care if I never set foot in it again, 'cept that I ain't been able to find another place yet."

"One house is very like another, you'll find. Best to stick with what you've got."

"'At's what they"—Becky jerked her chin toward the kitchen—"all say. A bird in the 'and is worf two in the bush."

Mrs. Kendricks took the sieve and shook out the last drops of liquid into the pitcher. "But you're not so sure, are you? Can you find me the funnel?"

Becky shrugged, and opened the cupboard under the table. "Oh, I'm a good girl. I mind my place. Save me breath to cool me porridge. Ask me no questions an' I'll tell you no lies." She slapped the tin funnel onto the worktable.

"What's happened to you here, Becky?"

"Oh, right! I tell you and you run right over to tell Mrs. Needles. No fanks."

Mrs. Kendricks ignored this childish play on her cousin's name. She had already heard enough to lose the girl her place. Now, however, was not the time to mention this. "Have you a cheese cloth?" Becky rolled her eyes and ducked her head down into the cupboard again, coming up with loose-woven, bleached cloth. Mrs. Kendricks took it to wrap the mouth of the funnel before she set it into the bottle.

"You know," she said as she began to pour the cordial carefully from pitcher to bottle. "If you really were unhappy, my Miss Thorne might be able to find you a new place." Becky made no answer. "Quiet like, of course. Better not to have anyone know when you're looking to leave, isn't it?"

Becky looked toward the door to the main kitchen. "Would she really?"

Mrs. Kendricks nodded. "There's always a place for a clever girl who knows her work."

"Thank you, Mrs. Kendricks. And thank Miss Thorne if she would. That is, I'd like another place, but they're so hard to find!"

Mrs. Kendricks set the pitcher down. "What is it, girl?" she asked Becky gently. "Come on and tell us, one woman in service to another. Was it . . ." She glanced toward the door, which stayed firmly closed. "Was it the young master? Gentlemen can make trouble for a good girl and everybody knows it."

Becky bit her lip. "Weren't the young master. I've got sharp enough elbows an' 'e wasn't bad like some. Didn't bother me more than once or twice. 'Twas the mistress."

"Now that doesn't surprise me," murmured Mrs. Kendricks. "The tales my Miss Thorne has to tell about them both, mother and daughter." She shook her head.

"Yeah, well, I'd be given to fits, too, with a mother who moves heaven and earth to get me engaged, and then goes and breaks it up!"

Mrs. Kendricks felt her jaw drop. "Now then, Becky, there's no call to be making things up."

"It's true! Hiller, her ladyship's maid, just about left her place because of it. Such scenes, and such goings-on behind everybody's back. She couldn't bear it. I heard her telling Mrs. Neill."

You hear a deal more than's good for you. Mrs. Kendricks stoppered the cordial bottle and wrung out the cloth over the slop bucket. "Well, *I've* never heard of such a thing. Are you sure?"

"Sure as sure," said Becky stoutly as she wielded her cloth to wipe down the bottle. "Hiller said Lady Edmund found out something she didn't like about Mr. Phineas, that was Miss Honoria's fiancé . . ." Mrs. Kendricks nodded. "But instead of telling

Miss Honoria about it, Lady Edmund starts tossing other girls in Mr. Phineas's path. Her guest lists were a sight. Not that your miss helped much."

"Now you watch yourself, Becky." Mrs. Kendricks set to work straining the lemon cordial into a clean pitcher. "Miss Thorne does a good deal to help all sorts, and yourself might be one if you'll recall."

"I'm sorry, but she must have scented something was up, and did nowt to stop it."

Mrs. Kendricks shook her head. It was possible. When Miss Thorne took on favors for other ladies, she usually had her own good reasons for doing things that might look a bit out of line. But those reasons, in Mrs. Kendricks's very private opinion, were not always as sound as Miss Thorne might believe.

"What kind of woman queers the pitch for her own girl?" Becky was saying. "Why not just come straight out and say the fellow's no good?"

"Well," sighed Mrs. Kendricks. "Many's the young lady who won't listen to her mother on the subject of young men." *Especially when they're trying to get out of a house that's no home at all.*

"I suppose. But that weren't . . ." Becky stopped.

Mrs. Kendricks set the pitcher down and turned fully toward Becky. "There was more?"

The girl looked up at her with pleading eyes. She was a talker, but she wasn't a fool. She knew as well as Mrs. Kendricks they'd ventured into dangerous territory. "You sure your Miss Thorne will help me?"

"She'll do her very best, I promise."

"Well." Becky moved closer, and started wrapping the funnel in a fresh length of cloth. "It was after Lady Edmund gets back from Switzerland, with Miss Honoria looking like she's had a six-months bellyache instead of a trip to the Continent . . ."

"You don't mean she was in trouble, do you?" whispered Mrs. Kendricks.

Now Becky looked shocked. "Oh, no! Not her. She's got the very devil of a temper, but she's not careless like some of them so-called ladies. She was just sour from all that time with her mother. And she had reason, I'd wager. But soon as they's back, that Lady Edmund starts setting spies on her own son. What kind of mother does that, I ask you?"

"No! Really?"

"My hand to God." Becky raised the hand in question. "She give me two shillings to watch the post and bring her any letters to or from Mr. Aimesworth before they went into the mail bag. An' I wasn't the only one she went to."

"But young Mr. Aimesworth had his own rooms, didn't he? He can't have written very many from this house."

"There was enough, I guess."

Mrs. Kendricks nodded, and for a moment paid attention to pouring the golden cordial into its fresh bottle. "And you did as you were told?"

"What choice did I have? It was take what was offered, or lose me place."

And incidentally, get accused of stealing that money, which would be why Lady Edmund paid it out in the first place. Mrs. Kendricks felt her jaw harden. She could probably add stealing the family letters to the charges as well.

"What on earth can she have wanted to know about so badly? Was he gambling? Or was it a woman?"

"Bound to be a woman, isn't it? With 'er ladyship so took up with everybody's marriages an' all. Strange, though, that they'd worry about that now. Everybody knows Mr. Jasper had his share of ladies, even before he went to university. What would be so special about this one?"

What indeed? Mrs. Kendricks corked the bottle. That was a question Miss Thorne would surely want answered.

CHAPTER 22

A Disorderly Progression

It is our duty to announce a great change likely to take place in the administration of A—m—k's. It has already been hinted at in several of the public papers that discontents of a serious nature have long existed among the high executive authorities of that society.

—Marianne Spencer Stanhope Hudson, *Almack's*

Society Notes
by A. E. Littlefield

FRESH SURPRISES AT ALMACK'S!
POWER TO CHANGE HANDS!

With the fashionable world still reeling from the recent, horrifying discovery of Mr. Jasper Aimesworth's tragic demise within the hallowed precincts of Almack's Assembly Rooms, there might not seem to be room for more surprise or scandal. But now the *haut ton* must prepare itself for a fresh shock. The *London Chronicle* has learned from a confidential source entirely informed of all details, that one of Almack's mighty

lady patronesses will be resigning her post before the
end of the season.

Even now, while the famed runners of Bow Street,
under the leadership of John Townsend and Adam "the
Watchdog" Harkness, are still actively engaged in
painstaking examination of each available clew in order
to discover how Mr. Aimesworth met his ultimate fate
in that place where so many of our finest young ladies
hope to meet their matches, all of society turns its
attention to the much grander and weightier question.
Who will the new lady patroness be?

Readers of the *Chronicle* and "Society Notes" are of
course familiar with the hallowed roll of the patronesses . . .

Rosalind lowered the paper. She sat in the comfortable violet parlor of Blanchard House, which had been set aside for her use when
writing her letters, doing her fancy work, or receiving callers.

Or reading Alice's breathless journalistic prose in the Sunday
Chronicle, and wishing she could feel more satisfied with her
progress.

The days that followed Jasper's funeral and Rosalind's arrival
at Blanchard House had been quiet ones. In fact, frustratingly so.
Her letters and calls to her various friends yielded nothing more
about Jasper's affairs than that vague gossip about money and
women which she had already heard. Indeed, the only interesting
news she had to add to her little store was Mrs. Kendricks's discovery that Lady Edmund had been worried enough about her
son's recent *amours* that she'd set the servants to spying on him.
But none of her housekeeper's careful inquiries had answered the
pertinent question: What caused Lady Edmund to take this step?
Was there really money involved, or was it strictly over an injudi-
cious affair? If the latter, just who was the lady in question?

Rosalind did hear that Mrs. Tillman-Edwards had just let her parlor maid go and was able to recommend for her a girl of good character and experience named Becky Lewis. That, at least, was something. But the news she craved most so far had eluded her.

She had no word of any kind from Lord Blanchard regarding the contents of White's betting book. Although a fortnight had passed since Jasper's death, Lord Blanchard had not broached the subject with her. He had not answered her first letter, nor her second, written while she was still resident at Little Russell Street. And in the two nights since Rosalind had arrived to begin her stay at Blanchard House, he had not been home to dinner.

Rosalind had been avoided before. She knew what it looked like. But this was incomprehensible. Who had better reason to wish the entire matter laid to rest than Lord Blanchard?

So far, it seemed the only two points on which Rosalind had succeeded was in distracting the attention of the popular press and in arranging a shopping trip with Devon's cousin, Louisa Winterbourne. Even these minute successes had taken far longer than she'd hoped. The murder had driven news of a patroness's departure out of the society columns until this issue, and Louisa had come down with a cold that kept her in bed for a solid week. All other avenues being blocked, Rosalind was now reduced to hoping that Devon at least would be willing to talk about Jasper, instead of being distracted by any remnants of their former relationship that still lay scattered about.

She had to hope the same about herself.

As Rosalind contemplated this uncomfortable point, the door opened to admit Collins, the footman, who carried a silver salver with not one, but three, visiting cards on it.

"Mrs. Nottingham is asking if you are at home, Miss Thorne," he informed her, holding out the tray. "Mrs. Fortnum and Miss Hall are with her."

Rosalind glanced at the mantelpiece clock. It was exactly eleven, the earliest possible moment for paying polite calls.

"Certainly I am at home," she said. "Please show them up, and ask Cook to send up a pot of tea."

Collins bowed and left, only to return a moment later with the three ladies tailing behind him, looking very much like a cluster of colorful and nervous goslings.

"Mrs. Nottingham, Mrs. Fortnum, Miss Hall," Rosalind greeted them all. "How very good to see you."

"Miss Thorne, good morning!" said Mrs. Nottingham as Rosalind invited them all to take a chair. "When I heard you were staying with Lady Blanchard, I felt I had to come 'round to thank you for all you've done so far to help my little gathering. I've just had my reply from Mr. Sanderson Faulks. Maxwell will be so pleased!"

Rosalind bowed her head modestly. "Mr. Faulks is always interested in the work of promising new artists. He was delighted when he heard Maxwell had returned to us." Which was stretching the truth, but Mr. Faulks would understand it was all in service of necessary *politesse*.

"I was saying to Mrs. Nottingham how very much we are looking forward to her party." Mrs. Fortnum was a small, plump woman. Her natal family was one of the oldest in Shropshire, and she had caused a minor scandal in marrying a returning Indiaman five years her junior. However, his fortune, combined with her dinner parties, had tidied all that away. "Hers are always such delightful entertainments, not at all too stuffy or crowded like some. And when she said you were assisting her, I of course said it could not fail to be anything but a delightful evening."

"So kind," Rosalind murmured. Collins and a maid arrived with the tea, and Rosalind busied herself with inquiring as to her guests' preferences and pouring out. According to the rules of such conversations, it would be Miss Hall's turn for flattery next, and Miss Hall did not disappoint.

"Have you seen the new fans at Harper and Grant's, Miss Thorne? I am very much hoping you'll consent to a shopping trip with me. You have the best taste and I'm sure I won't know which to choose."

"I would love to." Rosalind smiled. "We shall set a date."

The talk flowed, as did the flattery. Rosalind answered and inquired and exclaimed by turns. They chatted about Mrs. Nottingham's party and the guest list, but the whole while she saw how Mrs. Fortnum and Miss Hall kept glancing toward Mrs. Nottingham, waiting for her to get to the point that had brought them all here. Rosalind was sure she knew what it was, but etiquette forbade her from bringing it up herself.

At last, Mrs. Nottingham deemed the proper amount of casual conversation had been completed and set her half-empty teacup on the table. "Miss Thorne, I must confess, I've come to you because I'm very worried."

"I'm sorry to hear it. How can I help?"

The three ladies exchanged a glance, and several brief nods. "I'm sure you already have some idea," said Mrs. Nottingham. "It is this dreadful business with Almack's. The news has been so shocking and it simply won't stop! Of course we are all very sorry about young Mr. Aimesworth . . ."

Of course we are. Rosalind nodded solemnly.

"But, you know, Megan, my eldest girl, is to make her debut this season, and we have very high hopes for her. It is so important to be seen to do the thing properly, you know. And of course we want the very best."

"Naturally. She's a lovely girl." Rosalind knew Megan Nottingham only slightly, and found her a nervous little creature who stood in awe of her energetic mother and her voluble and

artistic brother. Rosalind personally thought what would be best
for the girl would be to find a dignified civil servant, the sort
who collected first editions and preferred to dine at home. She'd
already adjusted Mrs. Nottingham's guest list with this in mind.

Mrs. Nottingham leaned forward. "Miss Thorne, as you are
such very good friends with Lady Blanchard, we knew you
would be able to give us a true account of . . . matters." She
stopped. "There are rumors that the voucher lists are going to be
altered. That Lady Jersey is going to strike off those who haven't,
perhaps, been quite as supportive as she might like."

And there it was. All these women had applied for Almack's
vouchers. In a normal season, they would have received their
answers long before now.

"I have indeed heard those rumors, Mrs. Nottingham,"
Rosalind admitted. In fact, she'd been sitting beside Lady
Blanchard in several of the drawing rooms where they'd begun.
Mr. Faulks made himself useful by ensuring they reached the
clubs so the gentlemen could bear them home.

Mrs. Nottingham would have been utterly appalled to find
out that the delay in the issuing of the voucher lists had initially
been Rosalind's idea. Lady Jersey seized upon it as an opportunity to hear all the extended gossip and thus find out who the
truly faithful among the subscribers might be.

"And they . . . are just rumors, aren't they?" Mrs. Nottingham
had clearly been selected to speak for the trio. "We are good friends,
and if you'd heard . . . well . . . anything about us in particular, you
would let me know? It would be such a shame for us to have to
cancel Megan's debut . . ." Not to mention socially disastrous.

Rosalind nodded sympathetically. "You may be sure, Mrs.
Nottingham, if there was any such a change, I would let you
know the moment word reached me." She made sure to glance
at the others to let them know they were included in this.

The three ladies looked to one another, relief shining on all their faces, but of course, Rosalind could not remark on that. They chatted awhile longer about families and the upcoming seasons at the Opera and the Ancient Music. They talked about the Blanchards, and Rosalind made sure to mention the importance of the Konigsberg post and how vital Lord Blanchard's efforts there would be to the current government's plans for securing stability and British interests on the Continent. Mrs. Nottingham nodded and agreed easily, which was a relief. It meant she had not yet heard anything to the contrary.

The rules of visiting dictated that social calls could last only a quarter of an hour, and exactly on time, Mrs. Nottingham and the others rose to their feet to take their collective leave.

"So lovely to see you, Miss Thorne," Mrs. Nottingham said as they made their curtsies. "I do so look forward to seeing you at our little party. And perhaps you'd be so kind as to come dine with us next week?"

"And you mustn't forget our shopping trip!" beamed Miss Hall. "I'll write to you."

Nor was Mrs. Fortnum to be left out. "I'm having a small evening gathering, Miss Thorne. Just supper and cards, of course, nothing formal. But I may count on you, mayn't I?"

Rosalind accepted, with pleasure, said she would wait for their cards and letters, and summoned the footman to show Mrs. Nottingham and her party to the door.

She waited a moment, the compliments and the social worries still ringing through her mind. Then she took up her hems and went in search of Lady Blanchard.

She found her hostess still in her private apartment. In fact, she was still at her dressing table with her maid, Lacey, finishing her hair.

"No, not that one," Lady Blanchard said as Lacey lifted a

silver comb decorated with garnets and seed pearls out of its drawer in the jewel cabinet. "I'll have the tortoiseshell today. Good morning, Rosalind." She waved Rosalind in. "I understand you've already had callers today? I must seem so slothful to you!"

"Of course not," said Rosalind. "It was Mrs. Nottingham and some friends. They were most anxious to talk about the current state of the voucher lists."

"Your scheme is working then." As Lacey was arranging the last of her waves and curls, Lady Blanchard could not turn her head, but she did glance sideways and smile. "Sarah will be pleased."

"It's hardly a scheme," said Rosalind. "The funeral is over, the scandal has failed to break, and now everyone can return to worrying about being left out. It only made sense to hold back the voucher lists until they could become the focus of speculation, instead of . . . instead of Jasper. It's really just an extension of Lady Jersey's own game of exclusivity."

"Which is exactly why Sarah will be so pleased." Lady Blanchard touched the combs her maid set in place. "And we had better fly if we are to be on time for her. She does so hate it when other people are late. This will do very well, Lacey, thank you," she added to her maid, who curtsied, and began gathering up reticule, gloves, shawl, and other necessities for embarking on a social call.

Rosalind knew she should return to her room to receive her own items from Mrs. Kendricks, but she remained where she was. "Lady Blanchard, two weeks ago Lord Blanchard said he would check the betting book at White's, to see if Jasper had made a wager about being able to get into Almack's, but he has not yet told me anything about it. I was hoping he'd mentioned something to you."

"No. In fact, I'd rather forgotten the whole thing." Lady

Blanchard turned to let Lacey drape her white shawl over her shoulders. "Perhaps you should forget about it as well. We've so much to accomplish, the two of us. However difficult . . ." She stopped, and began again. "However difficult it may *seem* at times, we must keep our minds focused on the task at hand, mustn't we? And that task includes not being late for Lady Jersey."

What could Rosalind do but agree?

CHAPTER 23

The Concerns of
a Confidential Secretary

*This other basket, marked "Almack's Rejected," of course
contains all the applications which are not successful, from
which a list is to be made.*

—Marianne Spencer Stanhope Hudson, *Almack's*

As it happened, Lady Jersey was not in the least bit pleased.
Rosalind and Lady Blanchard had barely been ushered into
Lady Jersey's crimson morning room when she surged to her feet
and pushed a copy of the *London Chronicle* into Rosalind's
hands.

"There, Miss Thorne!" snapped Lady Jersey. "Do you see that?
Nothing about the gambling or foolishness of young men, which
you promised us! Not one word explaining that Mr. Aimesworth's death was due to his own carelessness! Nothing but more
dreadful calumnies about murderous reprobates and Bow Street
runners and their watchdogs and I know not what else!"

While Mrs. Drummond-Burrell and Lady Sefton watched
from their seats on the mahogany and gilt chairs rumored to
have been recently "acquired" from one of the former empress's

palaces in Paris, Rosalind folded the paper and laid it on the painted tea table.

"If you will forgive me, Lady Jersey," she said, "I do think that we are making progress, and the sort of progress you hoped for."

"The girl has lost her mind!" Lady Jersey cried. "This past week one could not keep from reading about the thing!"

"I've stopped taking the papers," said Mrs. Drummond-Burrell with a delicate shudder. "I cannot bear it."

Lady Sefton's mouth tightened, an expression speaking volumes about what she thought of such delicacy of feeling.

"That was last week, during the funeral, when it could hardly be avoided," Rosalind reminded them all. "Now, with this article, we see the tide has turned. Today, the paper expends much more ink on the history of the patronesses and the reputation of Almack's than they do on any other recent occurrences."

"But every last article on the subject mentions Aimesworth's death and the runners' interference!"

"Mentions the death, yes, but does not speculate on it," said Rosalind firmly. "The speculation is all saved for Lady Blanchard's likely successor. This will only increase as the season approaches."

Alice and George explained that Major Alway was a shrewd player at the newspaper game. Expert at doling out the news in the fashion most calculated to induce suspense, he had held back the announcement of a lady patroness's departure until the last drop of interest had been wrung from Jasper's funeral. Alice confidently predicted the name of the departing patroness would be revealed on Thursday. The pedigrees and biographies of potential replacements would appear the following Sunday, with the rumors of dark horse candidates and probable favorites to follow in succeeding weeks. All of this would be interspersed with articles decrying the "marriage mart" and the shame of allowing such a small group of ladies to exercise so much power over social London. Rosalind expected the other papers to follow suit. Unless, of course, it seemed one of the other papers was getting ahead in the race. Then all of the major's careful play would collapse into a rush to be first out with what he had.

Lady Jersey sniffed.

"I suspect you of being a very clever woman, Miss Thorne," she announced. "That is not a becoming attribute in a person such as yourself."

"So I have been informed. My mother did her best to correct the fault when I was younger, but it has sadly persisted."

Lady Jersey glowered at Rosalind, probably trying to work out whether she was joking. Rosalind bit the inside of her cheek and reminded herself that she was also facing a very clever woman, and a very powerful one.

"We have less than a month before our first assembly. The voucher lists have not even been sent out and I am *besieged* with letters." Lady Jersey waved toward her writing desk, which was indeed piled with correspondence. "Even Mr. Whelks can't keep up with it all. Every subscriber is asking what is happening."

Which was Rosalind's cue, and her opportunity. "Perhaps I could offer some assistance on this point? If you would permit me, I could update your visiting book and make certain your calling cards are in order, which will free Mr. Whelks for the more important work with the voucher lists."

"Thank you, Miss Thorne," said Lady Jersey. "So helpful and obliging." Apparently her recent remark questioning Rosalind's mental capacity was to be forgiven and forgotten. "If you'd just go and knock on Mr. Whelks's office door and tell him we need the secondary list. I feel that with the continuing"—she made sure Rosalind felt the full force of her glare—"gossip, we may need to make some changes to the calls for today."

"Certainly, Lady Jersey."

Rosalind left the room, carefully keeping her expression to one of polite neutrality. It was only once she was in the corridor that she pressed her hand over her mouth to muffle her heartfelt sigh of exasperation.

The office set aside for Mr. Whelks's labors was beside the Jerseys' great, and largely unused, library. Normally, a woman who had an unmarried man in her employ, let alone in her house, would be subject to endless ribald commentary. But because of Lady Jersey's power and standing, the wagging tongues remained largely mute—not in the least because no one wished to be summarily struck off the Almack's lists.

"Come," was the brisk answer to Rosalind's knock, and she entered softly, leaving the door open behind her.

The room was well carpeted, but otherwise as bare as a monk's cell, if monks' cells were ever supplied with cabinets for correspondence. Mr. Whelks hunched over a writing desk by the window, papers stacked about him in the tidiest, tallest piles Rosalind had ever seen. He finished the letter he labored over, blotted it, and set it aside on yet another stack. Someone's hopes for triumph were doubtlessly laid down on that page. Mr. Whelks carefully crossed off one line of a list, and closed the desk. Only then did he stand to make his bow.

"Good afternoon, Miss Thorne," he said solemnly. "How may I be of assistance?"

"Lady Jersey has asked for the secondary voucher lists, Mr. Whelks. In light of the continued talk surrounding Mr.

Aimesworth, she feels some adjustments may need to be made to the lady patronesses' visiting lists." According to the rules of Almack's, no one could receive a voucher who had not been visited, and approved, by a patroness. No one who had been struck from those visiting lists could hope to receive a voucher.

A small spasm flickered across Mr. Whelks's impassive features. Doubtlessly he was thinking of the vouchers he'd already written out and stacked so neatly, and how he would be the one responsible for reworking and redistributing the lists, and the cards, and the tickets, before the week was out. Two weeks was the absolute limit for sending out the vouchers. Mrs. Nottingham and her friends were only the beginning of a small regiment of ladies, not to mention a large army of London dressmakers, who were on pins and needles to see who would be the final recipients.

Mr. Whelks, however, was too much the consummate servant to make any remark on this. "You may tell her ladyship I will bring the lists at once."

Because, of course, those confidential writings could not be given into an outsider's hands. Mr. Whelks would never violate his patroness's trust in even such a small fashion.

Which was exactly the point in his character Rosalind was counting on.

"Mr. Whelks, there is a matter I very much hoped to take up with you. Quietly."

Mr. Whelks favored her with an assessing look that would have done his mistress proud. In answer, Rosalind assumed an attitude which, she hoped, radiated both meekness and humility.

"I know that Lady Jersey depends on you absolutely, so I feel I may trust you." She glanced up and thought she saw his expression soften, at least a little. Encouraged, she went on. "You know that sometimes great ladies, because of the constant demands on their time and attention, can overlook those matters that lie clos-est to them. At such times, it's up to their most loyal friends to help them, without . . . disturbing them."

"Your feelings do you credit, Miss Thorne, and yes, there have been times . . ." He sighed. "Well, that is neither here nor there."

Rosalind nodded in perfect sympathy and agreement. "It has been my heavy responsibility to help a few ladies who are less prudent than Lady Jersey through some unfortunate times. I must tell you, Mr. Whelks, we are entering the most delicate phase when it comes to managing a public affair of any sort. The unwelcome attention is waning, but it still might be brought back by any new revelation, and the gossips and the papers will be on the hunt for just that." She met his gaze now and spoke as one social veteran to another. "It is up to us to make sure nothing new arises between now and the first assembly that we do not know about."

"I understand you perfectly, Miss Thorne." Mr. Whelks glanced over his shoulder at his desk and made his decision. "I think I can assure you that should any . . . trifling matter arise that Lady Jersey herself perhaps should not be troubled with, you may expect a letter from me."

"Thank you so much, Mr. Whelks. I knew that I could count on you."

He bowed. "And thank you, Miss Thorne. It is always a privilege to work with a person of discretion and sense."

Rosalind took her leave rather more hopeful than when she had entered. With this little conversation, she now had an excuse to enter into regular communication with Mr. Whelks. She could work to loosen his hold on the information he carried, some of which was bound to be useful, if not now, then during the stormy season which was soon to come.

"Ah, Miss Thorne!"

Rosalind's head jerked up. She had been so lost in her own thoughts, she had failed to see the footman coming up the stairs, let alone the grand lady in a forest green morning dress following him.

Countess Lieven smiled brightly down at Rosalind.

"Your Grace." Rosalind remembered her manners and made her curtsy.

"I thought I might catch up with you here." The Russian countess glided up to her. "I've just come from Blanchard House, you know. You will find my card there for you when you return."

"I . . . Your Grace, that is most kind of you. I was hardly expecting—"

Countess Lieven waved her hand. "I understand Mrs. Nottingham is giving a little party to lighten up the little season."

"That she is, Your Grace."

"As she is your particular friend, I was wondering if you might hint at her that Lieven and I would adore being included. If you think she might still have room. It is such a bore to have to rearrange the table at the last minute!"

It took all of Rosalind's self-control to keep her jaw from dropping open. The countess beamed, and waited.

"I am certain Mrs. Nottingham would be delighted to include you and His Grace, the count. I will mention it to her." In fact, she would write the instant she was free from her tasks here.

The countess nodded. "Wonderful. I will expect your letter shortly. Or perhaps you will do me the favor of a call? Yes? That is also wonderful." With this she breezed past Rosalind, straight to the morning room and the other patronesses.

Rosalind stared after the departing countess. It was inconceivable that Dorothea Lieven should actually require Rosalind's help to gain any invitation. London had gone mad for all things Russian. This, added to her place among the patronesses, made the Countess Lieven one of society's most powerful and sought-after ladies. This meant only one thing. Either the countess had something she wished to say, or something she wished to hear.

And she wanted it to be well out of Lady Jersey's way. Rosalind paused. And possibly Lady Blanchard's.

CHAPTER 24

The Danger of Appearances

L'Angleterre est une nation de boutiquiers. *[England is a nation of shopkeepers.]*

—Napoleon Bonaparte

Bond Street was full to the brim with traffic, both in the streets and on the walks. There was scarcely a fortnight left before Easter week, and the all-important start of the season. The lady patronesses might not have finalized their lists yet, but there were plenty of others who had and now the fashionables were in a frenzy to complete their wardrobes.

As a result, the warehouse of Messrs. Taylor & Greene was at least as full as the streets outside. Women and men from every district of London moved between the counters, examining the samples of ribbons and patterned silk that the clerks held out for them. Once a selection was made and the price agreed upon, boys in aprons and shirtsleeves climbed ladders to bring down the bolts from their cubbyholes. The cloth was measured, cut, and wrapped in brown paper and white string while the clerk wrote out the receipt. In other quarters of the vast, sweltering building, the same scene was played out for those acquiring new lace, or for leather for gloves and boots, or for reels of thread for embroidery, beadwork, and tassels.

As it transpired, this trip had taken on a new significance for Rosalind. When they returned to Blanchard House from visiting Lady Jersey, her godmother had an additional piece of news.

"When you go shopping with Louisa Winterbourne, you must be sure to find yourself some good silk. I've gained Sarah's permission to give you one of my tickets for the opening assembly at Almack's."

"I . . . but . . ." *That's not possible. I'm little better than a servant. My family is a disgrace. I can write invitations, but I cannot attend as an equal!*

Lady Blanchard surely understood all the shocked words Rosalind could not speak aloud. She also waved them all away. "With all that has happened, do you think I could make it through that night without you? No. You will be there, and you must have something to stand up in that will pass muster with Sarah and the others. I have already made an appointment with Madame Giroux. Once you have your silk selected, she has promised a dress will be ready in time."

Rosalind advanced a few arguments, but it was a losing battle and she knew it by the determined set of her godmother's jaw. Her only choice was to swallow pride and worry, and accept. So it was that Rosalind now stood beside Louisa Winterbourne and her aunt, Mrs. Showell, at the counter with a senior clerk hurrying toward them.

"Ah, Miss Thorne!" Marcus Greene was the son of the Mr. Horace Greene, as well as head clerk. The gleam in his eye said clearly he remembered how many wealthy women Rosalind had steered toward this very spot. "How delightful to see you again! What can I do for you? Something for the young lady perhaps?" He turned his ingratiating smile on Louisa.

Louisa Winterbourne had been blessed with the family's

black hair; pale, clear skin; and bright gray eyes, although rather less of the family fortune. She was sponsored at school and at her first season by a range of female relatives who saw in her fresh beauty and the indulgence of the new duke a chance for a very good match, perhaps even a brilliant one. Louisa herself was one of those girls who seemed born for the game of society and sailed cheerfully through it all.

"Definitely something for Miss Winterbourne," said Rosalind, and was rewarded as the light of recognition sparked in the clerk's face. "And something for me as well. I hear tales of a stunning emerald green brocade you have just acquired."

She gave Marcus a moment to recover himself, and forgave him for his surprise that she should be asking for such fabric on her own behalf. "Ah, now that silk is in very limited supply and only for our most select and valued customers . . . but as it's you, Miss Thorne, I'll see what can be done."

With this faint protest, a sample of the emerald green was brought out, as well as a shimmering rose and a delicate blue far more suited to Louisa's complexion and age. All the cloths were closely inspected and haggled over. Marcus put up an excellent fight, but found himself faced with three formidable opponents, as well as the prospect of dressing not only an up-and-coming young lady connected to the Duke of Winterbourne, but someone on visiting terms with the lady patronesses. He accepted his loss gracefully and gave the order to his clerks so the silk could be measured, cut, and wrapped.

So it went with the laces and the ribbons, the Italian glass beads, and the silver bangles. It had been so long since Rosalind had been able to shop without counting each farthing in her mind, she felt a strange fear come over her with each acceptance, as if she were conducting some sort of illicit liaison right out in public. She told herself this was foolish, but the sensation would not be banished.

Nor was this her only reason to feel uneasy. As she moved between the counters with Louisa and her aunt, Rosalind glanced over her shoulder toward the edges of the crowd. Devon waited patiently near the entrance, his hands folded on his walking stick. Occasionally, she saw him engaging in casual conversation with other gentlemen who had brought their sisters and daughters to shop. At other moments he was quite alone, and watching her.

"Don't worry," murmured Louisa in knowing tones as she signed a receipt for some Belgian lace. "I've the matter in hand."

Rosalind raised an eyebrow at this, but offered no reply.

At last Aunt Showell snapped her book shut and tucked it into her black, beaded reticule. "That completes my list, Louisa," she said as the three of them made their way back to where Devon waited. "Are you ready to go? My feet ache, and I'm sure Casselmain has other things to do than squiring all of us about!"

Devon made some remark of polite denial, but Louisa turned one mischievous, Winterbourne-gray eye toward Rosalind. "Oh, but Aunt Showell, you do remember we are also invited to Mrs. Graves's theater party? I must still have something new for that and I've entirely changed my mind about the blue silk. Let's look again, shall we? Mrs. Graves is so very proper and you have the best eye for color . . ."

Still chattering, Louisa threaded her arm through her aunt's and pulled the older woman toward the nearest counter, leaving Rosalind standing beside Lord Casselmain, quite alone and unremarked on the edge of the jostling crowd.

Rosalind narrowed her eyes at Devon, who had the decency to look down at his hands and shift his stick uneasily.

"Goodness," murmured Rosalind. "One might almost suspect Miss Louisa of wanting to give us a moment in private."

Devon smiled. "You are not the only one who can arrange social matters, Miss Thorne."

"Did you buy her off with this trip?"

He chuckled uncertainly. "There was no need. Louisa likes you, and me, and she was perfectly willing to oblige when I asked her."

She doesn't want you to marry Honoria. Rosalind saw it in his face, or at least she thought she did. She must be careful of reading too much into Devon's expression.

One new dress and one shopping venture did not mean all was as it once was, or that the years since could be undone.

"Miss Thorne, I have something to ask you," said Lord Casselmain quietly. "Are you still . . . working on that matter Honoria talked to you about?"

This, of course, was the real reason that had dragged him out shopping on this raw, gray day. Rosalind was hard pressed not to blush with embarrassment at her sentimental thoughts. "Yes, I am. I have not yet discovered a satisfactory answer, however."

Devon stared out across the crowd. He located Louisa at the counter, and watched as she sent Marcus Greene after yet another bolt of cloth, this one a sprigged muslin. Apparently deciding she was at a safe enough distance, he said, "If I asked you to stop, for Honoria's sake and your own, what would you do?"

"I would wonder who you'd been talking to."

"As it happens, I've been talking to Lord Blanchard."

"Lord Blanchard?" *He'll talk to you, but not to me?* She closed her mouth firmly around the question. Of course he would. Lord Casselmain was a man of rank and understanding. She was the unwelcome and awkward spinster friend of his skittish wife, who might prove untrustworthy. Again.

Devon still wasn't looking at her. She could not tell if he was simply keeping an eye out for Louisa's return, or avoiding her gaze. "Blanchard's quite upset. The papers are saying this Watchdog Harkness has got it into his head that Jasper was murdered." Now Devon did turn to face her. "You don't seem surprised."

"Why would I be? It is, as you point out, in the papers, and it was always one of the possibilities."

"But Lord Blanchard said he told you about the bet."

"He said he thought there must be a bet, but he never told me that he found anything more about it. In truth, he's barely spoken two words to me since I came to the house."

Uncertainty flickered behind Devon's eyes, but it was quickly gone. "Rosalind . . . has this man, Harkness, bothered you?"

"He has not."

"But he has spoken to you? Did he tell you his ridiculous idea of a murder? Did you contradict it?"

"It should not be a surprise that he came to speak with me. I was there at the time, as were you," she reminded him tartly. "I imagine he'd like to speak with you as well, if you would agree."

Devon made a strangled sound deep in his throat. "Rosalind, you can't speak with this man anymore."

"Can't I?" Rosalind let her own gaze stray across the colorful crowd. Louisa had laid out some white ribbon against the sprigged fabric. "My voice seems to be working perfectly well."

"Damn . . . Rosalind, I am serious!" Devon struggled to maintain his hushed tones. "Listen, this Harkness is the youngest man ever promoted to—what was it—principal officer? He might be trying to impress his superiors, don't you see?"

"I'm afraid I don't, no."

"Now you're being deliberately obtuse," snapped Devon. "Rosalind, the man is trying to stir up trouble where there is none in order to keep his name in the papers and to justify his standing!"

Rosalind thought about the man who'd sat in her parlor, with his lively eyes and his charming smile. She thought about how easily Adam Harkness drew her out and engaged her assistance with his inquiries. Not that he'd had to work very hard. She had plenty of her own reasons for wanting to appear cooperative. With the Bow Street officer willing to talk with her, she stood a much better chance of getting the answers Honoria wanted, and of gauging whether any danger was, in fact, approaching Lady Blanchard.

Unless, of course, Adam Harkness wasn't telling her the truth.

"George Littlefield knows him," she said, to Devon and to herself. "And says he's an honest man." George did not, however, say that the accusations of bribery and collusion with criminals had ever been disproven.

"Honest men need to keep their masters happy as much as the dishonest do. You of all people know that."

"If you have something to say, Lord Casselmain, you will do me the favor of saying it straight out."

"I'm sorry, Miss Thorne. I'm losing the habit of plain speech. I am concerned about you, and so is Lord Blanchard. You say he hasn't talked to you. There's reason for that. He wasn't sure you'd listen to him, but thought I might . . . be able to convince you to be careful. If the man asks to talk with you again, you must refuse him absolutely."

"Lord Casselmain, I do not see that it is any of your business who I agree to speak with." *I am not under your protection or promise. We are barely friends anymore!*

Devon flushed scarlet and he leaned in far closer than he should have. "Of course it's my business!" he whispered angrily. "Rosalind, Harkness has been asking about your father!"

"What?"

"Blanchard told me. It's one of the reasons your godfather came to me in the first place. Apparently Harkness has got it into his head that since you were the one person in Almack's who knew all the others, including Jasper, you must have had something to do with the affair."

Rosalind closed her mouth.

"Blanchard says Harkness has found out about your father, and his debts, and is trying to trace him, and Charlotte as well."

She'd wondered why she'd heard nothing more from Mr. Harkness, or from Mr. Faulks since that day in her parlor at Little Russell Street. That could well be the reason. The room spun sharply. Rosalind pressed her hand to her mouth and forced herself to take deep breaths. "But they have—Father has—nothing to do with this."

"I know that, and so do you, but Harkness is putting together a story, do you understand?" Devon dropped his voice lower, forcing her to lean close enough to feel the heat of him against her cheeks. "Listen to me, Rosalind. I've had to deal with the courts since I inherited, trying to sort out the mess Hugh left behind. I've seen too well how they work. A clever lawyer will stand up and he'll tell a story to the bench. If the story's simple enough, and if he's enough of an orator and has enough law books in front of him, he'll be believed, whether that story's true or not." He reached out one hand and touched her, or at least the cuff of her sleeve. She knew she ought to pull away, but she did not. "You have never shied away from facts, Rosalind," Devon went on. "You need to take a hard look at your own right now. You're a debtor's daughter, who herself is short of money. You were in Almack's when you shouldn't have been at the same time a crime was committed. We're all vulnerable to scandal, Rosalind, but you're the one person who was there who has no protector."

"Lady Blanchard . . ."

"Hardly counts at this point. She's leaving London, which means her influence is all but over here, and Lord Blanchard may not be willing to let her extend what's left on your behalf. You know that, too."

Yes, I do know it. She remembered a year ago, when Lord Blanchard had stood in front of her, his hand clutching his lapel. She remembered his serious, sonorous voice explaining how he would not condemn her father to the gallows for his latest crime, but he also could not, would not, allow his name to be threatened or the peace of his house disturbed, not for anyone.

Especially not for a man who was not merely a debtor, but a forger.

Rosalind's hands remembered the light brush of the paper as Lord Blanchard laid the promissory note, the one Father had failed to burn, into her hands. It had Lord Blanchard's name on it, but he had not signed it. Father had put the false name to the bill, trusting that Blanchard would pay it off anyway.

I could have handed this to the magistrates at any time, Rosalind. I could do it now. But I won't, because despite all, you remain my goddaughter.

Forgery was a capital offense, and unlike thievery or debt, it was seldom forgiven, no matter what the rank of the condemned. If Father were found by Bow Street and the extent of his crime uncovered, he would hang.

Rosalind remembered Adam Harkness, his stillness and his sharp questions, and his talk of Peel's writings and reform and public good. She also remembered how at the time she thought he might be rather too dangerously aware of his own charm.

She closed her eyes. *Have I been nothing but a fool?* For a moment, that thought threatened to overwhelm her, but only for a moment.

"No," she said, and her eyes opened of their own accord, to

face the world around her, including Devon, who was both angry and anxious. But was all that emotion just for her?

"Something is wrong with this," she said. "It doesn't add up."

"Things don't add up in real life!" snapped Devon. "It's not one of your account books!"

"But perhaps it is."

"No, Rosalind, you have to stop! You're putting yourself at risk! What if the man decides to arrest you?"

"Well, then I shall just have to find out the truth before it comes to that, or at least a better story."

She said this placidly and now Devon wasn't just looking at her, he was staring, in open and flagrant outrage at her semblance of calm. "I beg you." His words rasped in his throat. "Don't do this. Honoria was angry when she asked you to find out about Jasper. I'll talk to her. She'll see that this can only damage you, and her. Us."

Rosalind lifted her chin so she could see between the nearest shoppers. Louisa was signing the receipt at the counter. Aunt Showell was consulting her book. They'd be back any moment. This conversation had to end. "It's not about Honoria, Devon, at least not just Honoria, and nothing you've told me changes that."

Devon swallowed, his face stricken. He watched his relations turn, and begin shouldering their way through the crowd. "Listen to me, Rosalind," he croaked. "The reason Lord Blanchard didn't tell you what he found in the betting book was he wanted to give me a chance to speak with you first. I've been delaying. I didn't . . . I hoped you would stop without my having to say."

"I don't understand." They had barely a few yards, a few seconds, left. He had to hurry. She could stop him, interrupt him. She didn't have to hear.

"I value your regard, Rosalind," whispered Devon, so softly

she could barely make out his words. "What little of it I have left. I had hoped . . . well, never mind that now." He took a deep breath and met her gaze. His mouth moved silently, shaping a single word. Rosalind was certain that word was *good-bye*.

"There is a bet in the White's book," Devon told her. "And it has Jasper's name signed to it, and mine."

CHAPTER 25

The Consequences of Memory

These gentlemen never failed to make hard terms for the borrower . . .

—Captain Rees Howell Gronow, *Recollections and Anecdotes of the Camp, the Court, and the Clubs*

Rosalind remembered very little of the carriage ride back to Blanchard House. Louisa did her best to keep up a steady stream of chatter with her aunt. In the end, however, Rosalind and Devon's mutual silence defeated her best efforts.

They arrived at Blanchard House and the driver put the step down. As courtesy dictated, Devon climbed out first to help Rosalind out. He bowed without taking his gaze from hers. He wanted her to see his pain, and his worry. He wanted her to see that he was sorry for what must come next.

"Don't make me use my name in this, Rosalind," he said. "Please. I have no wish to hurt you." Because if it came to any sort of public contest of words, it was Devon who would be believed, because he was Duke of Casselmain and the head of a family, and a gentleman. Rosalind, if she said anything that contradicted a statement of Devon's, would be left looking like a liar at best. At worst, she'd be labeled an hysteric.

"I do believe you," she murmured in response. "For all the good it does either of us."

A maid Rosalind did not know helped her off with coat and bonnet. Mrs. Kendricks was surely around somewhere. She should ask for her, but she could not muster the strength. But she had to talk to someone. She needed to find some kind anchor for all the thoughts swirling through her mind.

"Where might I find Lady Blanchard?" Rosalind asked the girl.

"I believe her ladyship is in her rooms, Miss Thorne. Shall I let her know you're asking for her?"

"No, that's all right. I'll go up myself."

But when she knocked at the door to Lady Blanchard's apartment, there was only a muffled response. Rosalind, aware she was being presumptuous, pushed the door open. The sitting room was empty, as was the boudoir. Lady Blanchard stood in her dressing room in front of her open jewelry cabinet. She held something in both hands.

"Lady Blanchard?" said Rosalind softly. "I beg your pardon. I—"

"Oh, Rosalind! I'm sorry." Lady Blanchard laid the comb back into its drawer. "You've caught me being a bit silly, I'm afraid. I managed to break the tooth of my tortoiseshell comb, and Lacey's out running an errand, something I'm sure I told her to do, and I thought I could manage to find my own replacement, only . . ." She turned to see Rosalind's face and she stopped. "My dear! What's happened?"

"I . . . I'm not sure. I . . . was out shopping with Louisa Winterbourne, and Devon . . . Lord Casselmain came as well and he, he had something to tell me and . . ."

Lady Blanchard did not let her get any further. She took Rosalind's arm and led her out into the sitting room. "Sit down, sit down." Matching action to words, she sat on the sofa, so

Rosalind could hardly remain standing. "Do you need some salts, Rosalind?"

"No. I am quite well." Rosalind swallowed against the patent lie. Temper and pride both flared. *I will control myself.* "But while we were out, Lord Casselmain told me that Lord Blanchard found a bet in the book at White's."

Lady Blanchard frowned. "Morgan said nothing to me. How—" She cut herself off. "What else did Casselmain say?"

"He said Lord Blanchard hadn't told me himself, because he thought Devon should speak first, because the wager was made by Jasper, and Devon."

Lady Blanchard went very still and very white. After a long moment she stood, and walked all the way back into her dressing room. Rosalind saw her close her jewel cabinet. By the time she returned, she was once again entirely composed.

"Thank you for telling me this, Rosalind," she said. "It explains why he did not tell me either. He would be concerned that I might let the matter slip before Casselmain had a chance to speak with you. This is very good." She spoke these words toward the doorway and the jewel cabinet. "Very good. It explains everything satisfactorily and now . . . now we can all get on with things."

"But there was more."

"What more could their possibly be!" cried Lady Blanchard. She immediately pressed her hand to her mouth. "Oh, forgive me, Rosalind. I didn't mean . . . I'm sorry."

Rosalind shook her head, indicating the outburst was of no importance. The question she had to ask now was, however. In fact, it was vital.

"Lady Blanchard, has my father contacted you since last year?"

The surprise on Lady Blanchard's face was immediate, and to Rosalind's inexpressible relief, it was genuine. "Oh my dear, what could your father have to do with this?"

"I don't know. But . . ." Forcing herself to speak calmly and clearly, Rosalind told Lady Blanchard about Devon's suspicions regarding the course of Mr. Harkness's inquiries. Lady Blanchard listened in absolute silence.

"So as you can see, I need to know if Father has contacted you looking for money, or anything else," Rosalind whispered finally. "If . . . if Lord Casselmain is right, and Mr. Harkness is looking for Father, and if he discovers that Father has been making mischief for anyone connected with me and this incident . . . I have to know."

Lady Blanchard touched the corner of one eye. "Of course you do, my dear. But you should know, Rosalind, that I have watched out for you even when you weren't under our roof." She smiled kindly. "I can say with confidence this matter has nothing to do with your father, or your sister. They have not been seen nor heard from, and if this man Harkness does try to trace them, that is what he will find. Not that there's any reason he should. Now that the wager has been found, the entire matter will be closed."

Rosalind's hands twisted in her lap. She stilled them with the force of long habit. "I want to believe that."

"Why wouldn't it be?"

"I'm not sure. But there's something. I was sure of it this morning, but now, I've been so worried about my father being dragged into this business it's driven everything out of my head." She paused again. "Lady Blanchard, that day . . . you were late coming out of Almack's. That's why I came in."

Lady Blanchard patted her hand and the consoling gesture sent a flash of irritation through Rosalind. "I was, and you cannot imagine how many times I have reproached myself for it since. I had mislaid one of my notebooks. You know how important our visiting cards are for determining who is allowed onto the subscribers lists. I stayed behind to hunt for it."

"But you said 'he' was supposed to have waited. What did you mean by that?"

"Did I say that?" Lady Blanchard blinked. "What an extraordinary thing. I don't remember. I was terribly shocked. I'm afraid I can recall nothing clearly."

She spoke smoothly and directly, without stammer or hesitation, and Rosalind felt a sensation inside her that was very close to heartbreak.

She kept her face still, and tried again. "Did you perhaps hear anything . . . untoward?"

She blinked, and for a moment, the mask slipped, but what Rosalind saw beneath was not distress. It was anger. "I heard many things," she said. "I could not begin to tell if any of them was untoward or not. Now." Lady Blanchard's normal decisiveness returned to her tone. "What you need is to lie down. I'll send Mrs. Kendricks to you with some tea."

"Thank you, but don't bother Mrs. Kendricks just yet." Rosalind saw Lady Blanchard get ready to protest and forced a smile. "I will lie down, and I promise I will ring for tea as soon as I've caught my breath."

"Excellent. You need your strength, Rosalind. There's still so much to come. I'm sorry, but it cannot be helped."

"It isn't your fault, Lady Blanchard."

She smiled again, and this time Rosalind saw the sadness in her eyes. "Go have your lie down, my dear. I'll see you later."

Rosalind returned to her rooms, but she did not lie down. Instead, she sat at her writing desk and stared out the window. The square beyond was filled with the day's traffic. Carriages, wagons, and persons of all kinds and classes on foot passed to and fro, all of them doubtlessly grateful for the sunshine the day most unexpectedly afforded.

Rosalind, though, saw all this only distantly. In her mind,

she was listening to Lady Blanchard talk about how she'd been late coming out of Almack's because she was looking for a missing notebook. It was perfectly believable. Lists, books, and letters—they not only regulated the social world, but also defined it. They told the tales of money, of welcome and hospitality, plans and hopes and dreams. They told of wins and losses and pending questions to be settled by future events. Even Mrs. Willis had her little book of notes of things to do and watch over. And Mr. Harkness had his. The lady patronesses certainly each had their own.

Rosalind remembered all the books and piles of papers in Mr. Whelks's office, and the steady, methodical way he wrote out the voucher cards. She remembered the solid hour she'd spent updating Lady Jersey's visiting book with the names of the women who wanted to secure their entrée to Almack's. She remembered the legions of matrons and daughters that had paraded through Lady Blanchard's sitting room in the past several days, to drink tea and try to find out if they would still be granted admission to the rooms, where they believed they could find the makings of a brilliant future, or at least a secure one, free of the least possibility of a drafty Bloomsbury flat and eggs boiled over the sitting room fire. Or worse.

She thought about the book at White's again, and Devon's declaration, and her hands remembered the touch of a paper, and her eyes remembered the sight of a signature and a promise of payment, and the revelation of a hanging offense.

And with that Rosalind knew what had killed Jasper Aimesworth. Not who, not why, but what.

And she remembered something else. It was another day like this, gray and sad and strange. She was standing in a lady's dressing room then, only this one was her mother's. Mother was applying her rouge, Rosalind recalled. She carefully rubbed the pale pink ointment into her skin and leaned forward to examine the effect in her mirror, while Rosalind attempted to explain how they should go at once to their friends, if any friends would consent to receive them.

"I will not run away as if something was wrong," Mother said. "I've told you a hundred times, Rosalind. Your father will be back shortly. I expect a letter from him with a bank draft momentarily."

"Mother, I don't think he is coming back," said Rosalind. "At least, not in time."

"I won't hear it, Rosalind. He would not have taken Charlotte if he did not mean to return."

"Perhaps he means to, but what if he can't? The men downstairs . . . they say he owes a great deal of money."

Mother held up a peach ribbon against her cheek. "This one will do, Marie." She passed it to the girl so it could be threaded into her curls.

"Mother, if we can't pay, they'll take the furniture."

"I can't understand you when you talk like that, Rosalind. Tell Phipps to deal with them."

"Phipps is gone, Mother."

"Then tell him when he gets back. Marie, I need my coral necklace."

But Phipps wasn't coming back any more than Father was. The only ones who stayed behind when Rosalind had to explain there was no money for wages on the quarter day were Marie, Cook, and Mrs. Kendricks, and she was no longer certain about Mrs. Kendricks. The housekeeper had not been seen all morning.

"Mother . . ."

"Oh, stop whining, Rosalind!" she snapped. "How many times must I say it? You will accord yourself with calm and dignity in front of me or you will not be allowed in this room at all." She turned toward Rosalind, and for the first time Rosalind saw the wild, empty look in Mother's eyes that would become the stuff of her nightmares. "Your father and Charlotte will return!" She shrieked and slammed both hands on the table. "Whatever *you* have done to drive them away, they will not desert *me*! They *will* be back for me!"

Rosalind fled. Out in the corridor she buried her head in her hands, and she shook from fear and from cold and from the knowledge that she was finally and entirely alone.

Eventually, the tremors eased, and Rosalind was able to straighten up. She went downstairs, because somehow the sneering men below had become less terrifying than her mother.

The reek of tobacco and onions filled the entrance hall. The bailiff's men sat on the velveteen sofa, playing cards on a packing crate.

"What will you take?" she asked them.

One of the men pulled out a wrinkled paper and held it to her. She looked at the column of figures. She read them all, but none of them made any sense. She had become like Mother up in her boudoir. Her mind simply would not hold any more horror.

A determined pounding rang through the hall. Rosalind jumped and turned toward the door. One of the bailiffs spat on the floor. Her heart hammering, Rosalind went to see who this new person might be. On the stoop stood a man in black coat and cravat, and next to him, like an angel from heaven, stood Lady Blanchard, with Mrs. Kendricks right behind her.

"Now, none o' that!" cried the bailiff's least shaven and greasiest man. "We was here first."

Lady Blanchard frowned. "Mr. Murrill." She gestured to the black-coated man. "You will deal with *those*. Rosalind, my dear." Lady Blanchard took both her hands and pressed them firmly. "You are not to worry. I'm here now and it will all be taken care of."

Pride fled in an instant and it was all Rosalind could do to keep from bursting into tears as Lady Blanchard sailed past the bailiff's men. "Your mother is upstairs, I assume? Excellent. We will go straight up."

"She won't hear me," said Rosalind as she hurried to catch up to her godmother. "I've tried to tell her what's happening, but she won't leave her room and she says she doesn't understand a word I say."

"Let's see what we can do."

What Lady Blanchard did was spend an hour pretending they were waiting for tea that wasn't going to come, ignoring the fact that the bailiffs downstairs, under Mr. Murrill's supervision, were carting away the furnishings and the carpets to which they were entitled. But in the end, Lady Blanchard had somehow managed to persuade Mother to come stay in the country with her, just for the week, until Sir Reginald came back.

"He is coming back," Mother said firmly. "He will not abandon me. I have kept up his appearances for twenty years, I have kept his house, kept his name, kept his children. Everything has always been perfect, no matter what he has done. He *owes* me for my years!"

Lady Blanchard did not argue. She told Mrs. Kendricks to pack up Mother's dresses and whatever Charlotte had left behind. Her godmother then led Mother down to her carriage to take her out "for some air," while Rosalind loaded her jewelry up into Mrs. Kendrick's bag, and the pocket under her skirt, so the housekeeper could storm out the back door, announcing loudly that she wouldn't stay in such a house a moment longer.

When Mother was installed into one of the guest rooms in the Blanchards' rambling country house, Rosalind went into Lady Blanchard's parlor to try to find the words to thank her. This was when she received her first lesson about Deportment When Abandoned.

"You may cry tonight, Rosalind," Lady Blanchard told her. "As much as you want. Tomorrow, however, that is over. It is you who must look after yourself and your mother, and that is not a state that allows any show of weakness. Do you understand?"

Rosalind understood. She went back to her room and wept until past midnight with Mrs. Kendricks holding her close. After that, she never shed another tear over her circumstances, never spoke a word in anger. At least, not where anyone could see.

Rosalind smoothed her hair back from her brow. *Why am I thinking about this now?*

But she knew. It was because of the relief in Lady Blanchard's face that accompanied the sorrow when she heard about the betting book. That should have seemed perfectly natural, of course. Anyone would be relieved that an unpleasant episode was over and life could continue on as normal.

But this was not the sole source of that relief, Rosalind was sure.

Men lie, Miss Thorne. Mr. Harkness's words came back to Rosalind with stunning clarity. Rosalind clenched both fists. *I will not hear you, Mr. Harkness.*

She could stop this right now, before it brought down any more unpleasantness. She had the perfect excuse. She could stand loyally beside those who had helped her, and never have it go any further. She could protect names and homes and family, by simply remaining still and silent. It was what was expected. It was the done thing. Nothing more, and nothing less.

It would simply mean keeping those same secrets that had made a ruin of her life. It would simply mean accepting that Lady Blanchard had perfectly good, personal reasons for lying when she told Rosalind she did not recall any words she spoke of Jasper Aimesworth's corpse.

Rosalind pulled the bell rope, then opened the writing desk.

Mrs. Kendricks arrived while she was signing her name to a fresh note:

Dear Mr. Harkness:

I have just received word from a normally reliable source that a wager regarding Almack's was found in the book at White's with Jasper Aimesworth's name attached. Have you been able to confirm this fact? It is important that I should know as soon as possible. I suspect some falsehood.

R. Thorne

"Mrs. Kendricks, I have a pair of letters that must go by hand. This one is to Mr. Harkness at Bow Street. The other is for Miss Aimesworth." She paused. "It is imperative that Lady Edmund not know about it, or about any reply."

She waited for Mrs. Kendricks to question her, but her servant just nodded. "You may leave it with me, miss. I believe it is my half day. I shall go visit my cousin Mrs. Neill."

Rosalind smiled. "Yes, of course, I had forgotten your half day."

She dipped her quill into the ink and began to write again.

Dear Honoria:

I may have made a significant error in judgment. I need you to come with me to search Jasper's rooms. Tell your mother you want to visit his grave . . .

Custom might refuse a woman the chance to attend a loved one's burial, but she was perfectly free to visit the grave after it was covered over. And Mrs. Kendrick's gossiping inquiries among the Tamwell House servants had yielded one piece of information of primary importance: the location of Jasper's bachelor rooms.

> *. . . and when she refuses to let you go alone, allow yourself to be talked into taking me with you.*
>
> *Let me know when. Mrs. Kendricks is waiting for your answer.*
>
> R.

Men lie, said Mr. Harkness once again from her memory.

Men lie, agreed Rosalind in the silence of her mind. *And they are not the only ones.*

CHAPTER 26

A Bachelor Establishment

*Now, it is impossible that a man who composes any ethics
at all, big or little should admire a thief . . .*
—Thomas De Quincy, *On Murder Considered as
One of the Fine Arts*

The response Mrs. Kendricks had brought back from Bow Street
and Mr. Harkness was brief, and completely unenlightening.

"The . . . officer says to thank you for your communication,
and that you will hear from him shortly."

Unfortunately this unsatisfactory message arrived on the
heels of another that was much more urgent. It came from Honoria, and was delivered to Mrs. Kendricks's hands at the back
door of Blanchard House by a rather greasy porter who tried to
barter for an additional sixpence, even though Honoria had
already paid him.

Honoria was as sparing in her words as Mr. Harkness. The
note read:

Have convinced her. Come tomorrow, one o'clock.

H.A.

Rosalind folded the paper and bit her lip. She had hoped to have Mr. Harkness with them on this particular errand, but with what Devon had told her about the officer's inquiries, perhaps it was for the best. If Devon had told the truth and Mr. Harkness was tracing her father, the result could be a disaster the like of which she had never imagined.

Unless, of course, Devon was trying to frighten her into giving up her inquiries. Rosalind's cheeks burned at the thought. Mr. Harkness had said a number of things, but at least he had not suggested Rosalind should hide away from whatever storm was to come.

The night passed and morning came. Rosalind sat beside Lady Blanchard to help receive early callers, most of them ladies anxiously inquiring about the state of the Almack's voucher lists and trying to find out if the opening assembly would be held as scheduled. Lady Blanchard answered them all patiently and sent them away much relieved. Most of them, at any rate. Mrs. Fort—who'd wanted to know if any vouchers had unexpectedly gone wanting, and could "dear Lady Blanchard" assist her to any that might have been left by ladies having been summarily dropped from the lists—was sent away with a flea in her ear.

Fortunately for both Rosalind and Honoria, Lady Blanchard had a letter she wished Rosalind to deliver to Lady Edmund. She said it was merely "a request to call."

"It's time we began our campaign," Lady Blanchard told Rosalind. "She has to make her impressions before anything . . . more occurs."

The receipt of Lady Blanchard's letter served to keep Lady Edmund's temper and her suspicions distracted while the two young women departed in a hired carriage, ostensibly to travel to the church yard and Jasper's grave. Her godmother had given Rosalind the perfect freedom to order the Blanchard carriage whenever she wished. Rosalind, however, did not want to risk Preston reporting back to his employers about where she and Honoria had actually gone.

Although enough time had passed that Honoria could be considered out of the first stage of mourning for her brother, she donned her heaviest black dress and a veil that entirely covered her face. But the moment the carriage drew away from the Aimesworth front door, Honoria threw the veil back so she could lean forward.

"Did Casselmain tell you?" she demanded. "About the betting book?"

"He did," Rosalind admitted.

"Jasper was hardly above foolish wagers," Honoria was saying. "I remember once he told me he kept a book for friends at university over a course of black beetle races. Apparently some of the students kept a whole stable of the insects, and a stud book and I don't know what all. Beetles! Men!" It was impossible to tell which she thought less of at that moment. When she spoke again, her tone was much softer and less certain. "Was I wrong? Was it all really an accident?"

"I don't know yet. That's why I still very much want to see Jasper's rooms." Devon may have confessed to making the bet, or at least knowing about its existence, but he was still hiding something important. In that, he was acting in common with Lord and Lady Blanchard, and now possibly Mr. Harkness.

Rosalind felt as if she held the shards of a stained glass window in her hands, and she was trying to piece it all together without cutting herself.

Not surprisingly, many of the *haut ton*'s young bachelors kept their rooms in the vicinity of St. James's Street and its famous "club row." The driver brought their carriage to a halt in front of a line of spruce, terraced houses. Honoria gave him an extra half crown to wait and climbed down behind Rosalind, drawing her veil across her face as she did so. Together they picked their way across the slush-covered walk. The door of the house in front of them opened, as if in welcome, but it was only to expel a pair of staggering young blades in tight white breeches and high-collared coats. The pair leaned hard against each other, laughing over something. As they passed the women at the foot of the stairs, one of them turned to the other and mumbled some remark that brought on a new fit of hilarity.

Honoria and Rosalind gripped each other's arms and hurried inside.

Inside was no great improvement, for the house had an over-used feeling about it. The cold and the damp had settled in, and neither the walls nor the stairs were as clean as they should have been. The entrance hall was cramped and bare, with white-washed walls and plain matting on the floor. There was no porter or footman on duty to greet them and learn their business.

In truth, it was a surprisingly dreary place, and not at all what Rosalind would have expected for Jasper to choose as a residence. Perhaps he had friends here.

"It should be up the stairs," said Honoria, and the pair of them began climbing.

The wooden stairs creaked badly beneath their half boots, and in the corridor below, a scarred door opened and a man with beady eyes peered up at them.

"If you're looking for Mr. Aimesworth, he ain't gonna be there," he announced. "Ain't been there for weeks."

Rosalind laid a hand on Honoria's wrist, signaling her to keep silent. "Can you say where might we find him?"

Like the building, the man was far from spotless. Grease stained his waistcoat and his shirtsleeves. His black cravat was barely tied and his collar gaped under his double chin. "You *might* try the churchyard. They do be sayin' he's gone and done a header in Almack's, over a girl or some such." He turned his head and spat on the hallway matting. "Or maybe two such."

"Mr. Aimesworth was my brother," said Honoria icily. "We've come to see about clearing out his rooms."

"Brother, is it?" The man, who was probably the landlord, narrowed his dark, glittering eyes. He also let those eyes travel up the pair of them from hems to bonnets, and then all the long way back down again. "Well, maybe that's so and maybe it ain't. Strikes me as funny you bein' his sister and not knowin' the rooms 'ave already been cleaned out."

What? The words hit hard enough to stagger Rosalind and Honoria both.

"When was this?" Honoria clutched at the stair railing. "By who?"

The landlord leaned his shoulder against the threshold. "By the family," he drawled. "Which you would know naturally, you bein' 'is *sister* and all." He looked her up and down again.

Which, for Honoria, was clearly the upper limit. She stormed down the stairs, leaving Rosalind to trail behind.

"Listen to me, you odious little man." Honoria poked the landlord with one sharp, gloved finger. "I am Honoria Aimesworth and the upstairs rooms in this hovel belonged to my brother, Jasper, and our father, *Lord* Edmund Aimesworth." This was not strictly true, but this did not seem to be the time to interrupt. "If you've allowed some thief to come in and make off with his possessions, I will see you in dock. I've no doubt you were well paid to open that door"—she jabbed her finger up toward the door in question—"with your keys!"

"Should I fetch the constables, Miss Aimesworth?" inquired Rosalind softly.

That finally wiped the grin off the landlord's round face.

"'Ere!" He squeaked. "There's no call for none a' that! 'Ow was I to know? Cove is dead, other cove shows up and says he's sent by the family, 'as the talk and all the names."

"Did he have the keys?" asked Rosalind. The landlord didn't answer, a fact which Honoria was quick to notice.

"Then you did let him in! You let him in without keys or written permission to rob my brother!"

"I did no such thing! 'E 'ad a letter! With a seal and all."

"What did it say?" asked Rosalind. Again, the man made no answer. "You didn't bother to actually read this letter, did you?"

"I didn't take no money from nobody," the man growled. "Ain't my fault the family leaves the young gent's personals lying about to get nicked, 'specially when anybody an' 'is uncle knows the gent's dead."

Honoria drew herself up to her loftiest height. "I am going to see my brother's rooms, and once I do, you had better hope I don't change my mind about sending my maid for the constables!"

"I didn't do nofink wrong!" bellowed the landlord.

"And who do you think they'll believe?" snapped Honoria. "You or me? Now, get out of my sight!"

The man growled like a sulky dog, and he eyed them both. He spat for good measure and muttered several rude words. He also shut himself back in his room.

Honoria grabbed her hems and stomped up the stairs. Rosalind followed closely, and glanced frequently over her shoulder, in case the landlord, or anyone else, decided to follow. Honoria's hand was shaking as she put the key in the lock.

Rosalind had been in many different sorts of rooms, both public and private, but never a bachelor's establishment. Although she knew it to be entirely ridiculous, it was not without a certain trepidation she entered these.

Jasper's rooms smelled of damp and dust, with no trace of the homey scents of candlewax or coal smoke left. The only light in the rooms was the gray, watery daylight that streamed through the windows, but it was more than enough to show them that the rooms had been stripped clean. Only the movable furniture remained: chairs, desks, the table in the dining room, the bed, and so forth. One lamp stood on the mantle, and a pair of silver candlesticks on the table in the dining room. But all the coverings had been stripped away, and the clothing emptied from closet and drawer.

"Who did this?" cried Honoria as she strode through the pillaged rooms.

Rosalind stayed in place, turning around slowly. This was wrong. Even the curtains from the bed and the windows had been taken. The dresser drawers gaped open. The floors were entirely without carpets. She stared at the bare room, and turned to stare again from a fresh angle. She thought of Mr. Harkness, and she wondered what he would see, from his stance as patrol officer.

"I'll have that landlord in dock, I swear I will!" Honoria shouted. "He probably works hand in glove with some foul pawnbroker!"

There. Honoria had said it, and now Rosalind understood.

"He probably does, but that's not who did this."

"I don't understand you." Honoria pulled her veil aside so Rosalind could see her angry glower.

"What sort of thief would take the bed curtains and leave silver candlesticks?" she said. "Did Jasper write letters?" Rosalind crossed quickly to the writing desk and lifted its lid. She also peered into the gaping drawers. There was one sheet of foolscap, and one broken quill. "A pawnshop wouldn't be interested in letters, or bills or any other correspondence, but somebody's emptied this desk. These rooms were cleared out to make it look like the work of thieves, but I think someone was trying to find some incriminating notebook or letters." She stood back and gestured toward the drawers, inviting Honoria to take a closer look if she so chose. Not that Honoria knew as much as she about what pawnbrokers would and would not buy. "And though that fellow downstairs knows Jasper's dead, he hasn't rented these rooms out again. That means someone has paid the rent at least until the end of the month." *And he thinks they might come back*, but she decided to keep that to herself.

Honoria closed her mouth. She also turned to stare about the rooms, seeing them with fresh eyes, and with some small trace of fear beneath her anger.

"We need to conduct a thorough search," Rosalind said firmly. "Something might have been left behind."

Honoria nodded. Rosalind made sure the door was locked, in case the landlord should change his mind and come to try to chase them out, or call the constables himself. That done, she turned her attention back to the desk while Honoria disappeared into the boudoir. Rosalind ran her hands through all the pigeonholes and pulled out the side drawers, but there was nothing. Then, when she pulled out the center drawer, a grimy piece of yellow paper fluttered down.

Rosalind leaned the drawer up against the desk, and claimed the paper. It was a receipt from Messrs. Jacobs, Thomas & Walsh, Jewelers, for a silver hair comb set with garnets and freshwater pearls, to be delivered to 12 Thurlough Square. The bill had been signed by Jasper Aimesworth.

The young maid Becky Lewis had been sure Jasper Aimesworth had a woman he didn't want his parents to know about. And here, to all appearances, was proof of that. Rosalind thought of the keys that Honoria had returned to her. Was one to a door in Thurlough Square?

Rosalind straightened up and turned. There was no sound from the boudoir, not even the rustle of skirts or the sound of footsteps. Frowning, she crossed into the other room. Honoria stood facing the bare dressing table, her head bowed and her fingertips resting on the polished surface. Her black gloves were smeared with pale dust, as were her skirts.

"Honoria?" said Rosalind, but the other girl shook her head.

"I'm trying to picture Jasper in here," she said quietly. "I'm trying to see him living in this place and drinking with those . . . persons on the stairs. But I can't. They've left nothing of him at all."

Rosalind stepped closer. She wished she were friends with Honoria. If they were friends, she could embrace her, or at least put a consoling hand on hers. But they were not friends, even though they did not seem to be exactly rivals anymore. There were no rules for them, and Rosalind did not know what to do.

"It will get easier to bear," Rosalind said. "I promise you."

"How would you know?" Honoria muttered.

"I've been left behind as well. I know what it's like."

Honoria sniffed, but she also lifted her head. For a moment their eyes met. Rosalind thought Honoria might say something, about the past, about the circumstances that brought their separate lives crashing back together. But she only asked, "Have you found anything?"

"It seems Jasper bought a gift." Rosalind showed her the yellowing bill.

"More than one." Honoria's hand had hidden a torn scrap of paper on the dressing table. She gave it to Rosalind. "I found it under the bed."

It was clearly a piece of another receipt, similar to the one Rosalind had found in the desk. The words "—*ver gilt*" were still visible, and a bit of Jasper's signature.

"Becky Lewis said he was seeing a woman." Rosalind held the receipts up to the window so she could examine them more closely. "And now it seems we have her address."

"We should go find the creature," said Honoria, some semblance of her usual spirit returning to her voice. "She could well be the thief the landlord's working with."

Rosalind shook her head. "I doubt that." She folded both the receipt and the scrap away in her reticule.

"Why?"

"This." Rosalind gestured about the room. "Stealing an entire apartment's worth of belongings is an enormous risk for someone who has so far kept herself hidden from the family. It took organization, and outlay. Not only would that letter have to be forged, but carters and porters would have to be hired." *Clearing out a house takes staff, and time. I've seen it done.* "A woman who can command jewelry and gifts from one young man would be no more likely to endanger herself that way than a thief would be to leave those candlesticks. She'd simply move on to another protector."

"But she still might know something."

"She might," Rosalind agreed slowly. But there was something else in the back of her mind, something she'd half forgotten, or perhaps half remembered. "Regardless, we should get out of here, in case I was wrong about that landlord, and he is working with a gang of thieves. They might not stop at burglary."

Honoria looked ready to take on an entire gang of hooligans. Fortunately, however, her practical side prevailed. She made no further complaint, but followed Rosalind out of the empty rooms and down the stairs.

But it was when they were being assisted into the carriage by the very relieved-looking driver that a fresh thought struck Rosalind.

"Wait here," she said to Honoria and the driver. Before either could question her, she hurried back to the house and banged on the scarred door the landlord had come out from previously. She heard a shout inside, which she took as an affirmative, and pushed her way through.

The landlord looked up from a battered desk surrounded by packing crates and papers.

"What's this?" he demanded. "You've 'ad your look, you and your mistress can be on your way. Sister, my eye." He spat again. "I know the quality, and I say she's—"

"She's his sister and a baronet's daughter and I'm the one who is keeping her from calling the watch," Rosalind replied evenly. "Now, tell me quickly, do you remember anything about the persons who came to clear the rooms? Could you tell me what he, or they, looked like?"

The landlord lowered his brows until they almost touched his bulbous nose, and for a moment Rosalind feared she'd overplayed her hand.

But then, he snorted. "Couldn't forget 'im. All in black, 'e was, like 'e'd just come from the undertakers, and thin as a darning needle. Not to mention bein' the tallest cove you ever clapped eyes on."

CHAPTER 27

The Evidence of the Betting Book

In the zenith of his popularity, he might be seen in the bow window of White's Club, surrounded by the lions of the day, laying down the law.

—Captain Rees Howell Gronow, *Anecdotes of the Camp, the Court, and the Clubs*

"Well, well." Sanderson Faulks carefully folded up Miss Thorne's letter of introduction. "I confess I am astonished, Mr. Harkness."

"I would not have thought a man such as yourself would be easily astonished, Mr. Faulks."

The first word that had come to Harkness's mind when he met Sanderson Faulks was "affected." Clearly one of the dandy set, his hair was brilliantly anointed with the macassar oil George Byron had made popular, and if his white breeches and bottle green coat had been any tighter, he would have asphyxiated. His hands were the whitest Harkness had ever seen. It might be a hazard of his profession, but Harkness distrusted any man whose hands were too clean. It usually meant they spent a great deal of time washing off the stains.

The rooms Faulks occupied were a match for the man. Harkness had never seen such a collection of paintings and statuary outside a public gallery. The furniture was all curved and carved

and curlicued, with enamel panels, marble tops, and an astound-
ing variety of marquetry decorations. It was all also so delicate
that Harkness felt afraid to move, lest he accidentally break
some priceless artifact.

"Oh, but I enjoy my astonishments," said Faulks, who in
contrast to his guest seemed perfectly at ease in these elaborate
and overcrowded environs. "Gives me something to wake up for
in the morning. Now." He steepled his fingers, and regarded
Harkness over their neatly kept tips. "Miss Thorne begs that I
offer you every assistance. Frankly, I had not thought to hear
that from her."

"Why not?"

"Because of her very close connection to Lady Blanchard, of
course. I would not think any lady patroness would want anything other than to close the books on Jasper Aimesworth."

"I am not employed by the lady patronesses," Harkness
reminded him. "And I understand from the papers that Lady
Blanchard is resigning her position."

In fact, the papers had been talking of little else since Sunday.
Harkness did not as a rule pay much attention to the society
columns, even at those times when they took up much of the front
pages. At the moment, however, he regarded reading them as part
of his inquiries. He also found himself looking longingly toward
the time when he could go back to his blissful ignorance of the
pending details of dresses and dances that didn't exist yet.

"Yes, the famed resignation. That does rather force a change
in perspective," Mr. Faulks acknowledged. "Still, when one leaves,
one generally wants to be sure there's something to come back to."

"Generally," Harkness agreed.

"Yes. So. Astonishing, as I say." Faulks offered no further
explanation but tucked Miss Thorne's letter into one of the
pigeonholes in his elaborately carved desk. "Still, I have seldom

ever refused Miss Thorne a favor, and I don't care to refuse this one. When shall we go to White's?"

"The sooner the better, as far as I'm concerned." It had been far too long since Miss Thorne had written out the letter of introduction, but the delay was unavoidable. Even when he was hired for private work, a principal officer's time could never be devoted to just one matter. There were only eight of them, after all, and with London, Westminster, and all the provinces clamoring for their attention, it was perhaps inevitable that the matter of Jasper Aimesworth slipped in importance. Harkness had to give testimony at court, assist the day patrol that was looking into the matter of the robbery of the Tassel Street Bank, and spend time with his fellow principal officer, Stephen Lavender, to help with the particularly tricky coinage case that had landed on his desk.

But yesterday a second letter arrived from Miss Thorne, this one hand-carried by Mrs. Kendricks. Harkness did not, however, feel any particular need to inform Mr. Faulks of its contents. At least, not yet.

"As it happens, you find me entirely at leisure. We can go at once if you like." Faulks pulled the embroidered and fringed bell rope and summoned an ancient valet.

Faulks's solemn and efficient manservant bundled the dandy into a cape lined and trimmed with sable and gloves of leather and sealskin. An ebony stick with a gold handle in the shape of a leaping stag completed his walking costume. By the time he was suitably attired, his well-sprung and comfortable barouche had been brought 'round to the front door.

The men rode in easy silence for a time, which gave Harkness a chance to study the man across from him. If this made Faulks uneasy, he gave no sign. As little as Harkness cared to admit it, it was taking him longer than usual to get the measure of the man beneath the highly polished surface. Faulks was slippery but not, Harkness thought, in the way of the habitual charlatan or aesthete.

"If I may, Mr. Faulks, how did you come to be a member at White's?" asked Harkness eventually. "I understood that . . . new men were not entirely welcome there."

Faulks chuckled. "I know I may not look it, Mr. Harkness, but I am a member of the old country gentry in very good standing. My family's lands are broad and only moderately encumbered. In addition, none of us has done a lick of work since the time of Charles the Second, and I have done my utmost to keep up our reputation for idleness and aristocratic display." He touched the sable collar of his cloak. "It also happens that I can be a useful fellow to know. I'm damnably lucky at dice, and yet very easy about repayments."

"You mean that men owe you money."

Mr. Faulks touched the side of his nose.

"And may I ask, how it is you came to know Miss Thorne?"

"Her father introduced us," said Faulks quietly.

Harkness raised his brows, and waited for the man to elaborate, but he did not. Instead, he peered out the carriage window. "Ah! Here we are."

White's had started its existence as a chocolate house, but had rapidly evolved into one of the most notorious of London's social clubs. On any given night, thousands of pounds might change hands at its famous gaming tables, and frequently did.

Not even the bitter winds outside could make Sanderson Faulks hurry. The man sauntered up the club's steps as if it were the mildest spring day. He waved his cane toward the liveried porter at the door, and doffed his hat to hand to the similarly attired boy who waited in the marble lobby to receive them.

"Now, as you aren't a member, it's quite against the rules for you to be in the club rooms," Faulks said as Harkness let himself be helped out of his blue great coat. "But you wait in the stranger's room and I'll see about having the book sent down."

"If you don't mind, I'd rather you sent down a waiter instead."

Faulks raised one eyebrow. "Any waiter in particular?"

"A boy named Toby Fergus."

"You intrigue me, Mr. Harkness. Again. All right. I'll have him sent through."

Faulks sauntered across the lobby to have a word with an older serving man who Harkness put down as the club's steward. The steward bowed and moved off, his face betraying neither surprise nor curiosity.

The stranger's room was off the entrance hall, about where the parlor would be in a private home. It was a sumptuous room, replete with gilding and stylish furniture, obviously meant to impress visitors as to the wealth and taste possessed by the club's members. There were newspapers and leather-bound books scattered about on the tables to amuse anyone waiting. There was no one to take advantage of this, however, except for one young lady who was perched on one of the chairs. She did not read, but sat with her hands tightly clasping her reticule, as if she feared she might be robbed at any moment. Harkness bowed, and she instantly dropped her gaze and blushed furiously.

As Faulks returned to Harkness's side, he also took note of the young woman. He touched Harkness's elbow in apology and went over to make his bow. The girl looked up at him, and Harkness saw she was on the edge of tears. Faulks whispered something in her ear and patted her hand. In answer, she clutched at his sleeve, and a spasm that might have been either distaste or anger crossed the dandy's face. Without another word, the girl got to her feet and hurried from the room.

Harkness raised an eyebrow. Faulks just shook his head.

"There's no excuse for a gentleman to treat a girl like that shabbily. None at all."

Before Harkness could ask another question, a short, slim young man in the club livery stepped into the room. He looked at Harkness, and he blanched.

"Hello, Fergus," said Harkness quietly.

"H . . . h . . ."

Harkness held up his hand. "Easy does it, Toby. You're not in trouble, at least none that I know about." For a minute, Harkness thought the boy might faint dead away from relief. "But this gentleman and I need the betting book brought down here. Quiet like. He's a member, so it's all right, isn't it? Will you oblige?"

"I . . . um . . ." Fergus's eyes narrowed and flickered back and forth. Considering the number and types of things that had once upon a time found their way into Tiny Toby's pockets, temporarily pinching a book shouldn't be a stretch of his skills. Fergus's father had been a poacher, and Toby had helped out the family by picking a few pockets on market days. That family, incidentally, had helped hide Red Lowell and his men a time or two. When Lowell was discovered in the Fergus's hut, Old Fergus had begged Harkness to let his boy, then only twelve years old, get away.

There were times when Harkness considered justice and the law to be separate matters. Young Toby did get away and Old Fergus went quietly to his fate, aware he'd done what he could for his son at the last.

Harkness watched the memory of all this flicker behind Toby's eyes. "Yes, sir," the young man said. "Since he's a member and all. Will you come up, Mr. Faulks?"

Faulks nodded and Harkness bowed and settled down to wait, patiently watching the hands of the case clock in the corner.

They had not advanced five full minutes before Toby and Faulks once more descended the stairs. The steward barely glanced in the young waiter's direction as the pair entered the stranger's room and Faulks brought the book out from under his coat.

"It'll be on the last page or so," Faulks said as Harkness turned over pages covered with all manner of handwriting, some of it barely legible. "Things get quiet out of season."

He was right. At the very bottom of the second to the last page waited a scrawled note:

Jasper Aimesworth wagers to five pounds, even odds, to Devon Winterbourne, Duke of Casselmain, that he can enter Almack's Assembly Rooms without having obtained a voucher or ticket.

There were the two signatures and a date.

"That would seem to settle the matter," said Faulks. He sounded a little disappointed.

Toby glanced nervously toward the entrance hall, probably looking out for the steward.

Harkness didn't bother to respond to either of them. On the strength of Miss Thorne's brief letter, he had fully expected the wager to be here. It was the rest of the book that interested him now. Harkness flipped through the pages, skimming them as quickly as he could decipher them. Some of the handwriting was so atrocious that it could only have been laid down by some very drunken men. God in heaven, what a thing it was to have money! There were bets on elections, marriages, births, deaths, and duels, as well as horse races and other of the more usual games. There were bets on the color of waistcoats, on the weather. Bets had been registered for ladies as well as club members.

Toby shifted his weight and glanced toward the hall again. Harkness closed the betting book and handed it back to the waiter. "That'll do." Clearly and openly relieved, the boy took the ledger, bowed, and hurried away.

Harkness didn't bother to look after him. He pulled his own book from his pocket and made a few notes.

Sanderson Faulks consulted his gold pocket watch against the time displayed on the case clock. "May I take it you are finished, Mr. Harkness? I'd like to get back home in time to dress for dinner. Can I drop you anywhere?"

"If you're passing by Bow Street, I would take it kindly, Mr. Faulks."

"Certainly."

The barouche was duly sent for and their coats brought. When they had settled themselves once more in the carriage, Faulks regarded Harkness with his lazy gaze. "Well, Mr. Harkness. You clearly didn't need my help to get into White's, or to get your hands on the book. Why did you come find me?"

"I am interested in Miss Thorne's friends."

"I believe I could take that very much amiss, sir."

"You shouldn't."

"I shouldn't yet, you mean." Faulks presented him with a narrow, false smile. Underneath his veneer, Faulks was an intelligent man, and his luster disguised a certain darkness. Probably he was more dangerous with that stick than most people would imagine.

"May I ask if you learned what you wanted to know?" inquired Faulks.

"I did, as it happens." *Including the fact that the betting book can be easily requested by a member, or simply filched by a waiter.*

"Intriguing." Faulks turned his stick in both hands, as if examining its surface for fresh scars. "Mr. Harkness, I am due to attend what I expect to be a terribly dull party. I wonder if you'd care to accompany me?"

The question was so unexpected, Harkness didn't have a chance to guard his expression, and Faulks laughed.

"Oh, don't worry, Harkness. You're not my sort, and neither, I expect, am I yours. This is purely a friendly invitation."

"And why would you invite me to a party?"

"I told you. I expect it will be terribly dull. You will add interest."

"I'm not an entertainer, Mr. Faulks."

Mr. Faulks bowed his head in acknowledgment of this stern truth. "No, you're not. But you are circumscribed in your movements by the little ways of society. I offer to open a door or two. It's one of my functions, as Miss Thorne herself could assure you."

"Again, why?"

"I told you before, I cannot bear to see men of rank treating women shabbily. It is coarse and undignified. I suspect Lord Casselmain has treated Miss Thorne shabbily, and while I cannot call him out on that matter, neither do I have to sit idly by."

"I shall consider it, Mr. Faulks."

"That, sir, is all I ask." Faulks smiled his thin, knowing, false smile.

CHAPTER 28

A Meeting with His Superiors

He seems to have impressed every one—thieves included—
with an idea of his infinite experience . . .

—Percy Hetherington Fitzgerald, *Chronicles of the*
Bow Street Police Office

As matters transpired, Harkness was soon presented with the opportunity to take Lord Casselmain's measure for himself.

After their informative sojourn into "clubland," Sanderson Faulks dropped Harkness off at the Bow Street station. He hadn't got halfway across the ward room when one of the office messengers—a man who went by the extremely unfortunate name of Charlie Crook—came up to him.

"Mr. Townsend's in his office, Mr. Harkness," said Crook. "He's been asking for you."

Harkness bit back an oath. He'd intended to spend this afternoon setting down his thoughts about what he'd found at White's while the adventure was all still fresh in his mind. After that, he needed to write to Miss Thorne to find out if they could arrange to meet privately. However, one did not keep John Townsend waiting. Not twice anyway.

"All right, Charlie. Tell him I'll be along directly."

As Harkness hung up coat and hat, he couldn't help noticing

how the handful of constables who were warming their feet and backsides at the wardroom fire studiously avoided meeting his gaze. He nodded to them, and received mumbled answers. It was not a good omen. Harkness straightened his black cravat, and his shoulders. Then he knocked on Mr. Townsend's door.

"That you, Harkness?" came an answering bellow. "Come in, man, come in!"

Harkness obeyed.

John Townsend was a man who displayed his prosperity, his connections, and his girth with equal enthusiasm. Compared to the ward room, and the patrol room, Townsend's office was a luxurious nest, with carpets, curtains, candlesticks, clocks, and paintings, many of them gifts from his aristocratic patrons. He never wore any hat but the wide-brimmed white one that the Prince of Wales had given him. It was widely known that he carried the prince's purse and watch when His Royal Highness ventured to the theater or the gaming houses.

Just now, Townsend sat behind a desk of good English oak, his hands folded across his gold and scarlet waistcoat. The fire-light gleamed on the silver buttons of his blue coat, and the gold signet ring on his hand. Neither was he alone. A well-dressed gentleman with black hair and startlingly bright gray eyes sat in one of two chairs in front of the desk. Compared to Townsend, his dark coat, buff waistcoat, and breeches were severely plain.

The gentleman rose as Harkness entered, his face cold and closed off.

Townsend heaved himself to his feet. "Well! Mr. Harkness! I was just telling His Grace you'd be along shortly." He clapped his meaty hands together. "Lord Casselmain, may I present Adam Harkness, principal officer and one of our finest men. Mr. Harkness, I introduce to you His Grace, the Duke of Casselmain."

Harkness made his bow, and received a polite nod from the duke.

"How do you do, Mr. Harkness?"

"Very well, Your Grace, an' I thank you." Privately, Harkness noted that His Grace had a wary, assessing look behind his hard eyes. For a man at the top of the ladder of London society, he was not at ease. Harkness wondered if this was inspired by his current surroundings, or something else altogether. Such as having treated Miss Thorne shabbily, as Mr. Faulks suspected.

"Sit down, Harkness." Townsend smiled expansively. "Now, I expect you're wondering what this is about."

"I expect it's about the Aimesworth matter," said Harkness carefully.

"And you'd be right at that." Townsend nodded vigorously. "The blessed thing's kept all of London talking for weeks now. I was fully expecting you to call on me, you know. A young fellow like you shouldn't be ashamed to talk to his seniors about a serious case."

He was being dressed down, gently and cheerfully, but dressed down all the same. Harkness didn't let his gaze stray to the duke, who maintained his silence, but gripped his gold-handled stick tightly.

". . . our very best officer, is what I said to His Royal Highness the other day," Townsend continued. "I've complete faith in Harkness. Practically a legend for how he broke up Red Lowell's gang. Still, two heads are better than one. Especially on such a sensitive affair." He touched the side of his nose. Harkness remembered Mr. Faulks making the exact same gesture.

"I didn't realize His Royal Highness had taken an interest," Harkness murmured.

"Oh yes, oh yes." Townsend leaned back, determined to relish the telling of this particular anecdote. "It was at the opera the other night, His Royal Highness turned to me and he said, straight out, as is his way, 'Now, Townsend, what about this Almack's business, eh? It's too bad the bottom ain't been plumbed yet.'"

Harkness said nothing.

"That's when I told him about you, and how you're our best and most thorough of men. Not the fastest, mind, but the best. When Adam Harkness is on the job, I assured him, he don't give up until he lays hands on the right answer. The *right* answer," Townsend repeated. "But still, as I say, I was waiting for you to come to me. Now . . ." Townsend glanced at Lord Casselmain. "Well, His Grace has kindly taken time out of his day to come down personally and give us the last piece of the puzzle. It was only what I was expecting to hear, of course, as I would have told you, and we could have had this all cleared up shortly after it happened."

Townsend was clearly prepared to continue working over this theme, unless someone stopped him.

"If I may, sir?" said Harkness quietly, and when Townsend nodded his permission, he turned to the duke. "Your Grace, are you here to tell us about the betting book at White's?"

"You've heard about it?" said Lord Casselmain, his voice tight.

"I have, Your Grace. I have, in fact, just returned from visiting the club."

"I see. It was Lord Blanchard who told you, I expect." The duke meant the statement to be casual, and he failed. Either the man was not used to this level of social deception, or he was not expert at it. He'd been the second son, hadn't he? That meant he would have been almost ignored by society's most ambitious, until the death of his brother catapulted him to the position of heir.

"I've seen the entry," Harkness said. There was a pause while Casselmain waited for him to say more. Now, however, it was

Harkness's turn to maintain his own silence. Townsend did not seem to notice the tension deepening around them. He kept his attention, and his determined smile, pointed at Harkness.

"I'm not proud of what I did." Casselmain spoke softly and, Harkness noticed, entirely to Mr. Townsend. "It was a moment's foolishness and then . . . this. I confess I wanted my name kept away from it because of my connection with the Aimesworth family. But when I saw the papers and how the speculation was all spiraling out of control, I felt I must say something." He paused. "The fact of the matter is I'd come down to Almack's that day to try to stop Jasper before he went in, but I got caught in the crush in Kings Street and I was too late. I will regret that to the end of my days."

"Now, now, Your Grace," said Mr. Townsend comfortably. "You can't have known how it would turn out. And we're most grateful to you for taking the trouble to come here now and clear the matter up. I will personally write to the papers, naming no names, of course, but confirming that we have found the whole of it to be a tragic accident. With the name of John Townsend, and the reputation of Bow Street, behind such a letter, you may be sure that an end will be made of any remaining rumors. I'll be writing a letter to Mr. Willis to that effect as well, of course, and Mr. Harkness here will be able to turn his attention to his other duties."

Which was, of course, meant to end the matter, and the interview. Lord Casselmain got to his feet. "I would like to pay your man's fees," said the duke. "Since it was my silence that caused such a waste of his time."

"That's very handsome, your lordship." Townsend beamed. "Very handsome, indeed."

"But not necessary," added Harkness. This got Casselmain to glance in his direction, if only briefly.

"I insist on it."

Townsend spread his hands, indicating his unwillingness to argue such a trifling matter with His Grace. "I'll have the clerk write up a receipt, and send it around, if you'll be so kind as to leave your address. Will that be satisfactory, sir?"

"Quite. Thank you, Mr. Townsend. Mr. Harkness."

They made their various bows. "I'll show His Grace out," said Harkness, more or less to see if Lord Casselmain would refuse the escort. He did not, however, and Harkness walked him through the main patrol room and the ward room, and out onto the steps, all the while watching the man silently struggle to make up his mind about some concealed point.

Outside, Lord Casselmain paused on the top step and faced Harkness fully. "I'm sorry you were put to all this trouble, Mr. Harkness." He held out his hand. "I never did believe the matter would go this far."

Which was probably truer than a number of things His Grace had said in Townsend's office. The real question, thought Harkness as he shook the duke's hand, was what had made the man lie?

But before Harkness could muster a reply, a muddy hired carriage pulled up to the foot of the stairs. For a moment, Harkness thought it must be Lord Casselmain's conveyance, but the man only frowned in evident confusion as the driver opened the door and helped out a woman dressed and veiled in unrelieved black. Lord Casselmain's face fell into an attitude of complete shock. Behind the first woman came another in a plain coat and bonnet, and all at once, Harkness and Lord Casselmain found themselves face-to-face with Rosalind Thorne.

"Good lord!" cried the woman in black as she grabbed her hems and climbed the steps. "Casselmain? What are you doing here?"

"I could ask you the same, Miss Aimesworth." The duke bowed, but he wasn't looking at Miss Aimesworth. He was looking past her to Miss Thorne, who was climbing the steps more slowly, and trying very hard to wipe the shock off her face.

"We've just come from Jasper's rooms," Miss Aimesworth told Lord Casselmain. "Who is this?"

Harkness bowed. "Adam Harkness, at your service, Miss Aimesworth."

Miss Thorne was still looking at Lord Casselmain, and still trying to bring her expression under some sort of control. Harkness could swear he saw fear as well as anger flicker across her pale features.

"His Grace had come to explain the nature of the wager in the betting book at White's," Harkness told the women.

"He did?" murmured Miss Thorne. Lord Casselmain met her gaze, and even Harkness could see the apology written across his face.

"I told you about it when we spoke yesterday, Miss Thorne," said His Grace. "I did not want you to be surprised when word of my folly reached the papers."

He was lying again. Harkness watched Miss Thorne closely. She was not taken in, but then, the lie wasn't for her, at least not directly. Miss Aimesworth felt her exclusion from their silent conversation, and her face turned thunderous. But that changed nothing. The duke's declaration was for Harkness, and any other listening ears. But there was also a warning on his face, and in his stance and his tone. That was entirely for Miss Thorne.

"And it's as well His Grace did come here," Harkness said. "I'd gone to the club myself, with Mr. Faulks, as you suggested, Miss Thorne, and I fully intended to write out a report explaining the reasons I believed that wager was a forgery."

They all turned to him, their shock and their anger written

plain. But the reasons behind those emotions were very different for each. Casselmain was angry that Harkness had sussed out the falsehood. Miss Thorne was stunned that he'd spoken at all. Miss Aimesworth was furious that she had not been heard.

"Forged!" Miss Aimesworth cried. "You cannot be serious!"

"Why would you think that?" snapped Lord Casselmain. "You—"

"He looked at the rest of the book," whispered Miss Thorne. "He saw that your name did not appear anywhere else in it." The wind blew hard and her eyes glittered.

"I did, as a matter of fact, and that is exactly what I saw." Mr. Harkness bowed his head in acknowledgment. Miss Aimesworth's face flushed scarlet. "What made you think of it, Miss Thorne?"

Her smile was faint. "Lord Casselmain abhors gambling. His brother ran up considerable debts before he died."

"Rosalind," breathed Casselmain. "Stop this."

Anger flashed in Miss Thorne's eyes, evaporating the tears that had threatened a moment before. But whether it was for the command, or the casual use of her Christian name, Harkness could not tell.

Miss Aimesworth did not seem to feel any such confusion. "You lied!" she shouted at Casselmain. "After everything we agreed! You lied to *me!*" Miss Thorne laid a hand on her arm, but Miss Aimesworth shook her off.

"I did not lie to you," said Lord Casselmain, but his voice faltered as he said it. "I made the wager with Aimesworth."

"And why would you do such an unspeakably stupid thing?" she demanded. "*That's* something you did not say!"

"Miss Aimesworth, this is not a conversation I care to have in the street," answered the duke stiffly. "May I call on you later?"

Lord Casselmain might not have wished to have this conversation in the street, but Miss Aimesworth looked perfectly ready to continue it, and at the top of her lungs. Miss Thorne leaned forward and whispered something in her ear that made the veiled woman turn sharply. Miss Thorne nodded, but when she spoke, it was to Harkness.

"We have some information to communicate, Mr. Harkness, but now does not appear to be convenient. Perhaps you could call at Blanchard House tomorrow? You will find me at home all morning."

Mr. Harkness bowed. "I would be glad to, Miss Thorne, thank you."

Rosalind nodded in acknowledgment and faced the other man. "Lord Casselmain," she said simply. He opened his mouth to answer, but Miss Thorne had already taken Miss Aimesworth's arm to walk her back toward the carriage, where the driver and his boy assisted them both inside and closed the door.

The driver touched up the horses and Casselmain rounded on Harkness. His face had gone hard with anger, but there was something more. Harkness had seen men's hearts break before, and he knew, to the depths of his soul, that's what he was seeing now.

"You intend to go, don't you?" Lord Casselmain planted his stick firmly onto the sidewalk and leaned heavily upon it. However briefly, Miss Thorne had managed to rob this young aristocrat of his strength.

"Is there a reason I shouldn't, Your Grace?" Harkness asked.

He expected a shout. But Lord Casselmain was not a shouter, any more than he was a gambler. He met Harkness's gaze, trying to get his measure, trying to find an argument that would reach him.

"If I told you that your interference will ruin an innocent woman absolutely and entirely, would you stop?"

"How could that be, sir?" Harkness answered him evenly. "Is there something else you've failed to mention? Something about Miss Thorne perhaps? Or are you referring to Miss Aimesworth?"

They were hard words, and deeply disrespectful. Harkness wanted to see how the duke would react to them, and he did not have to wait even a heartbeat for his answer. Casselmain walked forward, his stick clutched tight in his fist. Harkness held his ground. They were, of course, being watched from the station, probably by Townsend himself. Harkness would not be seen to strike the first blow.

But Casselmain did not strike, at least not with fist or stick.

"This is a private affair. Your business is done, your warrant is fulfilled," said Casselmain, with all the assurance of a man who knew law and custom were entirely on his side. "If I hear you have so much as mentioned Miss Thorne's name again, let alone had any contact with her, I will destroy you."

CHAPTER 29

The House in Thurlough Square

*There are few more delightful amusements than will be
afforded by a day's excursion in fine weather . . .*
—John Britton, *The Original Picture of London,
Enlarged and Improved*

"He lied!" fumed Honoria. "He looked in my face and he lied to me!"

"He did." The carriage curtains were closed, so Rosalind could not see what was happening on the station steps as they drove away.

"What does he think he's doing? As if this weren't enough of a mess, he has to go and do something so ridiculous, so shameful, so . . ."

Rosalind closed her eyes briefly, praying for patience. She also wanted to scream, and to lash out, but she wasn't sure if it was at Devon for his ill-conceived actions, or at Honoria because she could not be quiet for two minutes altogether. "I expect he thought he was protecting us."

"I don't want his protection!"

Neither do I. "It seems we are to have it anyway."

"You are," sneered Honoria. "He doesn't care two pins about me."

"Do you really believe that?"

Honoria stared at the curtains, which were waving in time with the rocking motion of the carriage. "No," she answered. Then she said, "He really hasn't told you, has he?"

"I beg your pardon?"

"Casselmain. He hasn't told you why we're marrying. I had assumed that was what that little shopping expedition was for."

Rosalind felt all the fibers of her body begin to tense, and it was a moment before she could speak and be sure her voice would remain even. "I did not ask."

Honoria waved this away. Of course, to her it would be entirely beside the point. "He's marrying me because I asked him to."

I have no wish to talk about this. I need to think about what has happened, about what we've done. About what Adam Harkness must be thinking now, and what he might well do next. "It is an eminently desirable marriage," she murmured. "And your mother seems to be in agreement with it." *Which must be a relief for you.*

Honoria faced her again. She said nothing, just looked hard at Rosalind from behind the shelter of her mourning veil.

"I don't want the marriage," said Honoria at last. "I want the divorce."

Rosalind stared blatantly, and with her mouth disgracefully wide open. Honoria sat back, her arms folded across her breasts. She stared at the waving curtains again.

"If I become a divorced woman, I'll be beyond all social salvation and Mother will finally have no further use for me."

To Rosalind it was as if Honoria had said she planned to run naked through the streets. She would deliberately conspire to lose all her standing, the protection of her family, their income, and their home? She was not angry. She was quite mad.

"Honoria, you don't have to do this."

"Then tell me what I can do," replied Honoria, quite calmly and with far less than her usual rancor. "Leave the house on my own? I have no relatives who will receive me, especially if it's understood I don't mean to go back. Live alone? Mother would never permit it and Father could override the lease on any house I tried to occupy. Once I am divorced, I will be free to leave the city for good. In fact, Mother might even arrange that herself. I'll be able to live on my own somewhere. Anywhere. No one will question it, because I'll already be disgraced." Under other circumstances, this might have been a shaft aimed at Rosalind. "I've my inheritance from Grandmother, and Casselmain promised a decent settlement. I'll be comfortable."

"There must be some other way." Rosalind's thoughts flew forward, skimming across possibilities. She knew Honoria was ruled by her anger, and her helplessness. She understood it. She knew what it was to live under the constant expectations of perfection. But Honoria could not possibly understand all that came with deliberately courting such ruin.

"If you find another way, please do let me know," Honoria said, and her words were flat and entirely devoid of that heated emotion that normally animated her. "As a single woman, I am controlled by my father, and my father is controlled by my mother. Casselmain agreed to the project when we were thrown together over Christmas. We will remain married for a year, possibly two, and then we will produce evidence of my having done . . . something. There are men who can be hired for such tasks. Casselmain will petition Parliament, there will be a trial to establish I did indeed fall into 'criminal conversation' with a man not my husband, after which I will be expected to retire permanently to Bath or Bristol or some other place."

Devon. Devon was willing to help Honoria ruin herself. It

was not possible. But then, he'd been lying about so many things of late, how could Rosalind be sure what he might do? "Why would Devon go along with such a scheme?"

"Because it will get society matchmaking mamas off his back, as well as his own mother. Since Hugh died, Lady Casselmain's become terrified that Devon will kick off early as well. He's all her security now. If he dies, the estate and much of its income will pass to some cousins. If he marries, however, there should soon be an heir, and all it implies." She paused and then added, "I also expect he's doing it to fill the time."

"The time until what?"

For a moment, Rosalind thought Honoria would refuse to answer. Her native stubbornness and disdain once again filled her features, but slowly, as if this once she fought against them. When she did speak, her voice shook. "He's waiting for you, Rosalind. He has been for years."

No. Devon was struggling, as she was. He'd worked to get past the feeling between them. He knew the gulf was too wide, just as she did. He knew, he felt, he *understood* . . .

Rosalind pressed her hand against her mouth.

"Why are you telling me this?"

"I rather thought as payment it would be worth more to you than the money."

A day ago it would have. A day ago, a week, a month. But Devon was lying to Mr. Harkness, and hiding more from her than she would have believed possible. What could it be worth to her now?

The carriage came to a halt, and rocked slightly as the driver climbed down and opened the door.

"Thank you for telling me, Honoria," Rosalind said.

Honoria shrugged with one shoulder. "You needn't come in.

I'll deal with Mother. Will you be at that thing of Mrs. Nottingham's tonight?"

"I had forgotten that was tonight." Which was unacceptable, and possibly unprecedented. "You mean to go?"

"Mother means to have me go." Honoria hunted in her reticule and came up with a pair of coins to hand to their driver. "With Casselmain, of course. It's been weeks since Jasper's funeral, so we are allowed to go into part mourning and since it's not the season yet, we may be seen at small friendly gatherings, although of course I cannot dance. I'm surprised Mother didn't tell you."

"I have been a little preoccupied. Perhaps she talked the matter over with Lady Blanchard."

"Probably. Your godmother's been here three or four times in the past week."

Rosalind caught herself right before she could begin staring. *She said nothing to me.* She swallowed this, as she had swallowed so many other words today. She had to think, and think quickly.

"Honoria, I need a favor of you."

Honoria waved wearily. "What is that?"

"I need you to keep your temper with Lord Casselmain and make sure he comes to Mrs. Nottingham's tonight."

"After what he did, that's a very large favor. Why?"

"Because I have a feeling time may be running short, and there are things I need to ask him."

Honoria pressed her lips into a hard, thin line. Then slowly, she nodded. "Very well. If it's necessary."

"I believe it is."

"But I'll call 'round tomorrow and we can work out how to tell that runner what we found." Honoria paused. "You never did say what that odious landlord told you when you went running back in there."

"I asked him if he could describe the men who removed Jasper's personal items. He denied being able to."

"I could have told you that would happen. Oh, well." Honoria sighed sharply. "I suppose it was worth trying."

Rosalind nodded, because she did not trust her voice, and Honoria strode up the steps to Tamwell House without looking back.

"Anywhere else, miss?" asked the driver.

Rosalind bit her lip. She pressed her hand onto her reticule where it lay in her lap.

"Yes," she said. "Number 12, Thurlough Square."

Had Rosalind allowed herself to think about this, she might have told the driver to turn around and return her to Blanchard House. But she did not allow herself to think. There had been too many revelations already, too many shocks and reversals. She needed this matter over and done with.

She needed to know which side to take on the war inside her—between the fear of Devon and all he had done, and the desperate yearning that rose up in her as Honoria's words repeated themselves in her dazed mind.

He's waiting for you. He has been for years.

She tried to deny this, but that denial would not come. The only thought she could muster in response was, *As you have been waiting for him.*

That was the real reason she'd guarded her gentility; that was the reason she'd struggled to keep her place in society. One of them, at any rate. But she had not wished to admit that particular reason even existed, until Honoria had dragged it up into the light.

Rosalind took a deep breath. Even if she must admit that

reason had been there all along, it changed nothing of present circumstance. She needed answers, not mistaken protection, or unresolvable affections. When she spoke again to Mr. Harkness, she needed to be able to tell him as much as possible.

Going alone to this place was a risk. She knew nothing about Thurlough Square, not even the portion of town where it was located. But there wasn't any possibility of stopping at Blanchard House and retrieving Mrs. Kendricks without alerting Lord or Lady Blanchard that something was wrong, and she had no way to send for Mr. Harkness. There was no time to be wasted, not to mention no additional money for the hackney's hire. Rosalind would have to hope, and trust to her native wit as a woman of the city.

Thurlough Square proved to be a new neighborhood. So new, in fact, that the square itself was still more dirt than cobbles, and the skeleton frames of several buildings stood sentry on its west side, waiting for better weather so the building could continue. Number 12 was a finished house at the northern corner, and a very neat one. It had a white pillared entranceway in the new style, with a freshly painted black door, and its shining brass appurtenances included two gleaming lamps.

Rosalind turned the bell and waited. When there was no answer, she knocked firmly and waited awhile longer, until her cheeks began to sting from the cold wind. Finally, she brought Jasper's key ring out from her reticule and selected the larger of the unidentified keys. It fitted easily into the lock, which turned smoothly.

The door came open on well-oiled hinges and Rosalind stepped inside.

Darkness enfolded her. The curtains were drawn, although the shutters were not. It was cold. Rosalind could see her breath steaming in the faint light. The silence around her was absolute, and there was no trace scent of candlewax or coal smoke in the still air of the entranceway.

If this was the home of the woman to whom Jasper had been sending expensive gifts, she had not been back recently.

However, those persons who had stripped down Jasper's bachelor rooms so thoroughly had left this place untouched. As Rosalind's eyes adjusted to the gloom of the entrance, she saw the cabinet table and the painting hanging above it. To the left was a tidy parlor, to the right, a comfortable sitting room. There were no dust covers on the furniture. The carpets still covered the floorboards. The draperies might be closed, but the house itself was not shut up, although with three weeks having passed since Jasper's death there had been plenty of time for the mistress of this place—whoever she was—to have ordered it done. That meant someone still planned to return, as they planned to return to Jasper's rooms.

That, in turn, meant that every moment she stood here, Rosalind risked being found.

With this thought goading her into action, she raced from one room to the other. All she found was in good taste, but not unduly luxurious or overcrowded with ornaments. A writing desk waited by one curtained window. Rosalind hurried to it, and opened the drawers. Inside was paper and quills and all other necessary items, but no letters or bills. Nothing that would give Rosalind the one thing she wanted, which was a name.

With a wordless cry of frustration, Rosalind slid the last drawer shut and turned to climb the stairs. A choice of four doors presented themselves to her in the upper corridor. She made for the one toward the back of the house and opened it.

In this at least, her luck was with her. The door lead to a woman's apartments, and a dressing room with a vanity table that still had its cosmetics, brushes, combs, and little scissors for trimming nails and curls, all neatly laid out. The casement window opened over the back garden, so Rosalind decided to take the risk and part the curtains a fraction of an inch to let in more light before turning her attention to the room. An unwound clock on the mantle stood silent sentry to her frantic search, but that did not matter. The maddened beating of her heart counted off the seconds as she riffled through the table and the jewel cabinet (still well filled with precious ornaments), and nightstands and dressers. Boxes and bags.

I've been here too long. There are too many places to search. It is impossible. Someone will be coming back any moment now. There can't be anything here.

The door in the room's right-hand wall opened to reveal a closet filled with tasteful clothing, neatly stored. Rosalind rummaged among the dresses and gowns. She dug through the shelves among the linens, in the drawers among the stockings.

I will be caught. I must stop. I don't even really know what I'm looking for. Surely there's nothing here to find . . .

Except there was. A black iron strongbox waited back among the glove boxes, stuffed hastily toward the rear of the shelves. It was abominably heavy, but Rosalind heaved it off the shelves and out onto the dressing table where she had better light.

Rosalind did not permit herself any further hesitation. She pulled Jasper's keys out from her reticule and selected the smallest one. She took a deep breath. She fit the key into the lock, and as with the door, it turned easily.

The lock snapped open and Rosalind lifted the lid.

Inside waited a tray of coins—guineas and sovereigns, crowns and half crowns, all glinted in the faint daylight. Rosalind lifted the tray out. It was astoundingly heavy, but the real astonishment was yet to come. The space beneath that tray was filled with banknotes.

"Dear Lord," whispered Rosalind. Slowly, she lifted out the banknotes, piling them to the side on the table. There were hundreds of pounds' worth, possibly thousands, rolls of notes tied with string, piles of notes clipped together, and others just lying loose.

Underneath the banknotes waited still other notes, these scrawled in a variety of hands, but all of similar purpose. They read:

Ignatius Shotwell promises to pay the bearer the sum of 200 pounds upon presentation of this note.

Or:

Albert Crane promises to pay 500 pounds to bearer.

Or simply:

I.O.U. 1,000 pounds. Bradford Fish

They were promissory notes, the sort gentlemen laid down for debts of honor. Thousands more pounds. A lifetime's worth of money and the promise of money, all in this one box.

Rosalind put the promissory notes back, and then the banknotes, and then the tray of coins. She closed the lid and locked it. She pressed both hands down on top of the box, hard, as if she thought it might fly away from her.

She imagined walking out of the house with this box and vanishing as thoroughly as her father and Charlotte. She'd never have to answer to anyone again. She'd never have to worry about appearances, about what she owed to whom. She could load her bag with jewelry, pack a case with dresses. She would never have to see Devon again or confront the tearing confusion inside her, or know what her godmother had or had not done.

She could never come back, of course, but she'd never have to want to.

I will have to apologize to Honoria. I should have been more understanding.

She understood what had been done, and now she had a fair idea how it had unfolded, and what Jasper's role in the business must have been.

The question now became, who owned this room? Rosalind found herself wondering if Mr. Whelks might know that as well.

CHAPTER 30

Dismissed

Forget the waste of time and anxiety, which this office will occasion you, the impertinence you will have to swallow, the rudeness you will have to commit . . . accept the appointment.

—Marianne Spencer Stanhope Hudson, *Almack's*

In the end, Rosalind was not caught out. She returned the strongbox and its contents to their hiding place, closed the draperies completely, got into the waiting hack carriage, and sat in silence, trying to sort out all she knew, and all she still did not know.

The conclusions were such as to leave her colder even than the damp March afternoon. That there had been forgery and fraud connected with Almack's was plain. That a great deal of money had been made from those forgeries was equally plain.

But who had run the scheme? And had Jasper been a participant, or had he simply discovered what was being done?

The drive across town from Thurlough Square to Blanchard House proved excruciating. An overturned carriage blocked one street and a broken cart another, forcing the man to turn down a maze of crowded streets and alleys. Rosalind was cold and hungry and overwhelmed with all that she'd learned and what she still suspected. She wanted desperately to retreat to her own room for a time, to gather her wits and her nerves.

But that did not seem to be a luxury she would be permitted, as the parlor maid informed her while she helped Rosalind off with her coat and bonnet.

"Lady Blanchard has been asking for you, Miss Thorne. She says you are to go to her at once."

Rosalind ran both hands across her hair to smooth it and suppressed a weary shiver. "Of course," she said. "Is she in her rooms?"

Upon receiving an affirmative, Rosalind climbed the stairs and turned into the corridor that led to the family wing. She knocked at Lady Blanchard's door and, schooling her expression into an acceptable attitude of calm, she pushed the door open.

"Rosalind!" Lady Blanchard started to her feet from her seat by her fire. "Where have you been?"

"I told you I was going with Honoria to visit Jasper's grave, Lady Blanchard." Rosalind had repeated the covering excuse to her godmother before she left. She felt some small guilt at the lie, but she had no wish to cause additional worry or disagreement by revealing the truth. "Has something happened?"

"Is that her?" roared a voice from out in the corridor. Lady Blanchard gripped Rosalind's hands hard, but had no time to speak before Lord Blanchard strode into the room, his face flushed and his shaggy hair standing on end.

"Morgan!" Lady Blanchard cried. "We agreed I should—"

Lord Blanchard cut her off with an abrupt gesture. "Miss Thorne, I brought you into this house on sufferance. My wife needed a companion, and you needed shelter from this disaster. I had thought you would display at least some modicum of gratitude!"

Rosalind looked to Lady Blanchard, but saw nothing except

a reflection of her own distress. "I don't understand, Lord Blanchard. I—"

"This!" Blanchard held up his fist to display a crumbled piece of paper. "Is a most impertinent note from that jumped-up fellow John Townsend, telling me I needn't worry anymore about the Aimesworth matter, it has all been laid to rest."

"But that should be good news—"

"*And* how it would be best if I hinted to Miss Thorne that she was in danger of making a public display of herself!" He snarled. "Those are his very words, *a public display!*"

Rosalind blanched. Of course John Townsend, who was welcome in all the great houses, had heard about her. Of course he had taken note of her standing with Lord Casselmain and Mr. Harkness on the steps of his station. And of course he had written to the man he knew to be keeping her under his roof.

Had she not gone to Thurlough Square, Rosalind might have beaten his letter home, and had a response ready. She might have even have thought to tell Lord and Lady Blanchard herself and show the thing in a better light. As it was, she must bow her head humbly. "I apologize, Lord Blanchard. I was only trying to help bring an end to the inquiry."

"Oh yes, quite. I'm certain you had your reasons," sneered Lord Blanchard. "But I have a reputation to protect, Miss Thorne, even if you do not, and I will not permit you to expose me and my wife to speculation and ridicule! Do I make myself clear?"

Rosalind lifted her chin. This was too far, even for the man in front of her. She waited for Lady Blanchard to speak, to defend Rosalind, or at least herself. But Lady Blanchard said nothing, and her silence squeezed so tightly, Rosalind felt sure one of them must be crushed by it.

"I understand you, Lord Blanchard," she told him. *I understand you are afraid.*

As she leveled her gaze against him, the blood slowly drained from Lord Blanchard's face. His gaze slid over her shoulder to his wife. Rosalind wished she could turn her head to see Lady Blanchard's face now, but she did not let her eyes so much as flicker from the man in front of her.

What is it that frightens you, Lord Blanchard? It cannot possibly be me.

Lord Blanchard thrust his jaw forward, but he said nothing. Instead, he turned on his heel and marched away. Rosalind forced her spine to stay straight. Her heart was pounding. For a moment she thought she would be quite sick. Not from Lord Blanchard's storm, but from Lady Blanchard's continued silence.

That silence which she must now turn and face. She met her godmother's gaze as determinedly and calmly as she had Lord Blanchard's. What she saw there shook her to her core. Because Lord Blanchard was not the only one who was afraid, or furious.

"Really, Rosalind!" snapped Lady Blanchard as she sat down, her hands clasped on her lap. "You of all people should have known better than to make a scene! I have always been able to trust to your discretion. Always!"

Is it my lack of discretion that worries you now? Rosalind felt her heart tremble. *Or your own?* "I promise you, Lady Blanchard, I did nothing untoward. I went to speak with Mr. Harkness to make sure he knew the truth about the betting book and—"

"And of course this means you and Miss Aimesworth were nowhere near her brother's grave today," said Lady Blanchard coldly. "I am truly disappointed that you would lie to me."

Rosalind made no answer.

"May I ask where you did go?"

Rosalind considered another lie, but as difficult as it was, she knew she needed to see this moment through to its end. "I went with Honoria to find Mr. Aimesworth's bachelor rooms."

"*What?*" cried Lady Blanchard. "How could you conceive of such an indecent sojourn?"

"There is a time when disaster must be faced head on. You taught me that," Rosalind reminded her. "We hoped to find some definitive clue as to what he was doing in Almack's when he died."

It was a long moment before Lady Blanchard was able to find voice enough to speak again. "What . . . what did you find?"

"We found nothing. The rooms had been stripped bare."

"Oh." Two pink spots appeared on Lady Blanchard's cheeks. Rosalind could not tell whether this was anger, or hope. "Of course, the Aimesworths—"

Now it was Rosalind's turn to interrupt. "The Aimesworths had not done it. Honoria was with me, you will recall, and she knew nothing of the matter. This was done by someone else."

"Oh. How terrible," Lady Blanchard murmured. "That he should die and his rooms be robbed . . ."

Rosalind found her patience at an abrupt and complete end. "Lady Blanchard," she said. "Is Jasper Aimesworth your son?"

"*What?*"

"Is—was—he your son by Lord Edmund?"

"How could you even think such a thing!" Which was the expected and appropriate answer, and Rosalind found herself deeply disappointed to hear it.

"Because it fits the facts," she answered. *And it is perhaps the lesser of the two possibilities.* "You have been unduly affected by Jasper's death since we found him. You have been visiting Tamwell House during their time of mourning without telling me, and this was after you said you wanted me to help you bring Lady Edmund into wider acceptance in society." She ticked off the points on her fingertips. "Lady Edmund must have some hold over you; otherwise you'd never consider her for the post of lady patroness let alone actively assist her. If Jasper was a bastard, she would have to be party to the secret. As Lord Edmund had no other heir, he might very well have chosen to acknowledge your baby as his own when Lord Blanchard would not. Even if Lord Edmund refused to tell his wife who Jasper's mother was, she would have years to find out, and she would very much want to find out." Rosalind paused a moment to make sure all this had sunk into her godmother's mind. "It also explains your anger at Almack's exclusivity and the lady patronesses' hypocrisies, as well as your impending retreat from London. We both know that a man may have as many outside children as he chooses, but for a lady it is different."

"Yes. I see." Lady Blanchard pressed her hand against her forehead. "But no. I can swear to you that Jasper Aimesworth was not my son by Lord Edmund, or anyone else."

Which only led to another question. Rosalind's hands gripped each other. *You don't have to ask this*, murmured a cowardly voice in her mind. *You don't have to find out yet if she'll tell another lie.*

But Rosalind did ask. "Then why did Lord Blanchard tamper with the betting book to deflect speculation from the death?"

"Rosalind!"

Rosalind steeled herself against the shock and the betrayal in her godmother's exclamation. From the first, she had hoped to take care of them both by bringing this matter to an eventual close, but now she saw how time was running short. Lord Blanchard's outrage showed her that. The longer she spun this thing out, the more she put herself at risk for idle speculation and that speculation would have long, cold consequences.

The forgery would have to have been done by somebody connected to the death. Devon hadn't done it. If Jasper did it, he would have had to take Devon into his confidence. That left

Lord Blanchard as the next most likely person. After all, he'd put the idea of a bet into Rosalind's head, and he'd been the one to tell Devon of the record in White's book.

Lady Blanchard looked at her for a very long time. Rosalind watched regret and calculation chase each other behind her god-mother's eyes and the pain of it shook her to her core. In the end, however, it was Lady Blanchard who looked away first.

"The truth is . . ." Lady Blanchard stammered. "The truth is that Morgan is in debt."

Rosalind said nothing.

"He told me about it before he told me about the posting. It is not on his own account," her godmother went on. "He agreed to back some friends in a stock-buying scheme. He signed several promissory notes for them, but the scheme collapsed and the notes are still there. It's not . . . an amount that can be brushed off." She took a deep, shuddering breath. "Now that he's taken the Konigsberg post, his creditors are pressing hard for the money. At least they were. Someone, I don't know who yet, has bought the notes, and is holding them over our heads. Morgan says . . . he says this person intends to use them as evidence of corruption in the foreign office if he doesn't pay and with interest."

"I see," said Rosalind slowly. "That means that all this time, you've been making inquiries to try to discover the blackmailer, and it's led you to the Almack's patronesses?"

"One of their husbands, I think," said Lady Blanchard. "That's why I need Lady Edmund, you see. Between her and you, I have an unquestionable reason to be making all sorts of calls and asking all sorts of questions. I should have told you," she said, "but I was afraid you might have felt it necessary to tell Honoria, or you might have inadvertently let it slip, and Hono-ria has no discretion whatsoever."

"I see," Rosalind said again.

It might be true. Rosalind remembered her own idea that Lord Blanchard had received his posting so that he might be quietly gotten out of London. Such debts would be reason enough for him to be sent away. But Mrs. Nottingham would surely have heard about any such scandal, and she would have at least hinted about it to Rosalind.

Which left the question of where this lie came from and why was it told? Was it told by Lord Blanchard to fool Lady Blanchard? Or was it being made up at this moment by Lady Blanchard to fool Rosalind?

Lady Blanchard's smile was weak and apparently filled with awareness of the irony of this moment. "As I believe I told you before, Rosalind, in society, two people can keep a secret when one of them is dead."

"Even when one of them is me," Rosalind finished, and Lady Blanchard nodded. A cold shudder ran down Rosalind's spine. *Oh, Godmother, I am so sorry it's come to this.*

There was a knock at the door and Lacey let herself in. "I'm sorry to disturb you, Lady Blanchard, but a letter has come from Lady Jersey."

"What?" Lady Blanchard blinked heavily, as if just awakening from her sleep. "Oh. Leave it on my desk."

"I'm afraid the man is waiting for a reply. I've put him in the Rose Salon."

"Go, Godmother." Rosalind mustered a smile. "I am tired and I think I should go lie down before it's time to change for Mrs. Nottingham's." *Then you won't have to come up with any more lies, and I won't have to hear them.*

Lady Blanchard rubbed her brow. "Oh, very well. I will go." Lady Blanchard gave Rosalind one more worried glance and hurried from the room.

Lacey glared at Rosalind as an unwelcome intruder in these

rooms. Rosalind lifted her chin and made to leave. Then, a sudden thought stopped her and she turned.

"Lacey? The man Lady Jersey sent with the message. Is it Mr. Whelks by any chance?"

For a heartbeat, she thought Lacey might refuse to answer, but the maid did finally relent. "I believe it is, miss."

"Thank you."

Rosalind stepped into the corridor, but she did not turn toward her own rooms. She moved in the opposite direction, toward the central stair. Even if Lady Blanchard gave only a spoken reply to whatever letter Lady Jersey sent, Rosalind should still be able to catch Mr. Whelks before he left and . . .

"Miss Thorne."

Lord Blanchard's voice cut harshly across Rosalind's thoughts, and turned her around before she had a chance to think. He stepped from the shadows of the side corridor. He hadn't smoothed his hair down, and he looked wild and entirely disdainful, of her and the rest of the world as well.

"Lord Blanchard," said Rosalind a little breathlessly. "Will you excuse me? Mr. Whelks is here and I was hoping to have a word—"

Lord Blanchard paced past her until he blocked her way to the stairs. "You may have your word with Mr. Whelks another time." He folded his hands behind him. "Right now you will hear what I have to say."

"But, sir . . ." Rosalind's eyes darted left and right, as if she was seeking escape. Perhaps she was.

Lord Blanchard shook his head slowly, decidedly. "I did not believe I would ever be saying these words to you again, Miss Thorne, but your actions leave me no choice. I have had time to think the matter over, and I believe it would be better for all of us if you packed yourself up and left this house."

He was as coldly serious as she had ever seen him. There was not even one iota of the regret he had expressed last time, when her father had come and made his threats.

"Yes, of course, sir," said Rosalind, because there was no other answer she could make. Perhaps, though, she could buy herself a moment of time. "Will tomorrow be soon enough?"

Her godfather nodded once, and Rosalind made her curtsy and turned. She walked away, back to her rooms, fully conscious that Lord Blanchard watched her every step of the way. So conscious was she of this, that it took a long time for another sad fact to surface in her mind. She had asked Lady Blanchard why her husband altered White's betting book.

Lady Blanchard had never answered.

CHAPTER 31

A Consequential Gathering

This beautiful England is always the same—an endless chain of perfections which appeal to the reason, but leave the imagination untouched.

—Countess Dorothea Lieven, from a letter to her
brother Alexander

The Nottinghams' London residence stood a mere two streets from St. James's Square. It was a tall, broad stone house that Rosalind always imagined to be peering keenly over its neighbors toward the seats of power.

Mr. and Mrs. Nottingham made an excellent team, both sharing an ambition to rise to political and social prominence, but both having the patience for the long work this must necessarily involve. Mrs. Nottingham had chosen the elegant, and—most important—not too ostentatious, house for them. Unlike Lord Edmund, she had the foresight to hire a fashionable builder to make her improvements (consulting, upon Rosalind's advice, with another prominent hostess before making her final choice). The result was an interior with proportionate and comfortable rooms that could display the Nottinghams' taste and prosperity without appearing grandiose.

"Lord Blanchard, Lady Blanchard." Mrs. Nottingham made

her curtsy as they entered the oak-paneled entrance hall. "And Miss Thorne. How very good of you to come."

Rosalind and her godparents made their courtesies and smiled and murmured the polite greetings. The carriage ride had passed entirely in silence. Lady Blanchard had not so much as looked at her husband, and Lord Blanchard had not taken his eyes off Rosalind. It was as if he feared that if he looked away, she might forget her promise to quit the premises and beg Lady Blanchard to let her stay on for good.

He would be most surprised if he knew what she did mean to say to Lady Blanchard as soon as she found a moment.

"How lovely everything looks, Mrs. Nottingham," said Rosalind to their hostess. "Has the Countess Lieven arrived yet?"

"The countess?" murmured Lady Blanchard. "I didn't realize Her Grace would be here this evening,"

Mrs. Nottingham smiled in triumph. "She's one of Miss Thorne's acquisitions for me. Rosalind has been such a tremendous help. I cannot think what I would have done without her."

Lady Blanchard smiled politely, but without feeling. "As I have always said. Now, Morgan, I believe I see Mr. Howell over there. I think you said you wished for a word?" Lord Blanchard grunted his assent, but turned another hard glare toward Rosalind. Fortunately, Mrs. Nottingham did not seem to notice.

"You'll be all right, Rosalind?" asked Lady Blanchard.

"Yes, of course. I see my friend Emma just there." She didn't, but it didn't matter. Her answer made it possible for Lady Blanchard to take her husband off and leave Rosalind, for the moment, to her own devices.

As Lord and Lady Blanchard moved through the crowd, Rosalind began a slow drift through the knots of party-goers that ended with her standing by the wall where she could better take in the scene around her.

The Nottinghams' house did not sport anything so grand as a ballroom, but it had several airy salons, which had been opened to the party. Brightly dressed men and women strolled about looking at the pictures and the *objets d'art* that the younger Mr. Nottingham had brought back from his trip to the Continent. The collection included several paintings by his own hand, which were being admired and discussed. Sanderson Faulks did not seem to be among the assembly yet, and Rosalind wondered if he meant to keep his promise to attend.

The succession of salons ended at a blue-painted music conservatory, where a trio of musicians played a sprightly country melody. A small set of young couples had assembled there, laughing gaily with—and at—each other as they stepped up and down the line.

Normally when Rosalind attended a party she'd helped to arrange, she looked about her with proprietary interest. She noted who spoke with whom and who needed a partner, or simply some attention, and dropped the occasional hint to the hostess. But as she looked about her now, all she felt was an uncertain dread. When would Countess Lieven arrive? It was imperative they speak. The countess might be able to help her arrange a meeting with Mr. Whelks. It had to be soon. Once word got about that she had been thrown out of Blanchard House, again, she would be welcome nowhere at all.

She must find out what was driving Lady Blanchard to lie so repeatedly and outrageously. She must know how to help and protect her godmother. She would not break faith with the woman who had saved her when no one else would, not until all possible choice had been removed.

"There you are, Rosalind."

It was Honoria, and Devon with her. They all made their bows, and Rosalind was conscious of an unforgivable flush rising in her cheeks, as frustration mixed with the memory of last seeing Devon on the steps of the policing station, and of all that Honoria had told her afterward. Devon glanced away.

"How very good to see you, Lord Casselmain, Miss Aimesworth," she murmured. "Is Miss Casselmain here as well?"

"Louisa had another engagement," Devon answered.

"Clever girl that she is," added Honoria. "This is going to be a very long night." She looked to Devon as she said it.

Honoria had begun the process her mother had described as "decorously stepping down" her mourning. Instead of unrelieved black, Honoria's gown was a charcoal gray bombazine, trimmed in pale gray ribbons. It actually looked rather well on her. Devon dressed in white silk breeches and black coat as befitted his station and the evening and looked thoroughly unhappy. Rosalind wondered what Honoria had said to him.

Behind them, the country dance finished, and the couples applauded. The man at the pianoforte sketched out the time, and the others struck up a smooth waltz.

"Oh, good," sighed Honoria. "Casselmain, waltz with Miss Thorne, would you? I can't dance and may as well sit down. There will be a thousand dowagers all oozing with condolences, and I want to get it over with."

They both stared at her and Honoria stared right back. Then, without ceremony or further comments, she set off determinedly for the gilt chairs by the drapes that covered the conservatory's French doors and kept out the drafts.

"She really is extraordinary," murmured Rosalind.

"She takes a great deal of getting used to," agreed Devon. "But one comes to appreciate her unique qualities." They both watched Honoria set herself down on the chair and glower at them. "I think we'd better dance."

"I think we'd better."

Devon's left hand, warm and strong, closed about hers, while his other hand rested politely against her back. It stunned her how familiar it felt. It had been years since they'd held hands like this, but her skin had not forgotten him.

If she closed her eyes, she could be in the Almack's ballroom again. It had been two in the morning then. She'd been flushed and exhausted and exultant. He'd smiled wide when he bowed.

I was going to give up on you, she'd told him then as he led her onto the floor.

But you never should, he had answered. *I was just waiting for the right moment.*

She snapped back to the present, and the feel of Devon's hand on the small of her back. They found the time, and they moved. She'd never been a proficient dancer, and had had little opportunity to practice of late. Devon, though . . . Devon moved lightly, smoothly. He had grown into this as he had all other aspects of his life.

He watched her eyes, and her face, and Rosalind knew she was coloring.

"Beautiful," Devon murmured.

"I beg your pardon?" she said, trying to muster some trace of indignation.

"You," he said. "You're so beautiful."

"Please don't. It does no good for either of us." *Not with you lying to me. To us.*

He turned them, and he turned them again. "I know. But it's still true."

"Not that it matters." Rosalind tried to smile, and she failed.

"It matters to me. It matters to me that you're beautiful and sad, and I can't get close to you."

"You're close to me now," she answered tartly, because pique was better than resignation. "In fact, I need to ask you to loosen your grip."

Now it was Devon who blushed. "I'm sorry," he murmured, and he did loosen his hold on her hand. "I keep thinking if I can just be near you, I'll remember what to say. I'll remember how to be."

"How have you forgotten?"

"By being a fool, Rosalind. By making one too many mistakes I can't undo."

Rosalind glanced past his shoulder, trying to make up her mind. He turned them. The room was a blur. They were alone in the middle of the world. No one could hear them, or would hear them over the sound of the music. For this brief moment, they could say anything to each other. She had so much to say and so much to do. She did not have the luxury of trying to make peace with Devon and their impossible situation. That would come later, if it came at all.

"Honoria told me about why you decided to marry her." Devon bit his lip, but made no answer. "Why on earth would you agree to such a plan?"

"Because we were friends as children," he said. "As you know."

"That's not enough, Devon. Not for something like this."

He sighed and glanced over her shoulder, steering them carefully about the small floor. "I agreed so she would not be tempted to do something worse."

Rosalind immediately wanted to protest that Honoria would never do such a thing, but she kept her mouth closed. Honoria would. She looked at Devon again, and saw the determination in him, and the sadness.

"It was still wrong."

"You wouldn't say that if . . ."

"If what? If I knew? Then *tell* me what's happened, Devon." She spat the words from between her teeth. "You keep saying how much you care, but you won't talk to me!"

"What happened was I waited," he said. "After I found out about your father, I waited. I told myself that when the scandal and the shock died away, I could ask you to marry me. But then your mother died, and I told myself I would have to wait until you'd mourned her, and then I could make my proposal. I wrote to her," he added abruptly. "I asked after you. I asked her to tender you my regards, and to call on me if you needed anything."

Rosalind's heart thumped. "She never told me."

"I wondered. I know she had a nervous condition."

She lost her mind. But they had enough to deal with between them without adding that.

"Then my brother died, and it broke my father, and he died as well, and there I was, with an estate that had been gutted and encumbered with thousands of pounds of debt." He looked at his feet. He looked past her shoulder. He turned them again. "And I was saddled with a title I didn't want because I knew you would see it as widening the gulf between us. As a second son, you might have been able to find enough room in your social principles to accept me, but as Lord Casselmain?" He shook his head. "It would be absolutely wrong."

Rosalind's face burned, but her hand, even cradled as it was by the warmth of Devon's hand, was ice cold.

"I was so angry. I hated everything—my place, my family, all of it. And then comes Honoria with her outrageous suggestion, and it seemed like this was something I could do, someone I could help. And once that was over . . . perhaps enough time would have finally passed that I could find a way to talk with you again." He glanced at his feet. "Or perhaps by then you would have found yourself married and I could at last manage to grieve and go on."

Devon's words beat against her mind and her heart in time to the rhythm of the waltz. *All this time, I did not see any of this.* She, who prided herself on her ability to understand the way the people of the world fit together, she had missed this entirely.

And the worst of it was, Devon had been exactly right about what her feelings and her reasoning were, and how absolutely she would have refused him.

It changed everything. It changed nothing. She could not give way to the longing inside her. She could not, heaven help her, let herself trust him, not yet, no matter how much she wanted to. They were still who they were and where they were, and he had done all he could to keep her from finding answers about what had happened to Jasper in Almack's.

The music slowed and swelled, signaling that the end of the dance was approaching. Their moment's respite from the prying eyes and listening ears was almost done.

"Devon," breathed Rosalind. "I need the answer to one question and I need you to give me your word of honor you will tell the truth."

"Rosalind . . ."

"Devon, please." She squeezed his arm urgently.

"All right. You have my word."

"Did you actually write the bet into the book? Or did you just agree to go along with the story of it?"

The music drew to its close. The couples, flushed and breathless, applauded politely. Under cover of that noise, Devon murmured his answer.

"I did not write the bet in. Lord Blanchard came to me and told me it had been done."

Lord Blanchard. Yes. Of course. He had plenty of time to write it, and he'd know you well enough to know you'd go along with the deed, for honor and for me, and Jasper and Honoria as well. Rosalind nodded. "Thank you."

The gentlemen led the ladies back to their friends and companions. Devon led Rosalind back to Honoria, so that all the world might see that she and his supposed intended were all friends. As they passed the threshold, Rosalind saw Sanderson Faulks leaning casually against a wall, his small, cynical smile set firmly on his face. He nodded toward her.

"Well, that's over with," announced Honoria as Rosalind and Devon reached her. "You've danced, we've been seen. Now what do we do?" She sent her sharp glance around the room. "And where's Mother got herself to?"

They all looked around. "Oh." Honoria waved her fan.

Lady Edmund was standing side by side with Lady Blanchard in the green salon. Together they surveyed the gathering. Rosalind, heart in her throat, saw the Countess Lieven, very grand in scarlet and black with a chain of diamonds at her throat, glide up to her godmother. Lady Blanchard gestured, one to the other, clearly making introductions. Lady Edmund curtsied, but not before giving the countess a long, measuring look.

"Well, won't Mother be full of herself now," muttered Honoria.

"I should probably get over to Lady Blanchard. She'll need me tonight. Thank you for the dance, Lord Casselmain. I'll speak with you soon, Honoria."

Devon bowed. His gray eyes were filled with questions, and with promises he wanted to make, but could not. Rosalind felt her heart crumble for the sorrow of it, and yes, the foolishness. She wanted to drag him out of here. She wanted to stand in the street like a fishwife, or Honoria, and scream at him until he told her all he was still hiding, and she could lose herself far enough in the violence of her emotion to confess all that she still hid from him.

Of course, what she did was turn away and make her slow, winding way through the crowd. But it wasn't the need to assist Lady Blanchard that guided her steps. It was the need to hear the conversation Lady Blanchard and Lady Edmund were carrying on with the Countess Lieven. But the rooms had filled up since the dance began, and Rosalind had to edge her way politely between the gathered persons. She must smile, and acknowledge their greetings, and make her curtsies to those who bowed to her. As fast as she might excuse herself, it was not fast enough.

For by the time Rosalind reached the countess, Lady Edmund was gone, and had taken Lady Blanchard with her.

CHAPTER 32

The Inner Workings of an Exclusive Society

For the female government of Almack's was a pure despotism, and subject to all the caprices of despotic rule.
—Captain Rees Howell Gronow, *Recollections and Anecdotes of the Camp, the Court, and the Clubs*

"Ah, Miss Thorne!" Countess Lieven bestowed her highly polished smile upon Rosalind. "How very fine to see you again. Do you enjoy yourself?"

"Very much, Your Grace," answered Rosalind, grateful for the politeness that was reflexive and covered over her distress. "Mrs. Nottingham's parties are always lovely." She let her gaze wander about the room, as if taking in the scene. She saw Lord Blanchard in a corner, next to a Grecian urn on its pedestal, listening to a small man in a cavalry officer's uniform. But she did not see Lady Blanchard at all.

". . . after their kind, and thanks in no small part to you, or so I am told," the countess was saying. Rosalind lowered her eyes modestly, which made the countess laugh.

"You are a charming girl, Miss Thorne. I wonder if you would consider coming to stay with us this summer? We have become quite English, you know, with a house in the country and all the . . . what is the phrase . . . all the trimmings!"

Startled, Rosalind almost fell out of her polite mannerisms. "That is most kind of you, Your Grace." She remembered her curtsy, which only made the Russian countess laugh again.

"Ah! You English. So many manners for a people who do not understand what you do."

"I don't understand you, I'm afraid."

"In Russia, it is simpler. Not better perhaps, but simpler." Countess Lieven waved her fan, which had been dyed the exact same shade of red as her dress. "In Russia, none of us has any ambition, except to be seen as the finest servant of the tsar. Everything we do is to magnify the tsar, and to make sure he knows it was us"—she tapped her chest with her fan—"who added so much to his glory."

"I don't see how that would be simpler."

"It means there is only one road, and one way to travel it, and one master over all. Here you may have your pick of masters, but if you pick the wrong one . . ." She clicked her tongue softly. "What a pity it is."

"I'd rather be able to choose my service, if I must serve." The cavalry officer moved away from Lord Blanchard, who folded his hands behind his back and scanned the room. Was he looking for his wife, too?

"We all must serve someone," the countess agreed. "But have you given any thought to what things will be like for you once Lady Blanchard leaves? Especially the way she is leaving." She nodded toward Lord Blanchard alone in his corner.

Rosalind took a moment to be sure of her voice before she answered. Her Grace's tone was entirely too arch and searching for anyone's comfort. "Lady Blanchard is leaving to accompany her husband to a diplomatic post," she said firmly. "There is nothing at all extraordinary in that."

"There would not appear to be, no."

Rosalind hesitated. This woman was clever. She was cultivated and ambitious. She was also very much playing her own game and could not be trusted. On the other hand, she very clearly had something she wanted to say to Rosalind, if she could be sure Rosalind was ready to hear it. A twisted hope seized hold of Rosalind. Perhaps the countess had heard this story of Lord Blanchard's debts and was about to tell it to Rosalind. If it was true . . . that could be the beginning and the end of Lady Blanchard's involvement in this terrible affair. Perhaps she really was just trying to find out who was trying to blackmail her husband.

"Your Grace, I have a question," said Rosalind.

"I am all attention, Miss Thorne."

"Lord Blanchard is a member of the foreign office, as is your husband." The countess nodded in acknowledgment. "Does Count Lieven perhaps have any business with him?"

"Minor matters from time to time, I believe. What is your interest?"

"There have been a few rumors. Nothing direct, of course, but some persons have been hinting that Lord Blanchard might have been experiencing some financial difficulties of late."

The countess kept her eyes fixed upon her party, but she did turn her head just slightly so that she could regard Rosalind out of the corner of one eye. "Hmm. I had not heard any such rumors, not from my husband, at least. But it is so seldom Lord Blanchard enters into what conversation I have with Lieven."

She's lying, Rosalind thought, irritatedly. *In a moment, she will say she recalls something.*

She was right. "But now that I stop to think on it, I believe I heard something . . . yes. From my dear Lord Palmerston, perhaps it was." She laughed. "Oh, you needn't look so distressed, Miss Thorne. There is no scandal. Simply ambitions which fell short, let us say." Rosalind's last hope shattered, but if the countess saw any hint in her expression, she took no notice. "Lord Blanchard has name, he has bearing and fortune and all that belongs to the great and good of the world. He has ambition, too. He wishes to soar." She waved her fan toward the ceiling.

Jane's not ambitious, she remembered Lord Blanchard saying. *Not in that way.*

"But somehow, he has not managed it, at least not to his own satisfaction. He is in good standing with his party and his friends, but they do not see him as a leader of men." The countess paused. "Some Englishmen trust too much in the family name. They assume all will flow smoothly from their friends to them, because they see it is so for others. They talk freely and lend freely—money and votes and favors. But they are not selective, or they make their selections badly and they find those favors are not repaid. Then they, for all their rank and fortune, are somehow left behind."

"I had not thought of it in that way." Across the room, Lord Blanchard was still on his own, glaring at them all, looking for someone. His wife? His political allies? This was a political party; he should be in the thick of it. But there he stood alone, and there he remained.

Rosalind struggled to collect her jumbled, frightened thoughts and return them to some semblance of order. There was one last thing this woman could tell her. One last chance that the worst of all possibilities would not prove true. "Your Grace, if it is not impertinent, may I ask another question?"

"Certainly, Miss Thorne. Whatever you like."

"The day Jasper Aimesworth died, Lady Blanchard was late in leaving the patronesses' meeting. Do you know why she was delayed?"

"Ah, now I have all this time been wondering when someone would ask that question. You see, that was a most unusual meeting."

"In what way?"

"Because Lady Blanchard was not there at all."

Rosalind's heart stopped. Her throat closed around her breath and all the warmth of the crowded room seemed to rush over her in a wave.

"But she was," Rosalind heard herself croak. "I was in the carriage when she was taken to Almack's." *She made such a point of having to be there, and of not wishing to be late . . .*

"Taken to Almack's she may have been, but she was not at the meeting. Lady Jersey told us she had been excused on a matter of urgent business."

"Did Lady Jersey say what the business was?" Because her godmother had talked about something being arranged, about having to wait. Was it possible that Lady Blanchard had missed the meeting, and Jasper's murder, because she'd been on some errand for Lady Jersey? That would make it all so innocent.

"Sarah did not favor us with further explanation." The countess arched her neatly plucked brows. "I find myself surprised you do not ask Lady Blanchard about the business yourself, Miss Thorne. She is, I believe, your godmother?"

And I have just tipped my hand. Now you know for certain that something is wrong, and you will make use of it. Because we are both still alive and this is society.

And now the secret is out.

"She has so much on her mind at the moment, I don't like to disturb her with a trivial matter," murmured Rosalind, even though she knew this thin veil of an excuse to be utterly useless.

"Ah, of course. Leaving the country is always such a monumental undertaking, and there is the matter of making her successor acceptable to Lady Jersey, and the rest of us, of course. So very much to do."

Rosalind followed her gaze across the busy room. Lord Blanchard was no longer alone. Lady Blanchard and Lady Edmund stood with him. While she watched, Honoria marched up to her mother and said something, accompanied by a great many broad gestures.

She could not see Devon anywhere.

"Is something wrong, Miss Thorne?"

"A sudden headache. I think I should get a bit of air."

"It is very close in here," agreed the countess. "But the night is hardly conducive to taking the air, and I say this as a Russian who understands the cold. Perhaps a walk in the gallery? For myself, I believe I shall indulge in a dance. How delightful it is to talk with you, Miss Thorne. I hope to make your better acquaintance very soon."

"Your Grace," murmured Rosalind as she curtsied. Then more softly she asked, "Why did you tell me these things?"

Countess Lieven winked. "We all must serve someone, Miss Thorne. I shall not serve my own master half so well if I have not Almack's, where I may see and be seen, let us say. Good luck in your hunting, or whatever it is you must do next."

With that, the countess sailed away, moving effortlessly as a swan through the crowd.

Across the room, Lady Edmund stood beside Honoria, who glared openly as Lord Blanchard and Lady Blanchard walked away. No. Lord Blanchard led Lady Blanchard away, his arm wrapped firmly around hers.

Getting her away from Lady Edmund. Why?

"Well, Miss Thorne, how is your evening thus far?" murmured a familiar voice at her shoulder. Rosalind closed her eyes briefly, struggling for patience before she turned to face him.

"Tiring, Mr. Faulks. And yours?"

"Dull, but I still find my little amusements. At the moment, I am composing a painting, Miss Thorne. A study of a supper party in all its elegance and complexity."

Rosalind resisted the urge to scream. "What have you seen?"

Mr. Faulks considered this, and her. "I have seen Mrs. Nottingham openly courting your favor and the Countess Lieven bringing you into her orbit. I have seen Lord and Lady Blanchard closer together, at least physically, than they have been in many years. I have seen Lord Casselmain becoming increasingly ill at ease with his situation and his decisions." He paused. "I have seen you, Miss Thorne, on the cusp of making either a great leap or a great fall." He turned his brilliant smile on her. "There! Now I make my self-portrait and it is as a grand and mysterious figure."

"So you do, and you can make up for it by answering a question."

He bowed. "I am at your service."

"When you went to White's with Mr. Harkness, did he ask you about my father?"

Sanderson paused, thinking carefully before he made his answer. "He did not. He did, however, ask about you, and Lord Casselmain."

"I see."

"I don't, and I don't mind confessing it. He looks on the world from a very different sort of perspective, does our Mr. Harkness, and at the moment I don't think he likes what he sees."

Rosalind remembered Devon's harsh assessment of the way in which Mr. Harkness might see things. She strained her eyes to see across the room. There. There was Devon, standing in front of Honoria and Lady Edmund. He was saying something, but for all she could hear, they might as well have been on the moon.

Now it was the Blanchards who were nowhere to be seen.

Mr. Faulks followed her gaze with his own, and sighed. "Perhaps I should have married you when your father suggested it," he murmured. "It might have saved us both a certain amount of trouble."

The words were filled with such a genuine and uncharacteristic melancholy that Rosalind turned toward him in surprise. "Oh, no, Sanderson, it would not have worked. You're many things, but a martyr to a marriage of convenience is not one of them."

Now he pulled a wounded face and laid his hand on his breast. "I'll have you know I will make a splendid husband one day."

Despite all, Rosalind smiled. "I have no doubt. If you're really looking for a wife, you could marry Alice. The money would certainly be welcome."

"Alas, I fear our Miss Littlefield has sailed far beyond my humble self into an entirely new existence, like a butterfly leaving behind her former fellow caterpillars. I will subscribe to her first novel, though, which I suspect will cause a sensation. Especially after she hears about the next act in our little play."

"What? Why? What are you . . ."

But Mr. Faulks put his finger to his lips and smiled. Then, he, too, made his way into the crowd, strolling nonchalantly toward the card room.

"Unless I'm mistaken, it is considered rude to leave a lady standing on her own."

Rosalind turned around and found herself face-to-face with Mr. Harkness.

CHAPTER 33

The Price of Admission

They formed a matrimonial market, where buyers and sellers were as eager, and sometimes the merchandise as unsuspecting and as passive, as in any other commercial traffic.

—E. Beresford Chancellor, *The Annals of Almack's*

"I surmise from your expression that Mr. Faulks did not tell you I would be here," said Mr. Harkness. "Or what state I'd be in."

"No, it's not that . . ."

Rosalind stopped, because she was lying and he could tell. Mr. Harkness was truly a sight. He must have borrowed his silk breeches, because they were at once too tight and too long, with the buckles digging hard into his calves. His jacket seams strained across his shoulders, but the cuffs had been turned back so as not to overhang his hands, and the buckled shoes were clownishly large.

And Mr. Harkness was *here*, where anyone could see him, and see her at his side. Including Lord Blanchard. Including Lady Blanchard.

Rosalind cast her panicked gaze about the room. She glimpsed Lady Blanchard and Lady Edmund in the conservatory, but could not spy Honoria, Devon, or Lord Blanchard.

"What's the matter?" asked Mr. Harkness, with none of the conventional nonsense about her looking unwell or faint. "What do you see?"

I don't know. But the words died unsaid. She did know. At least, she knew what she had seen up until now, and it was time to tell him.

But where on earth could she? Rosalind fell back at once on an old trick from her debut season.

"Mr. Harkness, I need you to step on my hem."

The principal officer peered at her to see if she was serious. Evidently deciding she was, he lifted his foot in its overlarge shoe and set the heel down on her gown's modest train. Rosalind gripped her skirt. With a silent apology to her mother's memory and to Mrs. Kendricks, who had worked so hard to keep the gown presentable, she yanked. Silk and lace tore, and Mr. Harkness lifted his foot to display a deplorable gap.

"I'm terribly sorry," he murmured. "Is there anything to be done?"

"My servant will be able to pin it up. She's in the retiring room."

"Where shall I wait so we can resume our conversation?"

"Mr. Nottingham has a private study at the top of the stairs."

He nodded his understanding and Rosalind smiled brightly in case anyone happened to look in their direction. She also curtsied, and hurried away.

In the retiring room, Mrs. Kendricks exclaimed and both pinned and stitched the gaping fabric closed. The seconds ticked relentlessly past until Rosalind felt herself in danger of genuine hysteria. What was happening downstairs? What were Lord and Lady Blanchard doing? What of Lady Edmund? She prayed Honoria was watching and would be able to tell her at least something when she returned.

For now, she had to do her best to steal down the shadowy

corridor that was not meant to be in general use for this party, let herself into a dark room she knew contained an unescorted man, and lock the door behind her.

She had been wrong in one respect. The room was not entirely dark. Mr. Harkness had used his time to light the candles on the mantle. The remaining shadows masked his ill-fitting clothing, but highlighted the strong planes of his face. Rosalind was glad she still stood in the darkness, so he could not see the outrageous way she stared at him.

"I'm afraid there will be trouble for you if we're caught together like this," Mr. Harkness said. He also did not move from his place by the black hearth.

"I am aware of that." She leaned toward the door, listening, but heard no sound of movement outside. "We should have a few moments, though, I think."

"What is it you want to say?"

She faced him, and opened her mouth, and closed it. Where, after all this, could she possibly begin?

"Mr. Harkness, what do you know of how Almack's works?"

A spasm of impatience crossed his shadowed features, but he smoothed it away. "Nothing at all, I'm afraid."

"It's complicated, and eccentric. What Almack's really is, is a series of assemblies given by the lady patronesses. Admission requires a ticket and only persons who have paid the subscription fee are eligible to receive those tickets.

"Is that unusual?"

"Not at all. It's quite the done thing, especially for charity concerts and the like. To become a subscriber to Almack's, you must apply to one of the ladies who arrange the assemblies."

"A patroness?"

"Yes. Now, in the normal run of things, a person giving a

subscription ball or assembly will grant tickets to anyone who pays until tickets run out."

"But not so at Almack's."

"No. You have to be granted permission to subscribe to Almack's." Now Mr. Harkness looked at her in frank disbelief, and all she could do was smile weakly in return. "To gain that permission, you must first be visited by a patroness. She judges your character, your taste, your rank and wealth, your *ton,* if you understand me." *That* ton *which does not allow for unmarried women to be alone with a man, incidentally.*

"Almost, I think." He frowned like a schoolboy working a particularly difficult sum. "So, if the lady patroness judges you to be of good enough *ton,* you are permitted to pay your fee and become a subscriber."

"Oh, no," said Rosalind. "Not yet. If you put on a good showing for the patroness who visits you, she takes your name to the others. You are discussed in a secret meeting and voted upon. Only if the whole of the board votes in your favor are you allowed to become a subscriber."

"Miss Thorne," choked Mr. Harkness. "Are you telling me people actually have to pass muster before a board of review in order to be allowed to give these women ten guineas?"

"Yes."

He stared at the fire for a long moment. "Perhaps this is why people say you have to be born to society. It's clearly beyond my tradesman's sensibilities." He sighed. "So, once you have been permitted to pay your money, you receive a voucher, and you can go to the ball?"

"Yes. A voucher entitles the subscriber to a certain amount of tickets for a certain number of assemblies. All the assemblies in May, for example, or two assemblies in August."

"The number of assemblies indicating the strength of the ladies' opinions of you?"

"You begin to understand, and I think . . ." She stopped. She had not said this out loud yet, and in this room, alone with this man, it suddenly seemed entirely absurd. But she remembered the strongbox, and she remembered the scrap of ledger Honoria showed her. And she remembered Jasper's eyes.

"I think someone has been forging Almack's tickets, and selling them."

Mr. Harkness did not answer immediately. He paced over to the window and eased the curtains back to look at the street outside. "I don't understand how that could work," he said. "You've just told me the patronesses personally know everyone who gets the tickets."

"No." Rosalind rubbed her hands together. Despite the cold of the room, her palms had gone damp inside her silk gloves. "The ladies know who gets the *vouchers,* or at least each lady personally knows who gets the vouchers she's approved. Say, for example, you are Mrs. Smith. You have two daughters and a son and you want them to be introduced to society. You apply to a patroness for admission to Almack's. You are found acceptable and pay your fee, and receive a voucher which entitles you to five tickets for the April assemblies; three ladies tickets and two gentlemen's tickets."

"Why two? I thought you said there was one son."

"Extra gentlemen's tickets are always given, to encourage more men to turn up. Now, the ladies tickets are transferrable . . ."

"I beg your pardon?"

"Transferrable. If Mrs. Smith cannot attend an assembly, she may give her ticket to another, within limits."

"So, the lady patronesses might *not* personally know everyone who holds the tickets," said Mr. Harkness slowly. "Are the tickets examined before the parties enter?"

"Yes, and the patroness who is assigned to preside over the assembly is supposed to be at the door to see who comes in and make sure they are appropriately dressed, and have their tickets."

"So that would be a barrier to a stranger's entry."

Rosalind tried to moisten her lips, but her mouth had gone entirely dry. "But not a very great one. The Almack's assemblies may be exclusive, but they are not small. On any given night, there can be as many as a thousand people coming and going. If one has a credible ticket and good enough clothing, one might very well slip in. All it would take was a certain steadiness of nerve at the door. Then, once inside, if there were extra people wandering about, it would be assumed that they were the guests of somebody else."

"It's an interesting hypothesis, Miss Thorne. I would like to know how you happened to hit on it."

He had gone still again, and he was waiting. Specifically, he was waiting to see if she would now lie to him.

Rosalind bowed her head. "I thought of forgery because my father is a forger, sir, as I think you already know."

"Yes, Miss Thorne, I do."

He said it softly and soberly. But that was all he said. He did not remind her that she was tainted by her father's crime. He did not suggest he had been searching for him, or for Charlotte. Rosalind pressed her hand against her stomach. She had ricocheted so many times between hope and fear tonight, every nerve felt weak and bruised. She must breathe. She could not compound the absurdity and discomfort of this moment by growing faint.

It was Mr. Harkness who broke the silence. "If this scheme is as you paint it, and it was discovered, I imagine the papers would pounce," he said. "The lady patronesses would go from ruling the fashionable world to being laughingstocks."

"Oh, worse." Rosalind told him. "Almack's reputation rests not only on its perfect exclusivity, but its perfect safety. Only the richest and most respectable gentlemen are allowed within reach of the most respectable girls. If the matchmaking mamas thought unacceptable parties, or poor fortune hunters, had been let near their darling children under false pretenses, the patronesses might very well find themselves cut dead throughout society."

"And you think Jasper Aimesworth might have been involved in this ticket-forging scheme?"

"I found a strongbox in a room that he had the key for. It had thousands in banknotes in it, and a thousand more in promissory notes."

"Which is very interesting, but not conclusive," Mr. Harkness said, gently, she thought. "He may have been lucky at the tables."

"Perhaps," said Rosalind. "But somehow, I doubt that. The last time Honoria, his sister, saw him alive, he was burning papers, and at least some of them were pages from a ledger of some sort."

"Which might have contained the names of people receiving tickets." Harkness's fists clenched.

"Honoria told me at the very beginning that Jasper Aimesworth was worried about money. The housekeeper at Tamwell House said he was badgering his father about it. I think he hit on a scheme to make some for himself. He forged and distributed the tickets in collusion with one of the lady patronesses . . ."

She looked at him, waiting for him to say "who might have been Lady Blanchard," but he did not. He just stood by the hearth and watched her with an air of weary sympathy that robbed Rosalind of her remaining breath. She was not used to being understood, not by strange men in the darkness certainly. But she was so alone, so broken by all the truths she had collided against, she needed someone, anyone, to cling to.

Oh, I have gone too far. There is no coming back from this.

"Miss Thorne, you do realize you're telling me that your god-mother, Lady Blanchard, might have killed a man."

His words dropped like stones into the cold stillness of the room. Rosalind wanted to kick them all away, but she could not even make herself move. "His skull was bashed in. That's hardly something a woman would do."

Mr. Harkness's smile was brief, and bitter. "Miss Thorne, I have seen women do as much and worse when they are angry, or desperate."

Which was hardly reassuring, but then, he did not mean it to be. He would not spare her. She should be grateful. She surely did not want any such protection now. She had been protected before this—first by her father and then by the Blanchards and Lord Casselmain—and look where it had gotten her.

"Lady Blanchard wasn't actually in Almack's when Jasper died," said Rosalind. Mr. Harkness stood perfectly still, waiting for her to go on. Rosalind did. "I just heard it from the Count-ess Lieven. I took Lady Blanchard to Almack's, but she never attended that patronesses' meeting. I think . . . I think she was meeting someone quite different."

"Who?" asked Mr. Harkness. "And why?"

"Mr. Whelks," she said. "I think Mr. Whelks found out about the forgeries, and was planning to tell Lady Jersey. I think Lady Blanchard was going to try to put him off, perhaps buy him off, but she didn't tell Jasper about it. Mr. Whelks never arrived to meet her. Jasper caught up with him in Almack's, thinking to kill him before he could reveal the secret."

"How would Aimesworth know Whelks had found out about the forgeries, much less care?" He stopped. "Because Lady Blanchard told him. Because Aimesworth and Lady Blanchard were colluding."

"Jasper came to kill Mr. Whelks, but in the struggle, Mr. Whelks killed Jasper instead. Perhaps it was an accident. Mr. Whelks knew he would be blamed for the death, and for allowing the forgeries to happen in the first place . . ."

"So he has been covering up the evidence," Mr. Harkness finished for her.

"He cleared out Jasper's bachelor rooms to make sure there was no ticket or letter, or anything else left to give the game away. And to try to find out which patroness was working with him."

"Which makes Whelks our key to this matter."

"If I'm right," Rosalind reminded him.

Harkness rubbed his chin. "I think you are, or at least, you are very close to right. Close enough that I'd better talk to Whelks before word gets out that you and I have spoken. I don't suppose he did us both the very great favor of coming to this little supper party?"

"No, I'm afraid not."

"Well then, I must bid you good night and go find him."

"I can't tell you his address but—"

Mr. Harkness held up his hand. "You must allow for the fact that I have some small skills of my own, Miss Thorne. I have already had some communication with Mr. Whelks and I do know where he lives."

Rosalind felt herself blush. "Oh. Of course you do."

He smiled, but only briefly. "Miss Thorne," he said seriously. "It might be best if you went home at once. If our person, or persons, feel matters are coming to a head, they could become desperate."

"You may rest assured, Mr. Harkness, that as soon as you are gone, I have every intention of succumbing to a sick headache."

"Very wise," he said solemnly. "I will leave you now." He

bowed once more but he did not move. He was watching her, much the way she had watched him when she first entered the room, taking note of the play of light and shadow, and something more. Rosalind knew she should turn away, should back away from that look, but she did not want to. She wanted reassurance, she wanted companionship. She wanted anything that might ease the cold and loneliness that filled her.

"You deserve better, you know," Mr. Harkness said softly. "A woman such as you should not be condemned to a life of polite artifice and deciding what fatuous man sits next to what prattling woman at dinner."

Her heart constricted. The pain of it reminded her she should not be here. This was the one situation, above all others, that she had been trained since birth to avoid, and yet she had walked right in, with her eyes open. She herself had locked the door so they would not be disturbed.

"I thank you for your good opinion," she murmured. "But what else am I to do?" She spread her hands. "I am shaped for one thing and one thing only—to marry a gentleman and run his house. If I had other choices, they were long since taken from me."

"That is not true," he said. "I will not let that be true."

He was moving toward her. The shadows covered his eyes like black silk. She wanted to kiss him. She had not wanted to kiss a man in a very long time and the impulse shocked her. She told herself it was not genuine desire. It was curiosity, perhaps. It was the feeling of already having passed all the boundaries. It was this desperate, terrible loneliness and the sense that all of her world had been torn away from her. Perhaps it was even some mad wish for revenge on Devon for agreeing to Honoria's marriage scheme instead of continuing to wait until she found her way to him.

That was the truth.

No, it wasn't.

It has to be.

"I cannot," she whispered as Mr. Harkness stopped in front of her. "It is impossible. Even if I wanted to."

"No. Only if you wanted to." He touched her cheek. "I am so far out of bounds, you should turn me out and complain to the magistrates."

"I should." She was trembling. His touch was reminding her how long she had been entirely alone. "I would, except I know you're going to stop now."

She watched his mouth and the play of the muscles of his face as he struggled to master himself. But he did lower his hand from her cheek, and he did step back. He folded his hands behind himself and she suspected he tightened those hands into fists.

"Please accept my apologies, Miss Thorne. I will let you know what I find."

He bowed, and he moved to the door. Even in his too-large shoes, he was absolutely silent. He paused, listening, before he undid the lock and slipped into the corridor.

Rosalind gripped the back of the nearest chair and held on until she was certain she would not stagger. Only then did she blow out the candles, and listen at the door for herself, and leave as she came; entirely alone.

She was so tired, it felt like a hundred years must have passed since she'd entered Mr. Nottingham's study. But the great case clock at the top of the stairs told her it had not even been half an hour. Rosalind leaned heavily on the polished banister as she descended. She needed to find a parlor maid to fetch Mrs. Kendricks. She needed to be gone from here. Perhaps she would not even return to Blanchard House. Perhaps it would be wisest to go straight to Little Russell Street. It would not be comfortable, but better that than—

Rosalind's thoughts broke off, sharply and suddenly, because

Honoria was shouldering her way through the gathering, rudely and quite alone.

Honoria grabbed her arm and dragged Rosalind into the shadow of the staircase. Rosalind's throat seized shut, even before the other girl spoke.

"Rosalind, I think there's trouble."

"What?" Rosalind croaked. "Why?"

"Lady Blanchard saw you go into Mr. Nottingham's study." Honoria dropped her voice to a harsh whisper. "And she saw that runner come out."

Rosalind's heart slammed against her ribs and she looked wildly around the room. "Where is she now?"

"She's gone, Rosalind. And Lord Blanchard went with her."

CHAPTER 34

The Final Race

*To expose the vices of fashionable life, in their original and
proudest sphere . . .*

—Marianne Spencer Stanhope Hudson, quoting
from the *Edinburgh Review*

Rosalind did not stop to think. She turned on her heels and
bolted, straight through the salons and the entrance halls, out
the door past astonished footmen and onto the steps of the Nottinghams' house. Cold engulfed her as she stared in desperation
at the cluster of carriages, at the drivers and link boys warming
their hands by the bonfires that had been lit on the cobbles, at
the few persons hurrying past.

Lord Blanchard was not among them. Lady Blanchard was
not among them. Neither was Mr. Harkness.

I have to stop her. I have to stop them! thought Rosalind frantically. From doing what, though? What did she really suspect? It
didn't matter. There was no good to come from them vanishing
so suddenly.

She ran back into the house, and up to an astonished footman who was keeping the door. "Did the Blanchards take their
carriage?" she demanded.

"They did, miss . . ." he stammered.

"And they were together?"

"Yes, miss."

"Rosalind!" Devon was pushing his way through the crowd, with Honoria right behind him. The crowd was staring, shifting and murmuring like members of a theater audience, trying to get a good look at the players.

I've finally done it, she thought with a kind of grim hilarity. *I'm making a scene.*

"I need a carriage," she said, not caring who answered, as long as somebody did. "I need to get to Blanchard House."

"I am at your service," said Devon at once.

"You came with us," Honoria reminded him. "I'll send for Michelson . . ."

But Devon was looking over her shoulder as Lady Edmund approached, slowly, like a storm cloud in her black and gray gown.

"Honoria?" she inquired icily. "Is something the matter?"

Honoria groaned and stomped her slippered foot. Rosalind felt her own temper overflow. There was no time for this. There was no time for anything.

"Honoria, go tell Mrs. Kendricks I'm leaving." She did not watch if she obeyed or not. Instead, she turned to Devon. "Lord Casselmain, find me a conveyance of some sort." Devon bowed. He also grabbed the nearest footman by the arm and dragged the poor man to one side. Rosalind left him to it. She stepped up so closely to Lady Edmund that she was nearly standing on her black hems. She leaned close, speaking in cool confidence. "Lady Edmund, you will let us go, and you will let us go quietly, or I will tell my reporter friends that you were involved in a scheme to sell false tickets to Almack's."

Lady Edmund smiled, brittle and sharp. But she was not surprised. "No one would believe you," she breathed.

"That hardly matters, does it? Your name will be salted throughout the *Chronicle* for weeks on end, and connected with your son's death. It will sell so many papers, they'll keep it on the front page for months."

Lady Edmund's eyes narrowed and there was poison in them. "You are as ludicrous as your mother was. Neither of you understand anything of the world." She looked past Rosalind to Devon, who had at some point released his captive footman and come up behind them. "You should disassociate yourself from her, Lord Casselmain, before she can utter her threats against you."

"Miss Thorne does not make threats," answered Devon evenly.

"Promises, yes, but not threats," remarked a new voice. Mr. Faulks slid easily and casually through the staring crowd and stepped up beside Lord Casselmain. "Miss Thorne," he said by way of greeting. "I see your woman is coming, with your things." He pointed his stick toward the stairs. He was right, Honoria was racing down, with Mrs. Kendricks beside her, and Rosalind's wraps trailing in her arms. "Are you leaving? Do you require an escort?"

"What's happening?" demanded someone among the guests.

"Don't know," someone else answered. "Ten pounds says it's nothing good."

"I'll take that!" cried another, drunker voice.

"You have finished yourself, Honoria," grated Lady Edmund.

"Oh good," her daughter answered with a great sigh. "It will save me the trouble of having to divorce Casselmain."

For a moment, Rosalind thought Lady Edmund was going to faint dead away. But there was no time to feel the irony or the justice of Honoria finally having found a way to shatter her mother's cold perfections. Devon was at their side again. "I have the carriage, it's being brought 'round."

"Quickly," said Rosalind, to Honoria and Devon, and Mr. Faulks, Mrs. Kendricks, and the world at large. "We may already be too late to stop them."

"Why do we have to stop them?" asked Honoria.

"One of them might be Jasper's murderer," answered Rosalind. "And may God have mercy on our souls."

London at night was hardly the place Harkness would have chosen for a horse race, but it was what he had. He leaned low over the gelding's neck, riding crop in hand, eyes fastened on the shifting dark. The wind whipped the tumult of voices, hoofbeats, carriages, and carts into a hurricane of sound around his ears. The horse did not like being run half-blind through the chaotic streets, and was coming near to panic. It took every ounce of Harkness's skill to hold the beast in check and on its course. How long had it been since he'd bolted from the Nottinghams'? He could not tell. He could not slow down for even a moment. Every instinct he possessed told him time was up.

He'd been seen. Like a raw recruit on his first patrol, he'd let himself be spotted in that damned party, as he'd never been spotted on the roads or in the woods. He'd taken the servants' stairs out of the private study, but instead of going straight out the back, as he should have done, like a fool, he'd slipped back into the salons to find Mr. Faulks. He'd wanted the man to keep an eye on Miss Thorne, and the rest of the gathering, in case something of note happened.

And it had. Lord Blanchard had seen him, and nearly dropped his whiskey glass.

Harkness drew back hard on the reins. The horse slowed and stopped, dancing uneasily under him. He patted the gelding's neck, trying both to calm his mount and to get his bearings.

London in the daytime was a maze of twisting streets and alleys with no rhyme or reason. London at night was ten times worse, with the ashy dark, the torches, and the traffic as the fashionables and their satellites made their way through its shadows.

This neighborhood was relatively quiet. The houses were low, and many were wood or old half-timber dwellings. No one had bothered with setting up streetlamps here yet, or sidewalks. The air smelled of smoke and horses and people's dinners.

On the corner slouched a group of porters, passing an earthenware jug back and forth between them. Harkness swung himself off the horse and dug in his waistcoat pocket for a shilling, which he tossed to the nearest man.

"There's another in it for you if you and the horse are still here when I get out. This is Bow Street business," he added, grateful that his great coat and the dark would hide his ill-fitting clothing.

The ruffian bit the coin, and touched his hat. Harkness prayed he wouldn't figure a horse in hand was worth more than the promise of another small coin. He turned and strode down the street, peering at the houses, until he found the right one.

It still seemed too fantastical to be true. Could a man really be murdered over tickets to a dance? Harkness hammered on the plain door. *He could if there was enough money involved.* And from Miss Thorne's description of what she found in the strongbox, there was more than enough.

Miss Thorne. He'd almost kissed her. And unless he was very much mistaken, she'd almost kissed him. How in the hell had he let that come about?

He would think about that later. Right now, there were footsteps sounding inside the house. A moment later the door opened, and Mr. Whelks, a flickering candle in hand, stooped to peer beneath the threshold at him.

"Who in the h—" But he didn't finish. He didn't need to.

Harkness saw recognition dawning, terrible and slow across the man's face.

"Principal Officer Adam Harkness of the Bow Street Police Office." Harkness pulled his white staff of office out of his great coat pocket and touched the man on the shoulder. "Here for a word with you, Mr. Thorvald Whelks."

"But they are not here, Miss Thorne," stammered the footman at Blanchard House. "They have not been here."

"What! That's not possible!" Rosalind raced up the stairs, stumbling over her own hems before she remembered to grab them out of the way.

"Breaking your neck is not going to help anyone," called Honoria behind her. Rosalind murmured a few words that would have gotten her expelled from school, and kept climbing. Her ball gown had never felt so heavy or awkward. Her breath was coming in tiny gasps and spots danced in front of her eyes. In the entrance hall below, the door slammed open again. Devon must have roused the grooms to deal with the carriage and horses. She didn't look back. Let them all follow as they would.

Lord and Lady Blanchard were in on the scheme together. That must be it. He had ambition. She had the social connections necessary to become a patroness. They'd realized Rosalind had found them out and so they ran. They'd meant to run in any case. There were no debts. It was to avoid the forgery scandal that Lord Blanchard had taken the Konigsberg post. That was why Rosalind had been so sure Lady Blanchard never meant to come back.

Lady Blanchard had invited her to stay to help cover their retreat, because she knew Rosalind to be loyal, and beholden. Rosalind would be willing and able to help her cover up any last-minute disasters.

Like Jasper's death.

Except that couldn't be it. Because Lord Blanchard was the one who'd created their covering story. He'd done it by forging the bet in White's book, and enlisting Devon in his lie. Because Lord Blanchard *had* been planning to come back.

Rosalind barged straight into Lady Blanchard's apartment and stared about her. The rooms were empty. Not even Lacey was there. The fire was lit, and all looked in order for the mistress's return. If Lady Blanchard had been here to grab a few things so she could fly away, there would be disarray.

Unless she had her bags packed. Rosalind ran to the boudoir, ducking into the dressing room and the closet. But all was in place. No case, no dress, no jewel box was gone from its accustomed place.

"Rosalind," said Devon from behind the door. "They've not been here. I've looked in Lord Blanchard's room."

"They must be," she said, turning in place, hardly seeing anything for the current of thoughts running through her mind. "They must be planning to leave tonight. They—"

Unless she'd been a fool.

Unless she wanted so much to believe in the goodness of Lady Blanchard, who had saved her, that she had not been willing to look at the final possibility.

Rosalind's heart was in her mouth. If she must make this accusation, she would be certain. Being right would be cold comfort in the hard days to come, but it might very well be all the comfort she had. Not to mention her only defense when this affair exploded through society like a cannon shell.

Rosalind moved back out into the dressing room. She was aware that Devon and Honoria had backed away from her. She ignored them and instead opened the jewel cabinet.

I could still be very wrong. I've been wrong about any number of things.

The third drawer held the hair combs.

They were laid out in tidy rows on the royal blue velvet. Gold, silver, tortoiseshell, etched with grand designs or set with sparkling stones. In the center of the second row was one made of silver. It was lovely, but not particularly ornate. An everyday accent to a lady's toilette, set with garnets and seed pearls. Rosalind lifted it out.

"Oh, Godmother," she breathed.

Because the gems were set in such a way as to form a pair of ornate curves. But when Rosalind turned the comb sideways, the curves turned into two stylized versions of the letter *J*. It could, of course, be *J* for Jane, Lady Blanchard's Christian name.

Or they could be *J* and *J* for Jane and Jasper.

That was why Lady Blanchard had been so shocked when Rosalind had suggested Jasper was her son. He was most emphatically not her son. There had always been two possibilities to explain why Lady Blanchard had been so stricken by Jasper's death. This was the second, the most obvious, and the one Rosalind had so badly not wanted to believe that she went chasing down every other path before she could make herself open this drawer.

Jasper Aimesworth's mysterious woman was Lady Blanchard. Did Lord Blanchard find out before or after the scheme of forging the tickets started? Did he drag his wife into it, or had she dragged him?

Jasper Aimesworth forged the tickets. Lady Blanchard distributed them and they collected the money. And when it all threatened to fall apart, she might have met him in secret, and killed him in anger. And in shock, in fear, confessed it to her husband.

It could easily have happened in just that way.

I could still be wrong. Rosalind slammed the drawer shut and turned to her friends. "I know where they are," she said. "They've gone to Thurlough Square."

Whelks led Harkness into the parlor. It was a Spartan place, with one chair drawn up in front of the fire, and one chair at the dining table. There was no evidence of a wife, never mind any children. The only luxury in the place was the small harpsichord under its tapestry cover by the window.

Whelks set the candle carefully on the mantle. "I trust I am allowed to dress before you take me with you?"

"Should I be taking you with me?" asked Harkness.

"Oh yes," said Whelks to the fire. "I killed Mr. Aimesworth. I am ready to confess it."

Give me patience. Harkness folded his arms. "You did not, and I can prove it, but I'd rather not have to take the time."

Whelks turned around, his eyes wide and astonished. "But—"

"I don't know who did it—yet, mind you, but I know it wasn't you. Was it your Lady Jersey?"

Whelks drew himself up to his full height, and it was impressive. If he'd been under the roof beam, he would have hit his very hard head. "You are insolent, sir!"

"I know," answered Harkness. "Look, man, you're not going to be able to stop the scandal, if that's what you're worried about. What you can do is make sure the proper parties pay for what they've done, before anyone else has to." He paused. The man was shrinking in on himself, shriveling like very tall men did to try to fit into the crowded world around them. "You've already seen how trying to hide this away has just made it worse."

"Yes," said Whelks softly. "Yes, I have." He slumped in the fireside chair.

Harkness grabbed up the chair from the dining table and brought it over.

"I'm sorry about this, Whelks," he said. "But I've got no time. I need you to talk, and quickly. What can you tell me about this business of the Almack's vouchers?"

Whelks rubbed his big hands against his knees.

"I found out last season." He paused so Harkness could nod and signal his understanding. "I was letting myself into the patronesses' office, to make sure it had been cleaned and that all was in order for the first meeting of the year. The room must be well aired and free of damp, with everything in its place. Willis is an excellent manager, but it is my job to be sure. Lady Jersey is quite particular, you understand."

And probably has the devil's own temper and if anything's out of place, it's your head on the block. "I understand."

"It was a Monday, of course, directly before the patronesses' meeting. I opened the door and . . . there was Lady Blanchard, and the young man was with her."

"Jasper Aimesworth?"

Whelks nodded. "It was a horrible breech of etiquette. No one is permitted in the lady patronesses' office except the ladies themselves."

"And you."

"Only when no business is being conducted." Whelks sniffed. "I was so shocked, I closed the door and stood there until her ladyship came out." He paused again. His fingers had started drumming restlessly against his thighs. It took Harkness a minute to realize the motion was that of a man playing a tune on a keyboard. "She said it was a joke. She begged me to say nothing. It would never happen again. She trusted my discretion.

"I, of course, was willing to overlook the matter. With the season coming on, there was no need for Lady Jersey to be distressed by something so small. I put it out of my mind, until I began to notice the discrepancies."

"More people were coming to the assemblies than showed up in the official books?" prompted Harkness.

Whelks's fingertips stilled. "Oh no, the lists were quite complete," he whispered. "But they were not in my handwriting."

"Someone was swapping them?"

He nodded. "Someone created false ledgers, copied from the originals, but with additions, and put them on the shelves. The copies were good, but well . . ."

Of course. Two sets of books. It was a standard trick among moneymen. It would work with other kinds of records as well. This way, if there was any question about admitted persons, and anyone did check the records, they would find all in order. Anyone, that is, except this man.

"I realized something was wrong, and I realized Lady Blanchard must be involved. It was a horrible accusation to make. I wanted to take my time and muster my evidence. But then, I heard about the Konigsberg appointment. I was so relieved." He paused and wiped his upper lip. "I thought that would end it. I need never say a word."

You would never be accused of carelessness, and perhaps dismissed from your post.

"Almack's would continue, and not a soul the wiser. Then . . ." He stopped and pressed his hand across his eyes.

"Then Jasper Aimesworth died," Harkness finished for him. Whelks nodded.

"Why didn't you say anything?"

"Because it would destroy Almack's, and my lady," he said, and Harkness saw a single tear trickle slowly down his cheek. "I could not take away everything she, and I, had worked for. It was all I had. He who steals my purse, Mr. Harkness, steals trash."

"But he who steals my good name . . ." Harkness continued the quotation. "But you said you'd mustered your evidence."

"Yes. I'd begun keeping copies of my own lists, so I could compare them to the ledgers in the office after the assemblies."

"And where are those ledgers?"

"I don't know," he said. "When I went to fetch them after . . . after. They were already gone."

Taken by somebody who had access to the office. Probably Aimesworth had gotten wind that the jig was up. He'd already been in and fetched the ledgers that morning, to take home and burn.

"But that was why you went and cleared out Aimesworth's rooms. You were looking for the ledgers. You assumed the landlord would be blamed when the theft was eventually discovered. It would be assumed he sold the young man's goods to a pawnbroker."

He nodded. "At that point, I just wanted to make it all go away, all evidence of . . . impropriety."

Because you were afraid, thought Harkness. *With good reason.*

Any servant, no matter how highly placed, could lose their position on the turn of a whim and the snap of a finger, and all of them knew it. If they were at all intelligent, they took great pains to make sure of the perfection of their actions. Mr. Whelks was very intelligent, and he knew it probable Lady Jersey would not forgive him for keeping such a secret from her.

"What did you do after you cleared out Aimesworth's rooms?"

"I went to Lord Blanchard with a letter, to warn him of his wife's deceptions."

Harkness got to his feet. Slowly he walked over and stood before a man who was not used to being loomed over. "You did *what?*"

"I wouldn't have done it, but Miss Thorne was still ferreting out the gossip. I thought Lord Blanchard could force her to be quiet. I was sure he would protect his name from scandal as I must protect . . ."

But Harkness was already across the room. He threw open the door, and reeled backward. A stunned and gasping Lord Casselmain staggered across the threshold.

"Harkness, come quick. Rosalind . . . Rosalind . . ."

Harkness just grabbed the duke by the arm and dragged him out into the dark.

CHAPTER 35

The Coldest Truth

I have often heard her say, "que le jeu d'Almack's ne valoit pas la chandelle" *["that the game of Almack's is not worth a candle"].*

—Marianne Spencer Stanhope Hudson, *Almack's*

Thurlough Square was absolutely black and silent when Rosalind and Honoria leapt from the carriage.

Devon had not wanted them to come. Devon had raged at them. But no one else could go to fetch Mr. Harkness, and Rosalind was finished with lying to Devon or playing the meek and obedient miss. Even then, she was sure he would have kept insisting if Mr. Faulks hadn't volunteered to drive.

Honoria stared about her at the blackened square. "Where are we?"

"I'll tell you later." Rosalind looked up at Sanderson. "Mr. Faulks?" They could not leave the horses and the carriage.

"Go," he said. "I'll tie up the horses and follow."

Rosalind grabbed Jasper's keys out of her reticule and ran up the steps, her slippers skidding on the damp stone. After several fumbling attempts, she found the lock and opened the door. The inside was as dark as the square, and as silent.

"I can't be wrong," she breathed as she grabbed up her hems and stumbled inside. Despite her coat and bonnet, she was chilled to the bone. She felt as if she would never be warm again.

"Why not? You were before." Honoria was leaning against the wall, trying to catch her own breath. Her curls had tumbled down from their formal dressing and trailed around her ears along with a tangle of ribbons.

"Because the money's here." Rosalind staggered forward and found the stairs. With her hems in her fists and Honoria right behind her, she climbed as fast as constricted breath and battered slippers allowed. "If they're fleeing the country, they'll need money."

There. The door to the lady's bedroom was open a crack, and there was a faint flickering light beyond. Rosalind ran, and when she reached the door, she pushed it open.

The first thing she saw was Lady Blanchard stretched out on the bed, the covers in disarray around her. Her head lolled at an unnatural angle. One white arm fell across her chest, the other dangled over the side of the bed.

"Lady Blanchard!" Rosalind cried and dashed forward.

"She's dead."

Rosalind froze in her tracks. Lord Blanchard stepped around the foot of the bed. The curtains had concealed him from Rosalind's view until now. He came forward, silent as a ghost and just as pale.

"My wife is dead," he said. "She took this." He held out a small, stoppered brown bottle. "She took it all."

Rosalind could not look away from him. The candlelight played across his ghastly features. He looked less alive than the woman on the bed. Rosalind raised the bottle to her nose and caught the too-sweet scent.

"Laudanum?" It was Honoria who spoke.

Lord Blanchard whipped around, seeing the other woman for the first time. He groaned. "I was too late. When she left the party, I followed, but not fast enough. God forgive me," he added. "You were too late, too."

His eyes shone oddly, but it was not tears. Rosalind took a step backward. Something was entirely wrong here.

She had it. Lord Blanchard said he followed his wife. *The footman said they'd left the party together.*

Movement caught her eye. Lady Blanchard's head shifted, just a little.

"She lives!" Rosalind cried. "Lord Blanchard, go shout for the watch! Faulks is outside! They can bring an apothecary! She lives!"

"I'll go!" Honoria was out the door and thudding down the stairs before Rosalind could stop her. She moved to dart forward to the bedside. There might be time. They might be able to get the poison out of her. She might . . .

Lord Blanchard stepped into her path. He did not even look behind him.

"She's dead, Miss Thorne," he breathed. "My wife is dead. I was too late and so were you."

"You can't mean this! Let me past!" She dodged sideways again, but he grabbed her wrist, holding it high and twisting hard.

"There is no help," he told her in that same soft, flat whisper. "How many times do I have to tell you? She is already dead."

Understanding fell heavily through her. Rosalind gulped air. "You knew. About Almack's, about the forged tickets."

"Yes, yes, I knew." He shoved her backward. "And now there's nothing to be done. You're a sensible woman, Miss Thorne. You can see how it had to end this way, can't you? She thought she could control you with your old loyalties. She thought she could control Lady Edmund with the bribe of an Almack's post. But she couldn't. And where would it end? She could not let the world know she'd killed her young lover with whom she'd colluded to sell fake tickets for Almack's. Her name would never survive it. She had to end her life. There was no choice."

His grip loosened, just enough. Rosalind drew her arm down slowly. She must not startle him. "Oh no. She never would. Not over such a man as she knew you to be."

His mouth closed.

"She was forging the tickets with Jasper. They were lovers, and they did it to get the money so they could run away together. You'd never grant her a divorce, and you'd ruin her if she tried to leave openly, because it would end your political ambitions. But you found out about the whole scheme . . ." Where was Honoria? Where was Mr. Faulks? She couldn't even hear voices in the street below. "And Jasper knew it. He'd gone to Almack's that day to warn Lady Blanchard."

"I thought he might be getting jumpy," said Lord Blanchard. "I was waiting to see if he'd show up and he did not disappoint." He snickered. "It was Aimesworth's idea to talk in the musicians' gallery. The young idiot thought he could put me off. *Me!* Said he'd tried to tell Jane I was wise to them as well as that blaggard Whelks. Said he burned the evidence that morning. He offered to hand over the money—thousands, he said—if I would just let her go. They were going anyway, he said. It was just a matter of whether they left quietly or loudly."

"And you killed him."

"Of course I killed him! That bitch and her insolent puppy were going to ruin my good name! I killed him right there, in pure and perfect Almack's, where everyone would rush to cover it all up and assign blame in every quarter, and never look twice at me, and never think to ask why it had happened, so there'd be no scandal involving my wife. What else was I supposed to do?" He spread his hands toward her. "And now, I must ask, what am I to do with you?"

Malice dripped from each word, and there was no mistaking the hatred, and the exhaustion.

Rosalind forced the panic down. She was not here alone. She'd not been such a fool. Honoria was outside, so was Mr. Faulks. They were bringing the watchmen, and an apothecary. She just had to buy herself some time.

Her eyes darted left, darted right, and she saw Blanchard's walking stick leaning against the wall. Her mind froze, then galloped forward. She wondered how many blows it had taken to kill Jasper, and how he'd dealt with the blood on his hands.

"It doesn't make any difference," she whispered. "I cannot tell anyone. They will not believe me."

"No, that's true. You're just a single woman alone. Prone to imaginings and hysterics. There's not a magistrate in the kingdom who would take your word over mine. Not when you've been abandoned by your family and living by your . . . wits." He chuckled rudely. "Especially once I've noised it about that I had to ask you to leave my house once before."

Rosalind listened to him reason with himself. She glanced toward the door. It was not so very far away. She could bolt. No. She was in slippers and corset and this ridiculous dress. If he tried even a little, he'd be on her in an instant.

"Still, Miss Thorne, we all know you are not an ordinary woman. You are so very useful. I can count on Lady Jersey and the rest of her scheming cats at that ridiculous little social club to keep quiet and safeguard their own reputations. But you, you might just be able to convince that man from Bow Street, or that harridan daughter of the Aimesworths, to say something out loud."

"I swear I will not tell anyone."

He shook his head ponderously, like it had suddenly grown too heavy for him. "I don't believe you. I can't believe you. You'll turn into a talking fool like any woman would."

He took a step toward her. He took another.

"Stop, Lord Blanchard. Think. Your wife . . ." She swallowed. Had Lady Blanchard moved again? Was she still alive? Was there any chance at all? "You're an intelligent man. You've fashioned an explanation for your wife's death, but what of mine? The watch will be here any moment."

He snickered. "What explanation do I need? I am Viscount Blanchard! What happens in my house is beyond question. You'll be buried and forgotten faster than that pathetic Aimesworth boy."

Rosalind turned. She dove forward, not for the door but for the walking stick. She seized on it and turned back to swing at her godfather's head, but Lord Blanchard ducked, and grabbed her wrists, twisting hard, until she cried out and dropped the stick.

One great hand closed about her throat.

"Now, now, Miss Thorne, it's best to go quiet. Even Jane saw that in the end."

Rosalind pried desperately at his fingers, but could not find purchase. She did the only thing she could. She grabbed his arm and let herself fall.

He wasn't ready to take all her weight, and he staggered. Rosalind twisted frantically and his death grip broke. She rolled sideways, struggling to get to her feet, but her skirts tangled her legs. She caught the dressing table and dragged herself upright.

"Help!" Rosalind screamed hoarsely. "Help!"

Blanchard was there, tall and broad and monstrous in the shadows. Rosalind snatched up the table's stool and swung it at him. He knocked it away easily and lunged for her, without seeing she now had hold of the tiny pair of silver scissors.

"Stop, Blanchard!" hollered a man's voice. "In the king's name, stop!"

It was too late. Blanchard's momentum had carried him too far forward. The scissors drove into his stomach and he howled in shock and pain and staggered backward.

Adam Harkness grabbed him from behind and bore him to the ground. Devon Winterbourne ran past and grabbed Rosalind.

"Are you hurt? Did he hurt you?"

Rosalind looked at her hands and saw the blood.

"I . . ."

She got no further before the blackness swallowed her whole.

CHAPTER 36

An Expectation of Return

Ladies Voucher
ALMACK'S
Deliver to _____,
___ Tickets for the Balls
on the Wednesdays of April, 1817

Society Notes
by A. E. Littlefield

We know that readers of the *Chronicle*, along with the whole of fashionable society, have been waiting with bated breath for the answer to one question—after all the drama and the danger of the little season, how was the opening assembly at the beating heart of fashionable life, Almack's Assembly Rooms?

There is but one word. Dazzling.

Never before has London, and therefore the world, witnessed such a collection of magnificence. Society seemed determined to show itself at its finest and its most glittering, wiping away all trace of tears from the beloved ballroom and banishing forever the darkness

that so recently threatened to blot out the shining star
of the fashionable . . .

Rosalind sipped her tea and listened to Alice read off confident descriptions of dresses and impending matches, of Lady Jersey and her poise, of Countess Lieven and her grace, not to mention Mrs. Drummond-Burrell and her vivacity. The fire crackled in the grate of her narrow parlor and Rosalind and Alice both sat with their feet resting on the fender. On the table between them lay the remains of their late breakfast, complete with muffins and a second pot of tea.

"Well?" Alice lowered the paper. "What do you think?"

"I think it's a scintillating description of the glittering opening of the Almack's season," Rosalind answered. "Especially considering that you weren't there."

"Neither were you, which is surprising. All the little birds say that you were granted a voucher, for services rendered."

"Little birds or Littlefields?" smiled Rosalind.

"There's not much difference in the end, is there?" Alice said. "But I'm being serious, Rosalind. If you have the voucher, why didn't you go?"

"I'm saving my tickets," she answered. "For later, when they might be useful."

"And I am still not forgiving you for not inviting me to the Nottinghams'." Alice picked up a remaining bit of muffin and popped it in her mouth. "How could you be so careless?"

"I had rather a lot on my mind," murmured Rosalind. "I promise it will not happen again."

"See that it doesn't," replied Alice grandly. Then, more softly and more seriously, she asked, "How is Lady Blanchard?"

"The doctors are quite hopeful," Rosalind said, glad that she could tell the truth about that. "As soon as she's strong enough, she'll go to her sister in Derbyshire."

"Permanently, I expect?"

Rosalind nodded in agreement.

"I'm sorry."

"That's what she said," Rosalind murmured. She did not want to remember how pale and weak her godmother had been when she did. She did not want to remember the way she even lacked the strength to take Rosalind's hand.

She was certain one day they would find their way back to some kind of understanding, and perhaps even forgiveness, but that day was a long way off yet. Lady Blanchard had meant to use her, to play upon her loyalty and her indebtedness to keep scandal away from her door, even after she'd realized her husband had murdered her lover. It was a great deal to have to forgive.

"And what of Lord Blanchard?" asked Alice quietly.

"He has succumbed to fever," said Rosalind. Her voice trembled shamefully. "They suspect blood poisoning from his wound. The doctors are doing what they can, but he is not expected to recover."

Alice took her hand and they sat like that for a long time.

The jangle of the doorbell cut the silence. Rosalind's head lifted.

"Visitors already? It's barely half past." Alice turned in her seat so she could see the door open. Mrs. Kendricks came in, ready to make her announcement, but there was no need. Honoria Aimesworth had decided not to wait.

"I thought you might be at home. You always did keep odd hours." Honoria dropped onto Rosalind's sofa and looked about the little room with undisguised interest. "So, this is your house?"

"Thank you, Mrs. Kendricks," said Rosalind to her housekeeper. "And yes, it is."

"Hello, Honoria," said Alice.

Honoria looked her up and down, especially noting how her feet still rested on the fireplace fender. "Hello, Alice. I'd wondered whatever happened to you."

"No more than's happened to you, from what I hear. What are you doing out this early?"

Honoria shrugged. "I felt like it, and I wanted to give Rosalind the news."

Rosalind arched her brows and waited.

"Mother's had enough," announced Honoria. "It seems Lady Jersey and the rest of them were utterly unmoved by her plea that she was trying to save them from Lord and Lady Blanchard by getting into their good graces and exposing the ticket scheme. She's giving up on society and going back to the Continent. Perhaps for good."

Rosalind could picture Lady Edmund sitting in her newly decorated parlor, delivering this news over cups of tea, perfectly calm, perfectly poised, and holding herself beyond possibility of questions, or arguments.

"Will you go with her?" she asked.

Honoria picked up the last whole muffin and broke it in two. "She's told me to." She spread strawberry jam across the muffin and popped it in her mouth. "But I think I'm going to stay and brazen it out this time."

"It's what you should have done that first time."

"Yes," she said around another bite of muffin. "I said as much then, as you'll recall."

"I do," admitted Rosalind with a sideways glance at Alice. "And I'm sorry. I should have listened."

Honoria shrugged and wiped her fingers on the nearest napkin. "Well, you will know better next time."

Silence fell between them, and Rosalind wondered how it could possibly be filled. She had been so very wrong about so many things, including this girl helping herself to muffins without being asked. It felt like much more than an apology was due her.

It was Alice, ever the newswoman, who found the right question. Or at least the most interesting one.

"What exactly was it your mother thought she was doing?"

Honoria tossed her head. "Oh. She found out that Jasper was having an affair with Lady Blanchard. Sentimental idiot that he was." Her chin trembled. "And she thought she could use that to blackmail herself into the patroness's position."

"I was Lady Edmund's blind," said Rosalind. "It was so well known in society how I manage things, that no one would ask how she got the post if it looked like I was on hand to arrange it."

"And Lady Blanchard was willing to go along with it, because it would serve Mother right when the ticket-forging scheme was discovered, and Almack's collapsed. After she and Jasper were safely away, of course," added Honoria. "And if you put that in your column, I'll deny all of it."

Now it was Alice's turn to shrug. "It's not the sort of thing that will interest the readers. They want Almack's to remain Almack's."

Which was probably nothing less than the truth, mused Rosalind. "If you're not fleeing to the Continent, Honoria, what will you do?"

"I don't know yet. I need some time to think. What about you, Rosalind?" At this, Rosalind and Alice both were treated to the most unusual sight of Honoria Aimesworth hesitating. "You could come stay at Tamwell House, if you like. I've money enough for two and I owe you rather a lot for what you did."

"It was not so much."

Honoria snorted. "It was a great deal more than that false modesty allows."

"It usually is," put in Alice.

Honoria rolled her eyes. She also got to her feet. "Well. I have let you see I am unchanged by sorrow and so on. I'm going now. Write and let me know if you want to come to me. I expect I'll be at home rather a lot for the rest of the season."

Rosalind thanked her and rang for Mrs. Kendricks to come with Honoria's things and help her on with her coat. As she buttoned her gloves, Honoria paused. She glanced at Alice, and then she shrugged.

"You can have him by the way."

"I'm sorry?" Rosalind frowned.

"Lord Casselmain. With Mother going and Father . . . disinterested, I find I'm in rather less of a rush to marry than previously. I've released him from his promise." She lifted her head and met Rosalind's gaze quite easily. "You should know that he did offer to see the thing through. He would have married me if I had still wanted it."

"Yes, I believe that he would." Rosalind remembered Devon's sad and serious voice. She remembered his hands holding hers, and his arms around her, catching her up, keeping her safe.

He had written her since she came back to Little Russell Street. Twice. She hadn't answered. Yet.

"Good-bye then." Honoria sounded a little disappointed. Rosalind met her gaze.

"Good-bye. And Honoria?" Honoria paused, her expression tired and impatient. "I think you're wrong,"

Honoria snorted. "About what?"

"About whether or not we could ever be friends."

Honoria did not answer. Even Alice held her peace. At last,

Honoria gave one small nod. Then she turned, and walked out the door.

Rosalind sighed and sat back down. She picked up the half of a muffin Honoria had left, and stared at it.

"If you're not going to go stay with Honoria, what are you going to do, Rose?" asked Alice. "After all this, society is going to be less than sure about you, Almack's voucher or no. How will you get on?"

"I'll find a way," said Rosalind, more to the broken muffin than to Alice. "I always do."

"Well, remember what I said about turning to writing." Alice got to her feet and came over to embrace her friend. "After what you've been through, you've material enough for ten novels!"

They laughed at this, but not too much, because there was such sadness behind it. And then Alice had to leave, because she had to meet with George and the major and lay out the next series of "Society Notes" now that there was no more murder and forgery to splash across the columns. Rosalind stood at the window and watched her leave. Then, she turned to her writing desk.

So much had happened, and so much waited for her. There was Devon, and there was Mr. Harkness. There was society and all its toils and there was still the need to make her way.

And there was this letter she had received yesterday afternoon. She lifted it up and read it again.

Dear Miss Thorne:

I hope you will forgive me, a woman to whom you've no connection at all, writing you in this fashion, but I have heard of you from the Countess Lieven. Her Grace spoke in such glowing terms of your courage and your cleverness in helping uncover the terrible forgery scheme for the lady patronesses of Almack's.

   I feel therefore I may lay before you my own troubles. I am in receipt of a series of letters of the most shocking nature, and no one can trace the blackguard responsible. I beg you to hear me and to advise me. Will you allow me to call? There will be no question of expense in this matter, if only you will help me . . .

And perhaps I can, thought Rosalind. *Perhaps I can.*